Praise for

Genghis

BIRTH OF AN EMPIRE

"A new series of brilliantly imagined and addictive historical fiction . . . Iggulden weaves a spellbinding story of an exotic and 'unforgiving land' and the enigmatic young man—charismatic, a brilliant tactician and capable 'of utter ruthlessness'—who sets out to tame it. This is historical fiction of the first order."
—*Publishers Weekly* (starred review)

"Vivid, fast, and brutal . . . it rings true."
—*Historical Novels Review*

"A rousing adventure."
—*Library Journal*

"Iggulden writes with sweep and immediacy."
—*Christian Science Monitor*

"Authentically detailed historical drama."
—*Booklist*

BY CONN IGGULDEN

Emperor: The Gates of Rome
Emperor: The Death of Kings
Emperor: The Field of Swords
Emperor: The Gods of War
Genghis: Birth of an Empire
Genghis: Lords of the Bow

BY CONN IGGULDEN
AND HAL IGGULDEN

The Dangerous Book for Boys

GENGHIS

BIRTH OF AN EMPIRE

Conn Iggulden

A DELL BOOK

GENGHIS: BIRTH OF AN EMPIRE
A Dell Book

PUBLISHING HISTORY
Delacorte Press hardcover edition published May 2007
Dell mass market edition / March 2008

Published by Bantam Dell
A Division of Random House, Inc.
New York, New York

This book is entirely fiction. The names, characters, and incidents portrayed in it, while based on historical events, are the work of the author's imagination.

Library of Congress Catalog Card Number: 2006102932

Dell is a registered trademark of Random House, Inc., and the colophon is a trademark of Random House, Inc.

ISBN: 978-0-440-24390-8

Printed in the United States of America

www.bantamdell.com

OPM 10 9 8 7 6 5 4 3 2 1

To my brothers
John, David, and Hal

ACKNOWLEDGMENTS

This book could not have been written without the people of Mongolia, who allowed me to live among them for a time and who taught me their history over salted tea and vodka while the winter eased into spring.

THE LANDS RULED BY THE MONGOL EMPIRE UNDER GENGHIS KHAN

HOLY ROMAN EMPIRE

POLAND

HUNGARY

SERBIA

BULGARIA

BYZANTINE EMPIRE

Mediterranean Sea

Black Sea

Dnepr

Volga

Sorai

Caspian Sea

Aral Sea

Lake Balkhash

Irtysh

Urgench

Kyzylkum Desert

Syr Dar'ya (Jaxartes)

KHARA KHITAI

Issyik Kul'

Kara Kum

Otrar

Balasagun

Tigris

Bukhara

Baghdad

Mervo

Amu Dar'ya (Oxus)

Samarkand

Kashgar

TIEN SHAN

Euphrates

Persian Gulf

KHWAREZM

Kabul

Delhi

GHORID SULTANATE

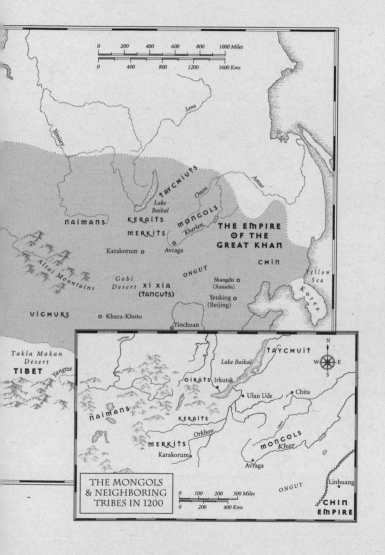

THE MONGOLS & NEIGHBORING TRIBES IN 1200

A multitude of rulers is not a good thing. Let there be one ruler, one king.

Homer, *The Iliad*

PROLOGUE

THE SNOW WAS BLINDING as the Mongol archers encircled the Tartar raiding party. Each man guided his pony with his knees, standing on the stirrups to fire shaft after shaft with withering accuracy. They were grimly silent, the hooves of their galloping ponies the only sound to challenge the cries of the wounded and the howling wind. The Tartars could not escape the whirring death that came out of the darkening wings of the battle. Their horses fell groaning to their knees, blood spattering bright from their nostrils.

On an outcrop of yellow-gray rock, Yesugei watched the battle, hunched deep into his furs. The wind was a roaring devil on the plain, tearing at wherever his skin had lost its covering of mutton grease. He did not show the discomfort. He had borne it for so many years he could not have been sure he even felt it anymore. It was just a fact of his life, like having warriors to ride at his word, or enemies to kill.

The Tartars did not lack courage, for all he despised

them. Yesugei saw them rally around a young warrior and heard his shouts carry over the wind. The Tartar wore a chain-mail vest that Yesugei envied, lusted after. With curt words of command, the man was preventing the raiders from scattering, and Yesugei saw the moment had come to ride. His *arban* of nine companions felt it, the best of his tribe, blood brothers and bondsmen. They had earned the precious armor they wore, boiled leather inscribed with the leaping figure of a young wolf.

"Are you ready, my brothers?" he said, feeling them turn to him.

One of the mares whinnied excitedly and his first warrior, Eeluk, chuckled.

"We will kill them for you, little one," Eeluk said, rubbing her ears.

Yesugei kicked in his heels and they broke effortlessly into a trot toward the screaming, roiling battlefield in the snow. From their height above the fighting, they could all see the full stretch of the wind. Yesugei murmured in awe as he saw the arms of the sky father reach around and around the frail warriors in great white scarves, heavy with ice.

They moved into a gallop without the formation changing and without thought, as each man judged the distances around him as he had for decades. They thought only of how best to cut the enemy from their saddles and leave them cold on the plains.

Yesugei's arban crashed into the center of the fighting men, making for the leader, who had risen in the last few moments. If he was allowed to live, perhaps he would become a torch for all his tribe to follow. Yesugei smiled as his pony hammered into the first of the enemy. Not today.

The impact broke the back of a Tartar warrior even as he turned to meet the new threat. Yesugei held his mount's mane in one hand, using his sword in single strikes that left dead men falling like leaves. He refused two blows where the blade of his father might have been lost, instead using the pony to trample the men down and the hilt as a hammer for one unknown soldier. Then he was past and had reached the knotted core of the Tartar resistance. Yesugei's nine followers were still with him, protecting their khan as they had been sworn to from birth. He knew they were there without looking, guarding his back. He saw their presence in the way the Tartar captain's eyes flickered to each side of him. He would be seeing his death in their flat, grinning faces. Perhaps he had also become aware of all the bodies around him, stiff with arrows. The raid had been crushed.

Yesugei was pleased when the Tartar rose in his stirrups and pointed a long red blade at him. There was no fear in the eyes, only anger and disappointment that the day had come to nothing. The lesson would be wasted on the frozen dead, but Yesugei knew the Tartar tribes would not miss the significance. They would find the blackened bones when the spring came and they would know not to raid his herds again.

Yesugei chuckled, making the Tartar warrior frown as they stared at each other. No, they would not learn. Tartars could starve to death deciding on a mother's tit. They would be back and he would ride out to them again, killing even more of their dishonest blood. The prospect pleased him.

He saw that the Tartar who had challenged him was young. Yesugei thought of the son being born to him over the hills to the east and wondered if he too would face a grizzled older warrior across the length of a sword one day.

"What is your name?" Yesugei said.

The battle had finished around them and already his Mongols walked among the corpses, taking anything of use. The wind still roared, but the question was heard and Yesugei saw a frown pass across the face of his young enemy.

"What is yours, yak penis?"

Yesugei chuckled, but his exposed skin was beginning to ache and he was tired. They had tracked the raiding party for almost two days across his land, going without sleep and surviving on nothing more than a handful of wet milk curd each day. His sword was ready to take another life and he raised the blade.

"It does not matter, boy. Come to me."

The Tartar warrior must have seen something in his eyes that was more certain than an arrow. He nodded, resigned.

"My name is Temujin-Uge," he said. "My death will be avenged. I am the son of a great house."

He dug in his heels and his mount surged at Yesugei. The khan's sword whipped through the air in a single stroke of perfect economy. The body fell at his feet and the pony bolted across the battleground.

"You are carrion, boy," Yesugei said, "as are all men who steal from my herds."

He looked around him at his gathered warriors. Forty-seven had left their *ger* tents to answer his call.

They had lost four of their brothers against the ferocity of the Tartar raid, but not one of twenty Tartars would return home. The price had been high, but the winter drove men to the edge in all things.

"Strip the bodies quickly," Yesugei ordered. "It is too late to return to the tribe. We will camp in the shelter of the rocks."

Valuable metal and bows were much prized for trade and to replace broken weapons. Except for the chain-mail vest, the pickings were poor, confirming Yesugei's thought that this was simply a party of young warriors out to skirmish and prove themselves. They had not planned to fight to the death on earth as hard as stone. He draped the bloody metal garment over his saddle horn when it was thrown to him. It was of good quality and would stop a dagger's blow, at least. He wondered who the young warrior had been to own such a valuable thing, turning his name over in his mind. He shrugged. It no longer mattered. He would trade his share of their ponies for strong drink and furs when the tribes met to trade. Despite the cold in his bones, it had been a good day.

The storm had not eased by the following morning, when Yesugei and his men returned to the camp. Only the outriders moved lightly as they rode, staying alert against sudden attack. The rest were so bundled in furs and weighed down with looted goods that they were shapeless and half frozen, rimed in dirty ice and grease.

The families had chosen their site well, against the lee of a craggy hill of rock and wind-blasted lichen, the gers almost invisible in the snow. The only light was a dim brightening behind boiling clouds, yet the returning warriors were spotted by one of the sharp-eyed boys who watched for attack. It lifted Yesugei's heart to hear the piping voices warn of his approach.

The women and children of the tribe could hardly be stirring yet, he thought. In such a cold, they dragged themselves from sleep only to light the iron stoves. The time of true rising came an hour or two later, when the great tents of felt and wicker had lost the snap of ice in the air.

As the ponies came closer, Yesugei heard a scream rise like the gray smoke coming from Hoelun's ger and felt his heart beat faster in anticipation. He had one baby son, but death was always close for the young. A khan needed as many heirs as his tents could hold. He whispered a prayer for another boy, a brother for the first.

He heard his hawk echo the high note inside the ger as he vaulted from the saddle, his leather armor creaking at each step. He barely saw the servant who took the reins, standing impassively in his furs. Yesugei pushed open the wooden door and entered his home, the snow on his armor melting instantly and dripping in pools.

"Ha! Get off!" he said, laughing as his two hounds jumped up in a frenzy, licking and bounding madly around him. His hawk chirruped a welcome, though he thought it was more a desire to be off on the hunt. His first son, Bekter, crawled naked in a corner, playing with curds of cheese as hard as stones. All these things Yesugei registered without his eyes leaving the woman on the furs. Hoelun was flushed with the stove's heat, but her eyes were bright in the gold lamplight. Her fine, strong face shone with sweat and he saw a trace of blood on her forehead where she had wiped the back of her hand. The midwife was fussing with a bundle of cloth, and he knew from Hoelun's smile that he had a second son.

"Give him to me," Yesugei ordered, stepping forward.

The midwife drew back with her wrinkled mouth puckering in irritation. "You will crush him with your big hands. Let him take his mother's milk. You can hold him later, when he is strong."

Yesugei could not resist craning for a sight of the little boy as the midwife laid him down, cleaning the small limbs with a rag. In his furs, he loomed over them both and the child seemed to see him, launching a ferocious bout of squalling.

"He knows me," Yesugei said, with pride.

The midwife snorted. "He is too young," she muttered.

Yesugei did not respond. He smiled down at the red-faced infant, then, without warning, his manner changed and his arm snapped out. He gripped the elderly midwife around the wrist.

"What is that in his hand?" he asked, his voice hushed.

The midwife had been about to wipe the fingers clean, but under Yesugei's fierce gaze, she opened the infant's hand gently, revealing a clot of blood the size of an eye that trembled with the tiniest movement. It was black and shone like oil. Hoelun had raised herself up to see what part of her newborn boy had caught Yesugei's attention. When she saw the dark lump, she moaned to herself.

"He holds blood in his right hand," she whispered. "He will walk with death all his life."

Yesugei drew in a sharp breath, wishing she had not spoken. It was reckless to invite an evil fate for the boy. He brooded in silence for a time, considering. The midwife continued nervously with her wrapping and cleaning, the clot quivering on the blankets. Yesugei reached for it and held it in his own hand, glistening.

"He was born with death in his right hand, Hoelun. That is fitting. He is a khan's son and death is a companion for him. He will be a great warrior." He watched as the baby boy was handed over at last to his exhausted mother, suckling ferociously on a nipple as soon as it was presented to him. His mother winced, then bit her lip.

Yesugei's expression was still troubled as he turned to the midwife.

"Throw the bones, old mother. Let us see if this clot of blood means good or evil for the Wolves." His eyes were bleak and he did not need to say that the child's life depended on the outcome. He was the khan and the tribe looked to him for strength. He wanted to believe the words he had used to avert the sky father's jealousy, but he feared that Hoelun's prophecy had been the truth.

The midwife bowed her head, understanding that something fearsome and strange had come into the birthing rituals. She reached into a bag of sheep ankle bones by the stove, dyed red and green by the children of the tribe. Depending on how they fell, they could be named horse, cow, sheep, or yak, and there were a thousand games played with them. The elders knew they could reveal more when cast at the right time and place.

The midwife drew back her arm to throw, but again Yesugei restrained her, his sudden clasp making her wince.

"He is my blood, this little warrior. Let me," he said, taking four of the bones from her. She did not resist, chilled by his cold expression. Even the dogs and hawk had grown still.

Yesugei threw the bones and the old midwife gasped as they came to rest.

"Aiee. Four horses is very lucky. He will be a great rider. He will conquer from a horse."

Yesugei nodded fiercely. He wanted to hold up his son to the tribe, and would have if the storm had not raged around the ger, searching for a way into the warmth. The cold was an enemy, yet it kept the tribes strong. The old did not suffer for long in such bitter winters. The weakling children perished quickly. His son would not be one of those.

Yesugei watched the tiny scrap of a child pulling at his mother's soft breast. The boy had gold-colored eyes like his own, almost wolf yellow in their lightness. Hoelun looked up at the father and nodded, his pride easing her worry. She was certain the clot was a dark omen, but the bones had gone some way toward calming her.

"Have you a name for him?" the midwife asked Hoelun.

Yesugei replied without a hesitation. "My son's name is Temujin," he said. "He will be iron." Outside, the storm roared on without a sign of ceasing.

PART
ONE

CHAPTER 1

ON A SPRING DAY in his twelfth year, Temujin raced his four brothers across the steppes, in the shadow of the mountain known as Deli'un-Boldakh. The eldest, Bekter, rode a gray mare with skill and concentration, and Temujin matched his pace, waiting for a chance to go past. Behind them came Khasar, whooping wildly as he moved up on the two leaders. At ten, Khasar was a favorite in the tribe, as lighthearted as Bekter was sullen and dark. His red-mottled stallion snorted and whickered after Bekter's mare, making the little boy laugh. Kachiun came next in the galloping line, an eight-year-old not given to the openness that made people love Khasar. Of all of them, Kachiun seemed the most serious, even secretive. He spoke only rarely and did not complain, no matter what Bekter did to him. Kachiun had a knack with the ponies that few others could match, able to nurse a burst of speed when the rest were flagging. Temujin glanced over his shoulder to where Kachiun had positioned himself, his balance perfect. He seemed to be idling along, but they had all been surprised before and Temujin kept a close eye on him.

Already some way behind his brothers, the smallest and youngest of them could be heard calling plaintively for them to wait. Temuge was a boy with too much love for sweet things and laziness, and it showed in his riding. Temujin grinned at the sight of the chubby boy flapping his arms for more speed. Their mother had warned against including the youngest in their wild tournaments. Temuge had barely grown out of the need to be tied to the saddle, but he wailed if they left him behind. Bekter had yet to find a kind word for Temuge.

Their high voices carried far across the spring grass of the plain. They galloped flat out, with each boy perched like a bird on the ponies' backs. Yesugei had once called them his sparrows and looked on with pride at their skill. Temujin had told Bekter that he was too fat to be a sparrow and had been forced to spend a night hiding out from the older boy's bad temper.

On such a day, though, the mood of the whole tribe was light. The spring rains had come and the rivers ran full again, winding across plains where dry clay had been only days before. The mares had warm milk for drinking and making into cheese and cool yoghurt. Already, the first touches of green were showing through the bones of the hills, and with it came the promise of a summer and warm days. It was a gathering year, and before the next winter, the tribes would come together in peace to compete and trade. Yesugei had decreed that this year the families of the Wolves would make the trip of more than a thousand miles to replenish their herds. The prospect of seeing the wrestlers and archers was enough to have the boys on their best behavior. The races, though, were what held them rapt and played across their imaginations as they rode. Except for Bekter, the boys had all seen their mother privately, asking Hoelun to put in a word with Yesugei. Each of them wanted to race the long distance or the sprints, to make a name for themselves and be honored.

It went unspoken that a boy who returned to his gers with a title such as "Exalted Rider" or "Master of Horse" might one day win their father's position when he retired to tend his herds. With the possible exception of fat Temuge, the others could not help but dream. It galled Temujin that Bekter assumed he would be the one, as if a year or two of age made a difference. Their relationship had become strained ever since Bekter had returned from his betrothal year away from the tribe. Though Temujin was still the tallest of the brothers, the older boy had grown in some indefinable way, and Temujin had found the new Bekter a humorless companion.

It had seemed an act at first to Temujin, with Bekter only pretending at maturity. The brooding boy no longer spoke without thinking and seemed to weigh every statement in his mind before he allowed it past his lips. Temujin had mocked his seriousness, but the months of winter had come and gone with no sign of an easing. There were moments when Temujin still found his brother's pompous moods amusing, but he could respect Bekter's temper, if not his right to inherit their father's tents and sword.

Temujin watched Bekter as he rode, careful not to let a gap grow between them. It was too fine a day to worry about the distant future, and Temujin daydreamed about all four brothers, brothers—all five with

Bekter, even—sweeping the board of honors at the tribal gathering. Yesugei would swell with pride and Hoelun would grip them one by one and call them her little warriors, her little horsemen. Even Temuge could be entered at six years of age, though the risks of a fall were huge. Temujin frowned to himself as Bekter glanced over his shoulder, checking his lead. Despite their subtle maneuvering, Yesugei had not yet given permission for any of them to take part as the spring came.

Hoelun was pregnant again and close to the end of her time. The pregnancy had been hard on her and quite different from the ones before. Each day began and ended with her retching over a bucket until her face was speckled with spots of blood under the skin. Her sons were on their best behavior while they waited for Yesugei to cease his worried pacing outside the gers. In the end, the khan had grown tired of their stares and careful silence, sending them off to run the winter out of the horses. Temujin had continued to chatter and Yesugei had picked him up in one powerful hand and tossed him at a stallion with a white sock. Temujin had twisted in the air to land and launch into a gallop in one movement. Whitefoot was a baleful, snappy beast, but his father had known he was the boy's favorite.

Yesugei had watched the others mount without a sign of his pride on his broad, dark face. Like his father before him, he was not a man to show emotion, especially not to sons he could make weak. It was part of a father's responsibility to be feared, though there were times when he ached to hug the boys and throw them up into the air. Knowing which horses they preferred showed his affection, and if they guessed at his feelings from a glance or a light in his eye, that was no more than his own father had done years before. He valued those memories in part for their rarity and could still recall the time his father had finally grunted approval at his knots and ropework with a heavy load. It was a small thing, but Yesugei thought of the old man whenever he yanked a rope tight, his knee hard into the bales. He watched his boys ride into the bright sunshine, and when they could no longer see him, his expression eased. His father had known the need for hard men in a hard land. Yesugei knew they would have to survive battle, thirst, and hunger if they were to reach manhood. Only one could be khan of the tribe. The others would either bend the knee or leave with just a wanderer's gift of goats and sheep. Yesugei shook his head at the thought, gazing after the dust trail of his sons' ponies. The future loomed over them, while they saw only the spring and the green hills.

The sun was bright on his face as Temujin galloped. He reveled in the lift in spirit that came from a fast horse straining under him, the wind in his face. Ahead, he saw Bekter's gray mare recover from a stumble on a loose stone. His brother reacted with a sharp blow to the side of the mare's head, but they had lost a length and Temujin whooped as if he were about to ride past. It was not the right moment. He loved to lead, but he also enjoyed pressuring Bekter, because of the way it annoyed him.

Bekter was already almost the man he would be, with wide, muscular shoulders and immense stamina.

His betrothal year with the Olkhun'ut people had given him an aura of worldly knowledge he never failed to exploit. It irritated Temujin like a thorn under his skin, especially when his brothers pestered Bekter with questions about their mother's people and their customs. Temujin too wanted to know, but he decided grimly that he would wait to find out on his own, when Yesugei took him.

When a young warrior returned from his wife's tribe, he was given the status of a man for the first time. When the girl came into her blood, she would be sent after him with an honor guard to show her value. A ger would be ready for her and her young husband would wait at its door to take her inside.

For the Wolves, it was tradition for the young man to challenge his khan's bondsmen before he was fully accepted as a warrior. Bekter had been eager and Temujin remembered watching in awe as Bekter had walked up to the bondsmen's fire, close to Yesugei's ger. Bekter had nodded to them and three men had stood to see if his time with the Olkhun'ut had weakened him. From the shadows, Temujin had watched, with Khasar and Kachiun silent at his side. Bekter had wrestled all three of the bondsmen, one after the other, taking terrible punishment without complaint. Eeluk had been the last, and the man was like a pony himself, a wall of flat muscle and wide arms. He had thrown Bekter so hard that blood had run from one of his ears, but then to Temujin's surprise, Eeluk had helped Bekter up and held a cup of hot black *airag* for him to drink. Bekter had almost choked at the bitter fluid mingling with his own blood, but the warriors had not seemed to mind.

Temujin had enjoyed witnessing his older brother

beaten almost senseless, but he saw too that the men no longer scorned him around the fires at night. Bekter's courage had won him something intangible but important. As a result, he had become a stone in Temujin's path.

As the brothers raced across the plains under a spring sun, there was no finishing line, as there would be at the great gathering of tribes. Even if there had been, it was too soon after winter to really push their mounts. They all knew better than to exhaust the ponies before they had a little summer fat and good green grass in their bellies. This was a race away from chores and responsibilities, and it would leave them with nothing but arguments about who had cheated, or should have won.

Bekter rode almost upright, so that he seemed peculiarly motionless as the horse galloped under him. It was an illusion, Temujin knew. Bekter's hands on the reins were guiding subtly, and his gray mare was fresh and strong. He would take some beating. Temujin rode as Khasar did, low on the saddle, so that he was practically flat against the horse's neck. The wind seemed to sting a little more and both boys preferred the position.

Temujin sensed Khasar moving up on his right shoulder. He urged the last breath of speed from Whitefoot, and the little pony snorted with something like anger as it galloped. Temujin could see Khasar's pony out of the corner of his eye, and he considered veering slightly, as if by accident. Khasar seemed to sense his intention and lost a length as he moved away, leaving Temujin grinning. They knew each other too well to race, he sometimes thought. He could see Bekter glance back and their eyes met for a second. Temujin raised his eyebrows and showed his teeth.

"I am coming," he called. "Try to stop me!"

Bekter turned his back on him, stiff with dislike. It was something of a rarity to have Bekter come riding with them, but as he was there, Temujin could see he was determined to show the "children" how a warrior could ride. He would not take a loss easily, which was why Temujin would strain every muscle and sinew to beat him.

Khasar had gained on both of them, and before Temujin could move to block him, he had almost drawn level. The two boys smiled at each other, confirming that they shared the joy of the day and the speed. The long, dark winter was behind, and though it would come back too soon, they would have this time and take pleasure in it. There was no better way to live. The tribe would eat fat mutton and the herds would birth more sheep and goats for food and trade. The evenings would be spent fletching arrows or braiding horsetails into twine; in song or listening to stories and the history of the tribes. Yesugei would ride against any young Tartars who raided their herds, and the tribe would move lightly on the plains, from river to river. There would be work, but in summer the days were long enough to give hours free to waste, a luxury they never seemed to find in the cold months. What was the point in wandering away to explore when a wild dog might find and bite you in the night? That had happened to Temujin when he was only a little older than Kachiun, and the fear had stayed with him.

It was Khasar who saw that Temuge had fallen, glancing back in case Kachiun was staging a late rush for the grass crown. Khasar claimed to have the sharpest eyes of the tribe, and he saw that the sprawled speck was not moving, making a decision in an instant. He whistled high-low to Bekter and Temujin, letting them know he was pulling out. Both boys looked back and then farther to where Temuge lay in a still heap. Temujin and his older brother shared a moment of indecision, neither willing to give the race to the other. Bekter shrugged as if it did not matter and reined his mare into a wide circle back the way they had come. Temujin matched him exactly and they galloped as a pair behind the others, the leaders became the led. It was Kachiun now who rode first amongst them, though Temujin doubted the boy even thought of it. At eight, Kachiun was closest in age to Temuge and had spent many long evenings teaching him the names of things in the gers, demonstrating an unusual patience and kindness. Perhaps as a result, Temuge spoke better than many boys of his age, though he was hopeless with the knots Kachiun's quick fingers tried to show him. The youngest of Yesugei's sons was clumsy, and if any of them had been asked to guess at the identity of a fallen rider, they would have said "Temuge" without a moment's hesitation.

Temujin jumped from his saddle as he reached the others. Kachiun was already on the ground with Khasar, lifting the supine Temuge into a sitting position.

The little boy's face was very pale and bruised-looking. Kachiun slapped him gently, wincing as Temuge's head lolled.

"Wake up, little man," Kachiun told his brother, but there was no response. Temujin's shadow fell across them and Kachiun deferred to him immediately.

"I didn't see him fall," he said, as if his seeing would have helped.

Temujin nodded, his deft hands feeling Temuge for

broken bones or signs of a wound. There was a lump on the side of his head, hidden by the black hair. Temujin prodded at it.

"He's knocked out, but I can't feel a break. Give me a little water for him."

He held out a hand and Khasar pulled a leather bottle from a saddlecloth, drawing the stopper with his teeth. Temujin dribbled the warm liquid into Temuge's open mouth.

"Don't choke him," Bekter advised, reminding them he was still mounted, as if he supervised the others.

Temujin didn't trouble to reply. He was filled with dread as to what their mother Hoelun would say if Temuge died. They could hardly give her such news while her belly was filled with another child. She was weak from sickness and Temujin thought the shock and grief might kill her, yet how could they hide it? She doted on Temuge and her habit of feeding him the sweet yoghurt curds was part of the reason for his chubby flesh.

Without warning, Temuge choked and spat water. Bekter made an irritable sound with his lips, tired of the children's games. The rest of them beamed at each other.

"I dreamed of the eagle," Temuge said.

Temujin nodded at him. "That is a good dream," he said, "but you must learn to ride, little man. Our father would be shamed in front of his bondsmen if he heard you had fallen." Another thought struck him and he frowned. "If he does hear, we may not be allowed to race at the gathering."

Even Khasar lost his smile at that, and Kachiun

pursed his mouth in silent worry. Temuge smacked his lips for more water and Temujin passed him the bottle.

"If anyone asks about your lump, tell them we were playing and you hit your head—understand, Temuge? This is a secret. The sons of Yesugei do not fall."

Temuge saw that they were all watching his response, even Bekter, who frightened him. He nodded vigorously, wincing at the pain.

"I hit my head," he said, dazedly. "And I saw the eagle from the red hill."

"There are no eagles on the red hill," Khasar replied. "I was trapping marmots there only ten days ago. I would have seen a sign."

Temuge shrugged, which was unusual in itself. The little boy was a terrible liar and, when challenged, he would shout, as if by growing louder they would be forced to believe him. Bekter was in the process of turning his pony away when he looked thoughtfully at the little boy.

"When did you see the eagle?" Bekter said.

Temuge shrugged. "I saw him yesterday, circling over the red hill. In my dream, he was larger than a normal eagle. He had claws as large as—"

"You saw a real eagle?" Temujin interrupted. He reached out and held his arm. "A real bird, this early in the season? You saw one?" He wanted to be certain it was not one of Temuge's idiotic stories. They all remembered the time he had come into the ger one night claiming to have been chased by marmots who rose up on their hind legs and spoke to him.

Bekter's expression showed he shared the same memory. "He is dizzy from the fall," he said.

Temujin noticed how Bekter had taken a firmer

hold on the reins. As slowly as he might approach a wild deer, Temujin rose to his feet, risking a glance to where his own pony cropped busily at the turf. Their father's hawk had died and he still mourned the loss of the great-hearted bird. Temujin knew Yesugei dreamed of hunting with an eagle, but sightings were rare and the nests were usually on cliffs sheer enough and high enough to defeat the most determined climber. Temujin saw that Kachiun had reached his pony and was ready to go. A nest could have an eagle chick for their father to keep. Perhaps Bekter wanted one for himself, but the others knew that Yesugei would be overcome with gratitude to the boy who brought him the khan of birds. The eagles ruled the air as the tribes ruled the land, and they lived almost as long as a man. Such a gift would mean they all could ride in the races that year, for certain. It would be seen as a good omen that an eagle had come to their father, strengthening his position with the families.

Temuge had made it to his feet, touching his head and wincing at the speck of blood that showed on his fingers. He did seem dazed, but they believed what he had said. The race of the morning had been a light-hearted thing. This one would be real.

Temujin was the first to move, fast as a dog snapping. He leapt for Whitefoot's back, calling "Chuh!" as he landed and startling the ill-tempered beast into a snorting run. Kachiun flowed onto his horse with the neatness and balance that marked all his movement, Khasar only an instant behind him, laughing aloud with excitement.

Bekter was already lunging forward, his mare's haunches bunching under him as he kicked in and went. In just a few heartbeats, Temuge was left standing alone on the plain, staring bemusedly after the cloud of dust from his brothers. Shaking his head to clear his blurred vision, he took a moment to vomit a milky breakfast onto the grass. He felt a little better after that and clambered up onto the saddle, heaving his pony's head from its grazing. With a last pull at the grass, the pony snorted and he too was off, jolting and bouncing behind his brothers.

CHAPTER 2

THE SUN WAS HIGH in the sky before the boys reached the red hill. After the initial wild gallop, each one of them had settled into a mile-eating trot their sturdy ponies could keep up for hours at a time. Bekter and Temujin rode together at the front in mutual truce, Khasar and Kachiun just behind. They were all tired by the time they sighted the great rock the tribes called the red hill, an immense boulder hundreds of feet high. It was surrounded by a dozen others of lesser size, like a wolf mother with her cubs. The boys had spent many hours climbing there the previous summer and knew the area well.

Bekter and Temujin scanned the horizon restlessly, looking for signs of other riders. The Wolves claimed no hunting rights to land this far away from the gers. Like so much else on the plains, the stream water, the milk, the furs and meat, everything belonged to whoever had the strength to take it or, better still, the strength to keep it. Khasar and Kachiun saw no further than the excitement of finding an eagle chick, but the two older boys were ready to defend themselves or run. Both carried knives and Bekter had a quiver and a small bow across his back that could be quickly strung. Against boys from another tribe, they would acquit themselves well, Temujin thought. Against fully grown warriors, they would be in serious danger and their father's name would not help them.

Temuge was again a speck behind the other four, persevering despite the sweat and buzzing flics that seemed to find him delicious. To his miserable eye, his brothers in their neat pairs seemed like a different breed, like hawks to his lark, or wolves to his dog. He wanted them to like him, but they were all so tall and competent. He was even clumsier in their presence than on his own, and he could never seem to speak the way he wanted to, except sometimes to Kachiun, in the quiet of the evenings.

Temuge dug his heels in viciously, but his pony sensed his lack of skill and rarely raised itself even to a trot, never mind a gallop. Kachiun had said he was too tenderhearted, but Temuge had tried beating the pony mercilessly when he was out of sight of his brothers. It made no difference to the lazy beast.

If he had not known his brothers' destination, he would have been lost and left behind in the first hour. Their mother had told them never to leave him, but they did it anyway and he knew complaining to her would earn him cuffs around the ears from all of them. By the time the red hill came into sight, Temuge was feeling thoroughly sorry for himself. Even from a distance, he could hear Bekter and Temujin arguing. Temuge sighed, shifting his buttocks where they had begun to ache. He felt in his pockets for more of the sweet milk curds and found the end of an old one. Before the others could see, he stuffed the little white stick into his cheek, hiding his blissful enjoyment from their sharp sight.

The four brothers stood by their ponies, staring at Temuge as he ambled closer.

"*I* could carry him faster than that," Temujin said.

The ride to the red hill had become a race again in the last mile, and they had arrived at full gallop, leaping off and tumbling in the dust. Only then had it occurred to them that someone had to stay with the ponies. They could be hobbled by wrapping reins around their legs, but the boys were far from their tribe and who knew what thieves were ready to ride in and snatch them away? Bekter had told Kachiun to stay at the bottom, but the boy was a better climber than the other three and refused. After a few minutes of argument, they had all nominated one of the others and Khasar and Kachiun had come to blows, with Khasar sitting on his younger brother's head while he struggled in silent fury. Bekter had cuffed them apart with a curse when Kachiun went a dark purple. Waiting for Temuge to get there was the only sensible solution and, in truth, more than one of them had taken a good look at the sheer face of the red hill and had second thoughts about racing his brothers up it. Perhaps more worrying than the bare rock was the complete lack of an eagle sign. It was too much to expect droppings, or even the sight of a circling bird guarding the nest or hunting. In the absence of any proof, they could not help but wonder again if Temuge had been lying, or spinning a wild tale to impress them.

Temujin felt his stomach begin to ache. He had missed the morning meal and, with a hard climb ahead, he didn't want to risk becoming weak. While the others watched Temuge approach, he picked up a handful of reddish dust and made it into a paste with a dribble of water from the saddle bottle. Whitefoot bared his teeth and whinnied, but did not resist as Temujin tied his reins to a scrub bush and drew his knife.

It was the work of a moment to nick a vein in the pony's shoulder and clamp his mouth to it. The blood was hot and thin and Temujin felt it restore his energy and warm his empty belly like the best black airag. He counted six mouthfuls before he took his lips away and pressed a bloody finger over the wound. The paste of dust and water helped the clotting, and he knew there would be just a small scab by the time he returned. He grinned, showing red teeth to his brothers and wiping his mouth with the back of his hand. He could feel his strength return now that his stomach was full. He checked the blood was clotting on Whitefoot's shoulder, watching a slow dribble reach down the leg. The pony didn't seem to feel it and resumed cropping the spring grass. Temujin brushed a fly away from the blood trail and patted the animal on its neck.

Bekter too had dismounted. Seeing Temujin feed himself, the older boy knelt and directed a thin trail of warm milk into his mouth from his mare's teat, smacking his lips in noisy appreciation. Temujin ignored the display, though Khasar and Kachiun looked up hopefully. They knew from experience that if they asked they would be refused, but if they ignored their thirst, Bekter might condescend to allow a warm mouthful to each boy.

"Drink, Khasar?" Bekter said, raising his head sharply.

Khasar did not wait to be asked twice and ducked his head like a foal to where Bekter held the dark teat, shining with milk. Khasar sucked greedily at the spray, getting some of it over his face and hands. He snorted, choking, and even Bekter smiled before he beckoned Kachiun over.

Kachiun looked at Temujin, seeing how stiffly he stood. The little boy narrowed his eyes, then shook his head. Bekter shrugged, releasing the teat with just a glance at Temujin before he stretched his back and watched the youngest of their brothers clamber down from his pony.

Temuge dismounted with his usual caution. For a boy of only six summers, it was a long way to the ground, though other children in the tribe would leap from the saddle with all the fearlessness of their older brethren. Temuge could not manage such a simple thing, and all his brothers winced as he landed and staggered. Bekter made a clicking sound in his throat, and Temuge's face darkened under their scrutiny.

"This is the place?" Temujin asked.

Temuge nodded. "I saw an eagle circling here. The nest is somewhere near the top," he said, squinting upwards.

Bekter grimaced. "It was probably a hawk," he muttered, following Temuge's gaze.

Temuge flushed even deeper. "It was an eagle! Dark brown and larger than any hawk who ever lived!"

Bekter shrugged at the outburst, choosing the moment to spit a wad of milky phlegm onto the ground.

"Maybe. I'll know when I find the nest."

Temujin might have replied to the challenge, but Kachiun had tired of their bickering and strode past them all, pulling at the waist cloth that held his padded *deel* in place. He let the coat fall, revealing just a bare-armed tunic and linen leggings, as he took his first hand-holds on the rocks. The soft leather of his boots gripped almost as well as his bare feet. The others stripped down as he had, seeing the sense in leaving the heaviest cloth on the ground.

Temujin moved twenty paces around the base before he saw another place to begin, spitting on his hands and taking a grip. Khasar grinned in excitement and threw his reins at Temuge, startling the little boy. Bekter found his own place and set his strong hands and feet in clefts, lifting himself up with a small grunt.

In a few moments, Temuge was alone again. At first, he was miserable and his neck ached from staring up at the climbing figures. When they were no larger than spiders, his stomach made its presence felt. With a last look at his more energetic brothers, he strolled over to steal a stomachful of milk from Bekter's mare. There were some advantages to being last, he had discovered.

After a hundred feet, Temujin knew he was high enough for the fall to kill him. He listened over his panting breath for his brothers, but there was no sound or sight of them in any direction. He clung by fingertips and boots, leaning out as far as he could to see a route higher. The air seemed colder and the sky was achingly clear above his head, without a cloud to spoil the illusion of climbing toward a blue bowl. Small lizards scurried away from his questing fingers and he almost lost his grip when one was trapped, squirming, under his hand. When his heart had stopped hammering, he brushed its broken body from the ledge where it had been enjoying the sun, watching it twist in the wind as it fell.

Far below, Temujin saw Temuge pulling at the teats of Bekter's mare and hoped he had enough sense to leave some. Bekter would thrash him if he found the milk gone, and the greedy little boy probably deserved it.

The sun was hard on the back of his neck, and Temujin felt a line of sweat touch his eyelashes, making him blink against the sting. He shook his head, hanging from just his hands as his feet scrabbled for a new place to rest. Temuge could have killed one of them with his stories of eagles, but it was too late for doubts. Temujin was not even sure he could get back down the sheer slope. At such a height, he had to find a place to rest, or he would fall.

The blood in his stomach gurgled as he moved, reminding him of its strength and making him belch its bitter smell. Temujin bared his teeth as he pulled himself higher. He could feel a worm of fear in his stomach, and it began to make him angry. He would *not* be afraid. He was a son of Yesugei, a Wolf. He would be khan one day. He would not be afraid and he would not fall. He began to murmur the words to himself, over and over as he climbed, staying close to the rock as the wind grew in force, tugging at him. It also helped to imagine Bekter's irritation if Temujin reached the top first.

A gust made his stomach drop with a sudden feeling that he would be plucked and thrown from the high rock, smashing into the ground by Temuge. He found that his fingers were shaking with each new grip, the first sign of weakness. He took strength from his anger and went on.

It was hard to guess how far he had come, but

Temuge and the ponies were only specks below and his arms and legs burned with effort. Temujin came to a ridge where he could stand out of the wind and gasped there, recovering. He could see no way to go farther at first, and craned around a shelf of rock. He would surely not be stuck there while the others found easier routes up? Only Kachiun was a better climber and Temujin knew he should take time to rest his aching muscles. He took a deep breath of the warm air, enjoying the view for miles around. He felt as if he could see all the way to the gers of their tribe and wondered if Hoelun had given birth. Surely many hours had passed since they had arrived at the red hill?

"Are you stuck?" he heard above him.

Temujin swore aloud as he saw Kachiun's face peering over the ledge. The boy met his gaze with the beginnings of a smile crinkling his eyes. Temujin shuffled along the ledge until he grasped a decent handhold. He had to hope it would lead to another above. With Kachiun looking on, he controlled his breathing and showed the cold face of the warrior. He had to jump up to reach for a second grip, and, for a moment, fear overwhelmed him. On the ground it would have been nothing, but on the ground he would have fallen only a little way. With the wind moaning around the crags, Temujin did not dare think of the emptiness at his back.

His arms and legs blurred as he shoved himself up by sheer strength and energy. To stop moving was to begin to fall, and Temujin roared as he made it to where Kachiun was kneeling, calmly watching his progress.

"Ha! Khans of the mountain do not get stuck," he told Kachiun, triumphantly.

His brother digested this in silence.

"The hill breaks apart just above us," he said. "Bekter has taken the south col to the peak."

Temujin was impressed at his brother's calm. He watched as Kachiun walked to the edge of the red boulder he'd climbed in panic, going close enough to have the wind pull at his braided hair.

"Bekter does not know where the eagles are, if they are here at all," Temujin told him.

Kachiun shrugged again. "He took the easier path. I don't think an eagle would build a nest where it could be so easily reached."

"There's another way, then?" Temujin asked. As he spoke, he scrambled up a shallow slope to get a better view of the summits of the red hill. There were two, as Kachiun had said, and Temujin could see Bekter and Khasar on the one to the south. Even from a distance, both boys could identify the powerful figure of their eldest brother, moving slowly but steadily. The northern peak that loomed above Temujin and Kachiun was a spike of rock even more daunting than the initial sheer slope they had climbed.

Temujin clenched his fists, feeling the heaviness in his arms and calves.

"Are you ready?" Kachiun asked him, nodding toward the northern face.

Temujin reached out and caught his serious little brother around the back of the head in a quick clasp. He saw that Kachiun had lost a fingernail from his right hand. There was a crust of blood running right along his forearm to the sinewy muscles there, but the boy showed no sign of his discomfort.

"I am ready," Temujin said. "Why did you wait for me?"

Kachiun grunted softly, taking a fresh hold on the rock. "If you fell, Bekter would be khan one day."

"He might be a good one," Temujin said, grudgingly. He did not believe it, but he remembered how Bekter had wrestled his father's bondsmen. There were aspects of the adult world he did not yet fully understand, and Bekter had at least the attitudes of a warrior.

Kachiun snorted at that. "He rides like a stone, Temujin. Who can follow a man who sits so badly?"

Temujin smiled as he and Kachiun began to climb.

It was a fraction easier with two of them working together. More than once, Temujin used his strength to support Kachiun's foot as the boy swarmed up the face like an agile spider. He climbed as well as he rode, but his young body was showing signs of exhaustion and Temujin saw he was growing pale as they put another hundred feet behind them. Both boys were panting and their arms and legs seemed too heavy to move.

The sun had crossed the highest point of the sky and begun its trail toward the west. Temujin eyed its position whenever he could find a place to snatch a moment of relief from the strain. They could not be caught on the face in the dark, or both of them would fall. More worrying was the sight of a looming ridge of clouds in the distance. A summer storm would tear them all off the red hill, and he feared for his brothers as Kachiun slipped and almost took them both to their deaths.

"I *have* you. Find another hold," Temujin grunted, his breath coming like fire from his open mouth. He could not remember being so tired and still the summit seemed impossibly far. Kachiun managed to take his weight off Temujin's arm, looking back for a moment at the bleeding scuff marks his boot had left on Temujin's bare skin. Kachiun followed his brother's gaze out over the plains and stiffened as he saw the clouds. The wind was difficult to judge as it gusted around the crags, but both boys had the feeling it was coming straight at them.

"Come on, keep moving. If it starts to rain, we're all dead," Temujin growled at him, pushing his brother upwards. Kachiun nodded, though he closed his eyes for a moment and seemed dazed. It was easy to forget how young he was at times. Temujin felt a fierce, protective pride for the little boy and vowed not to let him fall.

The southern peak was still visible as they climbed, though there was no sign of either Bekter or Khasar. Temujin wondered if they had reached the top and were even then on their way back down with an eagle chick safe under a tunic. Bekter would be insufferable if he brought one of the great birds back to their father's tents, and the thought was enough to lend a little extra energy to Temujin's tired muscles.

Neither boy understood at first what the high-pitched sounds meant. They had never heard the cries of young eagles, and the wind was a constant companion with its own sound over the rocks. The clouds had spread to fill the sky and Temujin was more concerned about finding a place for shelter. The thought of getting down with every handhold slick with rain made his heart sink. Even Kachiun could not do it, he was certain. One of them would fall, at least.

The threat of dark clouds could not completely hold the attention of the two boys as they dragged themselves up to a cleft stuffed with twigs and feathers. Temujin could smell the scent of rotting meat before he was able to bring his eyes up to the level of the nest. At last he realized that the whistling sound was from a pair of young eagles, watching the climbers with feral interest.

The adult birds must have mated early, as the chicks were neither scrawny nor helpless. Both still carried their lighter feathering, with only touches of the golden brown that would carry them soaring over mountains in search of prey. Their wings were stubby and ugly looking, though both boys thought they had never seen anything quite so beautiful. The claws seemed too large for the young birds, great yellow toes ending in darker spikes that looked already capable of tearing flesh.

Kachiun had frozen in wonder on the ledge, hanging from his fingertips. One of the birds took his stillness as some sort of challenge and hissed at him, spreading its wings in a show of courage that made Kachiun beam in pleasure.

"They are little khans," he said, his eyes shining.

Temujin nodded, unable to speak. Already he was wondering how to get both birds down alive with a storm on the way. He scanned the horizon at the sudden worrying thought that the adult eagles might be driven home before the clouds. At such a precarious height, an attacking eagle would be more than a match for two boys trying to shepherd fledglings to the ground.

Temujin watched as Kachiun drew himself up into a crouch on the very edge of the nest, seemingly oblivious to the precarious position. Kachiun reached out a hand, but Temujin snapped a warning. "The clouds are too close for us to get down now," he said. "Leave them in the nest and we can take them in the morning."

As he spoke, a rumble of thunder growled across the plains, and both boys looked toward the source. The sun was still bright over them, but in the distance they could see rain sheeting down in twisting dark threads, the shadow racing toward the red hill. At that height, it was a scene to inspire awe as well as fear.

They shared a glance and Kachiun nodded, dropping back from the nest edge to the one below.

"We'll starve," he said, putting his sore finger in his mouth and sucking at the crust of dried blood.

Temujin nodded, resigned. "Better that than falling," he said. "The rain is nearly here and I want to find a place where I can sleep without dropping off. It will be a miserable night."

"Not for me," Kachiun said, softly. "I have looked into the eyes of an eagle."

With affection, Temujin cuffed the little boy, helping him traverse the ridge to where they could climb farther up. A cleft between two slopes beckoned. They could wedge themselves in as far as possible and rest at last.

"Bekter will be furious," Kachiun said, enjoying the idea.

Temujin helped him up into the cleft and watched him wriggle his way in deeper, disturbing a pair of tiny lizards. One of them ran to the edge and leapt in panic with its legs outstretched, falling for a long time. There was barely room for both boys, but at least they were out of the wind. It would be uncomfortable and frightening after dark, and Temujin knew he would be lucky to sleep at all.

"Bekter chose the easy way up," he said, taking Kachiun's hand and pulling himself in.

CHAPTER 3

THE STORM BATTERED the red hill for all the hours of darkness, clearing only as dawn came. The sun shone strongly once more from an empty sky, drying the sons of Yesugei as they emerged from their cracks and hiding places. All four had been caught too high to dare a descent. They had spent the night in shivering wet misery; drowsing, then jerking awake with dreams of falling. As the dawn light reached the twin peaks of the red hill, they were yawning and stiff, with dark circles under their eyes.

Temujin and Kachiun had suffered less than the other pair because of what they had found. As soon as there was light enough to see, Temujin began to scramble out of the cleft to collect the first of the young eagles. He almost lost his grip when a dark shape swept in from the west, an adult eagle that seemed as large as he was.

The bird was not happy to find two trespassers so close to its young. Temujin knew the females were larger than the males, and he assumed the creature had to be the mother, as it screamed and raged at them. The chicks went unfed as the great bird took off again and again to float on the wind and look into the rock cleft that sheltered the two boys. It was terrifying and wondrous to be so high and stare into the black eyes of the bird, hanging unsupported on outstretched wings. Its claws opened and clutched convulsively, as if it imagined tearing into their flesh. Kachiun shuddered at the sight, lost in awe and fear that the huge bird would suddenly spear in at them, pulling them out as it might have done with a marmot in its hole. They had no more than Temujin's pitiful little knife to defend themselves against a hunter that could break the back of a dog with a single heavy strike.

Temujin watched the brown-gold head turn back and forth in agitation. He guessed the bird could remain there all day, and he did not enjoy the thought of being exposed on the ledge below the nest. One blow from a claw there and he would be torn loose. He tried to remember anything he had ever heard about the wild birds. Could he shout to frighten the mother away? He considered it, but he did not want to summon Bekter and Khasar up to the lonely peak, not until he had the chicks wrapped in cloth and close to his chest.

At his shoulder, Kachiun clung to the sloping red rock in the cleft. Temujin saw he had prized out a loose stone and was weighing it in his hand.

"Can you hit it?" Temujin asked.

Kachiun only shrugged. "Maybe. I'd have to be lucky to knock it down, and this is the only one I could find."

Temujin cursed under his breath. The adult eagle

had disappeared for a time, but the birds were skilled hunters and he was not tempted to be lured out of his safe haven. He blew air out of his mouth in frustration. He was starving, with a difficult climb down ahead of him. He and Kachiun deserved better than to leave empty-handed.

He remembered Bekter's bow, far below with Temuge and the ponies, and cursed himself for not having thought to bring it. Not that Bekter would have let him lay a hand on the double-curved weapon. His elder brother was as pompous about that as he was about all the trappings of a warrior.

"You take the stone," Kachiun said. "I'll get back up to the nest, and if she comes, you can knock her away."

Temujin frowned. It was a reasonable plan. He was an excellent shot and Kachiun was the better climber. The only problem was that it would be Kachiun who had taken the birds, not him. It was a subtle thing, perhaps, but he wanted no other claim on them before his own.

"You take the stone. I'll get the chicks," he replied.

Kachiun turned his dark eyes on his older brother, seeming to read his thoughts. He shrugged. "All right. Have you cloth to bind them?"

Temujin used his knife to remove strips from the edge of his tunic. The garment was ruined, but the birds were a far greater prize and worth the loss. He wrapped a length around each palm to have them ready, then craned out of the cleft, searching for a moving shadow, or a speck circling above. The bird had looked into his eyes and known what he was trying to do, he was certain. He had seen intelligence there, as much as any dog or hawk, perhaps more.

He felt his stiff muscles twinge as he climbed out into the sunlight. Once more he could hear thin screeching from the nest, the chicks desperate for food after a night alone. Perhaps they too had suffered without their mother's warm body to protect them from the storm. Temujin worried that he could hear only one call and that the other might have perished. He glanced behind him in case the adult eagle was soaring in to hammer him against the rock. There was nothing there and he pulled himself onto the high ledge, dragging up his legs until he crouched as Kachiun had the previous evening.

The nest was deep in a hollow, wide and steep-sided, so that the active young birds could not clamber out and fall before they could fly. As they caught sight of his face, both of the scrawny young eagles scuttled away from him, wagging their featherless wings in panic and cawing for help. Once more, he scanned the blue sky and said a quick prayer to the sky father to keep him safe. He eased forward, his right knee pressing into the damp thatch and old feathers. Small bones crunched under his weight and he smelled a nauseating gust from ancient prey.

One of the birds cowered from his reaching fingers, but the other tried to bite him with its beak, raking his hand with talons. The needle claws were too small to do more than lightly score his skin, and he ignored the sting as he held the bird up to his face and watched as it writhed.

"My father will hunt for twenty years with you," he murmured, freeing a strip from one hand and trussing the bird by wing and leg. The second had almost climbed out of the nest in panic, and Temujin was forced to drag it back by one yellow claw, causing it to wail and struggle. He saw that the young feathers had a tinge of red amidst the gold.

"I would call you the red bird, if you were mine," he told it, pushing them both down inside his tunic. The birds seemed quieter against his skin, though he could feel claws scrabble at him. He thought his chest would look as if he'd fallen in a thorn bush by the time he was down.

Temujin saw the adult eagle coming as a flicker of darkness above his head. It was moving faster than he would have believed possible, and he only had time to raise an arm before he heard Kachiun yell and their single stone thumped into the bird's side, knocking it off its strike. It *screamed* in rage as real as he'd ever heard from an animal, reminding Temujin that this was a hunter, with a hunter's instincts. He saw the bird try to flap its huge wings, scrabbling at the ledge for balance. Temujin could do nothing but crouch in that confined space and try to protect his face and neck from the lunging claws. He heard it screech in his ear and felt the wings beat against him before the bird fell, calling in anger all the way. Both boys watched the eagle spiral down and down, barely in control of the descent. One wing was still, but the other seemed to twist and flutter in the updraft. Temujin breathed more slowly, feeling his heart begin to slow. He had the bird for his father and perhaps he would be allowed to train the red bird for himself.

Bekter and Khasar had joined Temuge with the ponies by the time Temujin made his slow way down. Kachiun had stayed with him, aiding where he could so that Temujin never had to scramble for a hold, or risk his precious cargo. Even so, when he finally stood on the flat ground and looked up to the heights, they seemed impossibly far away; already strange, as if other boys had climbed them.

"Did you find the nest?" Khasar asked, seeing their answer in their pride.

Kachiun nodded. "With two eagle chicks in it. We fought off the mother and took them both."

Temujin let his young brother tell the story, knowing that the others would not understand what it had been like to crouch with the world under his feet and death beating against his shoulders. He had not been afraid, he'd found, though his heart and body had reacted. He had experienced a moment of exhilaration on the red hill, and it disturbed him too much to talk of it, at least for the moment. Perhaps he would mention it to Yesugei when the khan was in a mellow mood.

Temuge too had spent a miserable night, though he had been able to shelter with the ponies and had occasional squirts of warm milk to sustain him. It didn't occur to the other four to thank him for his sighting of the eagle. Temuge hadn't climbed with them. All he had from his brothers was a hard clip from Bekter when he discovered that Temuge had emptied the mare's teats during the night. The little boy howled as they set off, but the others had no sympathy. They were all parched and starving, and even the usually sunny Khasar frowned at him for his greed. They had soon left him behind as they trotted together across the green plain.

The boys saw their father's warriors long before they were in sight of the gers of the tribe. Almost as soon as they were out of the shadow of the red hill, they were spotted, the high-pitched horn calls carrying a long way.

They did not show their nervousness, though the presence of riders could only mean their absence had been noticed. Unconsciously, they rode a little closer together as they recognized Eeluk galloping toward them and saw that he did not smile in greeting.

"Your father sent us out to find you," Eeluk said, addressing the words to Bekter.

Temujin bristled automatically. "We've spent nights out before," he replied.

Eeluk turned his small, black eyes on him and ran a hand over his chin. He shook his head. "Not without warning, not in a storm, and not with your mother giving birth," he said, speaking sharply as if to scold a child.

Temujin saw Bekter was flushing with shame and refused to let the emotion trouble him. "You have found us, then. If our father is angry, that is between him and us."

Eeluk shook his head again, and Temujin saw the flash of spite in his eyes. He had never liked his father's bondsman, though he could not have said why. There was malice in Eeluk's voice as he went on.

"Your mother almost lost the child through worrying about the rest of you," he said.

His eyes demanded Temujin lower his gaze, but instead the boy felt a slow anger building. Riding with eagles next to his chest gave him courage. He knew his father would forgive them anything once he saw the birds. Temujin raised a hand to stop the others, and even Bekter reined in with him, unable just to ride on. Eeluk too was forced to turn his pony back to them, his face dark with irritation.

"You will not ride with us, Eeluk. Go back," Temujin said. He saw the warrior stiffen and shook his head, deliberately. "Today we ride only with eagles," Temujin said, his face revealing nothing of his inner amusement.

His brothers grinned around him, enjoying the secret and the frown that troubled Eeluk's hard features. The man looked to Bekter and saw that he was staring into nothing, his gaze fixed on the horizon.

Then he snorted. "Your father will beat some humility into your thick skins," he said, his face mottling with anger.

Temujin looked calmly at the older man, and even his pony was absolutely still.

"No. He will not. One of us will be khan one day, Eeluk. Think of that and go back, as I told you. We will come in alone."

"Go," Bekter said, suddenly, his voice deeper than any of his brothers'.

Eeluk looked as if he had been struck. His eyes were hidden as he spun his mount, guiding only with his knees. He did not speak again, but at last he nodded sharply and rode away, leaving them alone and shaking with an odd release of tension. They had not been in danger, Temujin was almost certain. Eeluk was not fool enough to draw steel on Yesugei's sons. At worst, he might have thrashed them and made them walk back. Still, it felt as if a battle had been won, and Temujin sensed Bekter's gaze on his neck the whole way to the river and his father's people.

They smelled the tang of urine on the wind before they saw the gers. After a winter spent in the shadow of Deli'un-Boldakh, the scent had sunk into the soil in a great ring around the families. There was only so far a man was willing to walk in the dark, after all. Still, it was home.

Eeluk had dismounted near their father's ger, obviously waiting to see them punished. Temujin enjoyed the skulking man's interest in them and kept his head high. Khasar and Kachiun took their lead from him, though Temuge was distracted by the smell of cooking mutton and Bekter assumed his usual sullen expression.

Yesugei came out as he heard their ponies whinny a welcome to the others in the herd. He wore his sword on his hip and a deel robe of blue and gold that reached down to his knees. His boots and trousers were clean and well brushed, and he seemed to stand even taller than usual. His face showed no anger, but they knew he prided himself on the mask that all warriors had to learn. For Yesugei it was no more than the habit of a lifetime to assess his sons as they rode up to him. He took note of the way Temujin protected something at his chest and the barely controlled excitement in all of them. Even Bekter was struggling not to show pleasure, and Yesugei began to wonder what his boys had brought back.

He saw too that Eeluk hovered nearby, pretending to brush down his pony. This from a bondsman who let his mare's tail grow thick with mud and thorns. Yesugei knew Eeluk well enough to sense his sour mood was directed at the boys rather than himself. He would have shrugged if he had not adopted a warrior's stillness. As it was, he dismissed Eeluk's concerns from his mind.

Khasar and Kachiun dismounted in such a way that Temujin was hidden for a moment. Yesugei watched closely and saw in a flash that Temujin's tunic was moving. His heart began to beat faster in anticipation. Still, he would not make it too easy for them.

"You have a sister, though the birth was harder for your absence. Your mother was almost blood lost with fear for you."

They did lower their gazes at that. He frowned, tempted to thrash each one of them for their selfishness.

"We were at the red hill," Kachiun murmured, quailing under his father's gaze. "Temuge saw an eagle there and we climbed for the nest."

Yesugei's heart soared at the news. There could only be one thing squirming at Temujin's breast, but he hardly dared hope for it. No one in the tribe had caught an eagle for three generations or more, not since the Wolves had come down from the far west. The birds were more valuable than a dozen fine stallions, not least for the meat they could bring from hunting.

"You have the bird?" Yesugei said to Temujin, taking a step forward.

The boy could not hold back his excitement any longer, and he grinned, standing proudly as he fished around inside his tunic.

"Kachiun and I found two," he said.

His father's cold face broke at this and he showed his teeth, very white against his dark skin and wispy beard.

Gently, the two birds were brought out and placed in their father's hands, squalling as they came into the light. Temujin felt the loss of their heat next to his skin as soon as they were clear. He looked at the red bird with an owner's eyes, watching every movement.

Yesugei could not find words. He saw that Eeluk

had come closer to see the chicks, and he held them up, his face alight with interest. He turned to his sons.

"Go in and see your mother, all of you. Make your apologies for frightening her and welcome your new sister."

Temuge was through the door of the ger before his father had finished speaking, and they all heard Hoelun's cry of pleasure at seeing her youngest son. Kachiun and Khasar followed, but Temujin and Bekter remained where they were.

"One is a little smaller than the other," Temujin said, indicating the birds. He was desperate not to be dismissed. "There is a touch of red to his feathers and I have been calling him the red bird."

"It is a good name," Yesugei confirmed.

Temujin cleared his throat, suddenly nervous. "I had hoped to keep him, the red bird. As there are two."

Yesugei looked blankly at his son. "Hold out your arm," he said.

Temujin raised his arm to the shoulder, puzzled. Yesugei held the pair of trussed chicks in the crook of one arm and used the other to press against Temujin's hand, forcing his arm down.

"They weigh as much as a dog, when they are grown. Could you hold a dog on your wrist? No. This is a great gift and I thank you for it. But the red bird is not for a boy, even a son of mine."

Temujin felt tears prickle his eyes as his morning's dreams were trampled. His father seemed oblivious to his anger and despair as he called Eeluk over.

To Temujin's eye, Eeluk's smile was sly and unpleasant as he came to stand by them.

"You have been my first warrior," Yesugei said to the man. "The red bird is yours."

Eeluk's eyes widened with awe. He took the bird reverently, the boys forgotten. "You honor me," he said, bowing his head.

Yesugei laughed aloud. "Your service honors me," he replied. "We will hunt with them together. Tonight we will have music for two eagles come to the Wolves." He turned to Temujin. "You will have to tell old Chagatai all about the climb, so that he can write the words for a great song."

Temujin did not reply, unable to stand and watch Eeluk holding the red bird any longer. He and Bekter ducked through the low doorway of the ger to see Hoelun and their new sister, surrounded by their brothers. The boys could hear their father outside, shouting to the men to see what his sons had brought him. There would be a feast that night and yet, somehow, they were uncomfortable as they met each other's eyes. Their father's pleasure meant a lot to all of them, but the red bird was Temujin's.

That evening, the tribe burned the dry dung of sheep and goats and roasted mutton in the flames and great bubbling pots. The bard, Chagatai, sang of finding two eagles on a red hill, his voice an eerie combination of high and low pitch. The young men and women of the tribe cheered the verses, and Yesugei was pressed into showing the birds again and again while they called piteously for their lost nest.

The boys who had climbed the red hill accepted cup after cup of black airag as they sat around the fires in the darkness. Khasar went pale and silent after the second drink, and after a third, Kachiun gave a low snort and fell slowly backwards, his cup tumbling onto the grass. Temujin stared into the flames, making himself night-blind. He did not hear his father approach and he would not have cared if he had. The airag had heated his blood with strange colors that he could feel coursing through him.

Yesugei sat down by his sons, drawing his powerful legs up into a crouch. He wore a deel robe lined with fur against the night cold, but underneath, his chest was bare. The black airag gave him enough heat and he had always claimed a khan's immunity from the cold.

"Do not drink too much, Temujin," he said. "You have shown you are ready to be treated as a man. I will complete my father's duty to you tomorrow and take you to the Olkhun'ut, your mother's people." He saw Temujin look up and completely missed the significance of the pale golden gaze. "We will see their most beautiful daughters and find one to warm your bed when her blood comes." He clapped Temujin on the shoulder.

"And I will stay with them while Eeluk raises the red bird," Temujin replied, his voice flat and cold. Some of the tone seeped through Yesugei's drunkenness and he frowned.

"You will do as you are told by your father," he said. He struck Temujin hard on the side of his head, perhaps harder than he had meant to. Temujin rocked forward, then came erect once again, staring back at his father. Yesugei had already lost interest, looking away to cheer as Chagatai stirred his old bones in a dance, his arms cutting the air like an eagle's wings. After a time, Yesugei saw that Temujin was still watching him.

"I will miss the gathering of tribes, the races," Temujin said, as their eyes met, fighting angry tears.

Yesugei regarded him, his face unreadable. "The Olkhun'ut will travel to the gathering, just as we will. You will have Whitefoot. Perhaps they will let you race him against your brothers."

"I would rather stay here," Temujin said, ready for another blow.

Yesugei didn't seem to hear him. "You will live a year with them," he said, "as Bekter did. It will be hard on you, but there will be many good memories. I need not say that you will take note of their strength, their weapons, their numbers."

"We have no quarrel with the Olkhun'ut," Temujin said.

His father shrugged. "The winter is long," he replied.

CHAPTER 4

TEMUJIN'S HEAD THROBBED in the weak dawn light as his father and Eeluk loaded the ponies with food and blankets. Hoelun was moving around outside, her baby daughter suckling inside her coat. She and Yesugei talked in low voices and, after a time, he bent down to her, pressing his face into the crook of her neck. It was a rare moment of intimacy that did nothing to dispel Temujin's black mood. That morning, he hated Yesugei with all the steady force a twelve-year-old boy can muster.

In grim silence, Temujin continued to grease his reins and check every last strap and knot on the halter and stirrups. He would not give his father an excuse to criticize him in front of his younger brothers. Not that they were anywhere to be seen. The ger was very quiet after the drinking the night before. The golden eagle chick could be heard calling for food, and it was Hoelun who ducked through the door to feed it a scrap of bloody flesh. The task would be hers while Yesugei was away, but it hardly distracted her from making sure her husband was content and had all he needed for the trip.

The ponies snorted and called to each other, welcoming another day. It was a peaceful scene and Temujin stood in the middle like a sullen growth, looking for the smallest excuse to lash out. He did not want to find himself some cow-like wife. He wanted to raise stallions and ride with the red bird, known and feared. It felt like a punishment to be sent away, for all he knew that Bekter had gone before and come back. By the time Temujin returned, Bekter's betrothed could well be in a ger with her new husband and his brother would be a man to the warriors.

The problem of Bekter was part of the reason for Temujin's sour mood. It had become his habit to prod the older boy's pride and see to it that he did not become too clearly their father's favorite. In his absence, Temujin knew Bekter would be treated as the heir. After a year had passed, his own right to inherit might be almost forgotten.

Yet what else could he do? He knew Yesugei's views on disobedient sons. If he refused to travel, he would be certain of a beating, and if he continued to be stubborn, he could find himself thrown out of the tribe. Yesugei often threatened such a thing when the brothers were too noisy or fought too roughly with each other. He never smiled when he made his threats, and they did not think he was bluffing. Temujin shuddered at the thought. To be a nameless wanderer was a hard fate. No one to watch the herds while you slept, or to help you climb a hill. On his own, he would starve, he was almost certain, or more likely be killed raiding a tribe for supplies.

His earliest memories were of cheerful shoving and bickering with his brothers in the gers. His people were never alone and it was difficult even to imagine what that would be like. Temujin shook his head a fraction as he watched his father load the mounts. He knew better than to show anything but the cold face. He listened as Eeluk and Yesugei grunted in rhythm, pulling the ropes as tight as they could possibly get. It was not a heavy load for just the two of them.

Temujin watched as the men finished, then stepped past Eeluk and checked each knot on his own pony one last time. His father's bondsman seemed to stiffen, but Temujin did not care about his hurt feelings. Yesugei had told him often enough that a man must not depend on the skill of lesser men. Even then, Temujin did not dare to check Yesugei's knots. His father's temper was too uncertain. He might find it amusing, or simply knock his son flat for his impudence.

Temujin frowned at the thought of the ride ahead, with just his father for company and none of his brothers to break the silences. He shrugged to himself. He would endure it as he had found he could endure any other discomfort. What was this but another trial? He had waited out storms, from both Yesugei and the sky father. He had suffered thirst and hunger until he was tempted to bite himself for the taste of his own blood. He had lived through winters where the herds froze to death and one summer that burned the skin, so that they had all had fat yellow blisters. His father had borne those things without complaint or sign of weakness, demonstrating limitless stamina. It lifted those around him. Even Eeluk lost his sour face in Yesugei's presence.

Temujin was standing as stiff and pale as a silver birch sapling when Hoelun ducked under the pony's neck and embraced her son. He could feel the tiny child at her breast wriggle as he smelled sweet milk and mutton grease. When she released him, the tiny little girl began to squawk, red in the face at the unwanted interruption. Temujin watched Hoelun tuck her flat breast back under the questing mouth. He could not look his mother in the eye and she glanced at where Yesugei stood nearby, proud and silent as he stared off into the distance. Hoelun sighed.

"Stop it, Yesugei," she said loudly.

Her husband jerked, his head coming round with a flush darkening his cheeks. "What are you—?" he began.

She interrupted him. "You know exactly what I mean. You haven't a kind word for the boy, and you expect to ride the next three days in silence?"

Yesugei frowned, but Hoelun wasn't finished with him.

"You took the boy's bird and gave it to that ugly bondsman of yours. Did you expect him to laugh and thank you for it?"

Yesugei's pale gaze flickered over Eeluk and his son, gauging the reaction to the speech.

"He is too young," he muttered.

Hoelun hissed like a pot on the stove. "He is a boy about to be betrothed. He is young and too proud, just as his stubborn father is. He is so much like you that you cannot even see it."

Yesugei ignored this, and Temujin did not know what to say as his mother looked back at him.

"He listens, though he pretends not to, Temujin,"

she murmured. "He is like you in that." She reached up to take his cheek in her strong fingers. "Do not be wary of the families of my people. They are good-hearted, though you must keep your eyes down around the young men. They will test you, but you must not be afraid."

Temujin's yellow eyes flashed. "I am not afraid," he said. She waited and his defiant expression altered subtly. "All right, I am listening as well," he said.

She nodded and from a pocket brought a bag of sweet milk curds, pressing it into his hand.

"There is a bottle of black airag in the saddlebag against the cold. These are for the journey. Grow strong and be kind to whichever girl is chosen for you."

"Kind?" Temujin replied. For the first time since his father had told him he was going, he felt a twinge of nervousness in his stomach. Somewhere there was a stranger who would be his wife and bear his children. He could not imagine what she might look like, or even what he wanted in such a woman.

"I hope she is like you," he said thoughtfully.

Hoelun beamed and hugged him with a brief clasp that set his little sister crying indignantly. "You are a good boy, Temujin. You will make her a fine husband," she said.

To his astonishment, he saw tears gleaming in her eyes. She rubbed at them even as he felt an answering pang. His defenses were crumbling and she saw his fear that he would be humiliated in front of Yesugei and Eeluk. Men on their way to be betrothed did not bawl with their mothers.

Hoelun gripped her son briefly around the neck, then turned away, exchanging a last few murmured words with her husband. The khan of the Wolves sighed visibly, nodding in reply as he mounted. Temujin leapt nimbly into his own saddle.

"Temujin!" he heard.

He smiled as he turned his white-footed pony with a gentle pressure on the reins. His sleepy brothers had roused themselves at last and come out to see him off. Temuge and Khasar clustered around his stirrups, adoration in their faces. Kachiun winced against the light as he took a moment to inspect a fraying front hoof. They were a noisy, lively group and Temujin felt the tightness in his chest begin to ease.

Bekter came out of the ger, his flat face impassive. Temujin regarded him, seeing a sparkle of triumph in the empty gaze. Bekter too had thought how much easier his life would be without Temujin there. It was hard not to worry for the younger ones, but Temujin would not shame them by voicing his concern. The bones had been thrown and the future laid out for all of them. A strong man could bend the sky to suit him, but only for himself, Temujin knew. They were on their own.

He raised a hand in final farewell to his mother and urged Whitefoot into a snorting trot at his father's side. He did not think he could bear to look back, so he did not. The sounds of the waking tribe and the whinnying calls of horses faded quickly, and after a short time there was just the thud of hooves and jingling harnesses, and their people were left behind.

Yesugei rode in silence as the sun rose ahead of them. Hoelun's people were closer than they had been in three years, and it would be a journey of only a few days alone with his son. By the end of it, he would know whether the boy had it in him to rule the tribe. He had known with Bekter, after only the first day. His oldest boy was no wild flame, it was true, but the tribe needed a steady hand and Bekter was growing into a fine man.

Yesugei frowned to himself as he rode. Some part of his mind scanned the land around them for a sight of an enemy or an animal. He could never become lost while every hill was sharp in his mind, and every clipped goat ear showed him the local tribes, like a pattern stretching over the land.

He had enjoyed the ride with Bekter, though he had taken pains not to show it. It was hard to know how a boy became a leader of men, but Yesugei was certain it was not through being spoiled or kept soft. He raised his eyes to the sky father at the thought of fat Temuge back in the gers. If the little boy had not had so many strong brothers, Yesugei would have taken him away from his mother's influence, perhaps to be fostered with another tribe. Perhaps he still would, on his return.

Yesugei shifted in the saddle, unable to maintain his usual drifting thoughts while Temujin rode at his side. The boy was too obviously aware of his surroundings, his head jerking at every new sight. Bekter had been a peaceful companion, but something about Temujin's silence chafed on his father.

It did not help that the route to the Olkhun'ut took them near the red hill, so that Yesugei was forced to consider his son's part in fetching the eagle chicks. He felt Temujin's eyes on him as he looked at the sharp slopes, but the stubborn boy would not give him an opening.

Yesugei grunted in exasperation, unsure why his temper was growling on such a fine, blue day.

"You were lucky to reach the nest at that height," he said.

"It was not luck," Temujin replied.

Yesugei cursed inwardly. The boy was as prickly as a thorn bush.

"You *were* lucky not to fall, boy, even with Kachiun helping you."

Temujin narrowed his eyes. His father had seemed too drunk to be listening to Chagatai's songs. Had he spoken to Kachiun? Temujin was not sure how to react, so he said nothing.

Yesugei watched him closely, and after a time, he shook his head and thought of Hoelun. He would try again, for her sake, or he might never hear the end of it.

"It was a fine climb, I heard. Kachiun said you were nearly torn off the rock by the eagle coming back to the nest."

Temujin softened slightly, shrugging. He was absurdly pleased that his father had shown an interest, though his cold face hid it all.

"He forced it down with a stone," he replied, giving measured praise with care. Kachiun was his favorite brother by far, but he had learned the good sense of hiding likes and dislikes from others, almost an instinct by the end of his twelfth year.

Yesugei had fallen silent again, but Temujin searched his thoughts for something to break the silence before it could settle and grow firm.

"Did your father take you to the Olkhun'ut?" he said.

Yesugei snorted, eyeing his son. "I suppose you are

old enough now to hear. No, I found your mother with two of her brothers when I was out riding. I saw that she was beautiful and strong." He sighed, and smacked his lips, his eyes gazing into the past.

"She rode the sweetest little mare, the color of storm water at dawn. Her legs were bare and very brown."

Temujin had not heard the story before and rode a little closer.

"You raided her from the Olkhun'ut?" he said. It should not have surprised him, he knew. His father enjoyed hunting and raiding and his eyes shone when he recalled his battles. If the season was warm and food was plentiful, he sent defeated warriors back to their families on foot, with red welts on their skin from the flats of swords. In the winter, when food was scarce, it was death to be caught. Life was too hard for kindness in the dark months.

"I chased her brothers away like a couple of young goats," Yesugei said. "I was hardly old enough to be out on my own, but I waved my sword above my head and I yelled at them."

Caught up in the memory, he put his head back and gave out an ululating whoop, ending in laughter.

"You should have seen their faces. One of them tried to attack me, but I was the son of a khan, Temujin, not some little dog to be cowed and sent running. I put an arrow through his hip and ran him off."

He sighed to himself.

"Those were very good days. I thought I would never feel the cold in my bones, back then. I had an idea that I would be given nothing in my life, that everything I had would be taken by my wits and my strength." He looked at his son, and his expression contained a regret Temujin could only guess at. "There was a time, boy, when I would have climbed for the red bird myself."

"If I had known, I would have come back and told you," Temujin began, trying to understand this great bear of a man.

Yesugei shook his head, chuckling. "Not now! I am too heavy to be dancing around on tiny ledges and cracks. If I tried it now, I think I would crash to earth like a falling star. What is the point in having sons if they cannot grow strong and test their courage? That is one truth I remember from my father, when he was sober. Courage cannot be left like bones in a bag. It must be brought out and shown the light again and again, growing stronger each time. If you think it will keep for the times you need it, you are wrong. It is like any other part of your strength. If you ignore it, the bag will be empty when you need it most. No, you were right to climb for the nest, and I was right to give the red bird to Eeluk."

There was no hiding the sudden stiffness that came into Temujin's bearing. Yesugei made a purring sound in frustration, deep in his throat like a growl.

"He is my first warrior, and deadly, boy, you should believe it. I would rather have Eeluk at my side than any five of the tribe—any ten of the Olkhun'ut. His children will not rule the families. His sword will never be as good as mine, do you understand? No, you are only twelve. What can you understand of what I say to you?"

"You had to give him something," Temujin snapped. "Is that what you mean?"

"No. It was not a debt. I honored him with the red bird because he is my first warrior. Because he has been my friend since we were boys together and he has never complained that his family were beneath mine amongst the Wolves."

Temujin opened his mouth to snap a reply. The red bird would be soiled by Eeluk's dirty hands, with their thick yellow skin. The bird was too fine for the ugly bondsman. He did not speak, and instead he practiced the discipline that gave him the cold face and showed the world nothing. It was his only real defense against his father's searching gaze.

Yesugei saw through it, and snorted.

"Boy, I was showing the cold face when you were the sky father's dream," he said.

As they made camp that night by a winding stream, Temujin set about the chores that would help sustain them the following day. With the hilt of his knife, he broke chunks of hard cheese from a heavy block, passing the pieces into leather bags half filled with water. The wet mixture would sit under their saddles, churned and heated by the ponies' skin. By noon, he and his father would have a warm drink of soft curds, bitter and refreshing.

Once that task was done, Temujin set about finding sheep droppings, pulling them apart in his fingers to see if they were dry enough to burn cleanly and well. He collected a pile of the best ones and drew a stick of flint across an old knife to light strands of them, building the sparks into a tongue of flame and then a fire. Yesugei cut pieces of dried mutton and some wild onions with sheep fat, the delicious smell making their mouths water. Hoelun had given them bread that would soon be hard, so they broke the flat loaves and soaked them in the stew.

They sat across from each other to eat, sucking the meat juices from their fingers between mouthfuls. Temujin saw his father's gaze fall on the pack that contained the black airag and fetched it for him. He watched patiently as the khan took a deep swig.

"Tell me about the Olkhun'ut," Temujin said.

His father's mouth curled in an unconscious sneer. "They are not strong, though there are many of them, like ants. I sometimes think I could ride in there and kill all day before they brought me down."

"They don't have warriors?" Temujin said incredulously. His father was not above making up some outlandish story, but he seemed serious.

"Not like Eeluk. You'll see. They use the bow rather than the sword, and they stand far off from their enemy, never coming close unless they have to. Shields would make a mockery of them, though they would kill the ponies easily enough. They are like wasps stinging, but if you ride in amongst them, they scatter like children. That is how I took your mother. I crept up, then I leapt on them."

"How will I learn to use a sword, then?" Temujin demanded.

He had forgotten his father's reaction to that tone and barely avoided the hand that came to smack a little humility into him. Yesugei went on as if nothing had happened.

"You will have to practice on your own, boy. Bekter had to, I know that. He said they didn't let him touch a bow or one of their knives from the first day to the day he left. Cowards, all of them. Still, their women are very fine."

"Why do they trade with you, with daughters for your sons?" Temujin asked, wary of another blow. Yesugei was already arranging his deel for sleep, lying back on the sheep-nibbled grass.

"No father wants unwed daughters cluttering the ger. What would they do with them, if I did not come with a son every now and then? It is not so uncommon, especially when the tribes meet. They can strengthen their blood with the seed of other tribes."

"Does it strengthen us?" Temujin asked.

His father snorted without opening his eyes.

"The Wolves are already strong."

CHAPTER 5

YESUGEI'S SHARP EYES spotted the Olkhun'ut scouts at exactly the moment they saw him. The deep notes of their horns carried back to the tribes, rousing the warriors to defend their herds and women.

"You will not speak unless they speak to you," Yesugei warned his son. "Show them the cold face, no matter what happens. Understand?"

Temujin did not respond, though he swallowed nervously. The days and nights with his father had been a strange time for him. In all his life, he could not remember having Yesugei's attention for so long, without his brothers crashing across the khan's field of vision and distracting him. At first, Temujin had thought it would be a misery to be stuck together for the journey. They were not friends, and could not be, but there were moments when he caught a glint of something in his father's eyes. In anyone else, it might have been pride.

In the far distance, Temujin saw dust rise from the dry ground as young warriors leapt onto their ponies, calling for weapons. Yesugei's mouth became a thin, hard line and he sat tall in his saddle, his back straight and unbending. Temujin copied him as best he could, watching the dust cloud grow as dozens of warriors came swarming out toward the lonely pair.

"Do not turn, Temujin," Yesugei snapped. "They are boys playing games, and you will shame me if you give honor to them."

"I understand," Temujin replied. "But if you sit like a stone, they will know you are aware of them. Would it not be better to talk to me, to laugh?"

He felt Yesugei's glare and knew a moment of fear. Those golden eyes had been the last sight of more than a few young tribesmen. Yesugei was preparing himself for enemies, his instincts taking over his muscles and reactions. As Temujin turned to return the stare, he saw his father summon an effort of will and visibly relax himself. The galloping Olkhun'ut did not seem so close and the day had grown a little brighter somehow.

"I will look a fool if they sweep us off the ponies in pieces," Yesugei said, forcing a stiff grin that would not have been out of place on a corpse.

Temujin laughed at his effort in genuine amusement. "Are you in pain? Try throwing your head back as you do it."

His father did as Temujin suggested and his effort reduced them both to helpless laughter by the time the Olkhun'ut riders arrived. Yesugei was red-faced and wiping tears from his eyes as the yelling warriors skidded to a halt, allowing their mounts to block the pair of strangers. The drifting cloud of dust arrived with them, passing through the group on the wind and making them all narrow their eyes.

The milling group of warriors fell silent as Temujin and Yesugei mastered themselves and appeared to notice the Olkhun'ut for the first time. Temujin kept his face as blank as possible, though he could barely hide his curiosity. Everything was subtly different from what he was used to. The bloodlines of their horses were superb and the warriors themselves wore light deels of gray with gold thread markings over trousers of dark brown. They were somehow cleaner and neater looking than his own people, and Temujin felt a vague resentment start in him. His gaze fell on one who must surely have been the leader. The other riders deferred to him as he approached, looking to him for orders.

The young warrior rode as well as Kachiun, Temujin saw, but he was almost a man grown, with only the lightest of tunics and bare brown arms. He had two bows strapped to his saddle, with a good throwing axe. Temujin could see no swords on any of the others, but they too carried the small axes and he wondered how they would be used against armed men. He suspected that a good sword would reduce their hatchets to kindling in just a stroke or two—unless they threw them.

His examination of the Olkhun'ut was being returned. One of the men nudged his pony close to Yesugei. A grimy hand stretched out to finger the cloth of his deel.

Temujin barely saw his father move, but the man's palm was striped with red before he could lay a finger on Yesugei's belongings. The Olkhun'ut rider yelped and pulled back, his pain turning to anger in an instant.

"You take a great risk riding here without your bondsmen, khan of the Wolves," the young man in a tunic said suddenly. "Have you brought us another of

your sons for the Olkhun'ut to teach him his manhood?"

Yesugei turned to Temujin and again there was that
odd light in his eye.

"This is my son, Temujin. Temujin, this is your
cousin Koke. His father is the man I shot in the hip on
the day I met your mother."

"And he still limps," Koke agreed, without smiling.

His pony seemed to move without a signal and he
came in range to clap Yesugei on the shoulder. The
older man allowed the action, though there was something about his stillness that suggested he may not have.
The other warriors relaxed as Koke moved away. He
had shown he was not afraid of the khan, and Yesugei
had accepted that he did not rule where the Olkhun'ut
pitched their gers.

"You must be hungry. The hunters brought in fat
spring marmots this morning—will you eat with us?"

"We will," Yesugei answered for both of them.

From that moment they were protected by guest
rights and Yesugei lost the stiffness that suggested he'd
rather be holding a sword. His dagger had vanished back
into his fur-lined robe. In comparison, Temujin's stomach felt as if it had dropped out. He had not fully appre-
ciated how lonely he would feel surrounded by
strangers, and even before they reached the outer tents
of the Olkhun'ut, he was watching his father closely,
dreading the moment when he would ride away and
leave his son behind.

The gers of the Olkhun'ut were a different shade of
white-gray from those Temujin knew. The horses were

held in great corrals outside the gathering of tents, too many for him to count. With cattle, goats, and sheep busy munching grass on every nearby hill, he could see the Olkhun'ut were prosperous and, as Yesugei had said, strong in numbers. Temujin saw little boys the age of his brothers racing along the outskirts of the camp. Each held a small bow and seemed to be firing directly into the ground, yelling and cursing alternately. It was all strange, and he wished Kachiun and Khasar were there with him.

His cousin Koke jumped down from his pony, giving the reins to a tiny woman with a face as wrinkled as a leaf. Temujin and Yesugei dismounted at the same time, and their ponies were taken away to be watered and fed. The other riders scattered through the camp, returning to their own gers or gathering in groups to talk. Strangers in the tribe were not common and Temujin could feel hundreds of eyes on him as Koke led the two Wolves through the midst of his people, striding ahead.

Yesugei grunted in displeasure at being forced to walk behind the young man. The khan walked even slower in response, pausing to inspect the decorative knotwork on the ger of a lesser family. With a frown on his face, Koke was forced to wait for his guests, or arrive at his destination without them. Temujin might have applauded the subtle way his father had turned the little game of status to his advantage. Instead of hurrying along after the younger man, they had made the trip a tour of the Olkhun'ut gers. Yesugei even spoke to one or two of the people, but never with a question they might not have answered, only with a compliment or a simple remark. The Olkhun'ut stared after the pair of

Wolves, and Temujin sensed his father was enjoying the tensions as much as a battle.

By the time they stopped outside a ger with a bright blue door, Koke was irritated with them both, though he could not exactly have said why.

"Is your father well?" Yesugei said.

The young warrior was forced to pause as he ducked into the ger. "He is as strong as ever," Koke replied.

Yesugei nodded. "Tell him I am here," he said, looking blandly at his nephew by marriage.

Koke colored slightly before disappearing into the darkness within. Though there were eyes and ears all around them, Temujin and Yesugei had been left alone.

"Observe the courtesies when we go in," Yesugei murmured. "These are not the families you know. They will notice every fault and rejoice in it."

"I understand," Temujin replied, barely moving his lips. "How old is my cousin Koke?"

"Thirteen or fourteen," Yesugei replied.

Temujin looked up with interest. "So he is alive only because you shot his father in the hip and not the heart?"

Ycsugei shrugged. "I did not shoot for the hip. I shot to kill, but I had only an instant to loose the shaft before your mother's other brother threw an axe at me."

"Is he here as well?" Temujin asked, looking round.

Yesugei chuckled. "Not unless he managed to put his head back on."

Temujin fell silent as he considered this. The Olkhun'ut had no reason to love his father and many to hate him, yet he sent his sons to them for wives. The certainties he had known among his own people were vanishing, and he felt lost and fearful. Temujin drew on his determination with an effort, composing his features into the cold face. Bekter had withstood his year with the tribe, after all. They would not kill him and anything else was bearable, he was almost certain.

"Why has he not come out?" he murmured to his father.

Yesugei grunted, breaking off from staring at some young Olkhun'ut women milking goats.

"He makes us wait because he thinks I will be insulted. He made me wait when I came with Bekter two years ago. No doubt he will make me wait when I come with Khasar. The man is an idiot, but all dogs bark at a wolf."

"Why do you visit him first, then?" Temujin said, dropping his voice even lower.

"The blood tie brings me safe amongst them. It galls them to welcome me, but they give your mother honor by doing it. I play my part, and my sons have wives."

"Will you see their khan?" Temujin asked.

Yesugei shook his head. "If Sansar sees me, he will be forced to offer his tents and women for as long as I am here. He will have gone hunting, as I would if he came to the Wolves."

"You like him," Temujin said, watching his father's face closely.

"The man has honor enough not to pretend he is a friend when he is not. I respect him. If I ever decide to take his herds, I will let him keep a few sheep and a woman or two, perhaps even a bow and a good cloak against the cold."

Yesugei smiled at the thought, gazing back at the

girls tending their bleating flock. Temujin wondered if they knew the wolf was already amongst them.

The inside of the ger was gloomy and thick with the smell of mutton and sweat. As Temujin ducked low to pass under the lintel, it occurred to him for the first time just how vulnerable a man was as he went into another family's home. Perhaps the small doors had another function apart from keeping out the winter.

The ger had carved wooden beds and chairs around the edges, with a small stove in the middle. Temujin felt vaguely disappointed at the ordinary look of the interior, though his sharp eyes noticed a beautiful bow on the far wall, double curved and layered in horn and sinew. He wondered if he would have the chance to practice his archery with the Olkhun'ut. If they forbade him weapons for the full turn of seasons, he might well lose the skills he had worked so hard to gain.

Koke stood with his head respectfully bowed, but another man rose as Yesugei came to greet him, standing a head shorter than the khan of the Wolves.

"I have brought another son to you, Enq," Yesugei said formally. "The Olkhun'ut are friends to the Wolves and do us great honor with strong wives."

Temujin watched his uncle in fascination. His mother's brother. It was strange to think of her growing up around this very ger, riding a sheep, perhaps, as the babies sometimes did.

Enq was a thin spear of a man, his flesh tight on his bones, so that the lines of his shaven skull could be easily seen. Even in the dark ger, his skin shone with grease, with just one thick lock of gray hair hanging from his scalp between his eyes. The glance he gave Temujin was not welcoming, though he gripped Yesugei's hand in greeting and his wife prepared salted tea to refresh them.

"Is my sister well?" Enq said as the silence swelled around them.

"She has given me a daughter," Yesugei replied. "Perhaps you will send an Olkhun'ut son to me one day."

Enq nodded, though the idea did not seem to please him.

"Has the girl you found for my elder son come into her blood?" Yesugei asked.

Enq grimaced over his tea. "Her mother says that she hasn't," he replied. "She will come when she is ready." He seemed about to speak again and then shut his mouth tight, so that the wrinkles around his lips deepened.

Temujin perched himself on the edge of a bed, taking note of the fine quality of the blankets. Remembering what his father had said, he took the bowl of tea he was offered in his right hand, his left cupping his right elbow in the traditional style. No one could have faulted his manners in front of the Olkhun'ut.

They settled themselves and drank the liquid in silence. Temujin began to relax.

"Why has your son not greeted me?" Enq asked Yesugei slyly.

Temujin stiffened as his father frowned. He put aside the bowl and rose once more. Enq stood with him, and Temujin was pleased to find he was the man's equal in height.

"I am honored to meet you, Uncle," he said. "I am

Temujin, second son to the khan of Wolves. My mother sends you her greetings. Are you well?"

"I am, boy," Enq replied. "Though I see you have yet to learn the courtesies of our people."

Yesugei cleared his throat softly and Enq closed his mouth over whatever he had been going to add. Temujin did not miss the flash of irritation in the older man's eyes. He had been plunged into an adult world of subtlety and games, and once more he began to dread the moment when his father would leave him behind.

"How is your hip?" Yesugei murmured.

Enq's thin mouth tightened as he forced a smile. "I never think of it," he replied.

Temujin noticed that he moved stiffly as he took his seat once more, and felt a private pleasure. He did not have to like these strange people. He understood that this too was a test, like everything else Yesugei set his sons. He would endure.

"Is there a wife for him in the gers?" Yesugei asked.

Enq grimaced, draining the dregs of his tea bowl and holding it out to be refilled.

"There is one family who have not been able to find a match for their daughter. They will be pleased to have her eating someone else's meat and milk."

Yesugei nodded. "I will see her before I leave you. She must be strong and able to bear children for the Wolves. Who knows, one day she could be mother to the tribe."

Enq nodded, sipping at the salty liquid as if in deep concentration. Temujin wanted nothing more than to be away from the man's sour smell and his gloomy ger, but he forced himself to remain still and listen to every word. His future hung on the moment, after all.

"I will bring her to you," Enq said, but Yesugei shook his head.

"Good blood comes from a good line, Enq. I will see her parents before I leave."

Reluctantly, Enq nodded. "Very well. I had to take a piss anyway."

Temujin rose, standing back as his uncle ducked through the door. He could hear the noisy spatter of liquid begin almost immediately. Yesugei chuckled deep in his throat, but it was not a friendly sound. In silent communication, he reached out and gripped Temujin around the back of the neck, then both of them stepped out into the bright sunshine.

The Olkhun'ut seemed to be burdened with an insatiable curiosity about their visitors. As Temujin's eyes adjusted to the light, he saw many dozens of them had gathered around Enq's ger, though Yesugei hardly spared them a glance. Enq strode through the crowd, sending two yellow dogs skittering out of his way with a kick. Yesugei strolled after him, meeting his son's eyes for a moment. Temujin returned the gaze coolly until Yesugei nodded, reassured in some way.

Enq's stiffness was far more visible as they walked behind him, every step revealing his old injury. Sensing their scrutiny, his face became flushed as he led them through the clustered gers and out to the edges of the encampment. The chattering Olkhun'ut followed them, unashamed in their interest.

A thunder of hooves sounded behind their small party, and Temujin was tempted to look back. He saw his father glance and knew that if there was a threat, the khan would have drawn his sword. Though his fingers twitched at the hilt, Yesugei only smiled. Temujin listened to the hoofbeats getting closer and closer until the ground trembled under their feet.

At the last possible moment, Yesugei moved with a jerk, reaching up in a blur to snatch a rider. The horse galloped on wildly, bare of reins or saddle. Freed of its burden, it bucked twice and then settled, dropping its head to nibble at dry grass.

Temujin had spun round at his father's movement, seeing the big man lowering a child to the ground as if the weight were nothing.

It might have been a girl, but it was not easy to be sure. The hair was cut short and the face was almost black with dirt. She struggled in Yesugei's arms as he put her down, spitting and wailing. He laughed and turned to Enq with raised eyebrows.

"The Olkhun'ut grow them wild, I see," Yesugei said.

Enq's face was twisted with what may have been amusement. He watched as the grubby little girl ran away screeching. "Let us continue to her father," he said, flashing a glance at Temujin before he limped away.

Temujin stared after the running figure, wishing he had taken a better look.

"Is she the one?" he said aloud. No one answered him.

The horses of the Olkhun'ut were out on the ragged edge of the tribe, whinnying and tossing their heads in the excitement of spring. The last of the gers sat on a piece of dusty ground by the corrals, baked and bare of any ornament. Even the door was unpainted wood, suggesting the owners owned nothing more than their lives and their place in the tribe. Temujin sighed at the thought of spending his year with such a poor family. He had hoped at least to be given a bow for hunting. From the look of the ger, his wife's family would be hard-pressed even to feed him.

Yesugei's face was blank, and Temujin tried hard to copy it in front of Enq. He had already resolved not to like the thin uncle who had given them such a reluctant welcome. It was not difficult.

The father of the girl came out to meet them, smiling and bowing. His clothes were black with old grease and dirt, layer upon layer that Temujin suspected would remain on his skin regardless of season. He showed a toothless mouth when he smiled, and Temujin watched as he scratched at a dark spot in his hair, flicking some nameless parasite away with his fingers. It was hard not to be revolted after the clean ger his mother had kept all his life. The smell of urine was a sharp tang in the air, and Temujin could not even see a latrine pit nearby.

He took the man's dark hand when it was offered and went inside to drink yet another bowl of the salty tea, moving to the left after his father and Enq. His spirits sank further at the broken wood beds and lack of paint. There was an old bow on the wall, but it was a poor thing and much mended. The old man woke his wife with a hard slap and set her to boiling a kettle on the stove. He was clearly nervous in the presence of strangers and muttered to himself constantly.

Enq could not hide his cheerful mood. He smiled around at the bare felt and wooden lattice, repaired in a hundred places.

"We are honored to be in your home, Shria," he said

to the woman, who bowed her head briefly before pouring the salt tea into shallow bowls for them. Enq's good humor was growing visibly as he addressed her husband. "Bring your daughter, Sholoi. The boy's father has said he wants to see her."

The wiry little man showed his toothless gums again and went out, pulling his beltless trousers up at every second step. Temujin heard a high voice yelling and the old man's curt reply, but he pretended not to, covering his dismay with the bowl of tea and feeling his bladder grow full.

Sholoi brought the grubby girl back in, struggling all the way. Under Yesugei's gaze, he struck her three times in quick succession, on the face and legs. Tears sprang into her eyes, though she fought them with the same determination as she had fought her father.

"This is Borte," Enq said slyly. "She will make your son a good and loyal wife, I am certain."

"She looks a little old," Yesugei said doubtfully.

The girl writhed away from her father's grip and went to sit on the other side of the ger, as far from them as she could possibly get.

Enq shrugged. "She is fourteen, but there has been no blood. Perhaps because she is thin. There have been other suitors, of course, but they want a placid girl instead of one with fire in her. She will make a fine mother for Wolves."

The girl in question picked up a shoe and threw it at Enq. Temujin was close enough to snatch it out of the air, and she stared malevolently at him.

Yesugei crossed the ger and something about him made her go still. He was large for his own people and larger still for the Olkhun'ut, who tended toward delicacy. He reached out and touched her gently under the chin, lifting her head.

"My son will need a strong wife," he said, looking into her eyes. "I think she will be beautiful when she has grown."

The little girl broke her unnatural stillness and tried to slap at his hand, though he was too fast for her. Yesugei smiled, nodding to himself.

"I like her. I accept the betrothal."

Enq hid his displeasure behind a weak smile.

"I am pleased to have found a good match for your son," he said.

Yesugei stood and stretched his back, towering over them all.

"I will return for him in a year, Enq. Teach him discipline, but remember that one day he will be a man and he may come back to pay his debts to the Olkhun'ut."

The threat was not lost on Enq and Sholoi, and the former clenched his jaw rather than reply before he had mastered himself.

"It is a hard life in the gers of the Olkhun'ut. We will give you back a warrior as well as a wife for him."

"I do not doubt it," Yesugei replied.

He bent almost double to exit through the small door and, in sudden panic, Temujin realized his father was leaving. It seemed to take forever for the older men to follow, but he forced himself to sit until only the wizened wife was left and he could leave. By the time he stood blinking against the light, his father's pony had been brought. Yesugei mounted easily, looking down on them all. His steady gaze found Temujin at last, but he said nothing and, after a moment, he dug in his heels, trotting away.

Temujin stared after his father as he rode, returning to his brothers, his mother, everything he loved. Though he knew he would not, Temujin hoped Yesugei would glance back before he was out of sight. He felt tears threaten and took a deep breath to hold them back, knowing it would please Enq to see weakness.

His uncle watched Yesugei leave and then he closed one nostril with a finger, blowing the contents of the other onto the dusty ground.

"He is an arrogant fool, that one, like all the Wolves," he said.

Temujin turned quickly, surprising him. Enq sneered.

"And his pups are worse than their father. Well, Sholoi beats his pups as hard as he beats his daughters and his wife. They all know their place, boy. You'll learn yours while you are here."

He gestured to Sholoi and the little man took Temujin's arm in a surprisingly powerful grip. Enq smiled at the boy's expression.

Temujin held silent, knowing they were trying to frighten him. After a pause, Enq turned and walked away, his expression sour. Temujin saw that his uncle limped much worse when Yesugei was not there to see it. In the midst of his fear and loneliness, that thought gave him a scrap of comfort. If he had been treated with kindness, he may not have had the strength. As things stood, his simmering dislike was like a draft of mare's blood in his stomach, nourishing him.

Yesugei did not look back as he passed the last riders of the Olkhun'ut. His heart ached at leaving his precious son in the hands of weaklings like Enq and Sholoi, but to have given Temujin even a few words of comfort would have been seen as a triumph for those who looked for such things. When he was riding alone across the plain and the camp was far behind, he permitted himself a rare smile. Temujin had more than a little fierceness in him, perhaps more than any other of his sons. Where Bekter might have retreated into sullenness, he thought Temujin might surprise those who thought they could freely torment a khan's son. Either way, he would survive the year and the Wolves would be stronger for his experiences and the wife he would bring home. Yesugei remembered the fat herds that roamed around the gers of his wife's tribe. He had found no true weaknesses in the defenses, but if the winter was hard, he could picture a day when he would ride amongst them once more, with warriors at his side. His mood lightened at the thought of seeing Enq run from his bondsmen. There would be no smiles and sly glances from the thin little man then. He dug in his heels to canter across the empty landscape, his imagination filled with pleasant thoughts of fire and screaming.

CHAPTER 6

TEMUJIN CAME ABRUPTLY from sleep when a pair of hands yanked him off his pallet and onto the wooden floor. The ger was filled with that close darkness that prevented him from even seeing his own limbs, and everything was unfamiliar. He could hear Sholoi muttering as he moved around, and assumed it was the old man who had woken him. Temujin felt a surge of fresh dislike for Borte's father. He scrambled up, stifling a cry of pain as he cracked his shin on some unseen obstacle. It was not yet dawn and the camp of the Olkhun'ut was silent all around. He did not want to start the dogs barking. A little cold water would splash away his sleepiness, he thought, yawning. He reached out to where he remembered seeing a bucket the evening before, but his hands closed on nothing.

"Awake yet?" Sholoi said somewhere near.

Temujin turned toward the sound and clenched his fists in the darkness. He had a bruise along the side of his face from where the old man had struck him the evening before. It had brought shameful tears to his eyes, though he'd seen that Enq had spoken the truth about life in that miserable home. Sholoi used his bony hands to enforce every order, whether he was moving a dog out of his path, or starting his daughter or wife to some task. The shrewish-looking wife seemed to have learned a sullen silence, but Borte had felt her father's fists more than a few times on that first evening, just for being too close in the confined space of the ger. Under the dirt and old cloth, Temujin thought she must have been covered in bruises. It had taken two sharp blows from Sholoi before he too kept his head down. He'd felt her eyes on him then, her gaze scornful, but what else could he have done? Killed the old man? He didn't think he would live long past Sholoi's first shout for help, not surrounded by the rest of the tribe. He thought they would take a particular delight in cutting him if he gave them cause. His last waking thought the night before had been the pleasant image of dragging a bloody Sholoi behind his pony, but it was just a fantasy born of humiliation. Bekter had survived, he reminded himself, sighing, wondering how the big ox had managed to hold his temper.

He heard a creak of hinges as Sholoi opened the small door, letting in enough cold starlight for Temujin to edge around the stove and past the sleeping forms of Borte and her mother. Somewhere nearby were two other gers with Sholoi's sons and their grubby wives and children. They had all left the old man years before, leaving only Borte. Despite his rough ways, Sholoi was khan in his own home, and Temujin could only bow his head and try not to earn too many cuffs and blows.

He shivered as he stepped outside, crossing his arms

in his thick deel so that he was hugging himself. Sholoi was emptying his bladder yet again, as he seemed to need to do every hour or so in the night. Temujin had woken more than once as Sholoi stumbled past him, and he wondered why he had been pulled from the blankets this time. He felt a deep ache in his stomach from hunger and looked forward to something hot to start the day. With just a little warm tea, he was certain he would be able to stop his hands shaking, but he knew Sholoi would only cackle and sneer if he asked for some before the stove was even lit.

The herds were dark figures under the starlight as Temujin emptied his own urine into the soil, watching it steam. The nights were still cold in spring and he saw there was a crust of ice on the ground. With a south-facing door, he had no trouble finding east, to look for the dawn. There was no sign of it and he hoped Sholoi did not rise at such an early hour every day. The man may have been toothless, but he was as knotted and wiry as an old stick, and Temujin had the sinking feeling that the day would be long and hard.

As he tucked himself in, Temujin felt Sholoi's grip on his arm, pushing at him. The old man held a wooden bucket, and as Temujin took it, he picked up another, pressing it into his free hand.

"Fill them and come back quick, boy," he said.

Temujin nodded, turning toward the sound of the nearby river. He wished Khasar and Kachiun could have been there. He missed them already and it was not hard to imagine the peaceful scene as they awoke in the ger he had known all his life, with Hoelun stirring them to begin their chores. The buckets were heavy as he headed back, but he wanted to eat and he did not doubt Sholoi would starve him if he gave him an opportunity.

The stove had been lit by the time he returned, and Borte had vanished from her blankets. Sholoi's grim little wife, Shria, was fussing around the stove, nursing the flames with tapers before shutting the door with a clang. She had not spoken a word to him since his arrival. Temujin looked thirstily at the pot of tea, but Sholoi came in just as he put the buckets down and guided him back out into the quiet darkness with a two-fingered grip on his biceps.

"You'll join the felters later, when the sun's up. Can you shear?"

"No, I've never had..." Temujin began.

Sholoi grimaced. "Not much good to me, boy, are you? I can carry my own buckets. When it's light you can collect sheep turds for the stove. Can you ride herd?"

"I've done it," Temujin replied quickly, hoping he would be given his pony to tend the Olkhun'ut sheep and cattle. That would at least take him away from his new family for a while each day. Sholoi saw his eagerness and his toothless mouth curled like a wet, grubby fist.

"Want to run back to your mother, boy, is that it? Frightened of a little hard work?"

Temujin shook his head. "I can tan leather and braid rope for bridles and saddles. I can carve wood, horn, and bone." He found himself blushing, though he doubted Sholoi could see in the starlit darkness. He heard the old man snort.

"I don't need a saddle for a horse I don't have, do I? Some of us weren't born into pretty silks and furs."

Temujin saw the old man's blow coming and

slipped it, turning his head. Sholoi wasn't fooled and thumped at him until he fell sideways into the darker patch where the urine had eaten at the frost. As he scrambled to get up, Sholoi kicked his ribs and Temujin lost his temper. He sprang up fast and stood wavering, suddenly unsure. The old man seemed determined to humiliate him with every word, and he couldn't under- stand what he wanted.

Sholoi made a whistling sound of exasperation and then spat, reaching for him with his gnarled fingers. Temujin edged backwards, completely unable to find a response that would satisfy his tormentor. He ducked and protected himself from a rain of blows, but some of them found their mark. Every instinct told him to strike back and yet he was not sure Sholoi would even feel it. The old man seemed to have grown and become fear- some in the dark, and Temujin could not imagine how to hit him hard enough to stop the attack.

"No more," he cried out. "No more!"

Sholoi chuckled, holding the edge of Temujin's deel in his unbreakable grip and panting as if he had run a mile in the noon sun.

"I've broken ponies better than you, boy. With more spirit, too. You're no better than I thought you were."

There was a world of scorn in his voice, and Temujin realized he could see the old man's features. The sun's first light had come into the east, and the tribe was stirring at last. Both of them sensed they were being watched at the same time, and when they turned, Borte was there, staring.

Temujin flushed with shame more painful than the actual blows. He felt Sholoi's hands fall away under

Borte's silent scrutiny, and the old man seemed discom-
fited somehow. Without another word, he pushed past
Temujin and disappeared into the fetid darkness of
the ger.

Temujin felt an itching drip of blood come from his
nostril onto his top lip, and he smeared it with an angry
gesture, sick of all of them. The movement seemed to
startle Sholoi's daughter and she turned her back on
him, running away into the dawn gloom. For a few precious moments he was on his own, and Temujin felt lost
and miserable. His new family were little better than animals from what he had seen, and it was only the beginning of the first day.

Borte ran through the gers, dodging obstacles and flying
past a barking dog as it tried to chase her. A few swift
turns and it was left behind to yap and snarl in impotent
fury. She felt alive when she ran, as if nothing in the
world could touch her. When she stood still, her father
could reach her with his hands, or her mother take a
whip of silver birch to her back. She still carried the
stripes from knocking over a pail of cool yoghurt two
days before.

The breath rushed cleanly in and out of her lungs,
and she wished the sun would stay frozen on the distant
horizon. If the tribe remained asleep, she could find a
little quiet and happiness away from their stares. She
knew how they talked of her and there were times when
she wished she could be like the other girls in the tribe.
She had even tried it when her mother had cried over
her once. One day was enough to become tired of
sewing and cooking and learning how to ferment the

black airag for the warriors. Where was the excitement in that? She even looked different from the other girls, with a thin frame and nothing more than tiny buds of breasts to spoil the rack of ribs that was her chest. Her mother complained she did not eat enough to grow, but Borte had heard a different message. She did not want big cow bosoms that would hang down for a man to milk her. She wanted to be fast like a deer and skinny like a wild dog.

She snorted as she ran, reveling in the pleasure of feeling the wind. Her father had given her to the Wolf puppy without a second thought. The old man was too stupid to ask her whether she would have him or not. No. He would not have cared either way. She knew how hard her father could be, and all she could do was run and hide from him, as she had a thousand times before. There were women in the Olkhun'ut who let her spend the night in their gers if old Sholoi was raging. Those were dangerous times, though, if their own men had been at the fermented milk. Borte always watched for the slurred voices and sweet breath that meant they would come grasping at her after dark. She had been caught once like that and it would not happen again, not while she carried her little knife, at least.

She raced past the final gers of the tribe and made a decision to reach the river without being conscious of it. The dawn light revealed the snaking black line of the water, and she felt the speed was still there in her legs. Perhaps she could leap it and never come down, like a heron taking off. She laughed at the thought of running like those ungainly birds, all legs and pumping wings. Then she reached the riverbank and her thighs bunched and released. She flew and, for a moment of glory, she looked up into the rising sun and thought she would not have to come down. Her feet caught the far edge of the shadowed riverbank, and she tumbled onto grass still stiff with frost, breathless at her own flights of imagination. She envied the birds who could drift so far from the land beneath them. How they must delight in the freedom, she thought, watching the sky for their dark shapes rising into the dawn. Nothing would give her more pleasure than to simply be able to spread wings and leave her mother and father behind like ugly specks on the ground. They would be small beneath her, she was sure, like insects. She would fly all the way to the sun, and the sky father would welcome her. Until he too raised his hand against her, and she had to fly again. Borte was not too sure about the sky father. In her experience, men of any stripe were too similar to the stallions she saw mounting the mares of the Olkhun'ut. They were hot enough before and during the act, with their long poles waving around beneath them. Afterwards, they cropped the grass as if nothing had happened, and she saw no tenderness there. There was no mystery to the act after living in the same ger as her parents all her life. Her father took no account of his daughter's presence if he decided to pull Shria to him in the evenings.

Lying on the cold ground, Borte blew air through her lips. If they thought the Wolf puppy would mount her in the same way, she would leave him with a stump where his manhood had been. She imagined carrying it away with her like a red worm and him being forced to chase and demand it back. The image was amusing and she giggled to herself as her breathing calmed at last. The tribe was waking. There was work to be done around the gers and with the herds. Her father would have his hands full with the khan's son, she thought, but she should stay close in case he still expected her to work on the untanned hides, or lay out the wool for felting. Everyone would be involved until the sheep were all sheared, and her absence would mean another turn with the birch whip if she let the day go.

She sat up in the grass and pulled a stalk to chew on. *Temujin.* She said it again aloud, feeling the way it made her mouth move. It meant a man of iron, which was a good name, if she hadn't seen him flinch under her father's hand. He was younger than her and a little coward, and this was the one she would marry? This was the boy who would give her strong sons and daughters who could run as she could?

"Never," she said aloud, looking into the running water. On impulse, she leaned over the surface and stared at the blurry vision of her face. It could have been anyone, she thought. Anyone who cut their own hair with a knife and was as dirty as any herder. She was no beauty, it was true, but if she could run fast enough, none of them could catch her anyway.

Under the noon sun, Temujin wiped sweat from his eyes, his stomach rumbling. Borte's mother was as sour and unpleasant as her husband, with eyes as sharp. He dreaded the thought of having a wife so ugly and sullen. For breakfast, Shria had given him a bowl of salt tea and a curd of cheese as long as his thumb and as hard as a bit of bone. He had put it into his cheek to suck, but it had barely begun to soften by noon. Sholoi had been given three hot pouches of unleavened bread and spiced mutton, slapping the greasy packages back and forth between his hands to ward off the morning chill. The smell had made Temujin's mouth water, but Shria had pinched his stomach and told him he could stand to miss a few meals. It was an insult, but what was one more?

While Sholoi greased leathers and checked the hooves of every Olkhun'ut pony, Temujin had carried great bales of fleeces to where the women of the tribe were laying them out on felting mats of ancient cloth. Each one was heavier than anything he had ever carried before, but he had managed to stagger with them across the camp, attracting the stares and excited chatter of small children. His calves and back had begun to burn before the second trip was over, but he was not allowed to stop. By the tenth bale, Sholoi had ceased greasing to watch his faltering progress, and Temujin saw some of the men grinning and muttering bets to each other. The Olkhun'ut would bet on anything, it seemed, but he was past caring when he fell at last, his legs limp under him. No one came to help him up and he thought he'd never been so desperately unhappy as in that moment of silence while the Olkhun'ut watched him rise. There was no pity or humor on a single one of the hard faces, and when he finally stood, he felt their dislike feed his spirit, raising his head. Though the sweat stung his eyes and every panting breath seemed to scorch him, he smiled at them. To his pleasure, some of them even turned away under his gaze, though most narrowed their eyes.

He knew someone was approaching from the way the expressions of the others changed. Temujin stood with the bale balanced on a shoulder and both arms up to steady it. He did not enjoy the feeling of vulnerability as he turned to see who had caught the eye of the crowd.

As he recognized his cousin, he saw that Koke was enjoying the moment. His fists hung loosely at his side, but it was easy to imagine them thumping into his unprotected stomach. Temujin tried to tense his belly, feeling it quiver in exhaustion. The bale weighed down heavily on him and his legs were still strangely weak. He showed Koke the cold face as he approached, doing his best to disconcert the boy on his home ground.

It didn't work. Koke came first, but there were other boys of the same age behind him, bright-eyed and dangerous looking. Out of the corner of his eye, Temujin saw the adults nudge each other and laugh. He groaned to himself and wished he had a knife to wipe the arrogance off their faces. Had Bekter suffered in this way? He had never mentioned it.

"Pick that bale up, boy," Koke said, grinning.

As Temujin opened his mouth to answer, he felt a push that overbalanced the bale and he almost went with it. He staggered into Koke and was shoved roughly away. He had been in too many fights with his brothers to let that go and threw a straight punch that rocked Koke's head back. In moments, they were rolling on the dusty ground, the fallen bale forgotten. The other boys did not cheer, but one of them rushed in and kicked Temujin in the stomach, winding him. He cried out in anger, but another one kicked him in the back as he struggled away from Koke and tried to rise. Koke was bleeding from his nose, though the blood was hardly more than a trickle, already clotting in the dust. Before Temujin regained his feet, Koke grappled him again, pressing his head into the earth while two more boys sat on his chest and legs, flattening him with their weight. Temujin was too tired to throw them off after so long carrying the bales. He struggled madly, but the dust filled every breath and soon he was choking and clawing at them. He had one of the other boys around the throat and Koke was punching at his head to make him let go. After that, he lost a little time and the noise seemed to go away.

He did not wake exactly, nor had he slept, but he came back as if he were surfacing from a dream when a bucket was upended over his head. Temujin gasped at the cold water running down him in streams of diluted blood and muddy filth. Sholoi held him upright and Temujin saw that the old man had sent the boys scurrying away at last, still jeering and laughing at their victim. Temujin looked into Sholoi's eyes and saw nothing but irritation as the old man clicked his fingers in front of his face to catch his attention.

"You must fetch more water now that I've emptied this bucket," he heard Sholoi say as if from far away. "After that, you will help beat the fleeces until we eat. If you work hard, you will have meat and hot bread to give you strength." He looked disgusted for a moment. "I think he's still dizzy. He needs a thicker skull, this one, like his brother. That boy had a head like a yak."

"I hear you," Temujin said irritably, shaking off the last of his weakness. He snatched the bucket, not troubling to hide his anger. He could not see Koke or the others, but he vowed to finish the fight they had started. He had endured the work and the scorn of the Olkhun'ut, but a public beating was too much. He knew he could not rush blindly at the other boy. He was enough of a child to want to, but enough of a warrior to wait for his moment. It would come.

As Yesugei rode between peaks in a vast green valley, he saw the moving specks of riders in the far distance and set his mouth in a firm line. From so far away, he could not tell if the Olkhun'ut had sent warriors to shadow him back to his gers, or whether it was a raiding party from a tribe new to the area. His hope that they were herdsmen was quickly dashed as he looked around at the bare hillsides. There were no lost sheep nearby and he knew with a grim feeling that he was vulnerable if the group turned to chase him.

He watched their movement out of the corner of his eye, careful not to show them a tiny white face staring in their direction. He hoped they would not trouble to follow a single horseman, but he snorted to himself as he saw them turn, noting the rise of dust as they kicked their mounts into a gallop. The farthest outriders of his Wolves were still two days away, and he would be pushed to lose the raiders on such open land. He started his gelding galloping, pleased that it was strong and well rested. Perhaps the following men had tired horses and would be left behind.

Yesugei did not glance over his shoulder as he rode. In such a wide valley, he could see for five or six miles and be seen in turn. The chase would be a long one, but without a wealth of luck, they would catch him unless he found shelter. His eyes traveled feverishly along the hills, seeing the trees on the high ridges, like distant eyelashes. They would not hide him, he thought. He needed a sheltered valley where woods stretched across the bones of the earth, layering it in ancient leaves and gray pine needles. There were many such places, but he had been spotted far from any of them. With irritation growling deep in his chest, he rode on. When he did look back, the riders were closer and he saw there were five of them in the pursuit. Their blood would be up for the chase, he knew. They would be excited and yelling, though their cries were lost far behind him. He showed his teeth in the wind as he rode. If they knew whom they were chasing, they would not be so rash. He touched his hand to the hilt of his sword, where it lay across the horse's hindquarters, slapping the skin. The long blade had belonged to his father and was held by a thong of leather, to keep it safe while he rode. His bow was tied securely to his saddle, but he could string it in moments. Under his deel, the old shirt of chain mail he had won in a raid was a comforting weight. If they pressed him, he would butcher the lot of them, he told himself, feeling the twinges of an old excitement. He was the khan of Wolves and he feared no man. They would pay dearly for his skin.

CHAPTER 7

TEMUJIN WINCED as the raw wool snagged his red fingers for the hundredth time. He had seen it done before in the camp of the Wolves, but the work was usually left to older boys and young women. It was different with the Olkhun'ut and he could see that he had not been singled out. The smallest children carried buckets full of water to sprinkle on each layer of the woolen fleeces, keeping them constantly moist. Koke and the other boys tied the fleeces onto upright skins on frames and beat them with long, smooth sticks for hours until the sweat ran off them in streams. Temujin had done his part, though the temptation to crack his stick into Koke's grinning face had been almost overwhelming.

After the fleeces had been thrashed into softness, the women used the width of their outstretched arms to measure out one ald, marking the fleeces with chalk. When they had their width, they stretched them on the felting cloths, smoothing and teasing the snags and loose fibers until they resembled a single white mat.

More water helped to weigh the rough felt down in layers, but there was real skill in finding the exact thickness. Temujin had watched his hands redden and grow sore as the day wore on, working with the others while Koke mocked him and had the women giggling at his discomfort. It did not matter, Temujin had discovered. Now that he had decided to wait for his moment, Temujin found he could bear the insults and the sneers. In fact, there was a subtle pleasure in knowing that the time would come when no one else was around and he would give Koke back a little of what he deserved. Or more than a little, he thought. With his hands smarting and painful scratch lines up to his elbows, it made a pleasant picture in his mind.

When the mats were smooth and regular, an Olkhun'ut pony was backed up and the great expanse of white wool rolled onto a long cylinder, worn perfectly smooth with the labor of generations. Temujin would have given a great deal to be the one who dragged it for miles away from those people. Instead, the job went to laughing Koke, and Temujin realized he was popular in the tribe, perhaps because he made the women smile at his antics. There was nothing for Temujin to do but keep his head down and wait for the next break of mare's milk and a pouch of vegetables and mutton. His arms and back ached as if someone had stuck a knife in him and twisted it with every movement, but he endured, standing with the others to heave the next batch of beaten fleeces onto the felting cloth.

He was not the only one to suffer, he had noticed. Sholoi seemed to supervise the process, though Temujin did not think he owned sheep himself. When one small boy ran too close and sent dust over the raw fleeces, Sholoi grabbed his arm and beat him unmercifully with a stick, ignoring his screaming until there was nothing but whimpering. The fleeces had to be kept clean or the felt would be weak, and Temujin was careful not to make the same mistake. He knelt on the very edge of the matting and allowed no small stone or drift of dust to spoil his patch.

Borte had worked across from him for part of the afternoon, and Temujin had used the opportunity to take a good look at the girl his father had accepted for him. She seemed skinny enough to be a collection of bones, with a mop of black hair that hung over her eyes and a cake of snot under her nose. He found it difficult to imagine a less attractive girl, and when she caught him glaring, she cleared her throat to spit before she remembered the clean fleeces and swallowed it. He shook his head in amazement at her, wondering what his father could have seen to like. It was just possible that Yesugei's pride had forced him to accept what he was given, thus shaming small men like Enq and Sholoi. Temujin had to face the fact that the girl who would share his ger and give him children was as wild as a plains cat. It seemed to fit his experience of the Olkhun'ut so far, he thought miserably. They were not generous. If they were willing to give a girl away, it would be one they wanted rid of, where she would cause trouble for another tribe.

Shria smacked his arms with her felting stick, making him yelp. Of course, the other women all chuckled and one or two even imitated the sound, so that he flushed with fury.

"Stop dreaming, Temujin," Borte's mother said, as she had a dozen times before.

The work was dull and repetitive and the women either kept up a stream of chatter or worked almost in a trance, but that was a luxury not allowed to the newcomer. The slightest inattention was punished and the heat and sun seemed endless. Even the drinking water brought round to the workers was warm and salty and made him gag. He seemed to have been smashing his stick into stinking wool, or removing lice from it, or rolling it or carrying it forever. He could hardly believe it was still his first day.

Somewhere to the south, his father was riding home. Temujin could imagine the dogs leaping around him and the pleasure of teaching the twin eagles to hunt and return to the wrist. His brothers would be part of the training, he was sure, allowed to hold bits of meat aloft on trembling fingers. Kachiun would not flinch as the red bird took the lure, he was certain. He envied them the summer they would have.

Shria smacked him again and he reached up with lightning speed to pull the stick from her hands, laying it gently on the ground by him. She gaped at him for an instant before reaching for it, but he put his knee on its length and shook his head, feeling light-headed as his heart hammered. He saw her eyes flicker to Sholoi, who was standing nearby, watching over a new batch of the wet fleeces as they were lowered to the ground. Temujin waited for her to screech and then, to his astonishment, she shrugged, holding out her hand for the stick. It was an awkward moment, but he made a choice and handed it back to her, ready to duck. She hefted it in her hands for a moment, clearly undecided, then simply turned her back and walked away from him. He kept her firmly in his vision for a while longer as his fingers resumed the smoothing and tugging, but she didn't return, and after a while, he was lost in the work once more.

It was Enq, his uncle, who brought a pot filled with fermented milk to give them the strength to finish. As the sun touched the hills in the west, each of them had a ladleful of the clear liquid known as black airag, which looked like water, but burned. It was hotter than the milky tea in the gers, and Temujin choked on his, coughing. He wiped his mouth and then gasped with pain as the liquid found his broken skin and stung like fire. Koke was off rolling the felt behind his pony, but Sholoi saw his discomfort and laughed until Temujin thought he would have a seizure and die right in front of him. He hoped it would happen, but the old man survived to wring tears from his eyes and wheeze his way back to the pot for another ladleful. It was difficult not to resent the second cup for one who had done practically nothing, but no one else seemed to mind. The light slowly faded and the last felting mat was rolled into a cylinder and tied behind another horse.

Before anyone could object, Borte leapt into the saddle, surprising Sholoi as he stood holding the reins. No words passed between them, but the old man's toothless mouth worked as if he had found a bit of gristle that he couldn't reach. After a moment's indecision, he slapped the rump of the pony and sent her out into the gloom to roll the felt into flatness and strength. It would keep the winter chill out of the gers, and make heavy rugs and horse blankets. The rough cuts would be used for babies too young to use a latrine pit without falling in. Temujin sat on his heels and stretched his back, closing his eyes against the aches. His right hand had gone numb, which worried him. He used his left to massage the blood into the fingers, but when it came, the pain brought tears to his eyes. He had never worked so hard, he thought, and wondered if it would make him stronger.

Sholoi came over as he dragged himself to his feet, and Temujin started slightly as he registered the old man's presence. He hated his own nervousness, but there had been too many sudden blows for him not to be wary. The draft of fermented milk made him belch sourly as Sholoi took him in the two-fingered grip he was beginning to know well, pointing him back toward the ger.

"Eat now and sleep. Tomorrow you'll cut wood for winter."

Temujin was too tired to respond and followed him in a daze of exhaustion, his limbs and spirit heavy.

Yesugei had found a place to camp that seemed safe enough. The valley where he'd sighted the group of riders had come to an end, and he'd galloped straight through a short pass between hills, hoping to find some shelter that would confuse his trail. He knew it would not be hard to track him on the dusty ground, but he could not go on all night and risk breaking his pony's leg in a marmot hole. Instead, he forced the courageous little gelding up a steep slope to the patchy tree line, dismounting to lead with reins and constant encouragement. It was a hard and dangerous climb and the horse's eyes were white-rimmed with fear when its hooves slipped on the loose mulch. Yesugei had moved fast, wrapping the reins around the bole of a tree and hanging on desperately until the gelding found its footing. Even then, his shoulder and chest muscles ached terribly by the time he reached the top and the gelding was blowing noisily enough to be heard a mile away. He did not think they would follow him into the trees as the darkness came. All he had to do was stay out of sight and they could search in vain for a trail that disappeared in the mat of dead pine needles. He would have chuckled at the thought if he had been able to see them, but he could not. His prickling neck told him his pursuers were still somewhere close, looking and listening for some sign of him. He worried that his mount would whinny to their horses and give his position away, but the animal was too tired after the climb and the hard ride. With a little luck, and a night without a fire, they would abandon the search and go on their way the following morning. It did not matter if he came back to the gers of the Wolves a day late, after all.

High on the crest of the hill, he pulled a pair of stunted bushes together and tied the reins, watching with amusement as the pony eased itself down onto its knees and found that it could not lie flat as the reins grew taut. He left the saddle on its back in case he had to move quickly, loosening the belly rope a couple of notches along the braiding. The gelding snorted at the attention and made itself comfortable as best it could. After a while, he saw it close its eyes and doze, its soft muzzle falling open to reveal solid yellow teeth.

Yesugei listened for a sign that his pursuers had not given up. It would be hard for them to come close without alerting him on such broken ground. He untied the leather strap that kept his sword in the scabbard and then drew it in one smooth movement, examining the blade. It was good steel and enough of a prize on its own to make him a target for thieves. If Eeluk had been with him, he would have challenged the men on the plain, but five was probably too many for him, unless they were unblooded boys who could be scared with a shout and a few quick cuts. His father's blade was as sharp as ever, which was all to the good. He could not risk them hearing him stroke it with his stone that evening. Instead, he took a few gulps from his leather water bottle, with a grimace at its lightness. The gelding would be thirsty come the morning. If the streams nearby had run dry, he would have a hard day, whether the riders saw him or not. He shrugged to himself at the thought. He had lived through worse.

Yesugei stretched and yawned, smiling at the sleeping pony as he pulled dried mutton from his saddlebags and chewed on it, grunting in pleasure at the spicy taste. He missed Hoelun and his boys and wondered what they would be doing at that moment.

As he laid himself down and pulled his hands back inside his deel for sleep, he hoped Temujin had the spirit to endure Hoelun's people. It was difficult to know whether the boy had the strength at such a young age. Yesugei would not have been surprised to find that Temujin had run away, though he hoped he would not. It would be a difficult shame to live down, and the story would spread around the tribes in less than a season. Yesugei sent a silent prayer to help his son. Bekter had suffered, he knew. His eldest boy spoke with little liking for the Olkhun'ut when Hoelun was not around. It was the only way to speak of them, of course. Yesugei grunted softly to himself and thanked the sky father for giving him such a fine crop of sons. A smile touched his lips then, as he slipped into sleep. Sons and now a daughter. He had been blessed with strong seed and a good woman to bear them. He knew of other wives who lost one miserable scrap of red flesh for every one that came alive into the world, but Hoelun's children all survived and grew strong. Grew fat, in the case of Temuge, which was still a problem he would have to face. Sleep took him at last then, and his breath came slow and steady.

When his eyes snapped open, the first light of dawn was in the east, with a strip of gold on the far hills. He loved this land and, for a moment, he gave thanks for having lived to see another day. Then he heard men moving close by and the breath stilled in his throat. He eased himself away from the frozen ground, pulling his hair from where it had stuck to the frost. He had slept with his sword bare under the deel and his fingers found the hilt, curling around it. He knew he had to rise so that they could not rush him while he was still stiff, but he did not yet know if he had been seen. His eyes slid left and right and he strained his senses, searching out the source of the noise. There was a chance it was just a herder looking for a lost goat, but he knew that wasn't likely. He heard a horse snort nearby and then his own gelding woke and whinnied, as he had feared it would. One of his pursuers rode a mare and she answered the call no more than fifty paces to his right. Yesugei rose like smoke, ignoring the twinge from his knees and back. Without hesitation, he took his bow from the saddle and strung it, pulling a long shaft from his quiver and touching it to the string. Only Eeluk could fire an arrow farther, and he did not doubt his eye. If they were hostile, he could drop one or two of them before they could come within a sword's length. He knew to look for the leaders for those first quick strikes, leaving only men weak enough to fall to his blade.

Now that they knew his position, there was no more sound from the group, and he waited patiently for them to show themselves. He stood with the sun behind him, and after a moment's thought, he unbuttoned his deel and reversed it. His heart was in his mouth as he lay down his sword and bow, but the dark inner cloth would blend with the bushes better than the blue, making him a poor target. He took up his weapons once more and stood as still as the trees and bushes around him. He caught himself humming under his breath and killed the sound. Sleep was just a memory and the blood flowed quickly in his flesh. Despite the threat, he found he was enjoying the tension.

"Hello the camp," a voice called from off to his left.

Yesugei cursed inwardly, knowing they had circled around. Without a thought, he left the gelding and moved deeper into the trees, heading toward the voice. Whoever they were, they would not kill him easily, he vowed. It crossed his mind that they might not be a threat, but a man would have to be a fool to risk his life, his horse, and his father's sword on a vague hope. On the plains, even a strong man survived only with caution, and he knew he was a valuable prize for a raiding party, whether they realized it or not.

A line of sweat prickled down from his hairline as he waited.

"I can't see him," another voice came from only a few paces away.

Yesugei eased down into a crouch, drawing back on the bow with a creak.

"His horse is here, though," a third man said, the

voice deeper than the others. They all sounded young to Yesugei's ear, though he wondered at their tracking skill. Even as close as they were, he could not hear them move.

With infinite care, he turned his head to glance behind him. Through the bushes, he could see a man pulling at the knot he had tied with the gelding's reins. Yesugei grimaced in angry silence. He could not let them steal his horse and leave him there.

He took a deep breath, and rose to his full height, startling the stranger by the gelding. The man's hand jumped for a knife, but then registered the drawn bow and froze.

"We're not looking for a fight, old man," the stranger said loudly.

Yesugei knew he was alerting his companions, and an answering rustle from his right sent his heart tripping at higher speed.

"Step out where I can see you, then, and stop creeping around behind me," Yesugei said, his voice ringing across the clearing.

The rustling stopped and the young man who stood so coolly under his arrow nodded.

"Do as he says. I don't want to get stuck before I've had breakfast this morning."

"Call out before you move," Yesugei added, "or die, one or the other."

There was a long silence and the young man sighed.

"Step out here, all of you," he snapped, his coolness fraying visibly under the arrow point that never wavered from his heart.

Yesugei watched with narrowed eyes as the other four men came noisily through the brush. Two of them had bows with arrows notched and ready. They were all armed and wore thickly padded deels—the sort of garment designed to stop an arrow from penetrating too far. Yesugei recognized the stitching and wondered if they, in turn, would know him for who he was. For all the light manner of the one by the gelding, this was a Tartar raiding party and Yesugei knew hard men when he saw them, out to steal what they could.

When they were all in sight, the one who had spoken first nodded to Yesugei.

"I did call the camp, old man. Will you grant us guest rights while we eat?"

Yesugei wondered whether the rules of courtesy would apply when they were not in danger from his bow, but with two of them bending bows of their own, he nodded and eased the tension on his string. The young men all relaxed visibly and their leader twitched his shoulders to relieve stiffness.

"My name is Ulagan, of the Tartars," the young man said with a smile. "You are from the Wolves, unless you stole that deel and sword."

"I am," Yesugei replied, then added formally, "You are welcome to share food and milk in my camp."

"And your name?" Ulagan said, raising his eyebrows.

"Eeluk," Yesugei said, without hesitating. "If you make a fire, I can find a cup of black airag to warm your blood."

All the men moved slowly as they set about preparing a meal, careful not to startle each other with a sudden movement. It took longer than usual for them all to gather rocks and nurse a flame with flint and steel, but as the sun rose, they ate well with the dried meat from

Yesugei's saddlebags and some rare honey that Ulagan brought from a pouch under his deel. The sweetness was wonderful to Yesugei, who had not tasted any since the time the tribe found a wild nest three years before. He licked his fingers to get every last drip of the golden fluid, rich with waxy fragments, yet his hands never strayed too far from his sword and the arrow remained ready on the ground in front of him. There was something uncomfortable in the gaze of Ulagan as he watched him eat, though he smiled whenever Yesugei met his eyes. None of the others spoke as they broke their fast, and the tension remained in every movement.

"Are you finished?" Ulagan asked after a time.

Yesugei sensed a subtle tautness in them as one of the men moved to one side and dropped his trousers to defecate on the ground. The man did not try to hide himself, and Yesugei had a glimpse of his manhood swinging loose as he strained.

"In the Wolves, we keep excrement away from the food," Yesugei murmured.

Ulagan shrugged. He stood and Yesugei rose with him rather than be at a disadvantage. He watched in astonishment as Ulagan crossed to the steaming pile and drew his sword.

Yesugei's own blade was in his hand before he had made a conscious decision, but he was not attacked. Instead, he watched Ulagan pull his blade through the stinking mass until its metal was slick with it along the whole length.

Ulagan wrinkled his nose and raised his head to the man whose efforts had created the pile.

"You have diseased bowels, Nasan, have I told you?"

"You have," Nasan replied without humor, repeating the action with his own blade. It was then that Yesugei realized this was no chance meeting on the plains.

"When did you know me?" he asked softly.

Ulagan smiled, though his eyes were cold.

"We knew when the Olkhun'ut told us you had come to them with a son. We paid their khan well to send a rider to our little camp, but he was not hard to persuade." Ulagan chuckled to himself. "You are not a popular man. There were times when I thought you would never come, but old Sansar was as good as his word."

Yesugei's heart sank with the news and he feared for Temujin. As he contemplated his chances, he tried to keep his enemy talking. He had already decided Ulagan was a fool. There was no point chatting to a man you were going to kill, but the young warrior seemed to be enjoying his power over him.

"Why is my life worth sending you out?" Yesugei asked.

Ulagan grinned. "You killed the wrong man, Wolf. You killed the son of a khan who was foolish enough to steal from your herds. His father is not one to forgive easily."

Yesugei nodded, as if he was listening intently. He saw that the other three men intended to poison their blades in the same filth, and without warning, he leapt forward and struck, cutting deep into Nasan's neck as he turned to watch them. The Tartar fell with a death cry and Ulagan roared in anger, lunging straight at Yesugei's chest with his blade. The Tartar was fast, but the blade

slid along the chain mail under the deel, cutting a flap
from the cloth.

Yesugei attacked quickly, needing better odds. The
blades rang twice as the three others fanned out around
him, and he felt the strength in his shoulders. He would
show them what it meant to be a khan of the Wolves.

Yesugei feinted his own lunge, then stepped back as
quickly as he could run forward, three sliding steps taking him outside the circle before it could form around
him. One of the other men turned to bring a blade down
in a great arc, and Yesugei stabbed him under the shoulder into the chest, wrenching his father's blade clear as
he fell. He felt a sharp pain in his back then, but another
step tore him clear and a quick slash felled another of
the group with half his jaw cut away.

Ulagan pressed forward, his face grim at the death
of three of his brothers in arms.

"You should have brought more to bring down a
khan," Yesugei taunted him. "Five is an insult to me."
He dropped suddenly to one knee to avoid Ulagan's cut.
With a savage jerk, Yesugei managed to chop his blade
into the younger man's shin. It was not a mortal wound,
but blood drenched Ulagan's boot and the Tartar warrior was suddenly not so confident.

As Yesugei came to his feet, he stepped left and
then right, keeping the pair off balance. He trained every
day with Eeluk and his bondsmen, and he knew that
movement was the key to killing with swords. Any man
could heave a blade around his head, but footwork sep-
arated a man from a master. He grinned as Ulagan
limped after him, gesturing for him to come closer. The
Tartar nodded to the one remaining warrior and Yesugei
watched as he moved to the side to take him. Ulagan

timed it well and Yesugei did not have space to dart away. He buried his sword in the chest of the unnamed man, but it snagged in the ribs and Ulagan struck with his full weight, punching his blade tip through the mail into Yesugei's stomach. Yesugei's grip was broken on his sword as it fell away. He felt a pang for his sons that was worse than the pain, but he used his right hand to hold Ulagan still against him. With his left, he drew a dagger from his belt.

Ulagan saw the movement and struggled, but Yesugei's grip was like iron. He looked down on the young Tartar and spat into his face.

"Your people will be torn from the land for this, Tartar. Your gers will burn and your herds will be scattered."

With a quick slash, he cut the young man's throat and let him fall away. As he crumpled, the Tartar blade slid out of Yesugei's wound and he bellowed in pain, falling to his knees. He could feel blood coursing down his thighs, and he used the dagger to cut a great strip from his deel, yanking and cursing the agony, with his eyes closed now that there was no one to see. His gelding pulled nervously at the reins, whinnying its distress. The animal was frightened by the smell of blood, and Yesugei forced himself to speak calmly. If the horse pulled free and bolted, he knew he would not make it back to his people.

"It's all right, little one. They have not killed me. Do you remember when Eeluk fell on the broken sapling and it went into his back? He lived through it, with enough boiling airag poured into the wound."

He grimaced at that thought, remembering how the usually taciturn Eeluk had screamed like a small child.

To his relief, his voice seemed to quiet the pony and it ceased yanking at the knot.

"That's it, little one. You stay and carry me home."

Dizziness threatened to overwhelm him, but his fingers tugged the cloth around his waist and tied the knots hard and tight. He raised his hands and sniffed at them, wincing at the smell of human filth from Ulagan's blade. That was an evil thing, he thought. They deserved death for that alone.

He wanted just to stay on his knees with his back straight. His father's sword was close by his hand and he took comfort from the touch of cold metal. He felt he might hold himself there for a long time and watch the sun rise. Part of him knew he could not, if Temujin was to live. He had to reach the Wolves and send warriors out for the boy. He had to get back. His body felt heavy and useless, but he summoned his strength yet again.

With a cry of distress, he pulled himself to his feet, staggering to the gelding, who watched him with the whites of its eyes showing. Resting his forehead against the pony's flank, he slid the sword into the saddle straps, taking sharp breaths through the pain. His fingers were clumsy as he undid the reins, but he managed somehow to get back into the saddle. He knew he could not make the steep slope down, but the other side of the hill was easier and he dug in his heels, his vision fixed far away, on his home and his family.

CHAPTER 8

AS EVENING CAME, Bekter let his mare graze while he sat on a high ridge, watching for his father's return. His back ached with tiredness after spending the day in the saddle with the herds. It had not been dull, at least. He'd rescued a goat kid that had fallen into a strip of marshy land by the river. With a rope around his waist, he had waded into the black muck to bring out the terrified animal before it drowned. It had struggled wildly, but he had pulled it out by an ear and placed it on the dry bank, where it glared at him as if the ordeal were his fault. As he moved his slow gaze over the plain, he scratched idly at a spatter of the black mud on his skin.

He enjoyed being away from the chatter and noise of the gers. When his father was absent, he sensed a subtle difference in the way the other men treated him, especially Eeluk. The man was humble enough when Yesugei was there to demand obedience, but when they were alone, Bekter sensed an arrogance in the bondsman that made him uncomfortable. It was nothing he could have mentioned to his father, but he walked carefully around Eeluk and kept his own counsel. He had found the best course was simply to remain silent and match the warriors at work and battle drills. There at least, he could show his skills, though it helped not to have Temujin's eyes on the back of his neck as he drew his bow. He had felt nothing but relief when Temujin went to the Olkhun'ut. In fact, he had taken satisfaction from the hope that his brother would have a little sense beaten into him, a little respect for his elders.

Bekter remembered with pleasure how Koke had tried to bait him on his very first day. The younger boy had not been a match for Bekter's strength or ferocity, and he had knocked him down and kicked him unconscious. The Olkhun'ut had seemed shocked by the violence, as if boys did not fight in their tribe. Bekter spat at the memory of their sheeplike faces accusing him. Koke had not risked taunting him again. It had been a good lesson to give early.

Enq had thrashed him, of course, with one of the felting sticks, but Bekter had borne the blows without a single sound, and when Enq was panting and tired, he had reached out and snapped the stick in his hands, showing his strength. They had left him alone after that and Enq had known better than to work him too hard. The Olkhun'ut were as weak as Yesugei said they were, though their women were soft as white butter and stirred him as they walked by.

He thought his betrothed would surely have come into her blood by now, though the Olkhun'ut had not sent her. He remembered riding out onto the plains with her and laying her down by the bank of a stream. She had struggled a little at first when she realized what he was doing, and he had been clumsy. In the end, he'd had to force her, though it was no more than he had a right to do. She should not have brushed past him in the ger if she didn't want something to happen, he told himself, smiling at the memory. Though she had cried a little afterwards, he thought she had a different light in her eye. He felt himself growing stiff as he recalled her nakedness, and wondered again when they would send her. Her father had taken a dislike to him, but the Olkhun'ut would not dare refuse Yesugei. They could hardly give her to another man after Bekter had spilled his seed in her, he thought. Perhaps she would even be pregnant. He did not think it was possible before the moon's blood began, but he knew there were mysteries there that he did not fully understand.

The night was growing too cold to be tormenting himself with fantasies, and he knew better than to be distracted from his watch. The families of the Wolves accepted that he would lead them one day, he was almost certain, though in Yesugei's absence they all looked to Eeluk for orders. It was he who had organized the scouts and watchers, but that was only to be expected until Bekter took a wife and killed his first man. Until that time, he would still be a boy in the eyes of seasoned warriors, as his brothers were boys to him.

In the gathering gloom, he saw a dark spot moving out on the plain below his position. Bekter rose to his feet instantly, pulling his horn free of the folds of his deel. He hesitated as he raised it to his lips, his eyes searching for more of a threat than a single rider. The height he had chosen gave him a view of a great expanse of the grassland, and whoever it was seemed to be alone. Bekter frowned to himself, hoping it was not one of his idiot brothers out without telling anyone. It would not help his status in the tribe if he called the warriors from their meal without cause.

He chose to wait, watching as the tiny figure came closer. The rider was clearly in no hurry. Bekter could see the pony was walking almost aimlessly, as if the man on his back was wandering without a destination.

He frowned at that thought. There were men who claimed allegiance to no particular tribe. They drifted between the families of the plains, exchanging a day's work for a meal or occasionally bringing goods to trade. They were not popular and there was always the danger that they would steal whatever they could lay their hands on, then disappear. Men without a tribe could not be trusted, Bekter knew. He wondered if the rider was one of those.

The sun had sunk behind the hills and the light was fading quickly. Bekter realized he should sound his horn before the stranger was lost in darkness. He raised it to his lips and hesitated. Something about the distant figure made him pause. It could not be Yesugei, surely? His father would never ride so poorly.

He had almost waited too long when he finally blew the warning note. The sound was long and mournful as it echoed across the hills. Other horns answered him from watchers around the camp, and he tucked it back into his deel, satisfied. Now that the warning had been given, he could go down to see who the rider was. He mounted his mare and checked that his knife and bow were within easy reach. In the silence of the evening, he could already hear answering shouts and the sound of horses as the warriors came boiling out of the gers. Bekter dug in his heels to guide his pony down the slope, wanting to get there before Eeluk and the older men. He felt a sense of ownership for the single rider. He had spotted him, after all. As he reached the flat ground and broke into a gallop, thoughts of the Olkhun'ut and his betrothed slipped away from his mind and his heart began to beat faster. The evening wind was cool and he hungered to show the other men that he could lead them.

The Wolves rode hard out of the encampment, Eeluk at their head. In the last moments of light, they saw Bekter kick his mount into a run and went after him, not yet seeing his reason for raising the alarm.

Eeluk sent a dozen riders left and right to skirt the camp, looking for an attack from another direction. It would not do to leave the gers defenseless while they went after a feint or a diversion. Their enemies were devious enough to draw the watchers away and then attack, and the last moments of light were perfect to cause confusion. It felt strange for Eeluk to be riding without Yesugei on his left, but Eeluk found he was enjoying the way the other men looked to him to lead them. He snapped orders and the arban formed around him with Eeluk on the point, racing after Bekter.

Another blast from a horn came from just ahead, and Eeluk narrowed his eyes, straining to see. He was almost blind in the gloom and to gallop was to risk his mare and his life, but he kicked his horse on recklessly, knowing Bekter would not have blown again unless the attack was real. Eeluk snatched at his bow and placed an arrow on the string by feel, as he had done a thousand times before. The men around him did the same. Whoever had dared to attack the Wolves would be met with a storm of whining shafts before they came much closer. They rode in grim silence, high on the stirrups, balancing perfectly against the rise and fall of their ponies. Eeluk pulled back his lips in the wind, feeling the thrill of the attack. Let them hear the hooves thundering toward them, he thought. Let them fear retribution.

In the dark, the riding warriors almost collided with two ponies standing alone on the open ground. Eeluk came close to loosing his arrow, but he heard Bekter shouting and, with an effort, he lowered himself into the saddle and eased his string. The battle blood was still strong in him and he felt a sudden fury that Yesugei's son had brought them out for nothing. Dropping his bow over the saddle horn, Eeluk leapt lightly to the ground and drew his sword. The darkness was on them and he did not yet know what was happening.

"Eeluk! Help me with him," Bekter said, his voice high and strained.

Eeluk found the boy holding the slumped figure of Yesugei on the ground. Eeluk felt his heart thump painfully as the last traces of battle rage slid away from him and he knelt by the pair of them.

"Is he injured?" Eeluk said, reaching out to his khan. He could hardly see anything, but he rubbed his fingers and thumb together and sniffed at them. Yesugei's stomach was tightly bound, but blood had soaked through.

"He fell, Eeluk. He fell into my arms," Bekter said, close to panic. "I could not hold him."

Eeluk laid a hand on the boy's to steady him, before standing and whistling for the other bondsmen to approach. He took a grip on the reins of one dark rider.

"Basan, you ride to the Olkhun'ut, and find the truth of this."

"Is it war, then?" the man answered.

"Perhaps. Tell them that if you are not allowed to leave freely, we will be riding behind you and I will see their gers burnt to ashes."

The warrior nodded and trotted away, the drumbeat of hooves fading quickly in the night.

Yesugei groaned and opened his eyes, feeling a sudden panic at the shadows moving around him.

"Eeluk?" he whispered.

Eeluk crouched at his side. "I am here, my khan."

They waited for another word, but Yesugei had passed back into unconsciousness. Eeluk grimaced.

"We must get him back to have his wound tended. Step away, boy; there's nothing you can do for him here."

Bekter stood stunned, unable to comprehend that it was his father lying helpless at his feet.

"He fell," he said again, as if dazed. "Is he dying?"

Eeluk looked down at the slumped man he had followed all his adult life. As gently as he could, he took Yesugei under the armpits and heaved him onto his shoulder. The khan was a powerful man, made even heavier in chain mail, but Eeluk was strong and he showed no sign of discomfort.

"Help me to mount, Bekter. He's not dead yet and we must get him to warmth. A night out here will finish it." A thought struck him as he draped Yesugei over his saddle, the long, limp arms reaching almost to the ground. "Where is his sword?" he asked. "Can you see it?"

"No, it must have fallen when he did."

Eeluk sighed as he mounted. He had not had a chance to think about what was happening. He could feel the blood warmth of Yesugei against his chest as he leaned forward to speak to the son.

"Mark the spot somehow, so you can find it again in the light. He won't thank you for losing his father's blade."

Bekter turned without thinking to another one of his father's bondsmen, standing nearby in shock at what he was witnessing.

"You will stay, Unegen. I must return to the gers with my father. Search in circles as soon as you can see, and bring the blade to me when you find it."

"I will do as you say," Unegen replied in the darkness.

Bekter moved to his pony to mount and did not see Eeluk's expression as he considered the exchange. The world was changing in those moments and Eeluk did not know what the day would bring for any of them.

Hoelun wiped tears from her eyes as she faced her husband's bondsmen. The men and women of the Wolves had come, hungry for news, as soon as word spread of the khan's injury. She wished she had something more to tell them, but Yesugei had not woken again and he lay inside the ger in the cool shadows, his skin burning. Not one of them had stirred from their watch as the day wore on and the sun rose high above their heads.

"He still lives," she said. "I have cleaned his wound, but he has not yet woken."

Eeluk nodded and she could not miss how the other warriors looked to him. Kachiun and Temuge were there with Khasar, standing shocked and pale after seeing their father helpless. Yesugei seemed smaller under the blankets, his weakness frightening his sons more than anything they had ever known. He had been such a force in their lives, it did not seem possible that he might never wake. She feared for them all, though she did not mention it aloud. Without Yesugei to protect them, she saw the glint of greed in the eyes of the other men. Eeluk in particular seemed to be hiding a smile when he spoke to her, though his words were deliberately courteous.

"I will tell you if he wakes," she told the warriors, ducking back into the ger, away from their cold interest. Her daughter, Temulun, was in the cradle there, crying to be changed. The sound seemed to match the screaming voice inside her that she barely held in check. She could not give way to it, not while her sons needed her.

Temuge had come with her into the ger, his small mouth quivering in grief. Hoelun gathered him into her arms and shushed his tears, though her own started just as strongly. They wept together at Yesugei's side and she knew the khan could not hear them.

"What will happen if he does not live?" Temuge asked.

She might have answered, but the door creaked open and Eeluk entered. Hoelun felt a grip of hot anger to have been seen at such a moment, and she wiped fiercely at her eyes.

"I have sent your other sons to the herds for the day, to keep their minds off their father," Eeluk said.

It may have been her imagination, but again she thought she saw a gleam of satisfaction as he looked at Yesugei's still form, quickly masked.

"You have been strong when the tribe needed it, Eeluk," she said. "My husband will thank you himself when he wakes."

Eeluk nodded as if he had barely heard, crossing the ger to where Yesugei lay. He reached down to press his hand against the khan's forehead, whistling softly at the heat there. He sniffed at the wound and she knew he could smell the corruption that tainted the flesh.

"I poured boiling spirits into the wound," Hoelun said. "I have herbs to ease the fever." She felt she had to speak, just to break the silence. Eeluk seemed to have changed in subtle ways since Yesugei had come back. He walked with a little more of a swagger with the men, and his eyes challenged her whenever she spoke. She felt the need to mention Yesugei every time they talked, as if his name would keep him in the world. The alternative was too frightening to consider and she did not dare look to the future. Yesugei had to live.

"My family has been bound to his from birth," Eeluk said softly. "I have always been loyal."

"He knows it, Eeluk. I'm sure he can hear you now and he knows you are first among his men."

"Unless he dies," Eeluk said softly, turning to her. "If he dies, my vows are ended."

Hoelun looked at him in sick horror. While the words remained unsaid, the world could go on and she could hold back the fear. She dreaded him speaking again for what he might dare to say.

"He will survive this, Eeluk," she said. Her voice quavered, betraying her. "The fever will pass and he will know you remained loyal to him when it mattered most."

Something seemed to break through to her husband's bondsman, and he shook himself, the guarded look in his eyes disappearing.

"Yes. It is too early still," he said, looking down at Yesugei's pale face and chest. The bandages were stained with dark blood and he touched them, coming away with a red smear on his fingers. "Still, I have a loyalty to the families. They must be kept strong. I must think of the Wolves, and the days to come," he said, as if to himself.

Hoelun could hardly draw breath as the certainties of her life came crashing down. She thought of her sons and couldn't bear the calculating expression on Eeluk's face. They were innocent and they would suffer.

Eeluk left without another word, as if the courtesies no longer mattered to him. Perhaps they did not. She had seen the naked desire for power in his face, and there was no taking it back. Even if Yesugei sprang healed from the bed, she did not think things would be the same again, now that Eeluk had woken his heart.

She heard Temuge sob and opened her arms to him once more, taking comfort from his desperate clasp. Her daughter cried in the cot, untended.

"What will happen to us?" the little boy sobbed.

Hoelun shook her head as she cradled him. She did not know.

Bekter saw the warrior he had left to look for his father's sword. The man was walking quickly through the gers with his head down in thought. Bekter hailed him, but he did not seem to hear and hurried on. Frowning, Bekter ran after him and took him by the elbow.

"Why have you not come to me, Unegen?" he demanded. "Did you find my father's sword?" He saw Unegen's eyes flicker over his shoulder, and when he turned, Eeluk was there, watching them.

Unegen could not meet his gaze as he looked back.

"No, no, I did not find it. I am sorry," Unegen said, pulling his sleeve away and walking on.

CHAPTER 9

UNDER WHITE STARLIGHT, Temujin peered through the long grass. It had been simple enough to walk away from Sholoi's ger, his urine still steaming behind him. Sholoi's wife and daughter slept soundly and the old man had staggered out to relieve his bladder only a short while before. Temujin knew he had only a little time before they noticed his absence, but he had not dared go near the horse pens. The Olkhun'ut guarded their mounts, and even if they hadn't, finding his own white-footed pony in the dark amongst all the others would have been almost impossible. It did not matter. His prey was afoot.

The plains were silver as Temujin moved gently through the grass, careful not to kick a stone that might alert the older boy ahead. He did not know where Koke was going. He did not care. When he had seen a figure moving through the gers, he had watched closely, standing completely still. After seven days among the Olkhun'ut, he knew Koke's swagger well. At the moment of the recognition, Temujin had slipped silently after him, his senses heightening for the hunt. He had not planned his revenge for that night, but he knew better than to lose a perfect chance. The world was asleep and, in the pale gloom, only two figures moved on the sea of grass.

Temujin watched the older boy with intense concentration. He loped along on light feet, ready to fall into a crouch if Koke sensed him. In the moonlight, he fancied for a while that he was following a ghost, lured out to where the darker spirits would steal the life from him. His father had told stories of tribesmen found frozen to death, their eyes fixed on some distant horror as the winter reached in and stopped their hearts. Temujin shivered at the memory. The night was cold, but he drew warmth from his anger. He had nursed it and sheltered it through the hard days with the tribe, through insults and blows. His hands ached to hold a knife, but he thought he was strong enough to beat Koke with his bare hands. Though his heart thudded, he felt exhilaration and fear together. This was being alive, he told himself as he followed. There was power in being the hunter.

Koke did not wander aimlessly. Temujin saw him make for a solid shadow at the foot of a hill. Whatever watchers the Olkhun'ut had posted would be looking outward for enemies. They would not see either boy in that deeper dark, though Temujin worried he would lose his prey. He broke into a trot as Koke crossed the black line and seemed to vanish. Temujin's breath came a little faster in his throat, but he moved with care as he had been taught, allowing no more sound than the pad of his soft boots. Just before he crossed the shadow boundary himself, he saw a pile of loose stones by the path, a cairn to the spirits. Without a thought, he stopped and picked up one the size of his fist, hefting it with grim pleasure.

Temujin blinked as he passed into complete darkness, squinting for some sign of Koke. It would not do to stumble across him, or worse, some group of Olkhun'ut boys out with a skin of stolen black airag. Even more disturbing was the thought that Koke was luring him deliberately to another beating. Temujin shook his head to clear it. His path was set and he would not turn from it now.

He heard low voices ahead and froze, straining to see the source. With the mountain blocking the moon, he was almost blind, and sweat broke out on his skin as each careful step brought him closer. He could hear Koke's low laugh and then another voice responded, lighter in tone. Temujin smiled to himself. Koke had found himself a girl willing to risk the anger of her parents. Perhaps they would be rutting and he could catch them unawares. He mastered the desire to stride in and attack, deciding to wait until Koke took the path back to the encampment. Battles could be won with stealth as well as speed and strength, he knew. He could not tell exactly where the couple lay, but they were close enough for him to hear Koke begin to grunt rhythmically. Temujin grinned at the sound, leaning back against a rock and waiting patiently to strike.

It did not take long. The moon shadow had moved a hand's breadth, lengthening the dark bar at the foot of the hill as Temujin heard the sounds of talking once more, followed by the girl's low laugh. He wondered which of the young women had come out into the darkness, and found himself imagining the faces of those he had come to know during the felting. One or two were agile and brown from the sun. He had found them strangely unsettling when they looked at him, though he supposed it was only what all men felt for a pretty woman. It was a shame he couldn't feel it for Borte, who seemed only irritated in his presence. If she had been long-limbed and supple, he might have found some small pleasure in his father's choice.

Temujin heard footsteps and held his breath. Someone was coming along the path and he pressed himself against the rock, willing them not to sense him. He knew too late that he should have hidden himself in the long grass. If they came together, he would have to attack them both or let them pass. His lungs began to pound and he could feel his pulse like a great drum in his ears. The breath seemed to expand inside him as his body cried out for air and the unseen figure came closer.

Temujin watched in excruciating discomfort as the walker passed within a few feet of him. He was almost certain it could not be Koke. The steps were too light and he sensed that the shadow was not large enough to be his enemy. His heart hammered as the girl passed and he was able to release his breath slowly. For a moment, he felt dizzy with the exertion, and then he turned to where he knew Koke would come, stepping out into the path to wait for him.

He heard more steps and let the older boy come close before he spoke, relishing the shock his voice would cause.

"Koke!" Temujin whispered.

The moving shadow jumped in terror.

"Who is it?" Koke hissed, his voice breaking in fear and guilt.

Temujin did not let him recover and swung the fist with the stone. It was a poor blow in the dark, but it made Koke stagger. Temujin felt an impact, perhaps an elbow into his stomach, and then he was punching in a wild fury, released at last. He could not see his enemy, but the blindness gave him power as his fists and feet connected again and again in a flurry until Koke fell and Temujin knelt on his chest.

He had lost the stone in the silent struggle and scrabbled for it while he held the dark figure down. Koke tried to call for help, but Temujin hit him twice in the face, then resumed his search for the stone. His fingers found it and curled around. He felt his anger surge as he lifted it, ready to smash the life out of his tormentor.

"Temujin!" a voice said out of the darkness.

Both boys froze, though Koke moaned at the name. Temujin reacted instinctively, rolling off his enemy and launching himself at the new threat. He thumped into a small body and sent it sprawling with a yelp he recognized. Behind him, he heard Koke come to his feet and sprint away, his steps rattling loose stones on the path.

Temujin held the arms of the new figure, feeling their wiry thinness. He cursed under his breath.

"Borte?" he whispered, knowing the answer. "What are you doing here?"

"I followed you," she said.

He thought he could see her eyes shining, catching some dim ray the mountain could not smother. She was panting with fear or exertion and he wondered how she had been able to remain on his trail without him seeing her.

"You let him get away," Temujin said. For a moment, he continued to press her down, furious with what she had taken from him. When Koke told the rest of the Olkhun'ut what had happened, he would be beaten or even sent home in shame. His future had been changed with a single word. With a curse, he let her go and heard her sit up and rub her arms. He could feel her accusing gaze on him, and in response, he threw the stone as far as he could, listening as it clicked somewhere in the distance.

"Why did you follow me?" he said in a more normal voice. He wanted to hear her speak again. In the darkness, he had noticed her voice was warm and low, sweeter without the distracting scrawniness and glaring eyes.

"I thought you were escaping," she replied.

She stood and he rose with her, unwilling to lose the closeness, though he could not have explained why.

"I would have thought you'd be pleased to see me run," he said.

"I . . . I don't know. You haven't said a kind word to me since you came to the families. Why should I want you to stay?"

Temujin blinked. In just a few heartbeats they had said more to each other than in the days before. He did not want it to end.

"Why did you stop me? Koke will run back to Enq and your father. When they find we're gone, they'll spread out to find us. It will be hard when they do."

"He is a fool, that one. But killing him would have been an evil thing."

In the darkness, he reached out blindly and found her arm. The touch comforted both of them and she spoke again to cover her confusion.

"Your brother beat him almost to death, Temujin. He held him and kicked him until he cried like a child. He is afraid of you, so he hates you. It would be wrong to hurt him again. It would be like beating a dog after it has loosed its bladder. The spirit is already broken in him."

Temujin took a slow breath, letting it shudder out of him.

"I did not know," he said, though many things had fallen into place at her words, like bones clicking in his memory. Koke had been vicious, but when Temujin thought about it, the older boy had a look in his eyes that was always close to fear. For an instant, he did not care and wished he had brought the stone down, but then Borte reached up and placed her hand against his cheek.

"You are ... strange, Temujin," she said. Before he could respond, she stepped away from him into the darkness.

"Wait!" he called after her. "We may as well walk back together."

"They will beat us both," she said. "Perhaps I will run away instead. Perhaps I will not go back at all."

He found he could not bear the thought of Sholoi hitting her and wondered what his father would say if he brought her back early to the gers of the Wolves.

"Then come with me. We'll take my horse and ride home."

He listened for her answer but it did not come.

"Borte?" he called.

He broke into a run and passed back into the starlight with a pounding heart. He saw her darting figure already far ahead and increased his pace until he was flying across the grass. A memory came to him of being forced to run up and down hills with a mouthful of water, spitting it out at the end to show he had breathed through his nose in the proper way. He ran easily and without effort, his mind dwelling on the day ahead. He did not know what he could do, but he had found something valuable that night. Whatever happened, he knew he could not let her be hurt again. As he ran, he heard the lookouts sound their horns on the hills all around, calling an alarm to the warriors in the gers.

The encampment was in chaos as Temujin reached it. Dawn was coming, but torches had been lit, spreading a greasy yellow light that revealed running figures. On the outskirts, he was challenged twice by nervous men carrying drawn bows. The warriors were already mounted and milled around, raising dust and confusion. To Temujin's eye, there seemed no focus to it, no center of authority. If it had been the Wolves, he knew his father would be dominating the scene, sending the warriors out to protect the herds from raiders. He saw for the first time what Yesugei had seen. The Olkhun'ut had many fine bowmen and hunters, but they were not organized for war.

He saw Enq hobbling through the gers and Temujin took him by the arm. With an angry sound, Enq shook himself free, then started, reaching out to hold Temujin in turn.

"He's here!" Enq shouted.

Temujin struck out from instinct, shoving his uncle onto his back to break his grip. He had a glimpse of warriors moving toward him, and before he could run, he was held in strong hands and practically carried across the bare ground. He fell limp then, as if he had fainted, hoping that they would relax their hold for a heartbeat and let him struggle free. It was a vain hope, but he could not understand what was happening and the men who held him were strangers. If he could reach a horse, he had a chance to get away from whatever punishment awaited him. They passed through a pool of torchlight and Temujin swallowed drily as he saw that his captors were bondsmen of the khan, grim and dark in boiled-leather armor.

Their master, Sansar, was a man Temujin had seen only from a distance in his days amongst the families. Despite himself, he struggled and one of the bondsmen cuffed him, making lights flash in his vision. They threw him down without ceremony at the door of the khan's ger. Before he could enter, one of them searched him with rough efficiency, then propelled him through the opening to land flat on a floor of polished yellow wood, glowing gold in the light of torches.

Outside, the whinnying of horses and shouts of the warriors continued, but Temujin rose to his knees into a scene of quiet tension. As well as the khan himself, there were three of his bondsmen standing guard with drawn swords. Temujin looked around at the faces of strangers, seeing anger and, to his surprise, more than a little fear. He might have stayed silent, but his gaze fell on a man he knew and he cried out in astonishment.

"Basan! What has happened?" he said, rising fully. The presence of his father's bondsman sent a clutch of fear into his stomach.

No one responded and Basan looked away in shame.

Temujin remembered himself and flushed. He bowed his head to the khan of the Olkhun'ut.

"My lord khan," he said, formally.

Sansar was a slight figure, compared with the bulk of Eeluk or Yesugei. He stood with his arms folded behind his back, a sword on his hip. His expression was calm and Temujin sweated under the scrutiny. At last Sansar spoke, his voice clipped and hard.

"Your father would be ashamed if he could see you with your mouth hanging open," he said. "Control yourself, child."

Temujin did as he was told, mastering his breathing and straightening his back. He counted to a dozen in his head, then raised his eyes once again.

"I am ready, my lord."

Sansar nodded, his eyes weighing him. "Your father has been grievously wounded, child. He may die."

Temujin paled slightly, but his face remained impassive. He sensed a malice in the khan of the Olkhun'ut and was suddenly determined he would show no more weakness in front of him. Sansar said nothing, perhaps hoping for some reaction. When it did not come, he spoke again.

"The Olkhun'ut share your distress. I will scour the plains for the wanderers who dared to attack a khan. They will suffer greatly."

The brisk tone gave the lie to the sentiment. Temujin allowed himself a brief nod, though his mind reeled and he wanted to scream questions at the old snake who could barely hide his pleasure at his distress.

Sansar seemed to find Temujin's silence irritating. He glanced at Basan, who sat like a statue on his right.

"It seems you will not complete your year with our

people, child. This is a dangerous time, when threats are spoken that are better left unsaid. Still, it is right that you return to mourn your father."

Temujin clenched his jaw. He could not keep silence any longer.

"Is he dying, then?" he asked.

Sansar hissed in a breath, but Temujin ignored him, turning to look at his father's bondsman.

"You will answer me when I ask, Basan!" he said.

The bondsman met his gaze then and raised his head a fraction, the tension showing. In the ger of another khan, Temujin was risking both their lives over a breach of custom, even after such news. Basan's eyes showed he knew the danger, but he too was a Wolf.

"He was badly wounded," Basan answered, his voice steady. "As strong as he is, he made it back to the families alive, but...it has been three days. I do not know."

"It is almost dawn," Temujin replied. He fixed his gaze on the khan of the Olkhun'ut and bowed his head once again. "It is as you say, my lord. I must return to lead my people."

Sansar grew very still at that, his eyes gleaming. "You go with my blessing, Temujin. You leave only allies here."

"I understand," Temujin replied. "I honor the Olkhun'ut. With your permission, I will withdraw and see to my horse. I have a long ride ahead of me."

The khan stood and drew Temujin into a formal embrace, startling him.

"May the spirits guide your steps," he said.

Temujin bowed a last time and ducked out into the darkness, Basan following.

When they had gone, the khan of the Olkhun'ut turned to his most trusted bondsmen, cracking the knuckles of one hand inside the other.

"It should have been clean!" he snapped. "Instead, the bones are flying and we don't know where they will fall." He took a skin of airag from a peg and poured a thin line of the raw fluid into the back of his throat, wiping angrily at his mouth.

"I should have known the Tartars could not even murder a man without causing chaos. I *gave* him to them. How could they have let him live? If he had simply disappeared, there would have been no hint of our involvement. If he lives, he will wonder how the Tartars knew to find him. There will be blood before winter. Tell me what I should do!"

The faces of the men with him were blank and worried as he looked around at them. Sansar sneered.

"Get out and quiet the camp. There are no enemies here except the ones we have invited. Pray that the khan of Wolves is already dead."

Temujin strode blindly through the gers, fighting for calm. What he had been told was impossible. His father was a warrior born and no two men amongst the Wolves could take him with a sword. He knew he should ask Basan for details, but he dreaded hearing them. As long as he did not speak, it might still be a lie or a mistake. He thought of his mother and his brothers and then suddenly came to a halt, making Basan stumble. He was not ready to challenge Bekter, if the news was true.

"Where is your horse?" he asked his father's man.

"Tethered on the north side of the camp," Basan replied. "I am sorry to bring such news...."

"Come with me first. I have something to do before I leave here. Follow my orders." He did not look to see how Basan responded, and perhaps that was why the man nodded and obeyed the young son of Yesugei.

Temujin strode through the Olkhun'ut as they scurried and recovered from the excitement. The alarms had sounded on Basan's approach, but they had reacted in panic. Temujin sneered to himself, wondering if he would one day lead a war party to these same gers. Dawn had come at last, and as he reached the outskirts, he saw the gnarled figure of Sholoi standing at his door with a wood axe in his hands. Temujin did not hesitate, walking up to within reach of the weapon.

"Is Borte here?" he said.

Sholoi narrowed his eyes at the change in manner in the boy, no doubt because of the warrior who stood so grimly at his side. Sholoi raised his head stubbornly.

"Not yet, boy. I thought she might be with you. Your brother tried the same with the girl they'd given him."

Temujin hesitated, losing his momentum. "What?"

"He took his girl early, like a couple of goats rutting. Didn't he say? If you've done the same, I'll cut your hands off, boy, and don't think I'm worried by your daddy's man, either. I've killed better with my hands alone. An axe will do you both."

Temujin heard the slide of steel as Basan drew his sword. Before a blow could be struck, Temujin laid a hand on the warrior's arm, stopping him with a touch.

"I have not harmed her. She stopped me fighting Koke. That is all."

Sholoi frowned. "I told her not to leave the tent, boy. That's what matters."

Temujin stepped closer to the old man. "I've learned more tonight than I wanted to know. Whatever the truth of it, I am not my brother. I will return for your daughter when the moon's blood is on her. I will take her for my wife. Until then, you will not lay a hand on her again. You will make an enemy of me if she takes a single bruise from you, old man. You do not want me as an enemy. If you give me cause, the Olkhun'ut will suffer."

Sholoi listened with a sour expression on his face, his mouth working. Temujin waited patiently for him to think it through.

"She needs a strong man, boy, to control her."

"Remember that," Temujin said.

Sholoi nodded, watching as the two Wolves walked away, the sight of the drawn sword scattering Olkhun'ut children before them. Sholoi hefted the axe onto his shoulder and hitched up his leggings, sniffing.

"I know you're here, girl, creeping around," he said to the empty air. There was no response, but the silence became strained and he grinned to himself, revealing black gums. "I think you've found yourself a good one, if he survives. Mind you, I wouldn't take a wager on those odds."

CHAPTER 10

TEMUJIN HEARD THE HORNS of the Wolves sound as he and Basan rode into view with the setting sun behind them. A dozen warriors galloped in perfect formation to intercept him, a spearhead of seasoned warriors well able to deal with a raiding party. He could not help comparing the instant response with the panic of the Olkhun'ut he'd left behind. It was hard to draw his mount back to a walk, but only a fool would risk being killed before he had been recognized.

He glanced at Basan, seeing a new tension there, overlaying the exhaustion. Temujin had pushed him hard to cover the distance home in only two days. Both of them had gone without sleep, surviving on water and drafts of sour yoghurt. Their time together had not begun a friendship, and as they came back into familiar territory, Temujin had sensed a growing distance between them. The warrior had been reluctant to speak, and his manner worried Temujin more than he cared to admit. It occurred to him that the arban of galloping warriors could now be enemies. He had no way of telling, and all he could do was sit tall and straight in the saddle, as his father would have wanted, while they came on.

When the warriors were within hailing distance, Basan raised his right arm, showing he did not carry a blade. Temujin recognized Eeluk amongst them and saw instantly how the others deferred to his father's bondsman. It was he who gave the signal to halt, and something about his confidence brought Temujin close to humiliating tears. He had come home, but everything had changed. He refused to weep in front of them all, but his eyes shone.

Eeluk laid a claiming hand on Temujin's reins. The others fell in around them and they began to trot as one, Temujin's mount matching the pace without a command from him. It was a small thing, but Temujin felt like yanking the reins away in childish anger. He did not want to be led back to his father's tribe like a small boy, but his wits seemed to have deserted him.

"Your father still lives," Eeluk said. "His wound was poisoned and he has been delirious for many days."

"He is awake, then?" Temujin said, hardly daring to hope.

Eeluk shrugged. "At times, he cries out and struggles against enemies only he can see. He is a strong man, but he takes no food and the flesh has melted off him like wax. You should prepare yourself. I do not believe he will live much longer."

Temujin bowed his head to his chest, overcome. Eeluk looked away rather than shame him at his moment of weakness. Without warning, Temujin reached out and tugged his reins away from Eeluk's grip.

"Who is responsible? Has he named them?"

"Not yet, though your mother has asked him whenever he wakes. He does not know her."

Eeluk sighed to himself and Temujin saw his own strain mirrored in the man. The Wolves would be stunned and fearful with Yesugei raving and close to death. They would be looking for a strong leader.

"What about my brother Bekter?" Temujin said.

Eeluk frowned, perhaps guessing the path of Temujin's thoughts.

"He has ridden out with the warriors to search the plains." He hesitated then, as if deciding how much he should share with the boy. "You should not hope to find your father's enemies now. Those who survived will have scattered days ago. They will not wait for us to find them."

His face was a mask, but Temujin sensed some hidden anger in him. Perhaps he did not like the thought of Bekter's influence on the warriors. The search had to be at least attempted and Bekter was an obvious choice, but Eeluk would not want new loyalties being forged away from him. Temujin thought he could read his father's bondsman well enough, despite his attempts to hide his private self. A man would have to be a fool not to think of the succession at such a time. Temujin was almost certainly too young and Bekter was on the edge of manhood. With Eeluk's support, either could rule the Wolves, but the alternative was obvious and chilling. Temujin forced a smile as he faced a man who was more of a threat than any of the Olkhun'ut he had left behind.

"You have loved my father, even as I have, Eeluk. What would he want for the Wolves if he dies? Would he want *you* to lead them?"

Eeluk stiffened as if he had been struck, turning a

murderous expression on the boy who rode at his side. Temujin did not flinch. He felt almost light-headed, but in that moment, he did not care if Eeluk killed him. No matter what the future held, he found he could return the gaze without a trace of fear.

"I have been loyal all my life," Eeluk said, "but your father's day has come and gone. Our enemies will be watching us for weakness as word spreads. The Tartars will come in the winter to raid our herds, perhaps even the Olkhun'ut, or the Kerait, just to see if we can still defend what is ours." He took a white-knuckled grip on his reins and turned away from Temujin, unable to go on with the pale yellow eyes watching him.

"You know what he would have wanted, Eeluk. You know what you must do."

"No. No, I do *not* know, boy. I do know what you are thinking, and I tell you now, you are too young to lead the families."

Temujin swallowed bitterness and pride in a hard knot.

"Bekter, then. Do not betray our father, Eeluk. He treated you like a brother all his life. Honor him now by helping his son."

To Temujin's astonishment, Eeluk kicked his heels in and rode ahead of the group, his face flushed and furious. Temujin did not dare look at the men around him. He did not want to see their expressions and know his world had crumbled. He did not see the questioning glances they shared, nor their sorrow.

The camp of the Wolves was still and quiet as Temujin dismounted by his father's ger and took a deep breath.

He felt as if he had been away for years. The last time he had stood on that spot, his father had been vital and strong, a certainty in all their lives. It was just not possible to think that world had gone and could not be recalled.

He stood stiffly in the open, looking out over the gers of the families. He could have named every man, woman, and child with just a glance at the design of their door. They were his people and he had always known his place amongst them. Uncertainty was a new emotion for him, as if there were a great hole in his chest. He found he had to summon all his courage just to enter the ger. He might have stood there even longer if he had not seen the people beginning to gather as the sun's rays faded. He could not bear their pity, and with a grimace, he ducked through the low door and closed it against their staring faces.

The night felt had not yet been placed over the smoke hole above his head, but the ger was stifling with heat and a smell that made him want to gag. He saw his mother's paleness when she turned to him, and his defenses crumbled as he rushed to her and fell into her embrace. Tears came beyond his control and she rocked him in silence as he gazed on his father's withered body.

Yesugei's flesh shuddered like a horse twitching at flies. His stomach was bound in crusted bandages, stiff as reeds with old fluids. Temujin saw a line of pus and blood move like a worm across the skin and into the blankets. His father's hair had been combed and oiled, but it seemed thin and there was more gray than he remembered in the wisps that reached down to his cheekbones. Temujin saw the ribs were starkly outlined. The face was sunken and dark in hollows, a death mask for the man he had known.

"You should speak to him, Temujin," his mother said. As he raised his head to respond, he saw her eyes were as red as his own. "He has been calling your name and I did not know if you would come in time."

He nodded, wiping a silvery trail of mucus from his nose onto his sleeve as he looked at the one man he had thought would live forever. The fevers had burnt the muscle off his bones and Temujin could hardly believe it was the same powerful warrior who had ridden so confidently into the camp of the Olkhun'ut. He stared for a long time, unable to speak. He hardly noticed his mother wet a cloth in a bucket of cold water and press it into his hand. She guided his fingers to his father's face and, together, they wiped the eyes and lips. Temujin breathed shallowly, struggling against revulsion. The smell of sick flesh was appalling, but his mother showed no distaste and he tried to be strong for her.

Yesugei shifted under the touch and opened his eyes, looking directly at them.

"It is Temujin, husband; he has come home safe," Hoelun said gently.

The eyes remained blank and Temujin felt fresh tears starting.

"I don't want you to die," he said to his father, beginning to sob in spasms. "I don't know what to do."

The khan of the Wolves took in a sharp breath, so that his ribs stood out like a cage. Temujin leaned over him and pressed his hand into his father's. The skin was impossibly hot and dry, but he did not let go. He saw his father's mouth move and dropped his head to hear.

"I am home, Father," he said. The grip tightened

enough to hurt. Temujin brought his other hand over to hold his father's fingers, and for a moment their eyes met and he thought he saw recognition.

"The Tartars," Yesugei whispered. His throat seemed to close on the words, and the pent-up air released in a great sigh that ended in a dry clicking. Temujin waited for the next breath, and when it did not come, he realized the hand he held had fallen limp. He held it even harder in a rush of despair, aching to hear another breath.

"Don't leave us here," he begged, but he knew he could not be heard. Hoelun made a choking sound behind him, but he could not tear himself away from the sunken face of the man he adored. Had he told him? He could not remember saying the words and he had a sudden fear that his father would go to the spirits without knowing how much he had meant to his sons.

"Everything I am comes from you," he whispered. "I am your son and *nothing* else. Can you hear me?"

He felt his mother's hands on his own.

"He waited for you, Temujin. He has gone now," she said.

He could not look at her.

"Do you think he knew how much I loved him?" he said.

She smiled through her tears and for a moment she looked as pretty as she must have been when she was young.

"He knew. He was so proud of you, he used to think his heart would burst with it. He used to look at me whenever you rode, or fought with your brothers, or argued with them. I could see it in his smile then. He did not want to spoil you, but the sky father gave him the sons he wanted and you were his pride, his private joy. He knew."

It was too much for Temujin to hear and he wept unashamedly.

"We must tell the families that he is gone at last," Hoelun said.

"What then?" Temujin replied, wiping his tears. "Eeluk will not support me to lead the Wolves. Will Bekter be khan?" He searched her face for some reassurance, but found only exhaustion and grief returning to cloud her eyes.

"I do not know what will happen, Temujin. If your father had survived a few more years, it would not matter, but now? There is no good time to die, but this..."

She began to weep and Temujin found himself drawing her head against his shoulder. He could not have imagined giving her comfort, but it seemed to come naturally and somehow it strengthened him for whatever was to come. He felt his youth as a weakness, but with his father's spirit close, he knew he had to find the courage to face the families. His gaze flickered around the ger.

"Where is the eagle I brought for him?"

His mother shook her head. "I could not care for it. Eeluk took it to another family."

Temujin struggled with a rising hatred for the man his father had trusted in all things. He drew away from his mother and Hoelun rose and looked down at the body of Yesugei. As Temujin watched, she leaned over her husband and kissed him gently on his open mouth. She seemed to shudder at the contact, her whole body quivering. With shaking fingers, she closed his eyes, then pulled a blanket over his wound. The air was sluggish with heat and death, but Temujin found the smell no longer troubled him. He breathed deeply, filling his lungs with his father's essence as he too rose to his feet. He splashed water from the bucket onto his face and then rubbed it away with a scrap of clean cloth.

"I will go out and tell them," he said.

His mother nodded, her eyes still fixed on a distant past as he walked to the small door and ducked out into the sharp air of the night.

The women of the families raised wailing voices to the sky father, so that he would hear a great man had passed from the plains. The sons of Yesugei gathered to pay their last respects to their father. When dawn came, they would wrap him in a white cloth and take him to a high hill, leaving his naked flesh to be taken into the hawks and vultures that were dear to the spirits. The arms that had taught them to draw a bow, the strong face, all of him would be torn into a thousand scraps to fly in hosts of birds under the sky father's gaze. He would no longer be tied to the earth as they were.

As the night wound on, the warriors met in clusters, moving from ger to ger until all the families had spoken. Temujin did not take part in the process, though he wished Bekter were there to see the sky burial and the recitals. As much as he disliked his brother, he knew it would hurt him to have missed the stories and tales told of Yesugei's life.

No one slept. As the moon rose, a great fire was built in the center of the encampment and old Chagatai the storyteller waited while they gathered, a skin of black airag ready against the cold. Only the scouting party and the lookouts remained on the hills. Every other man, woman and child came to hear and weep openly, giving Yesugei honor. They all knew that a tear shed into the ground would one day become part of the rivers that quenched the thirst of the herds and the families of all the tribes. There was no shame in weeping for a khan who had kept them safe through hard winters and made the Wolves a force on the plains.

Temujin sat alone at first, though many came to touch his shoulder and say a few quiet words of respect. Temuge was red-faced from crying, but he came with Kachiun and sat beside their brother, sharing their grief without words. Khasar too came to hear Chagatai and he was pale and wan as he embraced Temujin. The last to arrive was Hoelun, with her daughter Temulun asleep in the folds of her robe. She hugged her boys one after the other, then stared into the flames as if lost.

When the tribe were all there, Chagatai cleared his throat and spat into the roaring fire at his back.

"I knew the Wolf when he was a little boy and his sons and daughter were only dreams of the sky father. He was not always the man who led the families. When he was young, he crept into my father's ger and stole a comb of honey wrapped in cloth. He buried the cloth, but he had a dog in those days, a hound of yellow and black. The animal dug up the cloth and brought it to him while he was in the middle of denying he had even known the honey was there. He did not sit for days afterwards!" Chagatai paused as the warriors smiled. "As a man, he led war parties after only twelve summers, raiding the Tartars again and again for ponies and sheep. When Eeluk wanted to take a bride, it was Yesugei who raided ponies to give to her father, bringing in three red mares and a dozen cattle from a single night. He had the blood of two men bright on his sword, but even then there were few who could match him with a blade or a bow. He was a scourge to that tribe, and when he was khan, they learned to fear Yesugei and the men who rode with him."

Chagatai took a deep draft of the airag, smacking his lips.

"When his father was sky-buried, Yesugei gathered all the warriors and took them out for many days, making them live on just a few handfuls of food and barely enough water to wet the throat. All those who went on that trip came back with fire in their bellies and loyalty to him in their hearts. He gave them their pride and the Wolves grew strong and fat on mutton and milk."

Temujin listened while the old man recited his father's victories. Chagatai's memory was still sharp enough to remember what had been said and how many had fallen to his father's sword or bow. Perhaps the numbers were exaggerated, he did not know. The older warriors nodded and smiled at the memories, and as they emptied the skins of airag, they began to call out in appreciation as Chagatai painted the battles for them once more.

"That was when old Yeke lost three fingers from his right hand," Chagatai continued. "It was Yesugei who found them in the snow and brought them back to him. Yeke saw what he was carrying and said they should be given to the dogs. Yesugei told him it would be better to tie them to a stick. He said he could still use them to scratch himself."

Khasar chuckled at that, hanging on every word

with his brothers. This was the history of their tribe, the stories of the men and women who made them who they were.

Chagatai's manner changed subtly as he lowered the skin once more.

"He left strong sons to follow him, and he would have wanted Bekter or Temujin to lead the Wolves. I have heard the whispers in the families. I have heard the arguments and the promises, but the blood of khans runs in them and if there is honor in the Wolves, they should not shame their khan in death. He watches us now."

The camp fell silent, though Temujin heard some of the warriors murmuring agreement. He felt a hundred eyes on him in the flame-lit darkness. He began to rise, but in the distance, they all heard the lookout horns sound mournfully over the hills, and the warriors snapped out of their drunken trance, rising quickly to their feet and shaking themselves to alertness. Eeluk appeared on the fringes of the light, gazing malevolently at Chagatai. Temujin saw that the storyteller looked frail and tired now that the spell was broken. A breeze blew his white hair back and forth as he faced Eeluk without a sign of fear. As Temujin watched, Eeluk nodded sharply as if something had been decided. The bondsman's horse was brought to him and he mounted in one swift movement, riding out into the dark without looking back.

The horns ceased after only a short time when they realized it was the scouting party returning. Bekter came in at the head of a dozen warriors, riding up to the fire to dismount. Temujin saw they carried armor and weapons that were different from the ones he knew. In the light of the great fire, he saw rotting heads tied to Bekter's saddle by their hair. Temujin shivered suddenly at the sight of the open mouths flopping as if they still cried out. Though the flesh was black and flyblown, he knew he was looking at the faces of those who had killed his father.

Only his mother had also heard Yesugei whisper the name of his enemy in the tent, and neither she nor Temujin had shared the information with any other. It was somehow chilling to hear the Tartars named again by the returning warriors. They held up bows and deels splashed with dried blood, and the families gathered around them in horrified fascination, reaching out to touch the rotting faces of the dead.

Bekter strode into the firelight as if the leadership of the tribe were already settled. It would once have been a bitter scene in Temujin's imagination, but after his fears, he felt a savage pleasure. Let his brother take the tribe!

At first, the conversations were noisy and there were cries of shock at the description of what they had found. Five bodies lay rotting where they had ambushed the khan of Wolves. The gazes that fell on Yesugei's sons were bright with awe. Yet they fell silent when Eeluk drew up, leaping lightly down from his saddle to face the brothers. With deliberate resolve, Temujin came to stand at Bekter's shoulder and Khasar and Kachiun came with him. They faced Eeluk and waited for him to speak. Perhaps that was their mistake, for Eeluk was a powerful warrior and, next to him, they looked like the boys they were.

"Your father has gone at last, Bekter," Eeluk said. "It was not an easy passing, but it is at an end."

Bekter's hooded eyes regarded his father's bondsman, understanding the challenge and the danger. He raised his head and spoke, sensing he would never be stronger in his position than at that moment.

"I will be proud to lead the Wolves to war," he said clearly.

Some of the warriors cheered him, but Eeluk shook his head slowly, his confidence cowing the few who had shown support. Silence came again and Temujin found himself holding his breath.

"I will be khan," Eeluk said. "It is decided."

Bekter reached for his sword and Eeluk's eyes gleamed in pleasure. It was Temujin who gripped his brother's arm first, though Kachiun was there almost as quickly.

"He will kill you," Temujin said, as Bekter tried to free himself.

"Or I will kill him for the oath-breaking filth he is," Bekter snapped in response.

Locked in their own struggle, neither of them had time to react as Eeluk drew his sword and used the hilt as a hammer, smashing Bekter off his feet. He and Temujin went down in a tangle of limbs, and Kachiun threw himself at their father's bondsman unarmed, trying to stop him using the blade to kill his brothers. Hoelun cried out in fear behind them and the sound seemed to break through to Eeluk as he advanced, shaking Kachiun off with a flick of his arm. He glared at them all and then sheathed his sword.

"In honor to your father, I will not shed blood tonight," he said, though his face was heavy with anger. He raised his head to have his voice carry. "The Wolves will ride! I will not stay where the blood of my khan stains the earth. Gather your herds and horses. As the sun reaches noon, we will travel south."

He took a step closer to Hoelun and her sons.

"But not with you," he said. "I will not watch my back for your knives. You will stay here and take your father's body to the hills."

Hoelun swayed slightly in the breeze, her face white and pinched. "You will leave us to die?"

Eeluk shrugged. "Die or live, you will not be of the Wolves. It is done."

Chagatai loomed behind Eeluk then and Temujin saw the old man grip him by the arm. Eeluk raised his sword in reflex, but Chagatai ignored the bare blade so close to his face.

"This is an evil thing!" Chagatai said, angrily. "You dishonor the memory of a great man, left with no one to bring death to his killers. How will his spirit rest? You cannot leave his children alone on the plains. It is as bad as killing them yourself."

"Get away, old man. A khan must make hard decisions. I will not shed the blood of children or women, but if they starve, my hands are clean."

Chagatai's face grew dark with wordless fury and he scrabbled at Eeluk's armor, battering at him. His nails scored the flesh of Eeluk's neck, and the reaction was instantaneous. Eeluk drove his blade into the old man's chest and shoved him off it onto his back. Blood came from Chagatai's open mouth and Hoelun sank to her knees, weeping and rocking while her sons stood stunned. There were other screams at the murder and some of the warriors came to stand between Eeluk and the family of Yesugei, their hands ready on their swords.

Eeluk shook himself and spat at Chagatai as his blood poured into the parched soil.

"You should not have interfered, you old fool," he said, sheathing his sword and walking stiffly away.

The warriors helped Hoelun to her feet and women came to help her back to the ger. They turned their faces from the crying children, and to Temujin that was as bad as anything else that had happened that night. The families had deserted them and they were lost.

The gers of the Wolves left black circles on the hard ground when they were dismantled, littered with scraps of old bone and pieces of broken leather and pottery. The sons of Yesugei watched the process as outsiders, standing miserably with their mother and sister. Eeluk had been ruthless and Hoelun had needed all the others to hold Bekter back when the bondsman ordered their ger and everything in it to be packed with the rest. Some of the women had cried out at the cruelty, but many more had kept silent and Eeluk had ignored them all. The khan's word was law.

Temujin shook his head in disbelief as the carts were loaded and the herds urged into place with sticks and blows. He had seen that Eeluk wore Yesugei's sword as he strode about the encampment. Bekter had set his jaw tight as he noticed the blade, his fury evident. Eeluk had smiled to himself as he walked past them, enjoying their impotent glares. Temujin wondered at how Eeluk had kept such ambition hidden inside for so many years. He had sensed it when Yesugei gave him the red bird, but even then he would not have believed it possible to have Eeluk betray them so completely. He shook his head as he heard the eagle chicks crying when their wings were wrapped tight for the journey. He could not take it in. The sight of Chagatai's sprawled body tugged at his eyes over and over, reminding him of the night before. The old storyteller was going to be left where he had fallen, and that seemed as great a crime as any of the rest to the boys.

Though her sons were pale with despair, Hoelun herself radiated a cold rage that punished anyone foolish enough to meet her eyes. When Eeluk had come to order the khan's ger dismantled, even he had not looked at her, staring instead into a middle distance while the work went on. The great layers of heavy felt had been untied and rolled and the wooden lattice collapsed into its sections, the knots of dried sinew cut with quick slashes. Everything inside had been taken, from Yesugei's bows to the winter deels with their lining of fur. Bekter had cursed and shouted when he saw they would be left with nothing, but Hoelun had simply shaken her head at Eeluk's casual cruelty. The deels were beautifully made and too valuable to be wasted on those who would not survive. Winter would snatch them from life as surely as an arrow when the first snows came. Still, she faced the families with dignity, her face proud and dry of tears.

It did not take long. Everything was designed to be moved, and by the time the sun stood above them, the black circles were empty and the carts loaded, with men heaving at the ropes to tie everything down.

Hoelun shivered as the wind blew stronger. There was no shelter now that the gers had gone, and she felt exposed and numb. She knew Yesugei would have drawn his father's sword and taken a dozen heads if he were there to see it. His body lay on the turf, wrapped in cloth. In the night, someone in the families had wound an old piece of linen around Chagatai's withered frame, hiding his wound. They lay side by side in death and Hoelun could not bear to look at either of them.

The herdsmen shouted as Eeluk blew his horn, using sticks longer than a man to snap the animals into movement. The noise grew as sheep and goats bleated and ran to escape the stinging touch and the tribe began to move. Hoelun stood with her sons like a stand of pale birch and watched them go. Temuge was sobbing quietly to himself and Kachiun took his hand in case the little boy tried to run after the tribe.

The open ground quickly swallowed the cries of the herdsmen and their charges. Hoelun watched them until they were far away, at last breathing out some small part of her relief. She knew Eeluk was capable of sending a man circling back to make a bloody end to the abandoned family. As soon as the distance was too far for them to be seen, she turned to her sons, gathering them around her.

"We need shelter and food, but most of all, we need to get away from this place. There will be scavengers coming soon to sift through the ashes of the fires. Not all of them will walk on four legs. Bekter!" Her sharp tone snapped her son out of his trance as he stared after the distant figures. "I need you now to look after your brothers."

"What is the point?" he replied, turning back to watch the plain. "We're all dead."

Hoelun slapped him hard across the face and he staggered, his eyes blazing. Fresh blood started from where Eeluk had hit him the night before.

"Shelter, and food, Bekter. Yesugei's sons will not go quietly to their deaths, as Eeluk wants. Nor will his wife. I need your strength, Bekter, do you understand?"

"What will we do with . . . him?" Temujin said, looking at his father's body.

Hoelun faltered for an instant as she followed his gaze. She clenched her fist and shook with anger.

"Was it too much to leave us a single pony?" she said under her breath. She had a vision of tribeless men pulling the sheet from Yesugei's naked body and laughing, but there was no choice. "It's just flesh, Temujin. Your father's spirit is gone from here. Let him see us survive and he will be satisfied."

"We leave him for wild dogs, then?" Temujin asked, horrified.

It was Bekter who nodded. "We must. Dogs or birds, it doesn't matter. How far could you and I carry him, Temujin? It's already noon and we need to get up to a tree line."

"The red hill," Kachiun said suddenly. "There is shelter there."

Hoelun shook her head. "It's too far to reach before night falls. To the east, there is a cleft that will do until tomorrow. There are woods there. We'd die on the plains, but in woods, I'll spit on Eeluk ten years from now."

"I'm hungry," Temuge said, sniveling.

Hoelun looked at her youngest son and her eyes filled with shining tears. She reached into the folds of her deel and brought out a cloth bag of his favorite sweet curds. Each of them took one or two, as solemnly as if they were swearing an oath.

"We will survive this, my sons. We will survive until

you are men, and when Eeluk is old, he will wonder if it is you coming for him every time he hears hooves in the darkness."

They looked into her face in awe, seeing only fierce determination. It was strong enough to banish some of their own despair, and they all took strength from her.

"Now walk!" she snapped at them. "Shelter, then food."

CHAPTER 11

A THIN DRIZZLE FELL as Bekter and Temujin sat huddled together, wet to the bone. Before dark, they had reached a wooded cleft in the hills where a stream dribbled through sodden, marshy ground. The narrow crease in the land was host to black-trunked pines and silver birches as pale as bones. The echoing spatter of water was strange and frightening as the boys shivered on a great nest of dark roots.

Before the light faded, Hoelun had set them to lifting fallen saplings, dragging the great broken lengths of rotten wood through the leaves and mud to heave them into the crook of a low tree. Their arms and chests were scratched raw, but she had not let them rest. Even Temuge had carried armfuls of dead needles and piled them over smaller branches, tottering back again and again for more until the crude shelter was finished. It was not large enough for Bekter and Temujin, but Hoelun had kissed them both in gratitude and they had stood proudly as she crawled into the space with the baby. Khasar curled up like a shivering dog between her legs, and Temuge crept in after them, sobbing gently to himself. Kachiun had stood with his older brothers for a while, swaying gently from exhaustion. Temujin had taken him by the arm and pushed him after the others. There was hardly room even for him.

Their mother's head had sunk slowly onto her chest as the little girl nursed. Temujin and Bekter had moved away as quietly as they could, looking for anything that would keep the rain off their faces long enough to get to sleep.

They did not find it. The mass of roots had seemed a little better than simply lying down in the wet, but unseen lumps and twists made them ache however they lay. When sleep did come, a splash of icy water would strike their faces and bring them back for bleary moments, wondering where they were. The night seemed to last forever.

As Temujin woke yet again and moved his cramped legs, he thought about the day. It had been strange to walk away from his father's body. They had all looked back to see the pale speck growing smaller. Hoelun had seen the wistful glances and been annoyed with them.

"You have always had the families around you," she had said. "You have not had to hide from thieves and wanderers before. Now we *must* hide. Even a single herder can kill us all, and there will be no justice."

The hard new reality had chilled them as much as the rain that began to fall, dampening their spirits still further. Temujin blinked against a drip of water from somewhere above. He was not sure he had slept at all, though he sensed time had passed. His stomach was painfully empty and he wondered what they would do for food. If Eeluk had even left them a bow, Temujin could have fed them all on fat marmots. Without one, they could starve to death in just a few days. He looked up and saw that the rain clouds had passed, letting the stars shine through to the land beneath. The trees still dripped all around, but he hoped the morning would be warmer. The dampness had soaked every part of him, and his clothes were caked in mud and leaves. He felt the slippery muck on his fingers as he clenched a fist and thought of Eeluk. A pine needle or a thorn dug into his palm, but he ignored it, silently cursing the man who had betrayed his family. Deliberately, he clenched until his whole body shook and he could see green flashes under his eyelids.

"Keep him alive," he whispered to the sky father. "Keep him strong and healthy. Keep him alive, for me to kill."

Bekter grumbled in his sleep next to him, and Temujin closed his eyes again, aching for the hours to slip away until dawn. He wanted the same as the younger ones: to let his mother wrap him in her arms and solve all their problems. Instead, he knew he had to be strong, both for her and for his brothers. One thing was certain: they would survive and one day he would find and kill Eeluk and take Yesugei's sword from his dead hand. The thought stayed with him as he fell asleep.

They were all up as soon as it was light enough to see each other's dirty faces. Hoelun's eyes were puffy and bruised-looking with exhaustion, but she gathered her children around her, watching as the single water bottle was passed from hand to hand. Her tiny daughter was fussing and already slippery with fresh excrement. There were no spare cloths and the infant began a red-faced fit of screaming that showed no sign of lapsing. Hoelun could only ignore the cries as the baby refused the teat again and again in its distress. In the end, even their mother's patience was exhausted, and she left her bare breast hanging while the little girl clenched her fists and roared to the sky.

"If we are to live, we need to make somewhere dry and organize fishing and hunting," she told them. "Show me what you have with you, so that we all can see." She noticed Bekter hesitate and turned on him. "Hold nothing back, Bekter. We could all be dead in a single turn of the moon if we can't hunt and get warm."

In the dawn, it was easier to find a place where the thick mat of needles was damp rather than soaking. Hoelun removed her deel, shivering as she did so. They could all see the dark slick down her side where their sister's bowels had emptied during the night. The smell wafted over them all, making Khasar put a hand to his face. Hoelun ignored him, her mouth a thin line of irritation. Temujin could see she was barely holding her temper as she spread the deel on the ground. Gently, she placed her daughter on the cloth, the movement startling the tiny little girl into staring around at her brothers with tear-filled eyes. It hurt to see her shivering.

Bekter grimaced and took a knife from his belt, laying it down. Hoelun tested the blade with her thumb and nodded. She reached around her own waist to untie a heavy cord of braided horsehair. She had hidden it under her deel on the last night, looking for anything that would help them in their ordeal. Its coils were narrow but strong and it joined the blades of the brothers as they put them down in a pile.

Apart from his own small knife, all Temujin could add was the winding cloth that held his deel to him, though that was long and well woven. He did not doubt Hoelun would find some use for it.

They all watched in fascination as Hoelun brought a tiny bone box from one of the deep pockets in the deel. It contained a small piece of ridged steel and a good flint, and she laid those aside almost with reverence. The dark yellow box was beautifully carved and she rubbed her thumbs over it in memory while they watched.

"Your father gave this to me when we were married," she said, and then she picked up a stone and smashed the box into pieces. Each shard of bone was razor sharp and she sorted them with care, picking the best and holding them up.

"This one for a fishhook, two more for arrowheads. Khasar? You'll take the twine and find a good stone to grind the hook. Use a knife to dig for worms and find a sheltered spot. We need your luck today."

Khasar gathered his share without a trace of his usual light manner.

"I understand," he said, winding the horsehair length around his fist.

"Leave me enough to make a snare," she told him as he stood. "We need gut and tendons for a bow."

She turned to Bekter and Temujin, handing a sliver of sharp bone to each boy.

"You take a knife each and make me a bow from the birch. You've seen it done enough times."

Bekter pressed the point of the bone into his palm,

testing it. "If we had horn, or horsehide for the string..." he began.

Hoelun grew very still and her stare silenced him. "A single marmot snare won't keep us alive. I didn't say I wanted a bow that would make your father proud. Just cut something you can kill with. Or perhaps we should simply lie down in the leaves and wait for cold and hunger to take us?"

Bekter frowned, irritated at the criticism in front of the others. Without looking at Temujin, he snatched up his knife and strode away, his bone shard held tightly in his fist.

"I could lash a blade to a stick and make a spear, perhaps for fish," Kachiun said.

Hoelun looked gratefully at him and took a deep breath. She picked up the smallest of the knives and passed it into his hands.

"Good boy," she said, reaching out to touch his face. "Your father taught you all to hunt. I don't think he would ever have guessed it would matter this much, but whatever you learned, we need."

She looked at the pitifully small number of items left on the cloth and sighed.

"Temuge? I can light a fire if you find me something dry to burn. Anything."

The fat little boy stood up, his mouth quivering. He had not yet begun to recover from the terror of their new situation, nor its hopelessness. The other boys could see Hoelun was on the nervous edge of breaking, but Temuge still saw her as a rock and reached out to be embraced. She allowed him a moment in her arms before she eased him away.

"Find what you can, Temuge. Your sister can't take another night without a fire."

Temujin winced as the little boy broke into sobbing and, when Hoelun refused to look at him, ran away under the looming trees.

Temujin reached out clumsily to try to give his mother some comfort. He took her shoulder and, to his pleasure, she tilted her head so that her face briefly touched his hand.

"Make me a killing bow, Temujin. Find Bekter and help him," she said, raising her eyes to his.

He swallowed painfully against his hunger and left her there with the baby, the wailing cry echoing amongst the wet trees.

Temujin found Bekter by the sound of his blade hacking into a birch sapling. He whistled softly to let his older brother know he was approaching and received a surly glare for his trouble. Without a word, Temujin held the slender trunk steady for his brother's blade. The knife was a solid piece of edged iron and it bit deeply. Bekter seemed to be taking his anger out on the wood, and it took courage for Temujin to hold his hands still as blow after blow thumped near his fingers.

It did not take long before Temujin was able to press the sapling down and expose the whitish fibers of the young wood. The bow would be near to useless, he thought glumly. It was hard not to think of the beautiful weapons in every ger of the Wolves. Boiled strips of sheep horn and ground sinew were glued to birch cores and then left for an entire year in dry darkness. Each bow was a marvel of ingenuity, capable of killing over a distance of more than a hundred alds.

The bow he and his brother sweated to make would be little more than a child's toy in comparison, and this was the one on which their lives would depend. Temujin snorted in bitter amusement as Bekter closed one eye and finally held up the length of birch, still ragged with its paper bark. He saw Bekter's jaw clench in response and watched in surprise as his brother brought the length of wood back sharply and broke it over another trunk, throwing the splintered birch to the leaves.

"This is a waste of time," Bekter said furiously.

Temujin eyed the knife he was holding, suddenly aware of how alone they were.

"How far can they travel in a day?" Bekter demanded. "You can track. We know the guards as well as our brothers. I could get past them."

"To do what?" Temujin asked. "Kill Eeluk?" He saw Bekter's eyes glaze for a moment as he tasted the idea, then shook his head.

"No. We'd never get to him, but we could steal a bow! Just a single bow and a few arrows and we could eat. Aren't you hungry?"

Temujin tried not to think about the ache in his stomach. He had known hunger before, but always there was the thought of a hot meal waiting at the end. Here, it seemed worse and his gut felt sore and painful to the touch. He hoped it was not the first sign of the loose bowels that came from disease or poor meat. In such a place, any weakness would kill him. He knew as well as his mother that they walked a thin edge between survival and a pile of bones come the winter.

"I am starving," he said, "but we'd never get into a

ger without the alarm being raised. Even if we did, they'd track us back here and Eeluk would not let us go a second time. That broken stick is all we have."

Both boys looked at the ruined sapling and Bekter grabbed it in a show of mindless anger, wrenching at the unyielding wood and then throwing it into the undergrowth.

"All right, let's start again," he said grimly. "Though we don't have a string, we don't have arrows, and we have no glue. We have as much chance of catching an animal by throwing stones at it!"

Temujin said nothing, shaken by the outburst. Like all of his father's sons, he was used to someone knowing what to do. Perhaps they had become too used to that certainty. Ever since he had felt his father's hand go limp in his own, he had been lost. There were times when he felt the strength he needed begin to kindle in his chest, but he kept expecting it all to end and his old life to come back.

"We'll braid strips of cloth for a string. It will hold long enough to take two shots, I should think. We only have two arrowheads, after all."

Bekter grunted in reply and reached out to another birch sapling, supple and as thick as his thumb.

"Hold this steady, then, brother," he said, raising the heavy blade. "I'll make a bow good for two chances at the kill. After that fails, we'll eat grass."

Kachiun caught up with Khasar high into the cleft between the hills. The figure of his older brother was so still that he almost missed him as he climbed over rocks, but his gaze was drawn to where the stream had wid-

ened into a pool and he saw his brother on the edge.
Khasar had made himself a simple rod with a long birch
twig. Kachiun whistled to let him know he was there
and approached as silently as he could, staring down
into the clear water.

"I can see them. Nothing larger than a finger so
far," Khasar whispered. "They don't seem to want the
worms, though."

They both stared at the limp scrap of flesh that hung
in the water an arm's length from the bank. Kachiun
frowned to himself, thinking.

"We're going to need more than one or two if we're
all to eat tonight," he said.

Khasar grunted in response. "If you have an idea,
then say it. I can't *make* them take the hook."

Kachiun was silent for a long time, and both boys
would have enjoyed the peace if it had not been for the
ache in their bellies. At last, Kachiun stood and began to
unwind the orange waist cloth from his deel. It was
three alds long, stretching as far as three men lying head
to toe. He might not have thought to use it if Temujin
had not added his own to Hoelun's pile. Khasar glanced
up at him, a smile touching his mouth.

"Going for a swim?" he said.

Kachiun shook his head. "A net would be better
than a hook. We could get them all then. I thought I
might try to dam the stream with the cloth."

Khasar pulled his bedraggled worm out of the water, laying the precious hook down.

"It might work," he said. "I'll go farther upstream
and beat the water with a stick as I come back down. If
you can close off the stream with the cloth, you might
be able to scoop a few onto the bank."

Both boys looked at the freezing water reluctantly. Kachiun sighed to himself, winding the cloth around his arms.

"All right; it's better than waiting," he said, shuddering as he stepped into the pool.

The cold made them gasp and wince, but both boys worked quickly to tie the length of cloth across the path of the stream. A tree root made a perfect anchor point on one side, and Kachiun heaved a rock onto the other as he doubled the cloth and brought it back on itself. There was more than enough, and he forgot his chill for a time when he saw small fish touch the orange barrier and dart backwards. He saw Khasar cut a strip from the cloth and bind a knife to a stick to make a short stabbing spear.

"Pray to the sky father for some big ones," Khasar said. "We need to get this right."

Kachiun remained in the water, struggling not to shiver too violently as his brother walked away and was lost to sight. He did not need to be told.

Temujin tried to take the bow from his brother's hands, and Bekter rapped his knuckles with the handle of his knife.

"I have it," Bekter said, irritably.

Temujin watched as the older boy bent the birch to fit the loop of braided string over the other end. He winced in anticipation of the crack that would be the ruin of their third attempt. From the beginning, he had resented Bekter's bad-tempered approach to making the weapon, as if the wood and the string were enemies to be crushed into obedience. Whenever Temujin tried to help, he was roughly rebuffed, and only when Bekter failed again and again did he suffer his brother to hold the wood still as they bent it. The second bow had snapped and their first two strings had lasted just long enough to come under tension before they too gave way. The sun had moved over their heads and their tempers frayed as failure piled upon failure.

The new string was braided from three thin strips cut from Temujin's own waist cloth. It was childishly thick and bulky, vibrating visibly as Bekter eased the bow back from its bent position, wincing in anticipation. It did not snap and both boys breathed a sigh of relief. Bekter touched his thumb to the taut cord, making a deep twanging sound.

"Have you finished the arrows?" he said to Temujin.

"Just one," Temujin replied, showing him the straight birch twig with a needle of bone set firmly into the wood. It had taken forever to grind the shard into a shape he could bind, leaving a delicate tang that fitted between the split wood. He had held his breath for part of the process, knowing that if he snapped the head, there could be no replacement.

"Give it to me, then," Bekter said, holding out his hand.

Temujin shook his head. "Make your own," he replied, holding it out of reach. "This is mine."

He saw rage in Bekter's eyes then and thought the older boy might use the new bow to strike him. Perhaps the time they had spent on it prevented him from doing so, but Bekter nodded at last.

"I should have expected that, from you."

Bekter made a show of placing the bow out of

Temujin's reach while he found a stone to grind his own arrowhead. Temujin stood stiffly watching, irritated at having to cooperate with a fool.

"The Olkhun'ut do not speak well of you, Bekter, did you know that?" he said.

Bekter snorted, spitting on the stone and working the bone sliver back and forth.

"I don't care what they think of me, my brother," he replied grimly. "If I had become khan, I would have raided them the first winter. I would have shown them the price of their pride."

"Be sure to tell our mother that, when we go back," Temujin said. "She will be pleased to hear what you were planning."

Bekter looked up at Temujin, his small dark eyes murderous.

"You are just a child," he said, after a time. "You could never have led the Wolves."

Temujin felt anger flare, though he showed nothing.

"We won't know now, will we?" he said.

Bekter ignored him, grinding the bone into a neat shape for the shaft.

"Instead of just standing there, why don't you do something useful, like finding a marmot burrow?"

Temujin did not bother to reply. He turned his back on his brother and walked away.

The meal that night was a pitiful affair. Hoelun had nursed a flame into life, though the damp leaves smoked and spat. Another night in the cold might have killed them, but she was terrified the light would be seen. The cleft in the hills should have hidden their position, but still she made them cluster around the flame, blocking its light with their bodies. They were all weak with hunger and Temuge was green around the mouth where he had tried wild herbs and vomited.

Two fish were the product of their day's labors, both of them captured more by luck than skill in the river trap. As small as they were, the crisping black fingers of flesh drew the eyes of all the boys.

Temujin and Bekter were silently furious with each other after an afternoon of frustration. When Temujin had found a marmot hole, Bekter had refused to hand over the bow and Temujin had flown at him in a rage, rolling together over and over in the wet. One of the arrows had snapped under them, the sound interrupting their fight. Bekter had tried to snatch at the other, but Temujin had been faster. He had already decided to borrow Kachiun's knife and make his own bow for the next day.

Hoelun shivered, feeling ill as she held the twigs in the flames and wondered who would starve amongst her sons. Kachiun and Khasar deserved at least a taste of the flesh, but she knew her own strength was the most important thing they had. If she began to faint from hunger, or even died, the rest of them would perish. She set her jaw in anger as her gaze fell on the two older boys. Both of them bore fresh bruises and she wanted to take a stick to them for their stupidity. They did not understand that there would be no rescue, no respite. Their lives were in two tiny fish on the flames, barely enough for a mouthful.

Hoelun prodded at the black flesh with a nail, trying not to give in to despair. Clear liquid ran down a finger as she squeezed it and she pressed her mouth to the drip, closing her eyes in something like ecstasy. She ignored her complaining stomach and broke the fish into two pieces, handing one each to Kachiun and Khasar.

Kachiun shook his head. "You first," he said, making tears start in her eyes.

Khasar heard him and paused as he raised the fish to his mouth. He could smell the cooked meat and Hoelun saw saliva was making his lips wet.

"I can last a little longer than you, Kachiun," she said. "I will eat tomorrow."

It was enough for Khasar, who closed his mouth on the scrap and sucked noisily at the bones. Kachiun's eyes were dark with pain from his hunger, but he shook his head.

"You first," he said again. He held out the head of the fish and Hoelun took it gently from him.

"Do you think I can take food from you, Kachiun? My darling son?" Her voice hardened. "Eat it, or I will throw it back on the fire."

He winced at the thought and took it from her at once. They could all hear the bones breaking as he crunched it into a paste in his mouth, savoring every last drop of nourishment.

"Now you," Temujin said to his mother. He reached out for the second fish, intending to pass it to her. Bekter slapped his arm away and Temujin almost went for him again in a sudden rage.

"I do not need to eat tonight," Temujin said, controlling his anger. "Neither does Bekter. Share the last one with Temuge."

He could not bear the hungry eyes all round the fire and suddenly stood, preferring not to watch. He swayed slightly, feeling faint, but then Bekter reached out and took the fish, breaking it in two. He put the larger half in his mouth and held out the rest to his mother, unable to look her in the eye.

Hoelun hid her irritation, sick of the pettiness that hunger had brought to her family. They all sensed death was close and it was hard to remain strong. She forgave Bekter, but the last piece of fish went to Temuge, who sucked busily at it, looking round for more. Temujin spat on the ground, deliberately catching the edge of Bekter's deel with the clot of phlegm. Before his older brother could rise to his feet, Temujin had vanished into the darkness. The damp air cooled quickly without the sun, and they prepared themselves for another freezing night.

CHAPTER 12

TEMUJIN HELD HIMSELF very still as he sighted along the line of the shaft. Although the marmots had all scattered at his arrival, they were stupid creatures and it was never long before they returned. With a decent bow and feathered arrows, he would have been confident in taking a fat buck home for his family.

The closest warren to the cleft in the hills was still dangerously exposed. Temujin would have preferred a few small bushes for cover, but instead he had to sit perfectly still and wait for the timid animals to risk coming back. He kept watch on the hills around him at the same time, in case a wanderer came over a crest. Hoelun had fed them with her warnings until they were all fearful of shadows and watched the horizon whenever they left the shelter of the cleft.

The wind blew into Temujin's face so that his scent would not alarm his prey, but he had to hold the bow half drawn as the slightest movement sent them all diving back into their burrows like brown streaks across the ground. His arms were quivering with fatigue and always there was the little voice in his head telling him that he needed to make the kill this time, spoiling his calm. After four days surviving on tiny scraps and a handful of wild onions, Yesugei's sons and wife were starving to death. Hoelun had lost her energy and sat listless as her daughter pawed at her and screamed. Only the baby had fed well for the first three days, but then Hoelun's milk had begun to fail and their mother's sobbing had been pitiful to the boys.

Kachiun and Khasar had climbed far up the cleft, scouting the land and looking for any animal that might have strayed away from a herd and gone wild. Kachiun had made himself a small bow and three arrows with tips hard and black from the fire. Temujin wished them luck, but he knew he had a better chance of saving them, if he could only make a good strike. He could almost taste the hot meat of the marmot as it sat up twenty paces away. It was a shot a child could have made if the arrows had been flighted. As it was, Temujin was forced to wait while the agony built in his arms. He dared not speak aloud, but in his mind, he called to the nervous creatures, willing them to wander a little farther away from safety, a little closer to him.

He blinked stinging sweat from his eyes as the marmot looked around, sensing there was a predator nearby. Temujin watched as the animal froze, knowing the next movement would be a vanishing scuttle as the alarm went up. He released his breath and loosed the shaft, sick with the expectation of seeing it wasted.

It hit the marmot in the neck. The strike had been without any real force, remaining stuck as the animal struggled in a frenzy, pawing at it. Temujin dropped the bow and leapt to his feet, running toward his kill before it could recover and disappear underground. He saw the lighter belly fur and the legs jerking maniacally as he ran, desperate not to lose his chance.

He fell on the marmot, gripping it frantically. It went berserk and, in his weakened state, he almost lost it as it writhed in his grip. The arrow fell away and blood spattered on the dry ground. Temujin found there were tears of relief in his eyes as he pulled the neck out and twisted it. The marmot still kicked and jerked against his leg as he stood panting, but they would eat. He waited for dizziness to pass, feeling the weight of the animal he'd caught. It was fat and healthy and he knew his mother would have some hot meat and blood that night. The tendons would be ground into a paste and layered with fish glue onto his bow for strength. His next shot would be at a longer range, the kill more certain. He placed his hands on his knees and laughed weakly at his own relief. It was such a small thing, but it meant so much, he could hardly take it in.

Behind his back, he heard a voice he knew.

"What did you get?" Bekter said, walking across the grass toward his brother. He carried his own bow on his shoulder and he did not have the pinched and starving look of the others. It had been Kachiun who first voiced the suspicion that Bekter was not bringing his kills back to the family. He accepted his share readily enough, but in the four days since they had come to that place, he had brought nothing of his own to the fire. Temujin stood straight, uncomfortable with the way Bekter's eyes drifted over the prey he had taken.

"A marmot," he said, holding it up.

Bekter leaned closer to see and then snatched at it.

Temujin jerked backwards and the limp corpse fell sprawling into the dust. Both boys grabbed for it, kicking and punching wildly at each other. Temujin was too weak to do more than hold Bekter back before he was thrown off and left looking up at the blue sky, his chest heaving.

"I will take this one back to our mother. You would only have stolen it and eaten it yourself," Bekter said, smiling down at Temujin.

It was galling to have Kachiun's own suspicion thrown in his face and Temujin tried to struggle up. Bekter held him down with a foot and he could not fight him. His strength seemed to have vanished.

"Catch yourself another, Temujin. Don't come back until you do."

Bekter laughed then and snatched up the limp marmot, jogging away down the hillside to where the greenery became dark and thick. Temujin watched him go, so angry he thought his heart would burst. It fluttered in his chest and he wondered with a pang of terror if hunger could have weakened it. He could not die while Eeluk ruled the Wolves, or while Bekter had not been punished.

By the time he sat up, he had mastered himself once more. The foolish marmots had returned while he lay there, though they scattered as soon as he rose. Grimly, he returned to his arrow and notched it into the braided string, settling back into the stillness of the hunter. His muscles ached and his legs threatened to cramp under the strain, but his heart slowed to beat with force and need.

There was only one marmot to feed the family that night. Hoelun revived as Bekter brought it to her, and made a larger fire to heat stones. Though her hands shook, she nicked the belly neatly and scooped out the guts and organs, filling the space with pebbles hot enough to crack. She kept her deel wrapped around her hands, but twice she winced as the heat stung her fingers. The meat was seared from the inside and then the bloated skin rolled in the embers, charring it to crisp deliciousness. The heart too was roasted in the ashes until it sizzled. Nothing would be wasted.

The smell alone seemed to put a little color in Hoelun's cheeks, and she hugged Bekter, her relief turning to tears she did not seem to feel. Temujin said nothing of what had happened. She needed them to work together and it would have been cruelty to accuse his smiling brother when she was so weak.

Bekter basked in the attention, his gleaming gaze falling on Temujin at regular intervals. Temujin stared darkly back when his mother was not looking. Kachiun noticed as the evening faded to night, and he jogged his brother with an elbow.

"What's wrong?" the little boy whispered as they settled down to eat.

Temujin shook his head, unwilling to share his hatred. He could hardly think of anything else except the steaming scraps of meat pressed into his hands by Bekter, who chose the portions like a khan feeding his men. Temujin saw he kept the shoulder, the best piece, for himself.

None of them had ever tasted anything as fine as that meat. The family became a little happier, a little more hopeful, as it warmed them. One shot with the bow had brought about the changes, though Kachiun had added another three small fish and a few crickets to the fire. It was a feast that ached and burned inside them as the younger boys forced the morsels down too quickly and had to drink water against the heat. Temujin might have forgiven the theft if his brothers had not been so generous in their praise. Bekter accepted it as his due, his small eyes filled with an inner amusement only Temujin understood.

There was no rain that night and the boys slept in the second of the rough shelters they had constructed, a tiny part of their hunger laid to rest. It was still there, hurting, but they could hold it back once more and show the cold face to discomfort as they retreated from a ragged edge where no control was possible.

Temujin did not sleep. He rose on silent feet and padded out into the darkness, looking up at the moon and shivering. The summer would not last much longer, he realized as he walked. The winter was coming and it would kill them as surely as a knife in the chest. The marmots slept in their burrows in the cold months, far underground, where they could not be reached. The birds flew south and could not be trapped. Winter was hard enough for families in warm gers, surrounded by cattle and horses. It would be murder for the family of Yesugei.

As he stood and emptied his bladder onto the ground, he could not help thinking of the Olkhun'ut and the night he had crept out after Koke. He had been a child then, with nothing better to do than settle scores with other boys. He ached for the innocence of that night and wished Borte were there to hold. He snorted to himself at that thought, knowing Borte was warm and well fed, while his bones were showing.

Temujin sensed a presence behind him and spun, dropping low and ready to lunge or run.

"You must have good ears, brother," Kachiun's voice came. "I am like a silent breeze at night."

Temujin smiled at his brother, relaxing. "Why are you awake?"

Kachiun shrugged. "Hungry. I'd stopped feeling it all day yesterday, then Bekter brings in a handful of marmot meat and my stomach has woken up again."

Temujin spat on the ground. "*My* marmot. I killed it; he was just the one who took it from me."

Kachiun's face was difficult to read in the moonlight, but Temujin could see he was troubled.

"I guessed it. I don't think the others noticed."

He fell silent, a tiny grim figure standing in the dark. Temujin saw he had a bulge in his tunic, and he prodded it with a finger.

"What's that?" Temujin asked, curious.

Kachiun looked nervously back toward the camp before he pulled something out and held it for Temujin to see. It was another marmot carcass. Temujin took it, felt the bones in his hand, already angry. They were split exactly as a hungry man would break them to get at tiny scraps of marrow. Bekter hadn't risked a fire. The bones were raw, no more than a day old.

"I found it over where Bekter has been hunting," Kachiun said, his voice troubled.

Temujin turned the fragile little bones over in his hands, running his fingers along the skull. Bekter had left the skin on there, though the eyes were gone. He had killed it on a day when there was nothing else to eat in the camp for any of them.

Temujin knelt and searched for any small scrap of flesh. There was a smell of rot on the bones, but it would not have spoiled too much in a single day. Kachiun knelt with him and they sucked each of the broken bones again, teasing out even a whisper of flavor. It did not take long.

"What will you do?" Kachiun asked when they were done.

Temujin made up his mind and felt no regrets.

"Have you ever seen a tick on a horse, Kachiun?"

"Of course," his brother replied. They had both seen the fat parasites as large as the last joint on their thumbs. When they were pulled free, they left a trail of blood that took an age to clot.

"A tick is a dangerous thing when a horse is weak," Temujin said softly. "Do you know what you must do when you find one?"

"Kill it," Kachiun whispered.

When Bekter left the camp the following dawn, Temujin and Kachiun slipped out after him. They knew where he preferred to hunt and let him get far ahead, where he would not sense he was being watched.

Kachiun shot worried glances at Temujin as they crept along between the trees. Temujin saw the fear and wondered that he felt none of it himself. His hunger was a constant pain in his gut, and twice he had to stop and strain greenish liquid from his bowels, wiping himself with wet leaves. He felt light-headed and weak, but the starvation had burnt any sense of pity out of him. He thought he might have a light fever, but he forced himself on, though his heart bumped and fluttered weakly. This was what it was to be a wolf, he realized. No fear or regret, just a single drive to rid themselves of an enemy.

It was not hard to track Bekter on the muddy ground. He had not tried to conceal his path, and the only danger was that they would stumble across him when he had settled to watch for prey. Temujin and Kachiun padded silently behind, every sense straining. When they saw a pair of larks in a tree ahead, Kachiun touched his brother lightly on the arm in warning, and they walked a circle around the spot rather than have the birds cry an alarm.

Kachiun stopped and Temujin turned to him, wincing at the way his brother's skull was perfectly visible beneath the stretched skin. It hurt to see it and Temujin assumed he too looked as close to death. If he shut his eyes, it seemed to rob him of balance, so that he swayed and had to fight dizziness. It required an effort of will to take a long, slow breath and lower his heart's frantic pounding.

Kachiun raised an arm to point and Temujin stared ahead, freezing as he saw that Bekter had taken position a hundred paces farther on, overlooking the stream. It was hard not to be frightened of the figure kneeling like a statue in the bushes. They had all felt the force of Bekter's fists and his weight on them in childish games. Temujin watched Bekter, wondering how to get close enough to take a shot. There was no doubt in his mind. His vision seemed bright and slightly blurred and his thoughts were cold, slow-moving things, but his path was set.

Kachiun and Temujin jerked as Bekter loosed an arrow into the water from where he hid. Both boys stepped back into cover as they heard a flurry of wings and panic and saw three ducks take off wildly, calling their warnings too late.

Bekter jumped up and waded into the stream. He was lost to sight then behind a tree, but when he came back to the bank, they saw he held the limp body of a red duck.

Temujin peered through a tangle of branches and thorns.

"We'll wait here," he murmured. "Find a spot on the other side of this path. We'll take him on his way back."

Kachiun swallowed a lump in his throat, trying not to show his nervousness. He did not like the new coldness he saw in Temujin, and he regretted showing him the marmot bones the night before. In the light of day, his hands shook at the thought of what they were intending to do, but when Temujin looked at him, he did not meet his stare. The smaller boy waited until Bekter's back was turned and darted across the path, his bow ready.

Temujin narrowed his eyes as he watched Bekter retrieve the arrow and shove the duck into his tunic. He felt a pang of disappointment as Bekter stretched aching muscles and then strode away in the wrong direction, farther up the cleft. Temujin raised a flat palm to where Kachiun was hidden, though he could not see him. He thought of Bekter devouring the fat duck somewhere private, and he wanted to kill him right then. If he had been strong, with good milk and meat in his belly, he might have gone after him, but as weak as he was, only an ambush stood a chance of succeeding. Temujin eased his legs before they could begin to cramp. His gut sent a spasm of pain through him that made him close his eyes and curl up against it until it passed. He dared not drop his trousers while he waited, in case Bekter's sharp nose smelled it. Yesugei had raised them all to be aware, and Temujin did not want to lose his advantage. He shut out the discomfort and settled down to wait.

The worst moment was when a wood pigeon came to alight on a tree not far away from where the two boys crouched, hidden in the damp undergrowth. Temujin watched it in agony, knowing he could make the shot easily at just a few paces. The bird seemed unaware of them and his hunger made him cramp again and again as he tried to ignore it. For all he knew, Bekter was coming back already, and every bird nearby would rise out of the trees and give away their position if Temujin shot the pigeon. Still, he could not look away, and when it flew, he followed its flight as far as he could, hearing the clapping of its wings long after it had gone.

Bekter came back when the sun had crossed above the cleft and the shadows were lengthening. Temujin heard his footsteps and dragged himself out of a near trance. He was surprised to find so much time had passed and wondered if he had even been asleep. His body was failing and the stream water could not fill the aching pain in his stomach.

Temujin nocked his arrow and waited, shaking his head against dizziness and to clear his vision. He tried to tell himself that Bekter would kill him if he missed, to make his body come alive and serve just a little longer. It was hard, and he rubbed angrily at his eyes to sharpen them. He could hear Bekter's closeness and then the moment had come.

He stepped out into the path only a few paces from Bekter. Temujin drew the bow and Bekter gaped at him. There was an instant where Bekter scrabbled for the knife on his belt and then Temujin loosed, seeing the bone point punch into his brother's chest. At the same moment, Kachiun fired from behind and to one side, rocking Bekter forward with a second blow.

Bekter staggered and roared in rage. He drew his knife and advanced a step, then another before his legs went and he fell. Both arrows had struck him cleanly and Temujin could hear the great bubbling hiss of a punctured lung. There was no pity in him. In a daze, he stepped forward, dropping the bow and taking Bekter's knife from his fingers.

He looked across at Kachiun's horrified face, then grimaced, reaching down and shoving the blade into Bekter's neck, releasing his blood and his life.

"It is done," Temujin said, looking down at the staring eyes as they glazed over. He could not feel his own weight as he patted Bekter's deel and tunic, searching for the duck. It was not there, and Temujin kicked the body and staggered away from it, so dizzy he thought he would faint. He pressed his forehead against the cool wetness of a birch tree and waited for his pulse to ease its throbbing flutter.

He heard Kachiun approach, his steps soft on the leaves as they skirted their brother's body. Temujin opened his eyes.

"We had better hope Khasar brought something back to eat," he said. When Kachiun did not respond, Temujin took Bekter's weapons, pulling the drawn bow up around his shoulder.

"If the others see Bekter's knife, they will know," Kachiun said, his voice sick with misery.

Temujin reached out and held his neck, steadying himself as much as his brother. He could hear the panic in Kachiun and felt the first echo of it himself. He had not thought about what would happen after his enemy was dead. There would be no revenge for Bekter, no chance to win back their father's gers and herds. He would rot where he lay. The reality of it was only beginning to sink in, and Temujin could hardly believe he had actually done it. The strange mood before the shot was gone, and in its place, he had only weakness and hunger.

"I will tell them," Temujin said. He felt his gaze drawn down to Bekter's body once more as if pulled by an unseen weight. "I will tell them he was letting us all starve. There is no place here for softness. I will tell them that."

They walked down into the cleft once more, each taking comfort from the other's presence.

CHAPTER 13

HOELUN SENSED SOMETHING was wrong the moment she sighted the two boys returning to the camp. Khasar and Temuge sat with her, and little Temulun lay on a scrap of cloth near the fire's warmth. Hoelun rose slowly from kneeling, her thin face already showing fear. As Temujin came closer, she saw he carried Bekter's bow and she stiffened, taking in the detail. Neither Temujin nor Kachiun could meet her eyes, and her voice was just a whisper when it came at last.

"Where is your brother?" she said.

Kachiun stared at the ground, unable to reply. She took a step forward as Temujin raised his head and swallowed visibly.

"He was taking food, keeping it for himself...," he began.

Hoelun let out a cry of fury and slapped him hard enough to knock his head to one side.

"Where is your brother?" she demanded, shrilly. "Where is my son?"

Temujin's nose was bleeding in a red stream over his mouth, so that he was forced to spit. He bared red teeth at his mother and the pain.

"He is dead," he snapped. Before he could go on, Hoelun slapped him again, over and over, until all he could do was curl up and stagger backwards. She went with him, flailing in a misery she could not bear.

"*You* killed him?" she wailed. "What are you?"

Temujin tried to hold her hands, but she was too strong for him and blows rained down on his face and shoulders, wherever she could reach.

"Stop hitting him! Please!" Temuge called after them, but Hoelun could not hear him. There was a roaring in her ears and a rage in her that threatened to tear her apart. She backed Temujin up against a tree and grabbed him by the shoulders, shaking his thin frame with such violence that his head lolled weakly.

"Would you kill him as well?" Kachiun cried, trying to pull her away.

She tore her deel from his grasp and took Temujin by his long hair, wrenching his head back so that he had to look her in the eye.

"You were born with a clot of blood in your hand, with death. I told your father you were a curse on us, but he was blind." She could not see through her tears and he felt her hands tighten like claws on his scalp.

"He was keeping food from all of us, letting us starve," Temujin cried. "Letting *you* starve!" He began to weep under the onslaught, more alone than he had ever been. Hoelun looked at him as if he were diseased.

"You have stolen a son from me, my own boy," she replied. As she focused on him, she raised a hand over his face and he saw her broken nails shiver above his eyes. It was a moment that lasted a long time as he stared up in terror, waiting for her to tear at him.

The strength in her arms faded as suddenly as it had come, and she collapsed in a limp pile, senseless. Temujin found himself standing alone and shivering in reaction. His stomach cramped, forcing him to retch, though there was nothing but sour yellow liquid.

As he stepped away from his mother, he saw his brothers were staring at him and he shouted wildly at them, "He was eating fat marmots while we starved to death! It was right to kill him. How long do you think we would have lived with him taking our share on top of his own catch? I saw him take a duck today, but is it here to give us strength? No, it is in his belly."

Hoelun stirred on the ground behind him and Temujin jumped, wary of another attack from her. His eyes filled with fresh tears as he looked at the mother he adored. He could have spared her the knowledge if he had thought about it, perhaps inventing a story of a fall to explain Bekter's death. No, he told himself. It had not been wrong. Bekter had been the tick on the hide, taking more than his share and giving nothing back while they died around him. His mother would see that in time.

Hoelun opened bloodshot eyes and scrabbled to her knees, moaning in weary grief. She did not have the strength to come to her feet again, and it took Temuge and Khasar to help her up. Temujin rubbed a bloody smear on his skin and faced her sullenly. He wanted to run away rather than have her look at him again, but he forced himself to stand.

"He would have killed us," he said.

Hoelun turned an empty gaze on him and he shivered.

"Say his name," she said. "Say the name of my first-born son."

Temujin winced, suddenly overwhelmed by dizziness. His bloody nose felt hot and huge on his face and he could see dark flashes in his vision. All he wanted was to collapse and sleep, but he remained there, staring up at his mother.

"Say his name," she said again, anger replacing the dullness in her eyes.

"Bekter," Temujin replied, spitting the word, "who stole food when we are dying."

"I should have killed you when I saw the midwife open your hand," Hoelun said in a light tone more frightening than her anger. "I should have known then what you were."

Temujin felt he was being torn inside, unable to stop her hurting him. He wanted to run to her and have her arms wrap him against the cold, to do anything but see the awful vacant misery that he had caused.

"Get away from me, boy," his mother said softly. "If I see you sleeping, I will kill you for what you've done here. For what you have taken from me. You did not soothe him when his teeth came in. You were not there to draw out his fevers with herbs and rock him through the worst. You did not exist when Yesugei and I loved the little boy. When we were young and he was all we had."

Temujin listened, dull with shock. Perhaps his mother had not understood the man Bekter had become. The baby she had rocked had grown into a cruel thief, and Temujin could not find the words to tell her. Even as they formed in his mouth, he bit down on them, knowing they would be useless, or worse, that they would rouse her again to attacking him. He shook his head.

"I am sorry," he said, though as he spoke, he knew that he was sorry for the pain he had caused, not the killing.

"Take yourself away from here, Temujin," Hoelun whispered. "I can't bear to look at you."

He sobbed then and turned to run past his brothers, each breath hoarse in his throat and the taste of his own blood in his mouth.

They did not see him after that for five days. Though Kachiun watched for his brother, the only sign of him was in the prey he brought back and left at the edge of their small camp. Two pigeons were there the first day, still warm, with blood running from their beaks. Hoelun did not refuse the gift, though she would not speak about what had happened to any of them. They ate the meat in miserable silence, Kachiun and Khasar sharing glances while Temuge sniffled and wailed whenever Hoelun left him alone. Bekter's death might have been a relief for the younger boys if it had come while they were safe in the gers of the Wolves. They would have mourned him and taken his body for sky burial, taking comfort from the ritual. In the cleft in the hills, it was just another reminder that death walked with them. It had been an adventure for a while in the beginning, until starvation stretched their skin over their bones. As things stood, they lived like wild animals and tried not to fear the coming winter.

Khasar had lost his laughter in the cleft in the hills. He had begun to brood after Temujin went away, and it was he who cuffed Temuge for troubling their mother too often. In Bekter's absence, they were all finding new roles and it was Khasar who led the hunt each morning with Kachiun, his face grim. They had found a better pool farther up the cleft, though they had to pass where Bekter had been killed to reach it. Kachiun had searched the ground and seen where Temujin had dragged the body away and covered it with branches. Their brother's flesh attracted scavengers, and when Kachiun found a lean dead dog at the camp's edge on the second evening, he had to force himself to swallow every vital mouthful. He could not escape the vision of Temujin killing the animal as it worried at Bekter's body, but Kachiun needed the food and the dog was the best meal they had found since coming to that place.

On the evening of the fifth day, Temujin strode back into the camp. His family froze at his step, the younger ones watching Hoelun for her reaction. She watched him come and saw that he held a young kid goat in his arms, still alive. Her son looked stronger, she realized, his skin darkened by days spent on the hills in the wind and sun. It was confusing to feel such a wave of relief that he was all right and, at the same time, un-dimmed hatred for what he had done. She could not find forgiveness in her.

Temujin took his find by the ear and prodded it into the circle of his family.

"There are two herders a few miles to the west of here," he said. "They are alone."

"Did they see you?" Hoelun said suddenly, surprising them all.

Temujin looked at her and his steady gaze became uncertain.

"No. I took this one when they rode behind a hill. It might be missed, I do not know. It was too good a chance to ignore." He shifted his weight from one foot to the other as he waited for his mother to say something else. He did not know what he would do if she sent him away again.

"They will look for it and find your tracks," Hoelun said. "You may have brought them here after you."

Temujin sighed. He did not have the strength for another argument. Before his mother could protest, he sat down cross-legged by the fire and drew his knife.

"We have to eat to live. If they find us, we will kill them."

He saw his mother's face become cold again and he waited for the storm that would surely follow. He had run for miles that day and every muscle in this thin body was aching. He could not bear another night on his own, and perhaps that fear showed in his face.

Kachiun spoke to break the awful tension.

"One of us should scout around the camp tonight in case they come," he said.

Temujin nodded without looking at him, his gaze fixed on his mother.

"We need each other," he said. "If I was wrong to kill my brother, it does not change that."

The kid goat bleated and tried to make a dash for a gap between Hoelun and Temuge. Hoelun reached out and gripped it around the neck, and Temujin saw she was crying in the firelight.

"What should I say to you, Temujin?" she murmured. The kid was warm and she buried her face in its coat as it cried out and struggled. "You have torn my heart out and perhaps I do not care about whatever is left."

"You care about the others, though. We need you to live through the winter, or we're all finished," Temujin said. He straightened his back as he spoke and his yellow eyes seemed to shine in the light of the flames.

Hoelun nodded to herself, humming a song from her childhood as she fondled the ears of the little goat. She had seen two of her brothers die from a plague that left them swollen and black, abandoned on the plains by her father's tribe. She had heard warriors scream from wounds that could not be healed, their agonies going on and on for days until the life was dragged out of them at last. Some had even asked for the mercy of a blade opening their throat and been granted it. She had walked with death all her life and perhaps she could even lose a son and survive it, as a mother of Wolves.

She did not know if she could love the man who killed him, though she ached to gather him in and press away his sorrow. She did not, instead reaching for her knife.

She had made birch-bark bowls for the camp while her sons were hunting, and she tossed one to Khasar and Kachiun. Temuge scrambled forward to take another and then there were only two of the crude containers left and Hoelun turned sad eyes on her last son.

"Take a bowl, Temujin," she said, after a time. "The blood will give you strength."

He lowered his head on hearing the words, knowing that he would be allowed to stay. He found his hands were shaking as he took his bowl and held it out with the others. Hoelun sighed and took a firmer grip on the goat before jamming in the blade and cutting the veins in its neck. Blood poured over her hands and the boys jostled each other to catch it before it was wasted. The goat continued to struggle as they filled the bowls and drank the hot liquid, smacking their lips and feeling it reach into their bones, easing the aches.

When the flow was just a trickle, Hoelun held the limp animal in one hand and patiently filled her own bowl to brimming before she drank. The goat still pawed at the air, but it was dying or already dead, and its eyes were huge and dark.

"We will cook the meat tomorrow night, when I am sure the fire will not bring the herdsmen looking for their lost goat," she told them. "If they come here, they must not leave to tell where we are. Do you understand?"

The boys licked their bloody mouths as they nodded solemnly. Hoelun took a deep breath, crushing her grief somewhere deep, where she still mourned Yesugei and everything they had lost. It had to be locked away where it could not destroy her, but somewhere, she was crying, on and on.

"Will they come to kill us?" Temuge asked in his high voice, looking nervously at the stolen goat.

Hoelun shook her head, pulling him toward her to give and take a little comfort.

"We are Wolves, little one. We do not die easily." As she spoke, her eyes were on Temujin, and he shivered at her cold ferocity.

With his face pressed against the frozen white grass, Temujin stared down at the two herdsmen. They slept on their backs, wrapped in padded deels with their arms drawn into the sleeves. His brothers lay on their bellies at his side, the frost seeping into their bones. The night was perfectly still. The huddled gathering of sleeping animals and men were oblivious to those who watched and hungered. Temujin strained his eyes in the gloom. All three boys carried bows and knives and there was no lightness in their expressions as they watched and judged their chances. Any movement would have the goats bleating in panic, and the two men would jerk to wakefulness in an instant.

"We can't get any closer," Khasar whispered.

Temujin frowned as he considered the problem, trying to ignore the ache in his flesh from lying on frozen ground. The herdsmen would be hard men, well able to survive on their own. They would have bows close by and they would be used to leaping up and killing a wolf as it tried to steal a lamb. It would make no difference if the prey was three boys, especially at night.

Temujin swallowed past a hard knot in his throat, glaring down at the peaceful scene. He might have agreed with his brother and crept back to the cleft in the hills if it had not been for the scrawny pony the men had hobbled nearby. It slept standing up, with its head almost touching the ground. Temujin yearned to have it, to ride again. It would mean he could hunt much farther away than before, dragging even large prey behind him. If it was a mare, it might have milk, and his tongue tasted the sourness in memory. The men would have any number of useful things on their person, and he could not bear to simply let them go, no matter what the risk. Winter was coming. He could feel it in the air and the stabbing needles of frost forming on his exposed skin.

Without mutton fat to protect them, how long would they last?

"Can you see the dogs?" Temujin murmured. No one replied. The animals would be lying with their tails tucked in against the cold, impossible to spot. He hated the thought of them leaping at him in the dark, but there was no choice. The herdsmen had to die for his family to survive.

He took a deep breath and checked that his bowstring was dry and strong.

"I have the best bow. I will walk to them and kill the first man to rise. You come behind and shoot at the dogs when they go for me. Understood?" In the moonlight, he could see how nervous his brothers were. "The dogs first, then whoever I leave standing," Temujin said, wanting to be certain. As they nodded, he rose silently to his feet and padded toward the sleeping men, coming from downwind so his scent would not alarm the flock.

The cold seemed to have numbed the inhabitants of the tiny camp. Temujin came closer and closer to them, hearing his own breath harshly in his ears. He kept his bow ready as he ran. For one who had been trained to loose shafts from a galloping horse, it would not be hard, he hoped.

At thirty paces, something moved on the edge of the sleeping men, a dark shape that leapt up and howled. On the other side, another dog lunged toward him, growling and barking as it closed. Temujin cried out in fear, desperately trying to keep his focus on the herdsmen.

They came out of sleep with a jerk, scrambling to their feet just as Temujin drew and loosed his first shaft. In the dark, he had not dared to try for a throat shot, and his arrow punched through the deel into the man's chest, dropping him back to one knee. Temujin heard him calling out in pain to his companion and saw the second roll away, coming up with a strung bow. The sheep and goats bleated in panic, running madly into the darkness, so that some of them came past Temujin and the brothers, veering wildly as they saw the predators amongst them.

Temujin raced to beat the herdsman to the shot. His second shaft was in his waistband and he tugged at it, cursing as the head snagged. The herdsman fitted his own shaft with the smooth confidence of a warrior and Temujin knew a moment of despair. He could not free his own and the sound of snarling on his left made him panic. He turned as one of the dogs leapt at his throat, falling backwards as the herdsman's arrow hummed over his head. Temujin cried out in fear as the dog's teeth closed on his arm, and then Khasar's shaft hammered through its neck and the snarling savagery was cut off.

Temujin had dropped his bow and he saw the herdsman was calmly fitting a new shaft to his string. Worse, the one who had been downed was staggering back to his feet. He too had found a bow and Temujin considered running. He knew it had to be finished there or the men would follow and take them one by one under the moonlight. He yanked at his arrow and it came free. He pressed it to the string with shaking hands. Where was the other dog?

Kachiun's arrow took the standing herdsman high under his chin. For a moment, he stood there with his bow drawn and Temujin thought he would still fire before death took him. He had heard of warriors so trained that they could sheathe their sword even after they had been killed, but as he watched, the herdsman collapsed.

The one Temujin had wounded was scrabbling with his own bow, crying out in pain as he tried to draw it. Temujin's shaft had torn his chest muscles and he could not bend the weapon far enough to take a shot.

Temujin felt his heart settle, knowing the battle was won. Khasar and Kachiun came to his shoulder and all three of them watched the man as his fingers slipped off the bow again and again.

"The second dog?" Temujin murmured.

Kachiun could not draw his eyes away from the struggling man, now praying to himself as he faced his attackers.

"I killed it."

Temujin clapped his brother on the back in thanks.

"Then let us finish this."

The herdsman saw the tallest of the attackers take an arrow from one of the others and draw. He gave up his struggle then and let his bow fall, drawing a knife from his deel and looking up at the stars and moon. His voice fell still and Temujin's shot took him in the paleness of his throat. Even then, he stood for a moment, swaying, before he crashed to the earth.

The three brothers moved carefully toward the bodies, watching for any sign of life. Temujin sent Khasar after the pony, which had managed to jerk away from the smell of blood despite the reins around its legs. He turned to Kachiun and took him by the back of the neck, pulling him forward so that their foreheads touched.

"We will survive the winter," Temujin said, smiling.

Kachiun caught his mood and together they whooped a victory cry over the empty plains. Perhaps it was foolish, but though they had killed, they were boys still.

CHAPTER 14

EELUK SAT AND STARED into the flames, thinking of the past. In the four years since he had left the shadow of Deli'un-Boldakh and the lands around the red hill, the Wolves had prospered, growing in numbers and wealth. There were still those in the tribe who hated him for abandoning the sons of Yesugei, but there had been no sign of an evil fate. The very first spring of the following year had seen more lambs born than anyone could remember, and a dozen squalling infants had come into the gers. Not a single one had been lost in birth, and those who looked for signs were satisfied.

Eeluk grunted to himself, enjoying how his vision dimmed and blurred after the second skin of black airag. The years had been good and he had three new sons of his own to run around the camp and learn the bow and the sword. He had put on weight, though it was more a thickening than an excess of fat. His teeth and eyes were still strong and his name was feared among the tribes. He knew he should have been content.

The Wolves had ranged far to the south in those years, until they reached a land so infested with flies and wet air that they sweated all day and their skins grew foul with creeping rashes and sores. Eeluk had longed for the cool, dry winds of the northern hills, but even as he had turned the Wolves back on their old paths, he'd wondered what had become of the family of Yesugei. Part of him still wished he had sent a bondsman back to make a cleaner end to it, though not from guilt, but from a nagging sense of unfinished work.

He snorted, tilting back the skin and finding it empty. With an idle gesture, he signaled for another and a young woman brought it to his hand. Eeluk looked appreciatively at her as she knelt before him with her head bowed. He could not remember her name through the blurriness of the airag, but she was slim and long-legged, like one of the spring colts. He felt desire stir and he reached out to touch her face, raising it so that she had to look at him. With deliberate slowness, he took her hand and pressed it into his lap, letting her feel his interest. She looked nervous, but he had never minded that and a khan could not be refused. He would pay her father with one of the new ponies if she pleased him.

"Go to my ger and wait for me," he said, slurring, watching as she crept away from him. Fine legs, he noticed, and considered going after her. The urge faded quickly and he went back to staring at the flames.

He still remembered how the sons of Yesugei had dared to stare at him as he left them behind. If it had been that morning, he would have cut them down himself. Four years before, he had barely placed his hands on the reins of the tribe and did not know how much they would stand from him. Yesugei had taught him that much, at least. The tribes would bear a great deal from those who led them, but there was always a point to watch for, a line not to cross.

Surely the first winter had taken those skinny children and their mother? It was a strange thing to be moving back into an area with so many memories. The camp for that night was a temporary one, a place to let the horses grow fat again on good grass. In a month or so, they would be moving back to the lands around the red hill. Eeluk had heard the Olkhun'ut too had returned to the area, and he had brought the Wolves north with more than a few half-formed dreams of conquest. The airag heated his blood and made him itch for a fight, or the woman waiting in his ger.

Eeluk drew in a deep breath, reveling in the frozen air. He had lusted after cold on the humid nights in the south, when his skin was red with bites and strange parasites that had to be cut out with a knife tip. The air in the north felt cleaner and already the coughing sickness had dwindled among the tribe. One old man and two children had died and been left on the hills for the hawks, but the Wolves were lighthearted as they traveled back to lands they knew.

"Tolui!" Eeluk called, though the idea was only part formed. He glanced to one side, where his bondsman rose from a crouch to stand by his shoulder. Eeluk watched the massive figure as he bowed, and felt the same sense of satisfaction as when he looked over their swelling herds. The Wolves had done well in the last great gathering of tribes, winning two of the short races and only losing the longest by a single length. His archers had been honored and two of his bondsmen had wrestled their way to the final rounds of the competition. Tolui had reached the fifth bout and was given the title of Falcon, before being beaten by a man of the Naimans. Eeluk had made him a bondsman as a reward, and with a year or two more to grow his strength, he would wager on Tolui to beat all comers. The powerful young man was fiercely loyal and it was no coincidence that Eeluk called on one who had been raised up by his own hand.

"You were just a boy when we last rode in the north," Eeluk said. Tolui nodded, his dark eyes without expression. "You were there on the day we left the old khan's children and his wife."

"I saw it, but there was no place for them," Tolui replied, his voice deep and sure.

Eeluk smiled. "That is it. There was no place for them any longer. We have grown rich since we came south. The sky father has blessed us all."

Tolui did not respond and Eeluk let the silence grow as he considered what he wanted done. It was nothing more than ghosts and old wounds, but he still dreamed of Hoelun and woke, sweating. Sometimes she would be writhing naked under him and then he would see her bones jutting through the flesh. It was nothing, but the lands around the old mountain brought the past back from ashes.

"Take two men you can trust," Eeluk said.

Tolui grew tauter as he loomed over his khan, eager to please him.

"Where will you send us?" he said, waiting for an answer while Eeluk filled his mouth with the airag and swallowed.

"Return to the old hunting grounds," he said at last. "See if they still live, any of them."

"Should I kill them?" Tolui asked.

There was nothing but simple curiosity in his voice, and Eeluk rubbed his swollen stomach while he thought. At his side was the sword that had once belonged to Yesugei. It would be fitting to end his line with a few swift cuts from that blade.

"If they have survived, they will be living like animals. Do what you want with them." He paused for a time, remembering the defiance of Bekter and Temujin as he watched the flames. "If you find the oldest boys, drag them here, to me. I'll show them what the Wolves have become under a strong khan before we give them to the birds and spirits."

Tolui bowed his heavy head and murmured, "Your will," before turning away to gather his companions for the ride. Eeluk watched him go in the firelight, seeing how he walked with firm, certain steps. The tribe had forgotten the children of Yesugei. Sometimes he thought he was the only one who remembered.

Tolui rode out from the camp with Basan and Unegen. Both of his companions were approaching thirty years of age, but they were not men born to lead as he was. Tolui reveled in his strength, and though he had seen only eighteen winters, he knew they feared his temper. For the powerful young bondsman, it was something he kept only barely under rein, enjoying the nervous glances he earned from older men. He saw how they moved with care in the coldest months and how they favored their knees. Tolui could come from sleep and leap up ready to work or fight, proud of his youth.

Only Eeluk had never shown the slightest hesitation, and when Tolui had challenged him to wrestle, the khan had thrown him so hard he had broken two fingers and a rib. Tolui took a perverse pride in following the only man who could match his strength, and there was no one more loyal among the Wolves.

For the first three days, they rode without speaking. The older warriors kept a wary distance from Eeluk's favorite, knowing how quickly his mood could change. They scouted the land right up to the red hill, noting how the grass had grown thick and sweet for the herds Eeluk would drive before the tribe. It was good land and no other tribe had claimed it for this season. Only a few distant herders spoiled the illusion of being alone on the vast plains.

On the twelfth day, they sighted a solitary ger next to a river and galloped up to it. Tolui called *"Nokhoi khor"* to have the wanderer herdsmen hold their dogs, then jumped down onto the springy turf, striding to the low door and ducking inside. Basan and Unegen exchanged glances before following him in, their faces set hard and cold. Both men had known each other since they were boys, before even Yesugei had ruled the Wolves. It galled them to have the arrogant young Tolui leading them, but they had both grasped the chance to see what had become of those they had left behind.

Tolui accepted the bowl of milky salt tea in his huge hands, slurping it noisily as he sat on an ancient bed. The other men joined him after bowing their heads to the herdsman and his wife, who were watching the strangers in frank terror from the other side of their home.

"You have nothing to fear," Basan said to them as he accepted his tea, earning himself a scornful glance from Tolui. The young bondsman cared nothing for those who were not Wolves.

"We are looking for a woman with five sons and a daughter," Tolui said, his deep voice too loud in the small ger. The herdsman's wife looked up nervously and Basan and Unegen felt a sudden quickening of their pulses.

Tolui too had noticed the response.

"You know them?" he said, leaning forward.

The herdsman pressed himself backwards, clearly intimidated by the bulk of this strange warrior. He shook his head.

"We have heard of them, but we do not know where they are," he said.

Tolui held the man's gaze, his body utterly still. His mouth opened slightly, showing white teeth. A threat had come into the ger and they could all feel it.

Before anything else could be said, a young boy came running through the door, skidding to a stop when he saw the strangers in his parents' home.

"I saw the horses," he said, looking around with wide, dark eyes.

Tolui chuckled and before anyone else could move, he reached out and pulled the child onto his knee, turning him upside down and swinging him. The little boy giggled, but Tolui's face was cold and the herdsman and his wife stiffened in fear.

"We need to find them," Tolui said over the boy's laughter. He held him without apparent effort with his arms outstretched, flipping the child over so that he stood upright on Tolui's knees.

"Again!" the boy said, breathlessly.

Tolui saw the mother begin to rise and her husband grip her arm.

"You know them," Tolui said, with certainty. "Tell us and we will go." Once more, he swung their son upside down, ignoring the delighted cries. Tolui tilted his head to watch their reaction. The mother's face crumpled.

"There is a woman with boys, a day's ride to the north in a small camp. Just two gers and a few ponies. They are peaceful people," she said, almost in a whisper.

Tolui nodded, enjoying the power he had over her while her son chuckled oblivious in his arms. When they could not bear it any longer, he set the boy on the floor and pushed him toward his parents. The mother embraced her son, squeezing her eyes shut as she held him.

"If you are lying, I will come back," Tolui said. The danger was clear in his dark eyes and the hands that could so easily have broken their son. The herdsman would not meet his gaze, staring at his feet until Tolui and his companions had left.

As they mounted outside, Tolui noticed a heavyset dog come ambling out from behind the ger. The animal was too old to hunt and stared at the strangers with whitish eyes that suggested he was almost blind. Tolui bared his teeth at the dog and it responded with a low growl, deep in its throat. He chuckled then, stringing his bow in swift, sure movements. Basan watched frowning as Tolui sent a shaft through the dog's throat. The animal spasmed, making coughing sounds as they dug in their heels and rode away.

Tolui seemed to be in a fine humor when they cooked a meal for themselves that night. The dried mutton was not too old and the cheese was slightly rancid, sparkling on the tongue as they chewed and swallowed.

"What are the khan's orders for when we find them?" Basan asked.

Tolui glanced over at the older man, frowning as if the question were an intrusion. He enjoyed cowing other warriors with his glares, backed always by a strength that could knock a pony to its knees with a single blow. He did not answer until Basan had looked away from him and another little struggle had been won.

"Whatever I choose, Basan," he said, savoring the idea. "Though the khan wants the older boys dragged back. I will tie them to the tails of our mounts and make them run."

"Perhaps these are not the ones we are looking for," Unegen reminded the young warrior. "They have gers and ponies, after all."

"We'll see. If they are, we'll bring the mounts back with us, as well," Tolui said, smiling at the thought. Eeluk had not imagined there could be spoils, but no one would dispute Tolui's right to take the possessions of the family of Yesugei. Their fate had been shown on the day the tribe left them. They were outside the laws of hospitality, mere wanderers with no khan to protect them. Tolui belched to himself as he pulled his hands inside his deel for sleep. It had been a good day. A man could hardly ask for more.

Temujin wiped sweat from his eyes as he tied the last crosspiece of wood together to make a small corral for their sheep and goats to give birth. The small herd had grown, with only a few mouths to feed, and two years before, the brothers had gone amongst the wanderers to trade wool and meat for felt. They had bartered for enough to make two small gers, and the sight of them never failed to raise Temujin's spirits.

Khasar and Kachiun were practicing their archery nearby, with a target made from thick layers of felt wrapped in cloth. Temujin stood and stretched stiff muscles, leaning on the fence to watch them and thinking back to the first months when death and the winter stalked every step. It had been hard on them all, but their mother's promise had been good. They had survived. Without Bekter, the brothers had grown a bond of trust and strength between them as they worked every hour of daylight. It had hardened them all, and when they were not working with the herd or preparing goods for trade, they spent every moment honing their skills with weapons.

Temujin touched the knife at his belt, kept sharp enough to slice through leather. In his ger there was a bow the equal of anything his father had owned, a beautiful weapon with an inner curve of shining horn. It was like pressing a knife edge to the fingers to draw its string back, and Temujin had spent months hardening his hands to bear the weight. It had not yet killed a man, but he knew it would send a shaft straight and true if he needed it.

A cool breeze came across the green plains and he closed his eyes, enjoying the way it dried his sweat. He could hear his mother in the ger with Temuge and little Temulun, singing to both her youngest children. He smiled at the sound, forgetting for a time the struggle of their lives. He did not often find peace, even in fragments. Though they traded with single herdsmen and their families, it had come as a surprise to find there was another society beneath the great tribes grazing across the land. Some of them had been banished for crimes of violence or lust. Others had been born without the protection of a khan. They were a wary people and Temujin had dealt with them only to survive. To one born in a khan's ger, they were still tribeless men and women, beneath contempt. Temujin did not enjoy being one of their number, and his brothers shared the same frustration. As they grew into men, they could not help but remember the way their lives should have run. A single day had stolen all their futures, and Temujin despaired when he thought of scratching a life with a few goats and sheep until he was old and weak. That was what Eeluk had taken from them. Not just their birthright, but the tribe, the great family that protected each other and made life bearable. Temujin could not forgive those hard years.

He heard Kachiun shout with pleasure and opened his eyes to see a shaft in the very center of the target. Temujin straightened and strolled over to his brothers, his gaze automatically scanning the land around them as he had a thousand times before. They could never be safe and they lived with the fear that they would see Eeluk riding back with a dozen grim men at any moment.

That sense of foreboding was a constant in their lives, though it had dulled with time. Temujin had seen that it was possible to live beneath the notice of the great tribes as other wanderer families did. Yet it could all be taken from them by a single raiding party out for sport—at any moment, they could be hunted like animals and their gers torn apart or stolen.

"Did you see the shot, Temujin?" Kachiun said.

Temujin shook his head. "I was looking the other way, my brother, but it is a fine bow." Like the one in his ger, the double-curved length had been dried for a year before the boiled strips of sheep horn were glued and overlapped onto the frame. The fish glue had made the gers stink for weeks afterwards, but the wood had become iron hard with its new layers and they were proud of what they had made.

"Take a shot," Kachiun said, holding the bow out to his brother.

Temujin smiled at him, seeing again the way his shoulders had filled and the new height that seemed to come in bursts. Yesugei's sons were all tall, though Temujin had grown beyond the others, matching his father's height in his seventeenth year.

He took a firm grip on the shaft of the bow and notched an arrow with a bone head, drawing it back on the calloused pads of his fingers. He emptied his lungs and, at the moment when he might have taken a breath, he released the arrow and watched it plunge home beside Kachiun's.

"It is a fine bow," he said, running a hand along the yellow length of horn. His expression was somber as he faced them, and Kachiun was the first to notice, always sensitive to his brother's thoughts.

"What is it?" Kachiun asked.

"I heard from old Horghuz that the Olkhun'ut have come back to the north," Temujin said, looking out over the horizon.

Kachiun nodded, understanding immediately. He and Temujin had shared a special bond since the day they had killed Bekter. At first, the family had struggled simply to live through the winter and then the next, but by the third, they had enough felt for the gers and Temujin had traded a bow and wool for another pony to match the tired old mare they had taken from the herdsmen in the first days. The new spring of the fourth year had brought restlessness on the wind for all of them, though it affected Temujin particularly. They had weapons and meat and camped close enough to woods to hide from a force they could not handle. Their mother had lost her gauntness and, though she still dreamed of Bekter and the past, the spring had woken something of the future in her sons.

In his own dreams, Temujin still thought of Borte, though the Olkhun'ut had vanished from the plains, with no way of following them. Even if he had found them, they would have scorned a ragged wanderer. He did not have a sword, nor the means to barter for one, but the boys rode for miles around their little camp and they talked to the wanderers and listened for news. The Olkhun'ut had been sighted in the first days of spring, and Temujin had been restless ever since.

"Will you fetch Borte to this place?" Kachiun asked, looking around at the camp.

Temujin followed his gaze and he swallowed back bitterness at the sight of their rough gers and bleating sheep. When he had seen Borte last, it had been with the unspoken promise that she would marry him and be the wife of a khan. He had known his worth then.

"Perhaps she has already been given to another," Temujin said, sourly. "She will be what? Eighteen? Her father was not a man to leave her waiting for so long."

Khasar snorted. "She was promised to you. If she has married another, you could challenge him."

Temujin glanced at his brother, seeing again the lack of understanding that meant he at least could never have ruled the Wolves. Khasar had none of the inner fire of Kachiun, the instant grasp of plans and strategies. Yet Temujin remembered the night when they had killed the herdsmen. Khasar had fought at his side. He had something of his father in him after all, though he could never grasp the subtleties Yesugei had loved. If their father had lived, Khasar would have been taken to the Olkhun'ut himself the following year. His life had also been thrown from its course by Eeluk's treachery.

Temujin nodded reluctantly. "If I had a new deel, I could ride to them and see what has become of her," he said. "At least I would know for certain."

"We'll all need women," Khasar agreed cheerfully. "I have been feeling the urge myself and I don't want to die without having one under me."

"The goats would miss your love, though," Kachiun said.

Khasar tried to cuff him, but his brother swayed away from the blow.

"Perhaps I could take you to the Olkhun'ut myself," Temujin said to Khasar, looking him up and down. "Am I not the khan of this family now? You are a fine-looking lad, after all."

It was true, though he meant it as a joke. Khasar had grown into lean strength and was dark and wiry under a mop of uncut hair that reached right down to his shoulders. They did not trouble to braid their hair anymore, and when they could be bothered to take a knife to it, it was just to hack off enough to clear their vision for hunting.

"Ten of the ewes are carrying," Temujin said. "If we

kept the lambs, we could sell a few goats and two of the older rams. It would get us a new stitched deel, and maybe some better reins. Old Horghuz was fussing with a set while I talked to him. I think he wanted me to make an offer."

Khasar tried to hide his interest, but the cold face of the warrior had been lost between them for too long. They had no need to guard themselves the way Yesugei had taught, and they were out of practice. As poor as they were, the decision was Temujin's alone and the other brothers had long accepted his right to lead them. It raised his spirits to be khan even of some ragged ponies and a couple of gers.

"I will see the old man and bargain with him," Temujin said. "We will ride together, but I cannot leave you there, Khasar. We need your bow arm too much. If there is a girl come into her blood, I will talk to them for you."

Khasar's face fell and Kachiun clapped him on the arm in sympathy.

"What can we offer, though?" Khasar said. "They will know we have nothing."

Temujin felt his excitement ebb and spat on the ground.

"We could raid the Tartars," Kachiun said suddenly. "If we ride into their lands, we could take whatever we find."

"And have them hunt us," Khasar responded irritably. He did not see the light that had come into Temujin's eyes.

"Our father's death has never been settled," he said. Kachiun sensed his mood and clenched a fist as Temujin went on. "We are strong enough and we can strike before they know we are even there. Why not? The Olkhun'ut would welcome us if we come with cattle and horses, and no one will care if they bear Tartar brands."

He took his two brothers by their shoulders and gripped them.

"The three of us could take back just a little of what they owe us. For everything we have lost because of them." Khasar and Kachiun were beginning to believe, he could see, but it was Kachiun who frowned suddenly.

"We cannot leave our mother unprotected with the young ones," he said.

Temujin thought quickly. "We will take her to old Horghuz and his family. He has a wife and young boys. She will be as safe there as anywhere. I'll promise him a fifth of whatever we bring back with us and he'll do it, I know he will."

As he spoke, he saw Kachiun glance toward the horizon. Temujin stiffened when he saw what had attracted his brother's eye.

"Riders!" Kachiun yelled to their mother.

They all turned as she appeared at the door of the closest ger.

"How many?" she said. She walked out to them and strained to see the strangers in the distance, but her eyes were not as good as her sons'.

"Three alone," Kachiun said with certainty. "Do we run?"

"You have prepared for this, Temujin," Hoelun said softly. "The choice is yours."

Temujin felt them all look to him, though he did not break his gaze away from the dark specks on the plain. He was still lifted by the words he had spoken with his brothers, and he wanted to spit into the wind and challenge the newcomers. The family of Yesugei would *not* be cowed, not after they had come so far. He took a deep breath and let his thoughts settle. The men could be an advance party for many more, or three raiders come to burn, rape, and kill. He clenched his fists, but then made the decision.

"Get into the woods, all of you," he said, furiously. "Take the bows and anything you can carry. If they come to steal from us, we'll gut them, I swear it."

His family moved quickly, Hoelun disappearing inside the ger and emerging with Temulun on her hip and Temuge trotting at her side. Her youngest son had lost his puppy fat in the hard years, but he still looked fearfully behind him as they made for the woods, stumbling along beside his mother.

Temujin joined Khasar and Kachiun as they retrieved their shafts and bows, yanking bags onto their shoulders and running to the tree line. They could hear the riders shout behind them as they saw them run, but they would be safe. Temujin swallowed bitterness in his throat as he passed into the trees and paused, panting, looking back. Whoever they were, he hated them for making him run, when he had sworn no one would do it again.

CHAPTER 15

THE THREE WARRIORS RODE cautiously into the tiny camp, noting the wisp of smoke that still came from one of the gers. They could hear the bleating of goats and sheep, but otherwise the morning was strangely still and they could all feel the pressure of unseen eyes.

The small gers and the rickety corral lay by a stream at the bottom of a wooded hill. Tolui had seen the running figures disappear into the trees, and he was careful to dismount so that his pony's bulk hid him from an ambush or a stray shot. Under their deels, Basan and Unegen wore leather armor like his own, a layer that would protect their chests and give them an edge even against a direct attack.

Tolui kept his hands low behind his horse's neck as he signaled to the others. One of them had to check the gers before they moved on, or risk being shot at from behind. It was Basan who nodded, leading his mare into the shadow of the ger and using her to block the sight of him ducking inside. Tolui and Unegen waited while he searched, their eyes scanning the tree line. Both men could see heavy banks of thorn bush tied with twine amongst the trunks, forcing any pursuit to come on foot. The ground had been prepared by someone who had expected a raid, and they had chosen well. To reach the trees, the bondsmen would have to cross thirty paces of open ground, and if the sons of Yesugei were waiting with bows, it would be a hard, bloody business.

Tolui frowned to himself as he considered their situation. He no longer doubted the running figures were the sons they had left behind. The few wanderer families who scavenged on the plains would not have prepared for a battle as these had. He strung his bow by feel, never taking his eyes off the dark undergrowth that could be hiding an army. He knew he could ride away to return with enough men to hunt them down, but Eeluk would not have seen the rolls of thorns and he would think Tolui had lost his nerve. He would not have his khan believe that of him and he began to prepare himself for a fight. His breathing changed from long, slow inhalations to the sipping breath that raised his heartbeat and charged him with strength, while Basan entered the second ger and came out shaking his head.

Tolui clenched his fist, then spread three fingers in a sharp jab. Basan and Unegen nodded to show they had understood. They prepared their own bows and waited for his lead. Tolui felt strong and, in his leather armor, he knew only the most powerful arrow shot could hurt him. He raised his fist and the three men broke into a run together, splitting apart as they reached the open ground.

Tolui panted as he ran, watching for the slightest movement. To one side, he caught a flicker and threw himself into a wrestler's roll, coming up fast as something hummed over his head. The other two men jinked as they closed the gap, but Tolui had seen by then that there was no way through the first line of trees. Every single gap had been closed by the great rolls of tied thorns. The sons of Yesugei must have pulled the last one behind them and Tolui found himself hesitating, while his heart pounded at being so exposed.

Before he could make a decision, an arrow punched into his chest, staggering him. The pain was colossal, but he ignored it, trusting in the armor to have prevented it from sinking in too far. They had good bows, he realized.

The three Wolves came to a stop in the worst possible position, facing the rolls of thorns. Yet as archers, each of them could take a bird on the wing: the situation was not as disastrous as Tolui had feared. For their enemies to shoot, they had to show themselves, if only for an instant. If they did, one of the three bondsmen would send a shaft back in the flick of an eye, too fast to dodge.

The sons of Yesugei must have realized the weakness in their tactic as silence grew and spread through the trees. The birds had all flown at the sudden rush of the warriors, and the only sound was the panting of men in fear of their lives, slowly coming under control.

Tolui took two slow paces to his right, crossing one leg over the other in perfect balance as Basan and Unegen spread out to his left. Every sense was heightened as they watched, ready to kill or be killed. It was too easy to imagine an arrow tearing into their flesh, but Tolui found he was enjoying the sense of danger. He kept his head high, then, on impulse, called out to the hidden enemy.

"My name is Tolui of the Wolves," he said, his voice loud in the clearing. "Bondsman to Eeluk who was once bondsman to Yesugei." He took a deep breath. "There is no need to fight. If you grant us guest rights, we will go back to the gers and I will tell you my messages."

He waited for a response, though he did not really expect them to give themselves away so easily. Out of the corner of his eye, he saw Basan shift his weight slightly, betraying discomfort.

"We cannot stand here all day," Basan murmured.

Their eyes moved ceaselessly as Tolui hissed back, "You would let them run us off?"

Only Basan's lips moved to respond. "Now we know they are alive, we should take the news back to the khan. Perhaps he will have fresh orders."

Tolui turned his head a fraction to answer, and it was that movement that almost killed him. He saw a boy rise and pull smoothly back on an arrow. For Tolui, the world roared in his ears as he released his own shaft at the exact moment he was sent stumbling by another blow to his chest, just below the throat. The shot had been rushed, he realized over the pain. He heard Unegen shoot into the bushes and Tolui roared in anger as he rose, setting another arrow to the string.

Basan fired blindly where he saw something move. They heard no cry of pain and Tolui glanced to his left to see Unegen on the ground, a shaft through his throat from front to back. The whites of his eyes were showing and his tongue was hanging limply from his mouth. Tolui cursed, swinging his bent bow back and forth in a fury.

"You have asked for a hard death and I will give it to you!" he shouted. For an instant, he thought of running for the ponies, but his pride and fury kept him there, desperate to punish those who dared to attack him. His deel bristled with arrows and he snapped off two shafts with quick jerks of his hands when they interfered with his movement.

"I think I hit one of them," Basan said.

Once more the silence returned with the threat of another exchange.

"We should go back for the horses," Basan continued. "We can go around the thorns and come at them where it is clear."

Tolui showed his teeth in fury. The arrowheads had cut him and his chest throbbed with pain. He barked each word like an order.

"Hold your *ground*," he said, scanning the trees. "Kill anything that moves."

Temujin crouched behind the barrier of thorns he had prepared months before. It had been his arrow that took Unegen in the throat, and that gave him a savage satisfaction. He remembered how Unegen had passed his father's sword to Eeluk. Temujin had dreamed many times of taking his revenge. Even a small part of it was like the sweetness of wild honey to him.

He and his brothers had planned for just such an attack, though it had still been a shock to see bondsmen of the Wolves standing in their rough camp. Temujin had prepared a killing ground for raiders who would not have been as deadly as the men Eeluk had chosen for his best warriors. Temujin's chest felt tight with pride that they had downed one of them, though it was mingled with awe. These were his father's own warriors, the fastest and best. It felt a little like a sin to kill one of them, even Unegen. It would not stop Temujin trying to kill the others.

He remembered Tolui as a young boy with challenging eyes, not fool enough to interfere with the sons of Yesugei, but even then one of the strongest of the children in the Wolf encampment. From the glimpse Temujin had taken along the shaft of an arrow, Tolui had grown in strength and arrogance. He had prospered under Eeluk.

Temujin squinted through a tiny gap in the thorns, watching Tolui and Basan as they stood. Basan looked unhappy and Temujin recalled how he had been sent to the Olkhun'ut to bring him home. Had Tolui known that when he had chosen him? Probably not. The world had been different then and Tolui was just another grubby little brawler, always in trouble. Now he wore the armor and deel of a bondsman to a khan, and Temujin wanted to damage his pride.

Temujin kept himself completely still as he considered what to do. As slowly as he could, he turned his head to look over to where Kachiun had taken position. At any moment, he expected the movement to attract Basan's sharp gaze and an arrow to plunge through the thorns at him. Sweat trickled down his forehead.

When Temujin caught sight of his brother, he blinked in distress. Kachiun was looking back at him, waiting silently to be noticed. The younger boy's eyes were wide in pain and shock, and Temujin could see the shaft that had struck him right through his thigh. Kachiun had remembered the cold face on this morning where death had come for them. He sat like a statue, his features pinched and white as he looked back at his brother and dared not gesture. Despite his control, the feathers of the shaft quivered slightly and, with his senses heightened to the point of dizziness, Temujin could hear the faint movement of the leaves. Tolui would see, Temujin thought, and he would fire another shaft that would kill. It was not impossible that one of Eeluk's men would smell the blood on the breeze.

Temujin held Kachiun's gaze for a long time, each watching the other in mute desperation. They could not escape. Khasar was hidden from Temujin's sight, but he too was in trouble, whether he knew it or not.

Temujin turned his head back with infinite slowness until Tolui and Basan could be seen. They too were waiting, though Tolui was clearly furious and, as Temujin watched, he snapped two of the arrows that stuck in his chest. The young man's rage would have cheered Temujin if the shot that wounded Kachiun had not spoiled all their plans.

The standoff could not last forever, Temujin realized. There was a chance that Tolui would retreat, to return with more men. If he did that, he and Khasar would have enough time to take Kachiun to safety.

Temujin gritted his teeth, struggling with the decision. He did not think Tolui would tuck his tail between his legs and run for the ponies, not after losing Unegen. The man's pride would not allow it. If he ordered Basan forward, Khasar and Temujin would have to risk another shot, though finding the throat of an armored man was almost impossible when he kept his head down and ran. Temujin knew he had to move before Tolui could reach the same conclusion, and perhaps walk clear and come at them from another route. The boys had blocked the approaches to the woods around the camp, but there were places where a single warrior could force his way through.

Temujin cursed his luck. It had been only moments since the exchange of arrows, but time seemed to have distorted as his mind raced. He knew what he had to do, but he was afraid. He closed his eyes for a moment and summoned the will. A khan made hard decisions and he knew his father would already have moved. Basan and Tolui had to be drawn away before they could find Kachiun and finish him.

Temujin began to crawl backwards, still keeping an eye on the intruders whenever he caught a glimpse. They were talking, he could see, though he could not hear the words. When he had covered ten or twenty alds, he used a birch to hide his movement as he rose to his feet and drew another arrow from the quiver on his back. He could no longer see either man and would have to shoot from memory. He sent up a prayer to the sky father to grant him a few moments of confusion, then he pulled back the bow and sent the shaft through to where Tolui had been standing.

Tolui heard the arrow in the fraction of time it took to break through the leaves, coming from nowhere. His own shaft was released before the other reached him, tearing a long scratch down his forearm before spinning uselessly away. He yelled in pain and surprise and then he saw a figure running through the trees and he nocked and loosed another in the hope of a lucky shot. It was lost in the thick brush of the hill, and Tolui's anger overrode his caution.

"Get after him!" he shouted to Basan, who was already moving. They ran together to the east of the barriers, trying to keep the running figure in sight while they looked for a way into the trees.

When they found a gap, Tolui plunged through without hesitation, though Basan stayed back to watch in case the attack was a feint. Tolui climbed steadily and Basan ran to catch him in his rush up the hill. They could see that the young man carried a bow, and both of them felt the excitement of the hunt. They were well fed and strong and both were confident as they rushed past whipping branches and leapt over a tiny stream. The figure did not pause to look back, though they saw he took a path through the densest brush.

Tolui began to pant and Basan was red-faced with the climb, but they readied their swords and went on, ignoring the discomfort.

Kachiun looked up when Khasar's shadow fell across his face. His fingers scrabbled for his knife before he saw who it was and relaxed.

"Temujin has won us a little time," he said to his brother.

Khasar peered through the trees to where they could both see the men running higher and higher up the hill. The birch and pine reached only halfway up and they knew Temujin would be exposed until he could make it into the valley on the other side, where another wood lay. They did not know if he could escape the pursuers, but both brothers were shaken and relieved that Eeluk's bondsmen had left them.

"What now?" Khasar asked, almost to himself.

Kachiun tried to concentrate through the pain that seemed like something eating the flesh of his leg. Weakness came and went in waves as he struggled to remain conscious.

"Now we remove this arrow," he said, wincing at the thought.

They had all seen it done when the men returned from challenging raiders. The wound in his leg was clean enough and the blood flow had slowed to a trickle. Nonetheless, Khasar collected a thick pouch of leaves for Kachiun to bite on. He pressed the filthy mat into his brother's mouth and then took hold of the arrow shaft, snapping it cleanly and drawing it through as Kachiun's eyes widened, showing the whites. Despite himself, a low groan came through his lips and Khasar pressed his hand over Kachiun's mouth to muffle the sound, choking him until the pieces of arrow lay on the ground. With quick, neat movements, Khasar cut strips from his waist cloth and bound the leg.

"Lean on my shoulder," he said, heaving Kachiun to his feet. His younger brother was clearly dazed and light-headed as he spat out the wet leaves, but Khasar still looked to him for what they would do next.

"They will come back," Kachiun said, when he had recovered himself. "Bring the others here. If we're quick, we can take all the ponies and make for the second camp."

Khasar stayed with him long enough to put him in the saddle of Tolui's pony. He steadied Kachiun with a hand on his shoulder, pressing the reins into his fingers before racing off to where their mother was hidden with the other children. Temujin had prepared the bolt hole and Khasar gave thanks for his brother's foresight as he ran. The appearance of Eeluk's warriors had haunted all their dreams at some point in the years alone. It helped that Temujin had gone over and over the plans, though part of Khasar was sick at the thought of returning to the same dark cleft in the hills where they had spent their first few nights. Temujin had insisted on placing a tiny ger there, but they had not dreamed it would be needed so soon. They would be alone once again, and hunted.

As he ran, he prayed Temujin would escape his pursuers. When he made it back, he would know what to do. The thought that Temujin might not survive was too terrible for Khasar to contemplate.

Temujin ran until his legs were weak and his head swung with every step. At first, he had the strength and speed to leap and duck whatever crossed his path, but when his spit turned to bitter paste in his mouth and his energy faded, he could only blunder on, his skin whipped by a thousand branches and thorns.

The worst part had been crossing the top of the hill, as bare as a river stone. Tolui and Basan had launched shafts after him and Temujin had been forced almost to a walk to watch the arrows coming and jerk his tired body out of the way. They had gained on him across that vast empty space, but then he had found himself staggering among ancient trees again and had gone on, his vision blurring and every breath feeling as if it burned his throat.

He lost his bow when it snagged on a whip of briars, caught so firmly that he barely yanked at it before letting it go. He cursed himself for that as he ran, knowing he should have removed the string, or even cut it. Anything but lose a weapon that gave him some chance of fighting them off when they ran him down. His small knife would not help him against Tolui.

He couldn't outrun the bondsmen. The best he could do was search for a place to go to ground. As he staggered on through the brush, he looked for somewhere to hide. The fear was thick in his throat and he could not clear it. A glance backwards showed him a jolting vision of the two men coming steadily through the trees. They had unstrung their bows, and he knew despair. He had not planned on being pursued for miles, and it was pointless wishing he had prepared a cache of weapons or a deadfall of the kind used to trap wolves in the winter. His panting turned into a murmur, then a full sound as every breath was a cry from his body to stop. He did not know how far he had come. The sun still hung in the sky above his head and he could only go on and go on, until his heart burst or an arrow found his back.

A narrow stream crossed his path and his foot slipped on a wet stone, sending him tumbling in a great spray of icy water. The impact broke his trance and he was scrambling up and running with a little more control in just a few heartbeats. He listened as he ran then, counting his steps until he heard Tolui and Basan splashing through the same water. Fifty-three paces behind, easily close enough to drop him like a deer if he gave them a single clean shot. He raised his head and summoned his endurance to take him farther. His body was finished, but he remembered Yesugei telling him a man's will could carry him long after the weak flesh had given up.

A sudden hollow sent him out of their sight and he dodged through a stand of ancient birch. The briars were as high as a man there and he plunged into them without thinking, scrabbling madly against the scratching thorns to shove himself farther and farther into their gloomy protection. He was desperate and close to panic, but when the daylight had receded, he curled into a ball and held as still as he could.

His lungs screamed for air as he forced himself not to move. The discomfort swelled and fresh sweat broke out on his skin. He felt his face flush and his hands tremble, but he clamped every muscle of his mouth and cheeks tight as he blew a thin stream of air in and out, all he dared allow himself.

He heard Tolui and Basan crash past, calling to each other. They would not go far before they returned to search for him, he was certain. Though he wanted nothing more than to press his eyes shut and collapse, he used the precious time to wriggle farther into the dark core. Thorns scored him, but he could not cry out and simply pressed against them until they snapped off in his skin. Such little hurts did not matter compared with being caught.

He forced himself to stop his mindless crawling. For a little time, he had thought of nothing but darkness and safety, like a hunted animal. The part of him that was his father's son knew the shivering leaves would give him away if he could not cease all movement. That inner self watched his scrabbling with cold disdain, trying to regain control. In the end, it was the sound of Tolui's voice that made him freeze and close his eyes in something like relief. There was nothing more he could do.

"He's hiding," Tolui said clearly, frighteningly close.

Both men must have doubled back as soon as they lost sight of him.

Temujin's chest cramped and he pressed his hand into his sticky mouth to bite down against the pain. He concentrated on an image of his father in the ger and saw again the life that slipped out of him.

"We know you can hear us, Temujin," Tolui called, panting. He too had suffered over the miles, but the bondsmen were as hard and fit as a man could be and they were recovering quickly.

Temujin lay with his cheek pressed against ancient leaves, smelling the musty richness of old rot that had never seen the light of day. He knew he could escape them in the dark, but that would not be for many hours and he could not think of any other way to improve his chances. He hated the men who were searching for him, hated them with a heat he thought they would surely sense.

"Where is your brother, Bekter?" Tolui called again. "You and he are the only ones we want; do you understand?"

In a different tone, Temujin heard Tolui murmur under his breath to Basan. "He will have gone to ground somewhere around here. Search it all and call out if you see him."

The hard voice had regained some of its confidence, and Temujin prayed to the sky father to strike the man down, to burn him, or tear him apart with a bolt of lightning as he had once seen a tree destroyed. The sky father remained silent, if he heard him at all, but the rage kindled in Temujin's breast again with visions of bloody vengeance.

Temujin's searing breath had eased a fraction, but

his heart still pounded and he could barely keep himself from moving or panting aloud. He heard footsteps nearby, crunching through the thorns and leaves. There was a patch of light through to the outside and Temujin fixed his gaze on it, watching shadows move. To his horror, he saw a booted foot cross the light and then it was blotted out completely as a face peered in, the eyes widening as they saw him looking back, his teeth bared like a wild dog. For a long, long moment, he and Basan stared at each other, then the bondsman vanished.

"I can't see him," Basan called, moving away.

Temujin felt tears gather, and over the roar of blood in his ears, he could suddenly feel all the aches and wounds his poor battered body had taken in the chase. He remembered Basan had been loyal to Yesugei and the relief was shattering.

He heard Tolui's voice calling in the distance, and for a long time, he was alone with just the whisper of his breath. The sun sank toward distant hills unseen and darkness came early deep in the hill of briars. Temujin could hear the two men calling to each other, but the sounds seemed far away. Eventually, exhaustion stole his awareness in a sudden blow and he slept.

He woke to see a flicker of yellow flame moving across his field of vision. He could not at first understand what it was, or why he lay cramped and curled in brambles so dense he could barely move. It was frightening to be wedged in darkness and thorns, and he did not know how to get out without worming back the way he had come.

Through the gloom, he watched the torch burn

trails on his vision, and once he saw Tolui's face in its golden light. The bondsman still searched for him and now he looked grim and tired. No doubt the two men were hungry and stiff, just as Temujin was himself.

"I will tear the skin off you if you don't show yourself," Tolui shouted suddenly. "If you make me search all night, I'll beat you bloody."

Temujin closed his eyes and tried to stretch his muscles whenever the flame moved away. Tolui would not see the brambles quiver in the darkness, and Temujin began to prepare himself to run again. He eased his legs from where they were pressed against his chest, almost groaning with relief. Everything was cold and cramped and he thought his aches had woken him rather than Tolui's shouting.

He used his hands to rub knots of muscle in his thighs, loosening them. His first rush had to be fast to carry him away from them. All he needed was a little start and the darkness would hide him from their sight. He knew the family would have made it to the cleft in the hills, and if he pushed himself, he thought he could reach them before dawn. Tolui and Basan would never be able to track him over the dry grassland, and they would have to go back for more men. Temujin vowed silently that they would never catch him again. He would take his family far away from Eeluk's Wolves and start another life where they would be safe.

He was ready to move when the light from the torch fell across his patch of ground and he froze. He could see Tolui's face and the bondsman seemed to be looking straight at him. Temujin did not move, even when Eeluk's bondsman began pulling at the edges of the briars. The light from the torch cast shifting shadows and

Temujin's heart pounded in fear once again. He dared not turn to look, though he heard the flame crackle in the thorns around his legs. Tolui must have pushed the torch deep into the patch to cast light on his suspicions.

Temujin felt a hand scrabble at his ankle and, though he burst into life and kicked at it, the grip was like iron. He reached for the knife in his belt and yanked it free as he was dragged along the ground, coming out into the open with a cry of fear and anger.

Tolui had thrown down the torch to grasp him, and Temujin could barely see the man who grabbed hold of his deel and raised a fist. One huge hand crushed the wrist holding his knife and Temujin writhed helplessly. He hardly saw the blow coming before he was knocked into a darker world.

When he woke again, it was to the sight of a fire and the two men warming themselves around it. They had lashed him to a birch sapling, cold and chill at his back. There was blood on his mouth and Temujin licked at it, using his tongue to ease his lips apart from the gummy muck. His arms were high behind his back and he barely troubled to test the knots. No bondsman of the Wolves would have left a loose cord he could have reached with his fingers. In a few heartbeats, Temujin knew he could not escape and he watched Tolui through dull eyes, yearning for the bondsman's death with all the ferocity of his imagination. If there had been any god to listen, Tolui would have gone up in flames.

He did not know what to make of Basan. The man sat to one side, his face turned toward the fire. They had brought no food with them and it was clear that they preferred to spend a night in the woods rather than drag him back to their ponies in the dark. Temujin felt a trickle of blood going down his throat, and he gave a choking cough, causing both men to look round.

Tolui's bullish features lit up with pleasure at seeing him awake. He rose immediately, while behind him, Basan shook his head and looked away.

"I told you I would find you," Tolui said cheerfully.

Temujin looked at the young man he remembered as a boy with arms and legs too large for him. He spat a fleck of blood on the ground and saw Tolui's face darken. A knife appeared from nowhere in the bondsman's fist, and Temujin saw Basan rise from the fire behind him.

"My khan wants you alive," Tolui said, "but I can put out an eye, perhaps, in return for the chase? What do you think of that? Or cut your tongue in two like a snake?" He made a gesture as if to grab at Temujin's jaw and then laughed, enjoying himself.

"It's strange to think of the days when your father was khan, isn't it?" Tolui went on, waving the knife close to Temujin's eyes. "I used to watch you and Bekter when you were young, to see if there was something special about you, some part of you that made you better than me." He smiled and shook his head.

"I was very young. You can't see what makes one man a khan and another one a slave. It's in here." He tapped himself in his chest, his eyes gleaming.

Temujin raised his eyebrows, sick of the man's posturing. Tolui's odor of rancid mutton fat was strong, and as Temujin breathed its sourness, he had a vision of an eagle beating its wings into his face. He felt detached and suddenly there was no fear.

"Not in there, Tolui, not in you," he said slowly, raising his gaze to stare back at the massive man who threatened him. "You are just a stupid yak, fit for lifting logs."

Tolui brought his hand across Temujin's face in a sharp blow that knocked his head to one side. The second was worse and he saw blood on the palm. He had seen hatred and vicious triumph in Tolui's eyes, and he did not know if he would stop, until Basan spoke at Tolui's shoulder, surprising him with his closeness.

"Let him be," Basan said softly. "There's no honor in beating a tied man."

Tolui snorted, shrugging. "Then he must answer my questions," he snapped, turning to face his companion. Basan did not speak again and Temujin's heart sank. There would be no more help from him.

"Where is Bekter?" Tolui demanded. "I owe that one a real beating." His eyes seemed distant as he mentioned Bekter's name, and Temujin wondered what had gone on between them.

"He is dead," he said. "Kachiun and I killed him."

"Truly?" It was Basan who spoke, forgetting Tolui for a moment. Temujin played on the tension between them by replying directly to Basan.

"It was a hard winter and he stole food, Basan. I made a khan's choice."

Basan might have responded, but Tolui stepped closer, resting his huge hands on Temujin's shoulders.

"But how do I know you are telling me the truth, little man? He could be creeping up on us even now, and where would we be then?"

Temujin knew it was hopeless. All he could do was

try and ready himself for the beating. He set himself in the cold face.

"Be careful in your life, Tolui. I want you fit and strong for when I come for you."

Tolui gaped at this, unsure whether to laugh or lash out. In the end, he chose to thump a blow into Temujin's gut and then hammered at him, chuckling at his own strength and the damage he could do.

CHAPTER 16

TOLUI HAD BEATEN HIM again when he found the ponies gone. The young bondsman had been almost comically furious at the sheer nerve of Temujin's brothers, and one unwary smile from his captive had been enough for him to take out his anger in a fit of frustration. Basan had intervened, but the exhaustion and blows had taken their toll and Temujin lost hours of the dawn as he drifted in and out of consciousness.

The day was warm and gentle as Tolui burned the gers Temujin and his brothers had built. Ropes of black smoke reached up to the sky behind them, and Temujin had glanced back just once to fix it in his mind, to remember one more thing to repay. He stumbled behind his captors as they began their long walk, jerked on with a rope around his wrists.

At first, Tolui told Basan that they would take new ponies from the wanderers they had come across before. Yet when they reached that place after a hard day, there was nothing waiting for them but a scorched circle of black grass to mark where the ger had once been. Temujin hid his smile that time, but he knew old Horghuz would have spread the word among the wanderer families and taken his own far away from these hard warriors of the Wolves. They may not have been a tribe, but trade and loneliness bound together those who were weak. Temujin knew word of the return of the Wolves would spread fast and far. Eeluk's decision to come back to the lands around the red hill was like dropping a stone in a pool. All the tribes for a hundred days' ride would hear and wonder if the Wolves would be a threat or an ally. Those like old Horghuz who scraped by without the protection of the great families would be even more wary of the ripples and new order. Small dogs slunk away when Wolves roamed.

For the first time, Temujin saw the world from the other side. He might have hated the tribes for the way they strode on the plains, but instead, he dreamed that his tread would one day send other men running. He was his father's son and it was hard to see himself as one of the tribeless wanderers. Wherever Temujin was, the rightful line of Wolves continued in him. To give that up would have been to dishonor his father and their own struggle for survival. Through all of it, Temujin had known one simple truth. One day, he would be khan.

With nothing more than a little river water to ease his thirst and no hope of rescue, he could almost chuckle at the idea. First he had to escape the fate Tolui and Eeluk intended for him. He daydreamed as he trotted on his length of rope. He had considered coming forward and dropping a loop around Tolui's throat, but the powerful young man was always aware of him, and even if the right moment came, Temujin doubted he had the strength to crush the bondsman's massive neck.

Tolui was uncharacteristically silent on the march. It had occurred to him that he was returning with only one of the khan's children and not even the eldest, that the valuable ponies had been stolen, and that Unegen lay dead behind him. If it had not been for their single captive, the raid would have been a complete disaster. Tolui watched the prisoner constantly, worried he would somehow vanish and leave him with nothing but his shame to bring back. When night came, Tolui found himself jerking from restless sleep to check the ropes at regular intervals. Whenever he did, he found Temujin awake and watching him with hidden amusement. He too had considered their return and was pleased that his younger brothers had at least denied Tolui the chance to strut new honors in front of Eeluk. To come in on foot would be a great humiliation for the proud bondsman, and if he hadn't been so battered and miserable, Temujin might have enjoyed Tolui's sullen withdrawal.

Without supplies from the saddle pouches, they were all growing weak. On the second day, Basan stayed to guard Temujin while Tolui took his bow and headed up to a tree line on a high ridge. It was the chance for which Temujin had been waiting, and Basan saw his eagerness before he could even open his mouth.

"I will not let you go, Temujin, no. You cannot ask me," he said.

Temujin's chest deflated as if the hope had been let out of him with his breath. "You did not tell him where I was hiding," Temujin muttered.

Basan flushed and looked away. "I should have done. I gave you one chance, out of honor for your father's memory, and Tolui found you anyway. If it hadn't been dark, he might have realized what I had done."

"Not him. He is an idiot," Temujin said.

Basan smiled. Tolui was a rising young man in the gers of the Wolves, and his temper was becoming legendary. It had been a long time since Basan had heard anyone dare to insult him aloud, even when he wasn't in hearing. Seeing Temujin stand strong before him was a reminder that there was a world outside the Wolves. When Basan spoke again, it was with bitterness.

"They say the Wolves are strong, Temujin . . . and we are, in men like Tolui. Eeluk has raised new faces as his bondsmen, men of no honor. He makes us kneel to him and if someone makes him laugh or has brought back a deer, say, or raided a family, Eeluk throws a skin of black airag at him like a dog who has done well." As he spoke he stared up at the hills, remembering a different time.

"Your father never made us kneel," he said softly. "When he was alive, I would have given my life for him without thinking, but he never made me feel less than a man."

It was a long speech from the taciturn tribesman, and Temujin listened, knowing the importance of having Basan as an ally. He had no other in the Wolves, not any longer. He could have asked for help again, but Basan had not spoken lightly. His sense of honor meant he could not let Temujin run now that they had caught him. Temujin accepted it, though the open plains called to him and he ached to get away from whatever ugly death Eeluk intended. He knew better than to expect mercy a second time, now that Eeluk was secure in his position. When he spoke, he chose his words carefully, needing Basan to remember, to hear more than the pleading of a prisoner.

"My father was born to rule, Basan. He walked lightly with men he trusted. Eeluk is not so... certain of himself. He cannot be. I do not excuse what he has done, but I understand him and why he has brought men like Tolui to stand at his shoulder. Their weakness makes them vicious and sometimes men like that can be deadly warriors." He saw Basan was relaxing as he spoke, considering difficult ideas almost as if one of them were not the captive of the other.

"Perhaps that is what Eeluk saw in Tolui," Temujin mused. "I have not seen Tolui on a raid, but it may be he smothers his fear in wild acts of courage."

Temujin would not have said it if he believed it. The Tolui he had known as a boy had been a blusterer more likely to run wailing if he hurt himself. Temujin hid his pleasure behind the cold face when Basan looked troubled, considering some memory in the light of Temujin's words.

"Your father would not have had him as a bondsman," Basan said, shaking his head. "It was the greatest honor of my life to be chosen by Yesugei. It meant more then than having the strength and the armor to attack weak families and raid their herds. It meant..." He shook himself, retreating from his memories.

Temujin wanted him to go further down that path, but he dared not press him for more. They stood in silence for a long time, then Basan sighed.

"With your father, I could be proud," he muttered, almost to himself. "We were vengeance and death to those who attacked us, but never to the families, never to Wolves. Eeluk has us strut around the gers in our armor, and we do not work the wool into felt or break new ponies. He lets us grow fat and soft with gifts. The young ones know nothing different, but I have been lean and strong and certain, Temujin. I remember what it was to ride with Yesugei against the Tartars."

"You do him honor, still," Temujin whispered, touched by the man's memories of his father. In response, he saw Basan's face become calm and knew there would be no more from him that day.

Tolui returned triumphant with two marmots tied to his belt. He and Basan cooked them with hot stones sealed inside the skin, and Temujin's mouth was wet with saliva as he smelled the meat on the breeze. Tolui allowed Basan to throw one of the carcasses where Temujin could reach it, and he tore at the scraps with deliberate care, needing to remain strong. Tolui seemed to take pleasure in jerking the rope whenever he reached to put food into his mouth.

As they started off again, Temujin struggled against weariness and the pain and soreness in his wrists. He did not complain, knowing it would give Tolui satisfaction to see any weakness. He knew the bondsman would kill him rather than let him escape, and Temujin could see no opportunity to get away from the men who held him prisoner. The thought of seeing Eeluk again was a gnawing fear in his empty belly, and then as evening came, Tolui came to a sudden halt, his eyes fixed on something in the distance. Temujin squinted through the setting sun and despaired.

Old Horghuz had not gone far, after all. Temujin recognized his piebald pony and the cart it pulled, piled high with the family's meager possessions. Their small herd of goats and sheep went before them, the bleating carrying far on the breeze. Perhaps Horghuz had not understood the danger. It hurt Temujin to imagine the old man had stayed in the area to see what had become of the family he had befriended.

Horghuz was not a fool. He did not approach the walking bondsmen, though they could all see the paleness of his face as he turned to watch them. Temujin urged him silently to ride away as far and fast as he could go.

Temujin could do nothing but watch in sick anticipation as Tolui handed the rope to Basan and eased his bow from his shoulders, hiding it from view as he readied the string in his hands. He walked quickly toward the old man and his family, and Temujin could not bear it any longer. With a jerk that spun Basan around, he raised his hands and waved furiously at the old man, desperate for him to get away.

Horghuz hesitated visibly, turning in the saddle and staring back at the lone figure advancing toward him. He saw Temujin's frantic gesture, but it was too late. Tolui had reached his range and strung his bow with a foot on the shaft, raising the weapon whole in just a few heartbeats. Before Horghuz could do more than shout a warning to his wife and children, Tolui had drawn and loosed.

It was not a hard shot for a man who could fire at full gallop. Temujin moaned as he saw Horghuz dig in his heels and knew the tired pony would not be fast enough. The bondsmen and their prisoner followed the path of the arrow. Tolui had sent another rising after it,

which seemed to hang darkly in the air as the human figures moved too slowly, too late.

Temujin cried out as the shaft took old Horghuz in
the back, making his pony rear in panic. Even at such a
distance, Temujin could see the figure of his friend jerk,
his arms waving weakly. The second arrow fell almost
on the same track as the first, landing point first in the
wooden saddle as Horghuz slid to the ground, a heap of
dark clothing on the green plain. Temujin winced as he
heard the thump of the second strike an instant after he
had seen it land. Tolui roared his triumph and broke into
a hunter's trot, his bow held ready as he closed on the
panicking family as a wolf will pad toward a herd of
goats.

Horghuz's wife cut the pony loose from the cart and
put her two sons on the saddle after wrenching out the
upright shaft. She might have smacked the little animal
into a run, but Tolui was already shouting a warning. As
he raised his bow once again, the fight went out of her
and she slumped, defeated.

Temujin watched in despair as Tolui walked closer
still, casually fitting another arrow to his string.

"No!" Temujin shouted, but Tolui was enjoying
himself. His first arrow took the woman in the chest,
and then he picked off the screaming children. The
force of the impacts plucked them from the pony, leaving them sprawled on the dusty ground.

"What harm had they done to him, Basan? Tell me
that!" Temujin demanded.

Basan looked at him in mild surprise, his eyes dark
and questioning.

"They are not our people. Would you leave them to
starve?"

Temujin dragged his eyes from the sight of Tolui kicking one of the children's bodies out of the way to mount the pony. A part of him felt the crime in what he had witnessed, but he did not have the words to explain. There was no tie of blood or marriage with old Horghuz and his family. They had not been Wolves.

"He kills like a coward," he said, still searching for the idea. "Does he face armed men with so much pleasure?"

He saw Basan frown and knew his point had struck home. It was true that the family of old Horghuz would not have survived the season. Temujin knew Yesugei might even have given the same order, but with regret and an understanding that it would be a sort of mercy in a hard land. Temujin sneered as the bondsman rode back to them. Tolui was a little man despite his frame and his great strength. He had taken their lives to satisfy his own frustration, and he was beaming as he returned to those who had watched him. Temujin hated him then, but he made his vows in the privacy of his own thoughts and he did not speak to Basan again.

Tolui and Basan took turns to ride the piebald mare, while Temujin staggered and fell behind them. The bodies were left for scavengers once Tolui had recovered his arrows from their flesh. The little cart caught the bondsman's interest long enough to look through it, but there was little more than dried meat and ragged clothes. Wanderers like Horghuz did not have hidden treasures. Tolui cut the throat of a kid goat and drank the blood with obvious enjoyment before tying the body behind the saddle and driving the others along with them. They would have more than enough fresh meat to reach the gers of the Wolves.

Temujin had looked at the still, pale faces of Horghuz and his family as he passed them. They had made him welcome and shared salt tea and meat when he was hungry. He felt stunned and weak from the emotions of the day, but as he left them behind, he knew in a moment of revelation that they had been his tribe, his family. Not by blood, but by friendship and a wider bond of survival in a hard time. He accepted their revenge as his own.

Hoelun took Temuge by the shoulders and shook him. He had grown like spring grass in the years since they had left the Wolves, and there was no sign of his puppy-ish fat any longer. Yet he was not strong where it mattered. He helped his brothers work, but did only what he was told to do, and more often than not he would wander away and spend a day swimming in a stream, or climbing a hill for the view. Hoelun could have dealt with simple laziness as long as she had a switch to beat him. Temuge was an unhappy little boy, though, and he still dreamed of going home to the Wolves and everything they had lost. He needed time away from his family, and if it was denied him, he would grow nervous and sullen until Hoelun lost patience and sent him out to let clean air blow his thoughts like cobwebs.

Temuge was crying as the evening came, sobbing to himself in the tiny ger until Hoelun lost patience with him.

"What are we going to do?" he sobbed, wiping at a shining trail of mucus almost as wide as his nose.

Hoelun suppressed her irritation and smoothed down his hair with her hard hands. If he was too soft, it was no more than Yesugei had warned her would happen. Perhaps she had indulged him.

"He will be all right, Temuge. Your brother would never be easily caught." She tried to keep her voice cheerful, though she had already begun to consider their future. Temuge could weep, but Hoelun had to plan, and be clever, or she might lose them all. Her other sons were stunned and miserable at this blow to their lives. With Temujin, they had begun to know a little hope. To lose him was a return to the absolute despair of the first days alone, and the dark cleft in the hills brought it all back, like a stone hanging on their spirits.

Outside the ger, Hoelun heard one of the ponies whicker softly to itself. She considered the sound as she made decisions that seemed to tear the heart from her chest. At last, when Temuge was sniffing in a corner and staring at nothing, she spoke to them all.

"If Temujin has not come back to us by tomorrow night, we will have to leave this place." She had all their attention then, even little Temulun, who ceased playing with her colored bones and stared wide-eyed at her mother. "We have no choice now that the Wolves are coming back to the red hill. Eeluk will scout the area for a hundred miles and he will find our little hideaway here. That will be the end of us."

It was Kachiun who replied, choosing his words carefully.

"If we leave, Temujin will not be able to find us again, but you know that," he said. "I could stay and wait for him, if you take the ponies. Just tell me a direction and I will follow when he comes."

"And if he does not come?" Khasar said.

Kachiun frowned at him. "I will wait as long as I

can. If the Wolves come looking in the cleft, I will hide myself or travel by night after you. If we just leave, he might as well be dead. We will not find each other again."

Smiling, Hoelun clasped Kachiun by his shoulder, forcing herself to ignore her despair. Though she smiled, her eyes glittered uncomfortably.

"You are a good brother, and a fine son," she said. "Your father would be proud of you." She leaned forward, her intensity disturbing. "But do not risk your life if you see him caught, you understand? Temujin was born with blood in his hand—perhaps this is his fate." Her face crumpled without warning. "I cannot lose all my sons, one by one." The memory of Bekter brought a spasm of sudden weeping, shocking them all. Kachiun reached out and wrapped his arms around his mother's shoulders, and in the corner, Temuge began to sob on his own once more.

CHAPTER 17

EELUK SAT IN A GER twice the size of any other in the camp, on a throne of wood and polished leather. Yesugei had disdained such symbols of power, but Eeluk took comfort from being raised above his bondsmen. Let them remember who was khan! He listened to the crackle of torches and the far-off voices of the tribe. He was drunk again, or close to it, so that his hand blurred as he passed it in front of his eyes. He considered calling for enough airag to smash him into sleep, but instead, he sat in sullen silence, staring at the floor. His bondsmen knew better than to try to raise the spirits of their khan when he was brooding on better days.

His eagle perched on a wooden tree at his right hand. The hooded bird was a brooding presence that could be as still as bronze for the longest time, then suddenly jerk at a sound, tilting her head as if she could see through the thick leather. The red tinge to her feathers had remained, shimmering when her wings caught the light of torches. Eeluk was proud of her size and power.

He had watched her strike a kid goat and struggle into the air with the limp flesh dangling. He had not allowed her more than a single scrap of flesh for the kill, of course, but it had been a glorious moment. He had given Yesugei's eagle to another family, binding them in gratitude for a khan's gift. He longed to show the pair to Temujin or Bekter, and almost wished them alive just to experience their anger one more time.

He remembered the day he had been given the red bird by Yesugei's own hand. Against his will, sudden tears came to his eyes and he swore aloud and cursed the airag for bringing on his melancholy. He had been younger then and for the young everything is better, cleaner, and finer than for those who have let themselves grow thick-bodied and drunk every evening. Yet he was still strong, he knew it. Strong enough to break anyone who dared to test him.

Eeluk looked blearily around him for Tolui, forgetting for a moment that he had not returned. The Wolves had traveled slowly, drifting farther north since Tolui had left with Basan and Unegen. It should have been a simple enough matter to determine whether Yesugei's children still lived, or at least to find their bones. Eeluk thought back to his first winter as khan and shuddered. It had been bitter even on the trip south. For those in the north, it would have been cruelly hard, on the young and the old alike. Hoelun and her children would not have lasted long, he was almost certain. Yet it nagged at him. What could have delayed Tolui and the other men? The young wrestler was a useful man to have close, Eeluk knew. His loyalty was unquestioning, in comparison with some of the older men. Eeluk knew there were those who still denied his right to lead the tribe, fools who could not accept the new order. He made sure they were watched and, when the time came, they would find men like Tolui outside their gers one dawn. He would take their heads himself, as a khan should. It was never far from his thoughts that he had won the tribe with strength—and only strength could hold it. Disloyalty could grow unchecked until they found the courage to challenge him. Had he not felt the seeds of it long before Yesugei was killed? In his most secret heart, he had.

When the warning horns sounded, Eeluk lurched to his feet, taking his sword from where it lay propped against the arm of his chair. The red bird screeched, but he ignored it, shaking his head to clear it of fumes as he strode out into the cold air. He could already feel the rush of blood and excitement he relished. He hoped for raiders, or Tolui's return with the children of the old khan. One or the other would bring blood to his sword, and he never found sleep so sweet and dreamless as when he had killed a man.

His horse was brought for him and he mounted carefully rather than stumble. He could feel the airag in him, but it just made him stronger. He turned bleary red eyes on his bondsmen as they gathered and then dug in his heels, sending his stallion careering out to meet the threat.

Eeluk whooped into the cold wind as the riders formed around him in perfect formation. They were Wolves and they were to be feared. He never felt as alive as at that moment, when disloyalties were forgotten and a single enemy had to be faced. That was what he craved, rather than the petty problems and feuds of the families. What did he care about those? His sword and bow were ready for their defense, and that was all he had to give them. They could grow and increase their numbers, just as the goats did in their care. Nothing else mattered as long as the warriors rode and he led them.

At full gallop, Eeluk lowered his sword over the stallion's ears and called "Chuh!" for more speed, feeling the airag burn out of him. He wished there could be an enemy host coming against them, a battle to test his courage and make him feel again the intoxication of walking close to death. Instead, he saw only two figures on the plain, riding dark brown ponies too heavily laden to be a threat. The disappointment was bitter in his throat, but he quelled it, forcing the cold face. The Wolves would take whatever the two men owned, leaving them with their lives unless they chose to fight. Eeluk hoped they would as he drew close, his men riding around and taking positions.

With drunken care, Eeluk dismounted and walked to face the strangers. To his surprise, he saw that they were both armed, though they were not fool enough to draw their swords. It was rare to see long blades in the hands of wanderers. The skill to fold and beat steel was highly sought after amongst the tribes, and a good sword would be a valuable possession. Yet the pair did not look prosperous. Their clothes may once have been good quality, but were filthy with ancient dust and dirt. Through the vagueness of the black airag in his blood, Eeluk's interest was aroused.

As he strode closer, he watched the men carefully, remembering Yesugei's lessons on judging his enemies. One was old enough to be father to the second, but he looked strong despite his gray hair, braided and oiled into a queue down his back. Eeluk felt a prickling sense of danger in the way he was standing, and ignored the younger one, knowing by instinct to watch the elder for a first move. He could not have explained his decision, but it had saved his life more than once.

Despite being surrounded by mounted warriors, neither man bowed his head. Eeluk frowned at them, wondering at their strangeness and their confidence. Before he could speak, the older of the two men seemed to start, his sharp eyes picking out the leaping wolf on Eeluk's armor. He murmured something to his companion and both relaxed visibly.

"My name is Arslan," the older said clearly, "and this is my son, Jelme. We are pledged to the Wolves and we have found you at last." When Eeluk did not reply, the man looked around him at the faces of the bondsmen. "Where is the one called Yesugei? I have honored my vow. I have found you at last."

Eeluk glowered at the strangers as they sat in the warmth of his ger. Two of his bondsmen stood outside the door in the cold, ready to come at his call. Inside, only Eeluk was armed. Despite that, he felt a constant tension in their presence, for no reason he could bring clearly to his thoughts. Perhaps it was the utter lack of fear in both of them. Arslan had shown no surprise or awe at the great ger Eeluk had had constructed. He had handed over his own sword without a backwards glance. When Arslan's gaze drifted over the weapons on the walls, Eeluk was almost sure he had seen a faint sneer appear on his face, gone as quickly as it came. Only the red bird had held his attention, and to Eeluk's irritation, Arslan had made a clicking sound in the back of his throat and run a hand down the red-gold feathering of her chest. She had not reacted and Eeluk felt his own simmering anger increase.

"Yesugei was killed by Tartars almost five years ago," Eeluk said, when they had settled themselves and drunk their bowls of tea. "Who are you to come to us now?"

The younger man opened his mouth to answer, but Arslan touched him lightly on the arm and he subsided.

"It would have been earlier if you had stayed in the north. My son and I have ridden more than a thousand days to find you and honor the vow I made to your father."

"He was not my father," Eeluk snapped. "I was first among his bondsmen." He saw the two men exchange glances.

"It was no idle rumor then, that you abandoned Yesugei's sons and wife on the plain?" Arslan asked softly.

Eeluk found himself becoming defensive under the man's quiet scrutiny.

"I am khan of the Wolves," he replied. "I have ruled them for four years and they are stronger than they have ever been. If you are pledged to the Wolves, you are pledged to me."

Once again, he saw Arslan and his son glance at each other, and Eeluk grew angry.

"Look at me when I am talking to you," he ordered.

Obediently, Arslan faced the man on the throne of wood and leather, saying nothing.

"How did you come by long blades like the ones you carried?" Eeluk asked.

"It is my craft to make them, my lord," Arslan said softly. "I was once the armorer for the Naimans."

"You were banished?" Eeluk asked immediately. He wished he had not drunk as much before they came. His thoughts felt sluggish and he still sensed danger from the older man, for all his calm speech. There was an economy of movement about him, a suggestion of hardness that Eeluk recognized. The man may have been a swordsmith, but he was a warrior also. His son was as lean as a rope, but whatever it was that made a man dangerous was not there in him, and Eeluk could dismiss him from his thoughts.

"I left the khan after he took my wife for his own," Arslan replied.

Eeluk started suddenly, remembering a story he had heard years before.

"I have heard of this," he began, straining his memory. "You are the one who challenged the khan of the Naimans? You are the oath-breaker?"

Arslan sighed, remembering old pain. "It was a long time ago and I was younger, but yes. The khan was a cruel man and, though he accepted my challenge, he returned first to his ger. We fought and I killed him, but when I went to claim my wife, I found he had cut her throat. It is a tired story and I have not thought of it for many years."

Arslan's eyes were dark with grief but Eeluk did not believe him.

"I heard of it even in the south where the air is hot and wet. If you are the same man, you are said to be very skilled with the blade. Is it true?"

Arslan shrugged. "Stories always exaggerate. Perhaps I was once. My son is better than I am now. Yet I have my bellows and I can build a forge. I have my skills and I can still make weapons of war. I met Yesugei when he was hunting with his hawk. He saw the value for his families and offered to break tradition, to bring us back into a tribe." He paused for a moment, looking back over the years. "I was alone and despairing when he found me. My wife had been taken by another and I did not want to live. He offered me sanctuary with the Wolves, if I could bring her out with my son. He was a great man, I think."

"I am greater," Eeluk replied, irritated to have Yesugei praised in his own ger. "If you have the skills you claim, the Wolves will still welcome you with honor."

For a long time, Arslan did not respond or look away. Eeluk could feel the tension grow in the ger, and he had to force himself not to let his fingers drop to his sword hilt. He saw the red bird look up in her hood, as if she too felt the strained air between them.

"I pledged myself to Yesugei and his heirs," Arslan said.

Eeluk snorted. "Am I not khan here? The Wolves are mine and you have offered yourself to the Wolves. I accept you both and I will offer you a ger, sheep, salt, and safety."

Once again, the silence stretched and became uncomfortable, until Eeluk wanted to curse. Then Arslan nodded, bowing his head.

"You do us a great honor," he replied.

Eeluk smiled. "Then it is settled. You have come at a time when I will need good weapons. Your son will be one of my bondsmen if he is as quick with a sword as you say. We will ride to war with blades from your forge. Believe me when I say it is time for the Wolves to rise."

In the musty darkness of a new ger, Jelme turned to his father, keeping his voice low.

"Are we staying here, then?"

His father shook his head unseen in the gloom. Aware of the possibility of listening ears, he pitched his voice at barely more than a breath.

"We are not. This man who calls himself khan is just a yapping dog with blood on his hands. Can you see me serving another like the khan of the Naimans? Yesugei was a man of honor, a man I could follow without regret. He came across me when I was picking wild onions, with just a little knife. He could have stolen everything I had, yet he did not."

"You would have killed him if he had tried," Jelme said, smiling in the darkness. He had seen his father fight and knew that, even unarmed, he was more than a match for most swordsmen.

"I might have surprised him," Arslan replied without pride, "but he did not know that. He was hunting alone, and I sensed he did not want company, but he treated me with honor. He shared meat and salt with me." Arslan sighed, remembering. "I liked him. I am sorry to hear he has gone from the plains. This Eeluk is weak where he, Yesugei, was strong. I will not have my beautiful swords in his hands."

"I knew it," Jelme said. "You did not give him your oath, and I guessed. He did not even hear the words you used. The man is a fool, but you know he will not let us go."

"No, he will not," Arslan said. "I should have listened to the rumors about the new khan. I should not have brought you into danger."

Jelme snorted. "Where else would I go, Father? My place is at your side." He thought for a moment. "Shall I challenge him?"

"No!" Arslan said in a harsh whisper. "A man who could leave children on the plains to freeze with their mother? He would have you taken and beheaded without even drawing his own blade. We have made a mistake coming here, but now all we can do is watch for a time to leave. I will build my forge with new bricks of clay and that will take time. I will send you out for wood and herbs, anything to get you away from the camp. Learn the names of the guards and have them become used to you foraging for materials. You can find a place to store what we need and, when the time is right, I will bring the ponies out."

"He will send guards with us," Jelme answered.

Arslan chuckled. "Let him. I have not met a man I cannot kill. We will be gone from here by the end of summer, and the forge I will leave them will be useless for anything except scrap iron."

Jelme sighed for a moment. It had been a long time since he had seen the inside of a ger, and part of him did not relish the thought of returning to hard nights and the bitterness of the winters.

"There are some pretty women here," he said.

His father sat up as he heard the longing in his son's voice. He did not reply for some time.

"I have not given thought to it, my son. Perhaps I am being foolish. I will not marry again, but if you want to remain and make a place amongst these people, I will stay with you. I cannot drag you behind me for the rest of my life."

Jelme reached out in the dark to find his father's arm.

"I go where you go, you know that. Your vow binds me as much as it does you."

Arslan snorted. "A vow to the dead binds no one. If Yesugei had lived, or if his children survived, I would go to them with a clear heart. As it is, there is no life for us but here or on the plains with the real wolves. Do not answer me tonight. Sleep; we will talk again in the morning."

Eeluk rose at dawn, his head hammering with pain and slick sweat foul on his skin. He had called for more airag after Arslan and Jelme had gone to the ger, and at most he had slept for a hand's breadth of the stars moving in the sky. He felt terrible, but as he came out of his ger and surveyed the camp, he was startled to see Arslan and his son already awake. The two newcomers were exercising together, their swords drawn as they stretched and moved in what looked like a dance, to Eeluk's sleepy eyes.

Already, a few of the bondsmen had gathered around them, some of them laughing and making crude comments. The two men ignored the others as if they did not exist, and for those with an eye to see, the balance and agility they practiced revealed a very high level of skill. Arslan was bare-chested and his skin was a patchwork of scarring. Even Eeluk was impressed at the markings, from the white lattice of old cuts on his arms, to knots of burns and arrowheads on his shoulders and

chest. The man had fought and, as he spun in the air,
Eeluk saw only a few wounds in the paler skin of his
back. The pair were impressive, Eeluk admitted reluctantly. Arslan shone with sweat, though was not breathing heavily. Eeluk watched glowering, trying to recall the
conversation of the previous night. He noticed that the
bondsmen had fallen silent, and he snorted to himself as
father and son finished the routine. He did not trust
them. As he stood and scratched himself he saw two of
his bondsmen engage Arslan in conversation, clearly
asking questions about the exercises they had seen.
Eeluk wondered if the newcomers could be spies, or
even assassins. The older man, in particular, had the
look of a killer, and Eeluk knew he would have to force
a little obedience, or have his authority questioned in his
own camp.

Despite his misgivings, their arrival was a blessing
from the sky father, at a time when he planned a campaign against the Olkhun'ut. The Wolves were growing
and he felt the spring tide in his gut and blood, calling
him to war. He would need good swords for every
young warrior of the families, and perhaps Arslan was
the man to produce them. The armorer they had was an
old drunk and only his valuable craft prevented him being left out in the snow each winter. Eeluk smiled to
himself at the thought that Arslan would make chain
mail and blades for the Wolves to grow in strength.

When Eeluk dreamed, it was always of death. The
oldest woman had cast the bones in his ger and prophe-
sied a great bloodletting under his banners. Perhaps
Arslan was a messenger from the spirits, as the legends
told. Eeluk stretched, feeling his strength as his bones
cracked and his muscles tightened deliciously. He had

woken his ambition after the death of Yesugei. There was no telling where it would take him.

It was four days after the arrival of Arslan and his son that Tolui and Basan returned to the gers of the Wolves, dragging a battered figure behind them. Eeluk rode out with the others and he yelled hoarsely when he saw his men had returned with a live captive. He wanted it to be Bekter, but somehow it was sweeter still to see Temujin staring back at him through swollen eyes.

The journey had been hard on Temujin, but he stood as straight and tall as he could as Eeluk dismounted. He had been dreading the moment ever since they had caught him, and now that it had come, exhaustion and pain made him numb.

"Am I granted guest rights, then?" he said.

Eeluk snorted and backhanded a blow across his face that tumbled him to the ground.

"Welcome home, Temujin," Eeluk said, showing strong white teeth. "I have waited a long time to see you with your belly on the ground." As he spoke he raised his leg and pressed Temujin facedown into the dust. Little by little he increased the pressure, and there was a light in his eye that made the other warriors silent.

It was Basan who broke the silence. "My lord, Unegen is dead. The others escaped."

Eeluk seemed to drag himself back from far away to answer, releasing the silent figure under his boot.

"They all survived?" he said, surprised.

Basan shook his head. "Bekter is dead. I understand the others still live. We found their camp and burned it."

Eeluk did not care that Unegen had fallen. The man

had been one of the old bondsmen. None of them could truly see Eeluk as khan, he knew. As the years passed he was slowly leavening their numbers with younger men, hungry for blood and conquest.

"You have done well," he said, addressing Tolui and seeing how he swelled his chest with pride. "You may have the pick of my own horses and a dozen skins of airag. Get yourself drunk. You have earned a khan's praise."

Tolui was pleased and bowed as low as he could.

"You honor me, my lord," he said, stealing a sideways look at Temujin. "I would enjoy seeing him humbled."

"Very well, Tolui. You shall be there. The spirits need blood to feed their hunger. He shall be the stain on the ground that sends us on to victory and greatness. We have a swordsmith come to us. The son of a khan will be our sacrifice. The sky father will bring us sweet women and a thousand tribes under our feet. I can feel it in my blood."

Temujin struggled to his knees. His body was raw and aching from the journey and his wrists felt as if they were on fire. He spat on the ground and thought of his father as he looked around him.

"I have known sheep *shit* with more honor than you," he told Eeluk slowly. He tried not to wince as one of the bondsmen approached and used the hilt of his sword to batter him unconscious. It took three blows before he fell, his eyes still open on the dusty ground.

Temujin woke again with warm water spattering his clothes and face. He gasped and struggled to his feet, crying out in pain as he found one of his fingers had been broken and his right eye was too clotted with blood to open. He hoped they had not blinded him, but part of him was past caring. It was so dark, he could not understand where he was. Above his head, he could see bars blocking the distant starlight and he shivered. He was in a frozen hole, the wooden lattice too far above for him to jump. He pressed his good hand to the walls and found the earth was slick with wetness. His feet were submerged in water and above him he heard low chuckles.

To his horror, a soft grunt was followed by another rain of stinking liquid. The bondsmen were urinating into the hole and laughing as they did so.

Temujin covered his head with his hands and fought against a black despair. He knew he could end his life in that filthy hole, perhaps with rocks dropped in to break his legs and arms. There was no justice in the world, but he had known that ever since the death of his father. The spirits took no part in the lives of men once they had been born. A man either endured what the world sent his way, or was crushed.

The men grunted as they lifted a heavy stone onto the crisscross of branches. When they had gone, Temujin tried to pray for a little while. To his surprise, it gave him strength and he crouched against the frozen muddy walls until dawn, unable to do more than drift in and out of sleep. It was a small comfort that his bowels had nothing in them. He felt as if he had always been hungry and sore. There had been a life once where he was happy and could ride to the red hill with his brothers. He held on to the thought like a light in the darkness, but it would not stay with him.

Before dawn, he heard footsteps approach and a dark figure leaned out over the lattice, blocking more of the stars. Temujin winced in anticipation of another emptying bladder, but instead the dark figure spoke.

"Who are you?" came a low voice.

Temujin did not look up, but he felt his pride rekindle and he replied, "I am the eldest surviving son of Yesugei, who was khan to the Wolves."

For an instant, he saw flashing lights at the edges of his vision, and he thought he might pass out. He remembered old words his father had used, and he spoke them recklessly.

"I am the land, and the bones of the hills," he said fiercely, "I am the winter. When I am dead, I will come for you all in the coldest nights."

He stared up defiantly, determined not to show his misery. The shadow did not move, but after a time, it murmured a few words and then vanished, letting the light of the stars shine down into the pit.

Temujin hugged his knees and waited for the dawn.

"Who are you to tell me not to despair?" he murmured.

CHAPTER 18

TEMUJIN WATCHED THE SUN pass overhead, its fire damped by heavy cloud, so that he was able to gaze on the orange disk with only a little discomfort. The thin warmth was welcome each morning after the frozen night. When he drifted back to consciousness, his first act was to pull his feet free of the slurry of ice and mud, then stamp and pump his limbs until his blood began moving again. He had used one corner of the little pit for his wastes, but it was still practically underfoot, and by the third day, the air was thick and nauseating. Flies buzzed down through the lattice overhead and he spent time batting gently at them, keeping them alive as long as possible for sport.

They had thrown bread and mutton down to him, laughing at his attempts to catch the pouches before they fell into the slop. His stomach had squeezed painfully the first time he had eaten one from the ground, but it was that or starve, and he forced it down with nothing more than a shrug. Every day, he marked the moving shadows cast by the sun with small stones in the mud; anything to dull the passage of time and his own misery.

He did not understand why Eeluk had left him in the pit rather than give him a quick death. In the hours alone, Temujin fantasized about Eeluk being overcome with shame, or finding himself unable to hurt a son of Yesugei. Perhaps he had even been struck down by a curse or a disfiguring disease. It amused Temujin to imagine it, but in reality, Eeluk was probably just away hunting, or planning something vicious. He had long ago found the real world much less satisfying than his own imagination.

When the rock was removed and the lattice thrown aside, it was almost with a sense of relief that he realized death was coming at last. Temujin raised his arms and allowed himself to be dragged out. He had heard the voices of the families as they gathered, and guessed something of the sort was coming. It did not help that one of the men pulling him out took a grip on his broken finger, leaving him gasping as the bone grated.

Temujin fell to his knees as they let go. He could see more than a hundred faces around him, and as his eyes cleared, he began to recognize people he had once known. Some of them jeered and the smallest children threw sharp edged stones at him. Others looked troubled, the strain forcing them into the cold face.

He prepared himself for death, an ending. The years since the abandonment had been a gift, despite their hardship. He had known joy and sorrow, and he vowed to give up his spirit with dignity intact. His father and his blood demanded it, no matter what the cost.

Eeluk sat in his great chair, brought into the sun for

the occasion. Temujin glanced at him before looking away, preferring to watch the faces of the families. In spite of everything he had suffered, it was strangely comforting to see them all again. Ignoring Eeluk, Temujin nodded and smiled at some of the ones he had known well. They did not dare return his gestures, but he saw their eyes soften slightly.

"I would have brought him here in honor," Eeluk bellowed suddenly to the crowd. He lowered his great head and wagged it seriously back and forth. "But I found him living like an animal without the graces of men. Yet even a rat can bite, and when he killed my bondsman, I had this *tribeless* wanderer dragged back for justice. Shall we give it to him? Shall we show him the Wolves have not grown soft?"

Temujin watched the families as Eeluk's bondsmen cheered mindlessly. Some of them yelled agreement, but many more stood in silence and watched the dirty young man who stared back with his yellow eyes. Slowly, Temujin rose to his feet. He stank of his own filth and he was covered in fly bites and sores, but he stood unbending and waited for the blade to come.

Eeluk drew the sword with a wolf's head carved into the bone hilt.

"The spirits have abandoned his family, my Wolves. Look at his state now and believe it. Where is the luck of Yesugei?"

It was a mistake to mention the old khan's name. Many heads bowed automatically at its sound and Eeluk flushed in anger. It was suddenly not enough to take Temujin's head, and he sheathed the blade.

"Tie him to a pony," he said. "Drag him bloody

and then leave him in the pit. Perhaps I will kill him to-morrow."

As he watched, Tolui backed up a brown gelding and tied a long rope to the saddle. The crowd parted excitedly, craning to see this strange sport. As his wrists were fastened to the rope, Temujin turned his pale gaze on Eeluk for a few moments, then spat on the ground. Eeluk grinned hugely.

Tolui turned round in the saddle, his expression a mixture of smugness and malice.

"How fast can you run?" he said.

"Let's find out," Temujin said, licking cracked lips. He could feel sweat break out in his armpits. He had been able to summon courage to stand before a blade. The thought of being torn behind a galloping horse was more than he could bear.

He tried to brace himself, but Tolui dug his heels into the pony's flanks and yelled wildly. The rope snapped tight and Temujin was jerked into a run, his weak legs already stumbling. Tolui rode recklessly, enjoying himself. It did not take long for Temujin to fall.

When Tolui finally returned to the encampment, Temujin was a dead weight on the rope. It was difficult to see a patch of skin that was not scraped raw and bloody. His clothes had been reduced to dusty rags that fluttered in the breeze as Tolui cut the rope at last. Temujin did not feel it as he slumped to the ground. His hands were almost black and his mouth hung open, red spittle drooling from where he had bitten his tongue. He saw Basan standing at the door of his family ger, his face pale and strained as Temujin stared at him.

Eeluk strode out to greet Tolui, casting an amused

glance at the torn figure he had once considered important. He was glad he had not ended it too quickly. He felt lighter in step for the decision, as if a weight had been lifted. In fact, he was in the best of spirits and mock-wrestled with Tolui for a moment before the bondsman returned Temujin to the hole in the ground and dropped the lattice back into place.

Temujin sat in the icy filth, barely conscious of his surroundings. He had found a tooth in the muck at the bottom, large enough to have come from the jaw of a man. He did not know how long he had been sitting staring at it. Perhaps he had slept; he couldn't be certain. Pain and despair had exhausted his senses to the point where he could not be sure if he dreamed or was awake. He ached in every bone, and his face was so fat with bruising that he could see only through a slit around one eye. The other was still crusted with thick blood, and he dared not pick at it. He did not want to move at all, in fact, with the threat of pain from endless scrapes and cuts. He had never felt so battered in his life, and it was all he could do not to cry out or weep. He kept his silence, finding a strength of will he had not known he possessed until that moment. It was made hard in a furnace of hatred, and he relished the core of him that would not bend, nurturing it as he found he could endure and live.

"Where is my father? Where is my tribe?" he murmured, screwing his face up against the grief. He had ached to be returned to the Wolves, but they cared nothing for him. It was no small thing to cast off the last threads of his childhood, the shared history that bound him to them. He remembered the simple kindness of old Horghuz and his family, when he and his brothers were alone. For a time he could not measure, he stood slumped against the walls of earth, thoughts moving slowly like ice on a river.

Something grated above his head and he jerked in fear, coming awake as if he had been dreaming. Some part of him had been aware of a moving shadow on the floor of the pit. He looked blearily upwards and saw to his dull astonishment that the lattice had vanished. The stars shone down without restriction and he could only stare, unable to understand what was happening. If he had not been wounded, he might have tried to climb, but he could barely move. It was excruciating to see a chance to escape and not be able to take it. He had done his best to spread the damage as much as possible, but his right leg felt as if it had been shredded. It still seeped blood sluggishly into the muck around him, and he could no more jump than fly out of the hole like a bird.

He found himself chuckling almost hysterically at the thought that his unknown savior had left, expecting him to make his own way out. In the morning, the fool would find him still in the pit, and Eeluk would not leave him unguarded again.

Something came slithering down the wall and Temujin jerked away, thinking it was a snake. His mind was playing tricks as he felt the rough fibers of a braided rope and the beginnings of hope. Above him, he saw the shadow block the stars, and he strained to keep his voice low.

"I can't climb out," he said.

"Tie yourself on," came the voice from the night before, "but help me as I pull."

With clumsy fingers, Temujin tied it round his waist,

wondering again who would risk Eeluk's wrath. He did not doubt that if they were discovered, his rescuer would join him in the pit and suffer the same fate.

As the rope bit into his back, Temujin's legs scrabbled uselessly at the earth walls. He found he could dig his hands in as he climbed, though the effort was like setting his skin on fire. He felt a scream bubbling along inside him until involuntary tears squeezed out of the corners of his eyes. Still he made no sound until, at last, he lay on the frozen ground in a silent encampment.

"Get away as far as you can," his rescuer said. "Use the mud of the riverbanks to hide your scent. If you survive, I will come to you and take you farther away." In the starlight, Temujin could see he was gray-haired and had powerful shoulders, but to his surprise, he did not know the man. Before he could respond, the stranger pressed a bag into his hand and Temujin's mouth watered at the odor of onions and mutton. The bag was warm and he gripped it as if it were his last hope.

"Who are you to save me?" he whispered. Part of him was yelling that it didn't matter, that he had to run, but he couldn't bear not knowing.

"I was pledged to your father, Yesugei," Arslan replied. "Now go, and I will follow you in the confusion of the search."

Temujin hesitated. Could Eeluk have staged it all to find the location of his brothers? He could not risk telling a stranger of the cleft in the hills.

"When you leave," Temujin said, "ride five days north, sunrise to sunset. Find a high hill to watch for me. I will come if I can and lead you to my family. You have my thanks forever, nameless one."

Arslan smiled at the courage of the younger man. In

many ways, he reminded the swordsmith of his son, Jelme, though there was a fire in this one that would be hard to extinguish. He had not intended to give his name, in case the young warrior was captured and forced to reveal it. Under Temujin's gaze he nodded, making a decision.

"My name is Arslan. I travel with my son, Jelme. If you live, we will meet again," he said, taking Temujin's arm in a brief clasp that almost made him cry out in sudden pain. Arslan replaced the lattice and stone, then walked away, moving like a cat in the frozen starlight. Temujin could do no more than shuffle as he took a different direction, concentrating on staying alive and going as far as he could before the hunt began.

In the blue-gray light of dawn, two young boys dared each other to go to the edge of the pit and stare down at the captive. When they finally found the courage to peer over the edge, there was no one there looking back and they ran for their parents, calling an alarm.

When Eeluk came from his ger, his face was tight with excitement. The powerful red bird gripped a leather sleeve around his right forearm, her dark beak open far enough to show a sliver of dark tongue. Two hunting dogs leapt around him, sensing his mood and barking madly.

"Go out in threes," Eeluk shouted to his warriors as they gathered. "I will take the western point—and whoever brings him back will have a new deel and two knives with horn handles from my hand. Tolui, you are with me. Mount up, my brothers. Today we hunt."

He watched as the bondsmen and the lesser warriors formed their groups, checking equipment and supplies before leaping into the saddles of their ponies. Eeluk was pleased to see their mood was light, and he congratulated himself on the decision to bring Temujin back to the camp. Perhaps seeing him beaten and dragged bloody was a final proof that the sky father loved the new khan of the Wolves. There had been no lightning strike to punish Eeluk, after all. Even the oldest of the crones should be satisfied with what he had achieved.

It crossed his mind to wonder how Temujin had escaped the pit, but that was a problem for his return. The young man could not have gone far with his injuries. When they brought him in, Eeluk would ask him how he had climbed the slick walls, or who had helped him. He frowned at that thought. Perhaps there were traitors among the families. If there were, he would root them out.

He wound his reins around his fist and mounted, enjoying the feeling of strength in his legs. The red bird spread her wings to balance as he settled himself. Eeluk grinned tightly, feeling his heart begin to beat faster. It usually took a little time for him to come fully awake, but the prospect of hunting a wounded man had fired his blood and he was ready to gallop. The red bird sensed it in him and ducked her head, tugging at the hood with a long claw. Eeluk pulled away the leather restraint and the eagle flew from his forearm, lunging upwards with a screech. He watched her beat the air for height, his arm rising without her weight until it was almost a greeting or a farewell. On such a morning, he could feel the land. Eeluk glanced around the camp and nodded to Tolui.

"Come. Let's see how far he has managed to run."

Tolui grinned at his lord and master, digging in his heels and sending his mount surging forward. The hunting dogs broke off their howling to run alongside, hungry for a kill. The air was cold, but the warriors wore padded deels and the sun was on the rise.

Temujin lay very still and watched a fly crawl across the mud in front of his face. He had slathered himself in river clay to mask his scent, but he did not know whether it would work or not. He had gone as far as he could in the dark, though by the end he was limping and sobbing with every step. It was strange how much weakness he could show when he was on his own. He did not mind the sting of his tears on his raw skin when there was no one else to witness it. Every step was an agony and yet he had pushed himself on, remembering Hoelun's words on the first nights in the cleft in the hills. There would be no rescue; no end to their suffering unless they made it themselves. He kept going, relying on the dark to hide his movement from the watchers on the hills.

By the time dawn had come, he had been hobbling like a wounded animal, almost doubled over with pain and weakness. He had collapsed at last by the bank of a stream, lying panting there with his head turned to the pale sky that heralded the sunrise. They would discover his escape by first light, he realized. How far had he come? He watched the first gold spark touch the dark horizon, instantly too harsh on his eyes. He began digging his swollen hands into the clay, crying out as his broken finger jarred yet again.

He was mindless for a time and there was relief in that. The mud worked loose in a paste he could squeeze between his fingers as he smeared it over his skin and clothes. It was cool, but it itched appallingly as it dried.

He found himself staring at his broken finger, seeing the swollen joint and the purple skin beneath the mud. He jerked from a daze then, suddenly afraid that time was slipping away in his exhaustion. His body was at the very end of its endurance, and all he wanted to do was give up and pass out. At the heart of him, at the deepest part, there was still a spark that wanted to live, but it had been smothered in the muddy, dumb thing that wallowed on the bank and could barely turn its face to feel the sun move in the sky.

In the distance he heard dogs baying and he surfaced from the cold and the exhaustion. He had eaten Arslan's ration of food long before, and he was starving again. The dogs sounded close and he feared suddenly that the stinking river mud would be no protection at all. He heaved himself along the slope of the bank, hidden by the grasses on the edge as he moved in spasms, flopping and weak. The howling dogs were even closer and his heart beat in fluttery panic, terrified at the thought of them tearing at him, ripping his flesh from his bones. He could not yet hear the hooves of riders, but he knew he had not made it far enough.

With a groan at the icy sting, he pulled himself into the water, heading out to the deepest point and a thick bed of reeds. The part of him that could still think forced him to ignore the first patch. If they saw where he had been lying, they would search all around it.

The river numbed the worst of his pain, and though it was still shallow, he used the current to push himself downstream on his hands and knees, scrabbling in the soft mud. He felt live things move between his fingers, but the cold had reduced him to a core of sensation that had no link to the world. They would see the cloud of muck he had disturbed. It was surely hopeless, but he did not stop, searching for deeper water.

The river wound around a corner, under ancient overhanging trees. On the other side was a bank of blue ice that had survived the winter in constant shadow. The rushing water had eaten a shelf beneath it, and though he feared the biting cold, he made for it without hesitation.

He wondered vaguely how long he could survive in the freezing water. He forced his way in under the ridge of ice and knelt in the mud with just his eyes and nose above the surface. They would have to enter the water to see him, but he did not doubt the hunters would send dogs up and down the stream.

The cold had numbed every part of him and he thought he was probably dying. He jammed his jaw shut against chattering teeth, and for a little while, he forgot what was happening and simply waited like a fish, frozen and blank of thought. He could see his breath as mist on the surface of the clear water as the cloud of muck settled around him.

He heard the excited yelping of dogs nearby, but his thoughts moved too slowly to feel fear. Was that a shout? He thought it was. Perhaps they had found the trail he had made across the clay. Perhaps they had recognized it as the mark a man would make if he dragged himself on his belly like a beast. He did not care any longer. The cold seemed to have reached inside him and clutched at his heart, slowing it with a terrible force. He could feel each beat as a burst of warmth in his chest, but it was growing weaker with every passing moment.

The yelping of the dogs grew quieter after a time, though he remained where he was. In the end, it was not a conscious decision that made him move, more the impulse of flesh that did not want to die. He almost drowned as a wave of weakness struck and he struggled to keep his head above the water. Slowly, he pushed himself out into the deeper water, sitting in it with limbs so heavy he could barely move them.

He pushed himself to the far bank and lay on the dark clay again, scoring its perfect smoothness as he pulled himself up under the overhanging grass and passed out at last.

When he woke, it was still light, but there was no sound near him but the river itself, rushing past with snow melt from the mountains. Pain had woken him as the blood moved in his limbs, weeping into the water from his torn skin. He flopped one arm over and dragged himself a little farther from the water, almost sobbing at the pain of his awakening flesh. He managed to raise himself enough to peer through the trees and saw no one close.

Eeluk would not give up, Temujin was certain. If the first hunt failed, he would send the entire tribe out to search for him, covering the land for a day's ride around the camp. They knew he could not have gone farther, and they would certainly find him eventually. He lay staring up at the sky and realized there was only one place to go.

As the sun set, Temujin staggered to his feet, shivering so powerfully it felt as if he would shake himself apart. When his legs failed him, he crawled for a time across the grass. The torches of the camp could be seen from far away, and he realized he had not come such a great distance in his weakened state. Most of the hunters had probably taken a wider path to search for him.

He waited until the last rays of the sun had gone and the land was dark again and cold. His body seemed to be willing to bear him onward for a little longer, and he had long ceased to wonder at how far he could push his broken, damaged limbs. The river had unstuck his swollen eye and he found with relief that he could see out of it a little, though everything was blurred and it watered constantly, like tears.

He dreaded the dogs of the camp, though he hoped the river mud would keep his scent down. The thought of one of those vicious animals running out to savage him was a constant fear, but he had no other choice. If he stopped his hobbling crawl, he would be found in the second sweep of hunters in the morning. He went on, and when he looked back, he was surprised to see how far he had come.

He knew the ger he wanted and thanked the sky father that it was close to the edge of the quiet camp. He lay on his belly for a long time, at the edges, watching for the slightest movement. Eeluk had placed his sentries looking outward, but they would have needed the sight of an owl to see the muddy figure creeping forward on the dark earth.

After an age, Temujin reached out to touch the felt wall of a ger, feeling its dry coarseness with something like ecstasy. Every sense was heightened, and though his pain had returned, he felt alive and light-headed. He thought of trying to gain an entry under the wall, but it would have been pegged down and he did not want someone to shout in fear or think he was a wolf. He grinned to himself at the thought. He made a very ragged wolf, stealing down from the hills for warmth and milk. Clouds hid the stars and, in the darkness, he reached the little door to the ger and pushed it open, closing it behind him and standing panting in the deeper dark within.

"Who is it?" he heard a woman ask. To his left, he heard a rustle of blankets and another deeper voice.

"Who is there?" Basan said.

He would be reaching for a knife, Temujin knew.

"Temujin," he whispered.

Silence greeted his name and he waited, knowing his life hung in the balance. He heard the strike of flint on steel, the flash lighting their faces for an instant. Basan's wife and children were all awake and Temujin could only stare dully at them while Basan lit an oil lamp and shuttered the flame down to barely more than a glowing cinder.

"You cannot stay here," Basan's wife said.

Temujin saw the fear in her face, but he turned in mute appeal to his father's bondsman and waited.

Basan shook his head, appalled at the shambling figure that stood hunched in his home.

"They are looking for you," Basan said.

"Hide me, then, for a day, until the search is over," Temujin replied. "I claim guest rights." He did not hear an answer and he slumped suddenly, the last of his strength vanishing. He slid to his knees and his head lolled forward.

"We cannot send him away," he heard Basan tell his wife. "Not to be killed."

"He will kill us all," she said, her voice rising in volume.

Blearily, Temujin watched Basan cross the ger to her, holding her face in both his hands.

"Make him tea and find something to eat," he told her. "I will do this for his father."

She did not respond, though she moved to the kettle and began stoking the little iron stove, her face hard. Temujin felt himself lifted in Basan's strong arms and then darkness overwhelmed him.

Eeluk did not think to search the gers of the families. His initial good humor faded visibly as the second day passed and then the third with no sign of the fugitive. At the end of the fourth day, Basan returned to Temujin to report that Arslan and his son had also vanished. They had ridden north that morning with one of the bondsmen, but none of them had returned by sunset and Eeluk was beside himself with rage. He had sent men to the ger he had given the swordsmith and found that his most valuable tools had vanished along with him. No one was expecting the bondsman to come back, and the wailing of his family could be heard long into the night. The mood of the Wolves had soured and Eeluk had

knocked a man unconscious for questioning his decision to send them out again.

Temujin could barely remember the first two days.
A fever had set in, perhaps from the stinking air of the
pit. The freezing river had cleaned his skin and may have
saved him. Basan's wife had tended his wounds with
stern efficiency, bathing away the worst of the remaining filth and dabbing at the blood and pus with a cloth
dipped in boiled airag. He had groaned at her touch and
had a memory of her hand over his mouth to stifle the
sound.

Basan had left them to join the other men each
morning, after stern warnings to his two sons not to say
a word to anyone. They watched Temujin with owlish
curiosity, frightened by the stranger who said nothing
and bore such awful wounds. They were old enough to
understand that their father's life depended on their silence.

Eeluk had taken to drinking more and more heavily
as his search parties returned empty-handed day after
day. By the end of a week, he gave a drunken order for
the families to continue farther north, leaving the pit
and their bad luck behind them. That night, he retired to
his ger with two of the youngest girls in the tribe, and
their families had dared not complain. Basan took a late
watch from midnight until dawn, seeing a chance to
spirit Temujin out of the camp at last. The families were
unhappy and nervous and he knew there would be eyes
watching and listening whenever he moved. Though it
was fraught with danger, Temujin would be discovered
when the gers were dismantled, so it was that night or
nothing.

It was hard to do anything in the tight-knit society

of the tribe without it being noticed. Basan waited as close to midnight as he could, leaving the top felt off the ger and peering up at the stars as they crept across the bowl of sky above. As a result, they were all shivering by the time he judged the tribe was as quiet and still as it was going to get. Those who were still awake would not remark on a trusted bondsman going out to take his watch, though Basan had agonized over giving Temujin one of his ponies. He had eleven and loved them all as his children. In the end, he had chosen a small black mare and brought her to the door of his ger, tying on saddlebags with enough food to keep Temujin alive for the trip.

Temujin stood in the deepest shadow and struggled to find words to express his gratitude. He had nothing to give even the children, and he felt ashamed for the burden and fear he had brought into their home. Basan's wife had not warmed to him, though Basan's oldest son seemed to have lost his nervousness and replaced it with awe when he heard who the stranger was in their home. The little boy had visibly summoned his courage when Basan told them it would be that night, and approached Temujin with all the self-consciousness of his twelve years. To Temujin's surprise, the boy had gone down on one knee and reached out for his hand, pressing it down on the top of his head, where Temujin could feel his scalp lock of hair against the bristly skin.

Temujin found his throat tight with emotion at the boy's simple gesture. "Your father is a brave man," he murmured. "Be sure to follow his steps."

"I will, my khan," the boy replied.

Temujin stared at him and Basan's mother hissed in a breath. At the door, Basan heard the exchange and shook his head, troubled. Before Temujin could reply, the bondsman crossed the ger to his son and lifted him to his feet.

"You cannot give an oath to this man, little one. When the time comes, you will pledge your sword and your life to Eeluk, as I have." He could not meet Temujin's eyes as he spoke, but the little boy's resistance fled in his father's strong grip. He ducked away and scurried to his mother's embrace, watching them both from under the crook of her arm.

Temujin cleared his throat. "My father's spirit watches us," he murmured, seeing his frozen breath like a plume of mist. "You do him honor in saving me."

"Walk with me now," Basan said, embarrassed. "Do not speak to anyone and they will think you are another of the guards on the hills." He held open the door and Temujin ducked through it, wincing at the pain from his scabs. He wore a clean tunic and leggings under a padded winter deel that belonged to Basan. Beneath the thick layers, the worst of his wounds were heavily bandaged. He was far from healed, but he yearned to be placed in a saddle. He would find his tribe among the wanderers of the plains, and the Wolves would not catch him again.

Basan walked deliberately slowly through the encampment, trusting in the dark to hide the identity of his companion if anyone was fool enough to brave the cold. There was a chance someone might notice that he returned without his mare, but he had no choice. It did not take long to leave the gers behind, and no one challenged them. The two men walked together in silence, leading the pony by the reins until the camp of the Wolves was far behind. It was late and Basan would

have to work up a sweat to reach his post without causing comment. When they were hidden in the shadow of
a hill, he pressed the reins into Temujin's hands.

"I have wrapped my second bow and placed it
here," he said, patting a bundle tied to the saddle.
"There is a little food, but I have left you two arrows
with it, for when you need to hunt. Lead her on foot until you are far away, or the watchers will hear your
hooves. Stay in the shadow of the hills as long as you
can."

Temujin nodded, reaching out to clasp the bondsman by his arm. The man had been his captor with Tolui
and then saved his life and risked his own family to do it.
He did not understand him, but he was grateful.

"Watch for me on the horizon, Basan," he said. "I
have scores to settle with the Wolves."

Basan looked at him, seeing again the determination
that reminded him chillingly of Yesugei when he was
young.

"That is your father talking," he said, shivering suddenly.

Temujin returned his gaze for a long moment, then
clapped him on the shoulder.

"When you see me again, I promise your family will
be safe," he said, then clicked in his throat to start the
mare walking once more. Basan watched him go before
he realized he was late and began to run. By the time
Temujin passed out of the hill shadow, only Basan
would be there to see him go, and his horn would remain silent.

CHAPTER 19

KACHIUN SAT ALONE on a gentle slope, breaking his fast with a little hard bread and the last of the spiced mutton. He and Khasar had managed to recapture most of the herd Tolui had scattered, and Hoelun had slaughtered and smoked enough to keep him for many days of his lonely watch for his brother. The supply had dwindled despite his attempts to eat sparingly, and he knew he would have to hunt marmots and birds the following day if he was not to starve.

As he munched the dry meat, he found himself missing his family and wondered if they still lived. He knew as well as anyone that a family of wanderers was vulnerable on the plains, even if they moved by night. As the brothers had once ambushed a pair of herdsmen, so his family could be attacked for the little flock or the ponies they rode. He did not doubt Khasar would give a good account of himself, but against two or three warriors out to raid, there could be only one outcome.

Kachiun sighed to himself, sick of the way the world

had turned its face against them all. When Temujin had been there, they had dared to hope for something more than lives spent in fear of every stranger. Somehow his brother's presence made him stand a little taller and remember how it had once been when Yesugei was alive. Kachiun feared for them all and his imagination threw up unwanted bloody images as the days passed.

It was hard being alone. Kachiun had felt the strangeness of his position as Hoelun led her last three children away to the west. He had stood watch for many nights as a little boy, though always with an older warrior to see he did not fall asleep. Even those long hours had not prepared him for the dreadful loneliness of the empty plains. He knew there was a chance that he would never see his family again, his mother or Temujin. The sea of grass was vast beyond imagining, and if they were dead, he might not even find their bones.

After the first few days, he had found it comforting to talk aloud to himself as he scanned the distant hills, just to hear a voice. The place he had chosen was high up in the cleft, near where he and Temujin had killed Bekter, so long ago. He still shuddered as he passed that spot each dawn on his way up to the watching post. He told himself that Bekter's spirit would not stay there, but his knowledge of the rituals was hazy. Kachiun remembered old Chagatai referring to more than one soul. One would ride the winds far above, but wasn't a part of it bound to the earth? He didn't mind taking the path in the light of the morning sun, but when he left it too late and it was growing dark as he came back, it was easy to imagine Bekter standing there in the shadow of the trees, white and deadly. Kachiun shuddered at the thought. His memories of Bekter seemed to have become frozen in that single moment when he had released a shaft to punch into his back. What had gone before was just mist, a different life. He remembered his terror that Bekter would somehow pluck out the shaft and turn on him in fury. The world had changed when Bekter fell onto the damp leaves, and Kachiun sometimes wondered if he was still paying for that day. Temujin had said the spirits gave you just enough wit and strength to live and then took no further interest, but part of Kachiun feared there was a price to pay for every savage act. He had been a child, but he could have refused to follow Temujin.

He chuckled to himself at the idea. None of the brothers could refuse Temujin. He had more of his father about him than Kachiun had realized in the first days. It had become more and more evident as Kachiun saw Temujin bargain and trade with wanderer families like old Horghuz and his wife. Despite his age, he was never taken lightly, and if he had been killed, Kachiun would honor him by trying to follow the same path. He would find his mother and build a safe place somewhere with clean water and good grazing. Perhaps they would find a small tribe willing to take on a family. Hoelun could marry again, and they would be warm and safe.

It was a dream, and though he knew it, he spent many hours in the fantasy, imagining something that was more than a little like his childhood around the gers of the Wolves, with horses to race in the sun. He had not spent every day thinking of the future then, and he missed the certainty of his old life, the solid path before his feet. On the high hill with the wind blowing his hair, he missed it all and grieved again for Temujin. The wound in Kachiun's thigh was still sore, but Hoelun had stitched the red holes closed and Kachiun scratched idly at them as he sat and listened to the breeze.

Temujin had not escaped his pursuers, Kachiun was certain. He remembered Tolui as a spiteful bully, much given to pinches and sneers when no one else was looking. The thought of Temujin in his power made Kachiun twist his hands together in the sleeves of his deel. The family of Yesugei had been given a hard life, and no one could say they had not struggled. There had been times like the morning of Tolui's arrival when he had really begun to hope for a normal life. Now, it had all been taken from them, and though he waited, he no longer believed he would see Temujin return to the cleft in the hills. If the sky father was just, he would bring suffering to Eeluk and his bondsmen, but that too was just a dream. There was no justice in the world and evil men prospered. Kachiun struggled not to despair as he wrapped his deel around him, but there were times when he hated as ferociously as Temujin did. There should be justice. There should be revenge.

He finished the last of the meat, digging his fingers into the seams of the cloth bag in search of some final morsel. He was tired and stiff from sitting for so long, but the coldness was more than just the wind. Somewhere to the west, Hoelun might be riding into danger, and he was not there to kill for her and die with her. Only stubbornness kept him at his post as the days fled.

Temujin saw two men in the far distance, high on a hill. His heart soared that it might be Arslan and his son, though he made sure his bow was strung and ready. If they were raiders, he vowed he would have their hearts on a slow fire. His injuries would not prevent him from firing Basan's bow, and he was in no mood to be playing games after everything he had suffered.

Though it rubbed his bloody scabs away, he had ridden for five days, sunrise to sunset, as he had instructed Arslan to do. The cleft in the hills was many miles away from that desolate place, but by then he knew he could trust men who had deserted Eeluk. The new khan of the Wolves was not cunning enough to plan so far ahead, though Yesugei might once have been. Temujin shaded his eyes against the setting sun to watch the two men guide their ponies down a steep hill, leaning back in the saddles to balance. He grunted to himself as he saw one of them dismount and walk alone toward him, raising his hands. The meaning was clear and Temujin raised his bow in response. It could only be Arslan.

Temujin trotted forward, still keeping his bow ready. The man may have saved him from the pit, but it would be a long time before Temujin trusted anyone again. He stopped and let Arslan cross the final paces between them, seeing the man's sure step on the springy grass. He walked as Yesugei had walked, and the memory brought a sudden pain that never reached Temujin's face.

"I knew you would escape them," Arslan said, smiling gently as he came close. "I did not expect you for many more days, though I see you have found yourself a fine mare."

"She was a present from a man who remembered my father," Temujin said stiffly. "But tell me, what do you think will happen here?"

Arslan blinked and chuckled. "I think you will wave to my son to join us and we will sit and share our food. As the camp is ours, I grant you guest rights."

Temujin cleared his throat. He owed the man a huge debt and was uncomfortable with the burden of it.

"Why did you help me?" he asked.

Arslan looked up, seeing the barely faded bruising and the hunched way the young man sat in the saddle. Yesugei would have been proud of such a son, he thought.

"I swore my oath to your father, Temujin. You are his eldest surviving son."

Temujin's eyes glinted as he thought of Bekter. Would this man have come to aid his older brother? Temujin could only marvel at the turns of fate.

"You do not know me," he said.

Arslan became very still. "I do not. I thought about standing by while you rotted in that pit, but I am not a man who stands by. Even if I had not met your father, I would have pulled you out."

Temujin flushed. "I . . . am grateful that you did," he said, looking away at the hills.

"We will not talk of it," Arslan said. "It is behind. For now, I will say you do not know me, but you will learn my word is iron."

Temujin snapped a glance at the man, looking for mockery. Instead, he found only stern control.

"Your father used to say that, yes," Arslan went on. "It drew me to him and I believed it. If you are half the man he was, my son and I will take oath to you and bind ourselves in honor to your line."

Temujin stared back at the man, sensing the quiet strength in him. He carried no weapons, but the mare had taken three steps away from Arslan while they talked, aware like her rider of a predator under rigid control. He wondered if Arslan thought there was a host of warriors waiting for Temujin's return. The thought occurred to him that a man who weighed himself by his word might remain bound even when he discovered there was nothing but a few scrawny brothers hiding in the hills. The temptation was there, but Temujin ignored it, unable to play false with one who had saved his life.

"I have no tribe, nor wealth, nor anything but my own family in hiding," Temujin said. "I have nothing to offer you, or your son. If you choose to ride on, I will make my own way back to them and still bless you for your help."

"You said you were the land and the bones of the hills," Arslan said softly. "I believe you were speaking with the words of your father. I will follow you."

"Call your son to me, then," Temujin said, suddenly exasperated. He did not want to begin to hope, but he had been changed in his captivity. He could no longer be satisfied with mere survival. He looked down at Arslan and he imagined a trail of fire and blood across the tribes that would end in the gers of the Wolves. He had seen it in the darkest days in the pit. While the flies had buzzed around him, his imagination had been in flames.

As Jelme approached, Temujin dismounted and hobbled to the two men.

"If you will call me khan, your will is no longer yours," he said, remembering his father speaking the same words. "Kneel to me."

Both Jelme and his father went down on one knee, and Temujin pressed his damaged hands on their heads.

"I ask you for salt, milk, horses, gers, and blood."

"They are yours, my khan," both men said together.

"Then you are kin and we are of one tribe," Temujin

said, surprising them. "I call you brothers and we are one people."

Both Arslan and Jelme raised their heads, struck by his tone and everything it meant. The wind picked up, rushing down from the mountains. Temujin turned his head in the direction of where his family would be hiding. He knew he could find his tribe among men scorned by all the others, among the wanderers and the herdsmen. Men like old Horghuz and his family, killed by Tolui. They were few, but they were hardened in fire. They had been cast out and many would hunger as he did: for a tribe, and for a chance to strike back at a world that had abandoned them.

"It is begun here," Temujin whispered. "I have had enough of hiding. Let them hide from *me*."

When Kachiun saw the three men riding south, he did not know who they were. He took careful note of their path and slipped back into the cleft in the hills with his bow and quiver ready. He knew the lay of the land better than anyone, and he raced down the inner slopes, leaping over fallen trees and old wood until he was panting.

He took his position close to where they would pass, well hidden in the undergrowth. There was murder in his heart as he prepared himself. If Tolui and Basan had returned with their captive, Kachiun would risk two long shots and trust his skill. He had trained for it and neither Khasar nor Temujin were his master with the bow. He waited in silence for the clop of hooves, ready to kill.

When they came into sight, Kachiun's heart pounded with excitement as he recognized his brother.

Just seeing Temujin alive lifted his spirits from where they had sunk in the days alone. He pressed his lips tight and only then realized he had been murmuring his brother's name aloud. He had been too long on his own, he admitted to himself as he sighted down the arrow at the older of the pair riding with Temujin.

Kachiun hesitated, his sharp eyes taking in every detail of the three men. Temujin sat tall in the saddle and there was no sign of ropes or a rein tied to the other men. Would they trust a captive not to gallop away at the slightest chance for freedom? Something was wrong, and he adjusted his grip on the drawn bow, the powerful muscles of his shoulders beginning to quiver. He would not let them past—he could not—but if he fired a shot in warning, he would have lost his chance to kill them swiftly. Both men were armed with bows, though he saw they were unstrung. They did not ride like men in hostile territory. Kachiun saw they carried long swords like the one Yesugei had worn on his hip. Nothing about them made sense, and while he hesitated, they had drawn level with his position in the trees.

He risked it all.

"Temujin!" Kachiun roared, rising from his crouch and pulling the bowstring back to his ear.

Temujin saw the figure out of the corner of his eye.

"Hold! Hold, Kachiun!" he shouted, raising his arms and waving.

Kachiun saw the two strangers vanish from sight in the instant of his warning, as fast as cats. Both dropped on the far side of their ponies, using the animals to shield them from attack. Kachiun breathed in relief as Temujin nodded to him, leaning over to dismount with a terrible awkwardness.

Kachiun's heart thumped at the sight. The Wolves had hurt his brother, but he was here and he was safe. Temujin limped visibly as they ran together and Kachiun embraced him, overcome. It would be all right.

"I did not know if they were friends or enemies," Kachiun said breathlessly.

Temujin nodded, steadying him with a clasp around the back of his neck.

"Bondsmen, brother," Temujin said. "Arslan and Jelme, who brought me out of my captivity. They have come to us from our father's spirit."

Kachiun turned to the two men as they approached.

"Then you are always welcome in my camp," he said. "I have a couple of ducks to feed you if you are hungry. I want to hear the tale."

Temujin nodded and Kachiun realized he had not smiled since he had first caught sight of him. His brother had changed in his time away, grown darker somehow under the weight of his experiences.

"We'll stay the night here," Temujin confirmed. "But where is my mother and the others?"

"They have ridden west. I stayed alone in case you could make it back. I . . . was almost ready to leave. I had lost hope of seeing you again."

Temujin snorted. "Never lose faith in me, little brother. My word is iron and I will always come home."

To his astonishment, Kachiun found there were tears in his eyes. He blinked them away, embarrassed in front of the strangers. He had been too long alone and had lost his cold face completely. He struggled to bring his soaring emotions back under control.

"Come. I will make a fire and cook the meat," he said.

Temujin nodded. "As you say. We have ground to cover at first light. I want to catch up with our mother."

The three men followed Kachiun back to his camp, a damp place barely worthy of the name, with a litter of old bones around a small firepit. Kachiun set about starting a flame, his hands clumsy as he knelt over old ashes.

"There is a wanderer family half a day's ride to the west," he said as he worked the flint and steel. "Three men and two women. They came past here yesterday evening." He saw Temujin look up with interest and misunderstood the light in his eye.

"We can avoid them if we take a line directly south before cutting through the black hills," he said, grunting in satisfaction as the flame licked up around his tinder.

Temujin stared at the little fire. "I do not want to avoid them, brother. They may not know it, but they are my blood as much as you are yourself."

Kachiun paused and sat back on his haunches. "I do not understand," he said, seeing Arslan and Jelme exchange glances. "What do we want with wanderers?"

"They are the great tribe," Temujin replied, almost to himself. His voice was so quiet that Kachiun had to strain to hear. "I will give them a family again. I will bring them in and I will make them hard and I will send them against those who killed our father. I will write the name of Yesugei in Tartar blood and, when we are strong, I will come back from the north and scatter the Wolves in the snow."

Kachiun shivered suddenly. Perhaps it was his imagination, but he thought he heard the click of old bones on the wind.

PART
TWO

CHAPTER 20

KHASAR WAITED in the deep snow, his face numb despite the covering of mutton fat. He could not help feeling a little sorry for himself. His brothers seemed to have forgotten, but this was his sixteenth birthday. On impulse, he stretched out his tongue and tried to catch a few of the cold flakes. He had been there a long time and he was weary and bored. He wondered idly if he would find himself a woman in the Tartar camp, as he stared at it over a hundred paces of white ground. The wind was bitter and the clouds scudded by at great speed overhead, driven like pale goats before a storm. Khasar liked the image of the words and repeated them to himself. He would have to remember to tell Hoelun when they came back from the raid. Khasar considered sipping his airag to keep himself warm, but he remembered Arslan's words and resisted. The swordsmith had given him only a cupful of the precious fluid in a second leather bottle.

"I do not want you drunk," Arslan had said sternly.

"If the Tartars reach you, we'll need a steady hand and a clear eye."

Khasar liked the father and son Temujin had brought back, particularly the older man. At times, Arslan reminded him of his father.

A distant movement distracted Khasar from his wandering thoughts. It was difficult to stay focused on the task at hand when he thought he was slowly freezing. He decided to drink the airag rather than be too cold to act. He moved slowly so as not to disturb the layer of snow that had built up on his deel and blanket.

It stung his gums, but he gulped it quickly, feeling the warmth spread in his lower chest and up into his lungs. It helped against the cold, and now there was definitely activity in the Tartar camp. Khasar lay just to the west of them, invisible under his covering of snow. He could see running figures and, when the wind dropped, he could hear shouting. He nodded to himself. Temujin had attacked. Now they would know if it really was only a small group of Tartars or the ambush Arslan had warned about. The Tartars had offered a blood price for the small group of raiders who had come north into their lands. If anything, it helped Temujin to recruit warriors from the wanderer families, taking their wives and children into his protection and treating them with honor. The Tartars were helping Temujin to build himself a tribe out in the icy wastes.

Khasar heard the flat smack of arrows being released. From such a distance, he could not tell if they were from Tartar bows, but it did not matter. Temujin had told him to lie at that point with a white blanket over him, and that is what he would do. He could hear dogs barking and he hoped someone shot them before they could threaten Temujin. His brother still feared the animals and it would not be right for him to show weakness in front of new men, some of them still wary and untrusting.

Khasar smiled to himself. Temujin preferred to take warriors with wives and children. They could not betray him with their loved ones back at the camp under Hoelun's care. The threat had never been spoken and perhaps it was only Khasar who thought of it. His brother was clever enough, though, he knew, cleverer than all of them.

Khasar narrowed his eyes, his pulse doubling in a jerk as two figures came racing out of the camp. He recognized Temujin and Jelme and saw that they were sprinting with bows and shafts ready. Behind them came six Tartars in their furs and decorated cloth, baying and showing yellow teeth in the pursuit.

Khasar did not hesitate. His brother and Jelme belted past without looking down at him. He waited another heartbeat for the Tartar warriors to close, then rose up from the snow like a vengeful demon, drawing back to his right ear as he moved. Two arrows killed two men, sending them onto their faces in the snow. The rest skidded to a stop in panic and confusion. They could have fallen on Khasar then, tearing him apart, but Temujin and Jelme had not deserted him. As soon as they heard his bow, each man had turned and gone down onto one knee, punching arrows into the snow ready for their snatching hands. They hammered the remaining Tartars, and Khasar had time for one last shot, sending it perfectly through the pale throat of the man closest to his position. The Tartar warrior pulled at the shaft and almost had it out before he fell still. Khasar shuddered as the man died. The Tartars wore deels much like his own people, but the men of the north were white-skinned and strange and they seemed to feel no pain. Still, they died as easily as goats and sheep.

Temujin and Jelme recovered the arrows from the bodies, cutting them out with quick chops of their knives. It was bloody work and Temujin's face was spattered as he handed Khasar half a dozen shafts, wet and red down their full length. Without a word, he clapped Khasar on the shoulder and he and Jelme dog-trotted back into the Tartar camp, running almost crouched with their bows low to the ground. Khasar's racing heart began to slow and he arranged the bloody arrows neatly in case he had to kill again. With great care, he wrapped a piece of oiled cloth over his bowstring to keep it strong and dry, then settled himself back in position. He wished he had brought a little more of the airag as the cold seeped into his bones and the falling snow began to drift over him once more.

"No ambush, Arslan!" Temujin called across the Tartar camp.

The swordsmith shrugged and nodded. It did not mean it could not come. It meant this time it had not. He had argued against them raiding so often into Tartar lands. It made a trap too easy to set if Temujin pecked at every single opportunity they gave him.

Arslan watched the young khan stride among the gers of dead men. The wailing of women had started and Temujin was grinning at the sound. It signified victory for all of them, and Arslan had never known a man as remorseless as the son of Yesugei.

Arslan looked up into the softly falling flakes, feeling them alight in his hair and on his eyelashes. He had lived for forty winters and fathered two sons dead and one alive. If he had been alone, he knew he would have lived the last years of his life away from the tribes, perhaps high in the mountains where only the hardiest could survive. With Jelme, he could think only as a father. He knew a young man needed others of his own age and a chance to find himself a wife and children of his own.

Arslan felt the cold bite through the padded deel he had taken from the body of a dead Tartar. He had not expected to find himself holding a tiger by the tail. It worried him to see the way Jelme hero-worshipped Temujin, despite him being barely eighteen years old. Arslan thought sourly that in his youth a khan was a man tempered by many seasons and battles. Yet he could not fault the sons of Yesugei for their courage, and Temujin had not lost a man in his raids. Arslan sighed to himself, wondering if the luck could last.

"You'll freeze to death standing still, swordsmith," came a voice behind him.

Arslan turned to see the still figure of Kachiun. Temujin's brother maintained a quiet intensity that gave nothing away. He could certainly move silently, Arslan admitted to himself. He had seen him shoot and Arslan no longer doubted the boy could have taken them from cover when they rode back to the cleft in the hills. The whole family had something and Arslan thought they were heading for fame or an early death. Either way, Jelme would be with them, he realized.

"I don't feel the cold," Arslan lied, forcing a smile.

Kachiun had not warmed to him the way Khasar

had, but the natural reserve was slowly thawing. Arslan had seen the same coldness in many of the newcomers to Temujin's camp. They came because Temujin accepted them, but old habits were hard to break for men who had lived so long away from a tribe. The winters were too cruel to trust easily and live.

Arslan knew enough to see that Temujin chose his companions on the raids very carefully indeed. Some needed constant reassurance and Temujin let Khasar handle those, with his rough ways and humor. Others would not give up their simmering doubts until they had seen Temujin risk his life at their shoulder. For raid after raid, they saw that he was so completely without fear that he would walk up to drawn swords and *know* he would not be alone. So far, they had gone with him. Arslan hoped it would last, for all their sakes.

"Will he raid again?" Arslan asked suddenly. "The Tartars will not stand for this much longer."

Kachiun shrugged. "We'll scout the camps first, but they are dull and slow in winter. Temujin says we can go on like this for months more."

"But you know better than that, surely?" Arslan said. "They will draw us in with a fat target and men hidden in every ger. Wouldn't you? Sooner or later we are going to walk into a trap."

To his astonishment, Kachiun grinned at him.

"They are just Tartars. We can take as many as they want to send against us, I think."

"It could be thousands if you provoke them all winter," Arslan said. "The moment the thaw comes, they could send an army."

"I hope so," Kachiun said. "Temujin thinks it is the

only way to get the tribes to band together. He says we need an enemy and a threat to the land. I believe him."

Kachiun patted Arslan on the shoulder as if in consolation before strolling away in the snow. The swordsmith allowed the touch out of sheer astonishment. He didn't have a tiger by the tail after all. He had it by the ears, with his head in its mouth.

A figure came padding by him and he heard the only voice he loved.

"Father! You'll freeze out here," Jelme said, coming to a halt.

Arslan sighed. "I've heard the opinion, yes. I am not as old as you all seem to think."

He watched his son as he spoke, seeing the bounce in his step. Jelme was drunk on the victory, his eyes shining. As Arslan's heart swelled for his son, he saw the young man could hardly stand still. Somewhere nearby, Temujin would be holding his war council once again, planning the next assault on the tribe who had killed his father. Each one was more daring and more difficult than the last, and the nights were often wild with drinking and captured women away from the main camp. In the morning, it would be different, and Arslan could not begrudge his son the company of his new friends. At least Temujin respected his skill with a bow and sword. Arslan had given his son that much.

"Did you take a wound?" he asked.

Jelme smiled, showing small white teeth. "Not a scratch. I killed three Tartars with a bow and one with the blade, using the high pull stroke you taught me." He mimed it automatically and Arslan nodded in approval.

"It is a good one if the opponent is unbalanced," he replied, hoping his son could see the pride he felt. He could not express it. "I remember teaching it to you," Arslan continued lamely. He wished he had more words, but a distance had somehow sprung up between them and he did not know how to breach it.

Jelme stepped forward and reached out to grip his father by the arm. Arslan wondered if he had taken the habit of physical contact from Temujin. For one of the swordsmith's generation, it was an intrusion and he always had to master the urge to slap it away. Not from his son, though. He loved him too much to care.

"Do you want me to stay with you?" Jelme asked.

Arslan had to snort with barely suppressed laughter, tinged with sadness. They were so arrogant it pained him, these young men, but with the wanderer families, they had grown themselves into a band of raiders who did not question their leader's authority. Arslan had watched the chains of trust develop between them, and when his spirits were low, he wondered if he would have to see his son killed before him.

"I will walk the perimeter of the camp and make sure there are no more surprises to spoil my sleep tonight," Arslan said. "Go." He forced a smile at the end and Jelme chuckled, his excitement bubbling back to the surface. He ran off between the white gers to where Arslan could hear the sound of revelry. The Tartars had been far from their main tribe, he thought to himself. For all he knew, they had been looking for the very force that had crushed them mercilessly. The news would filter its way back to the local khans, and they would respond, whether Temujin understood it or not. They could not afford to ignore the raids. In the east, the great cities of the Chin would have their spies out, looking always for weakness in their enemies.

As he walked around the camp, he found two other men doing the same thing and adjusted his view of Temujin yet again. The young warrior listened, Arslan had to admit, though he didn't like to ask for help. It was worth remembering.

As he crunched his way through the deepening snow, Arslan heard soft sobbing coming from a thicket of trees near the outskirts of the Tartar gers. He drew his sword in utter silence at the sound, standing like a statue until the blade was completely clear. It could have been a trap, though he didn't think so. The women of the camp would have either stayed in the gers or hidden at the edges. On a summer night, they might have been able to wait out the raiders before making their way back to their own people, but not in the winter snow.

He hadn't reached forty years of age without sensible caution, so Arslan had his sword still drawn when he looked on the face of a young woman, half his age. With a pleased grin, he sheathed the blade and held out a hand to pull her to her feet. When she only stared at him, he chuckled low in his throat.

"You'll need someone to warm you in your blankets tonight, girl. You'd be better off with me than one of the younger ones, I should think. Men of my age have less energy, for a start."

To his immense pleasure, the young woman giggled. Arslan guessed she wasn't kin of the dead men, though he reminded himself to keep his knives well hidden if he intended to sleep. He'd heard of more than one man killed by a sweetly smiling capture.

She took his hand and he pulled her up and onto his shoulder, patting her bottom as he strode back through the camp. He was humming to himself by the time he found a ger with a stove and a warm bed to shut out the softly falling snow.

Temujin clenched a fist in pleasure as he heard the tallies of the dead. The Tartar bodies would not talk, but there were too many to be a hunting trip, especially in the heart of winter. Kachiun thought they had probably been a raiding party much like their own.

"We'll keep the ponies and drive them back with us," Temujin told his companions. The airag was being passed around and the general mood was jubilant. In a little while they would be drunk and singing, perhaps lusting after a woman, though without hope in that bare camp. Temujin had been disappointed to find that most of the women were the sort of hardy crones men might take into the wilderness to cook and sew rather than as playful objects of lust. He had yet to find a wife for Khasar or Kachiun, and as their khan, he needed as many loyal families around him as possible.

The old women had been questioned about their menfolk, but of course they claimed to know nothing. Temujin watched one particularly wizened example as she stirred a pot of mutton stew in the ger he had chosen as his own. Perhaps he should have someone else taste it, he thought, smiling at the idea.

"Do you have everything you need, old mother?" he said. The woman looked back at him and spat carefully on the floor. Temujin laughed out loud. It was one of the great truths of life that no matter how furious a man became, he could still be cowed by a show of force. No one, however, could cow an angry woman. Perhaps he should have the food tasted first, at that. He looked around at the others, pleased with them all.

"Unless the snow covered a few," he said, "we have a count of twenty-seven dead, including the old lady Kachiun shot."

"She was coming at me with a knife," Kachiun replied, nettled. "If you'd seen her, you'd have taken the shot as well."

"Thank the spirits you weren't hurt, then," Temujin replied with a straight face.

Kachiun rolled his eyes as some of the other men chuckled. Jelme was there with a fresh covering of snow on his shoulders, as well as three brothers who had come in only the month before. They were so green you could smell the moss on them, but Temujin had chosen them to stand by his side in the first chaotic moments of the fight in the snow. Kachiun exchanged glances with Temujin after looking in their direction. The small nod from his older brother was enough for him to embrace them all as his own blood. The acceptance wasn't feigned, now that they had proved themselves, and the three beamed around at the others, thoroughly enjoying their first victory in this company. The airag was hot on the stove and each of them gulped as much as he could to keep the cold out before the stew gave strength back to tired limbs. They had all earned the meal and the mood was light.

Temujin addressed the oldest of them, a small, quick man with very dark skin and unkempt hair. He had once been with the Quirai, but a dispute with the khan's son had meant he had to ride away with his brothers before blood was shed. Temujin had welcomed them all.

"Batu? It's time to bring my brother Khasar in from the cold, I think. There will be no more surprises this night."

As Batu rose, Temujin turned to Jelme. "I imagine your father is out checking the camp?"

Jelme nodded, reassured by Temujin's smile.

"I would expect no less," Temujin said. "He is a thorough man. He may be the best of us all." Jelme nodded slowly, pleased. Temujin signaled to the old Tartar woman to serve him the stew. She clearly considered refusing him, but thought better of it and gave him a large portion of the steaming mix.

"Thank you, old mother," Temujin said, ladling it into his mouth. "This is good. I do not think I have ever tasted anything better than another man's food eaten in his own ger. If I had his beautiful wife and daughters to entertain me, I would have it all."

His companions chuckled as they received their own hot food and laid into it, eating like wild animals. Some of them had lost almost all traces of civilization in their years away from a tribe, but Temujin valued that ferocity. These were not men who would think to question his orders. If he told them to kill, they killed until they were red to the elbows, regardless of who stood in their way. As he took his family north, he had found them scattered on the land. The most brutal had been alone, and one or two of those were too much like mad dogs to be trusted. Those he had taken out away from the gers, killing them quickly with the first blade Arslan had forged for him.

As he ate, Temujin thought of the months since coming back to his family. He could not have dreamed then of the hunger he saw in the men around him, the need to be accepted once again. Yet it had not always gone smoothly. There had been one family who joined him, only to steal away in the middle of the night with all they could carry. Temujin and Kachiun had tracked them down and carried the pieces back to his camp for the others to see before they left them for wild animals. There was no return to their previous lives, not after they had joined him. Given whom he had decided to take in, Temujin knew he could not show weakness, or they would have torn him apart.

Khasar came in with Batu, blowing and rubbing his hands together. He shook himself deliberately close to Temujin and Kachiun, scattering snow over them. They cursed and ducked against the soft pats of snow that spattered in all directions.

"You forgot about me again, didn't you?" Khasar demanded.

Temujin shook his head. "I did not! You were my secret, in case there was a last attack when we were all settled."

Khasar glared at his brothers, then turned away to get his bowl of stew.

As he did so, Temujin leaned close to Kachiun and whispered, "I forgot he was out there," loudly enough for them all to hear.

"I knew it!" Khasar roared. "I was practically frozen to death, but all the time I kept telling myself, 'Temujin won't have abandoned you, Khasar. He will be back any moment to call you in to the warm.'"

The others watched bemused as Khasar reached into his trousers and rummaged around.

"I think a ball has actually frozen," he said mournfully. "Is that possible? There's nothing but a lump of ice down there."

Temujin laughed at the wounded tone until he was in danger of spilling the rest of his own stew.

"You did well, my brother. I would not have sent a man I couldn't trust to that spot. And wasn't it a good thing you were there?"

He told the others about the rush of Tartar warriors that Khasar and Jelme had put down. As the airag warmed their blood, they responded with stories of their own, though some told them humorously and others were dark and bleak in tone, bringing a touch of winter into the warm ger. Little by little, they shared each other's experiences. Little Batu had not had the sort of archery training that had marked the childhood of Yesugei's sons, but he was lightning fast with a knife and claimed no arrow could hit him if he saw it fired. Jelme was the equal of his father with a sword or bow, and so coldly competent that Temujin was in the habit of making him second in command. Jelme could be depended upon, and Temujin thanked the spirits for the father and son and everyone who had come after them.

There were times when he dreamed of being back in that stinking pit, waiting to be killed. Sometimes, he was whole, his body perfect. Other times, it was roped with scars or still raw and bleeding. It was there that he had found the strange thought that still burned inside him. There was only one tribe on the plains. Whether they called themselves Wolves or Olkhun'ut or even tribeless wanderers, they spoke the same language and they were bound in blood. Still, he knew it would be easier to sling a rope around a winter mist than to bring the tribes together after a thousand years of warfare. He had made a beginning, but it was no more than that.

"So what next when we've finished counting our new horses and gers here?" Kachiun asked his brother, interrupting his thoughts. The rest of them paused in their eating to hear the answer.

"I think Jelme can handle the next raid," Temujin said. Arslan's son looked up from his meal with his mouth open. "I want you to be a hammer," Temujin told him. "Do not risk my people, but if you can find a small group, I want it crushed in my father's memory. They are not our people. They are not Mongols, as we are. Let the Tartars fear us as we grow."

"You have something else in mind?" Kachiun asked with a smile. He knew his brother.

Temujin nodded. "It is time to return to the Olkhun'ut and claim my wife. You need a good woman. Khasar says he needs a bad one. We all need children to carry on the line. They will not scorn us when we ride amongst them now.

"I will be gone for some months, Jelme," Temujin said, staring at Arslan's son. His yellow eyes were unblinking and Jelme could not meet them for long. "I will bring back more men to help us here, now that I know where to find them. While I am gone, it will be your task to make the Tartars bleed and fear the spring."

Jelme reached out and they gripped each other's forearms to seal the agreement.

"I will be a terror to them," Jelme said.

In the darkness, Temujin stood swaying outside the ger Arslan had chosen and listened to the sounds within, amused that the swordsmith had finally found someone to take the edge off his tension. Temujin had never known a man as tightly bound as the swordsmith, nor one he would rather have stood with in battle, unless it was his own father. Perhaps because Arslan was from that generation, Temujin found he could respect him without bristling or proving himself with every word and gesture. He hesitated before interrupting the man at his coupling, but now that the decision was made, he intended to ride south in the morning and he wanted to know Arslan would be with him.

It was no small thing to ask. Anyone could see how Arslan watched his son whenever the arrows were flying. Forcing him to leave Jelme alone in the cold north would be a test of his loyalty, but Temujin did not think Arslan would fail it. His word was iron, after all. He raised a hand to knock on the small door, then thought better of it. Let the swordsmith have his moment of peace and pleasure. In the morning they would ride back into the south. Temujin could feel bitterness stir in him at the thought of the plains of his childhood, swirling like oil on water. The land remembered.

CHAPTER 21

TEMUJIN AND ARSLAN TROTTED across the sea of grass. To Arslan's surprise, he had found he was comfortable with the silence between them. They talked at night around the fire, and practiced with swords until they had built a fine sweat. The blade Temujin carried was beautifully balanced and cut with a blood channel that allowed it to slide free from a wound without snagging. Arslan had made it for him and instructed him in maintaining its edge and oiling the steel against rust. The muscles of Temujin's right arm stood out in ridges as he became completely familiar with the weight, and with Arslan as his tutor, his skill improved daily.

The days riding were spent if not in thought then in the peaceful absence of it. To Arslan, it was just as he had traveled with his son, Jelme, and he found it restful. He watched as Temujin rode a little ahead or scouted up a hill to see the best route south. The young raider had a quiet assurance about him, a confidence that could be read in every movement. Arslan considered the twists of

fate that had led him to rescue Temujin from the
Wolves. They called him khan in their little camp,
though there were barely twenty men to follow him and
only a handful of women and children. Still, Temujin
walked with pride amongst them and they fought and
won raid after raid. There were times when Arslan wondered what he had unleashed.

It was no easy task to find the Olkhun'ut. They had
moved camp many times since Temujin had ridden
away from them with Basan, the news of his father's injury still fresh. It took two moons just to reach the lands
around the red hill, and still Temujin did not know
where to find them. It was even possible that they had
begun another drift to the south as they had years before, putting them beyond reach. Arslan saw the tension
grow in his young companion as they questioned each
wanderer and herdsman they met, searching for any
word of them.

It was no easy task for Temujin to approach strangers with Arslan at his side. Even when he strapped his
bow to his saddle and rode up with his hands in the air,
they were met with drawn arrows and the frightened
eyes of children. Temujin dismounted to speak to the
tribeless as he found them, though more than one galloped away as soon as he and Arslan were spotted. Some
he directed north, promising them a welcome in his
name. He did not know if they believed him. It was a
frustrating business, but a fearless old woman finally
nodded at the name and sent them east.

Temujin found no peace for his spirit in riding lands
he had known as a child. He also asked for news of the
Wolves, to avoid them. Eeluk was still somewhere in the
area and it would not do for Temujin to come across a

hunting party unprepared. There would be a reckoning between them, he knew, but not until he had gathered enough warriors to tear through the gers of the Wolves like a summer storm.

When they sighted the vast camp of the Olkhun'ut after another month of riding, Temujin reined in, over-come with memory. He could see the dust of outriders as they came out, buzzing like wasps around the edges of the tribe.

"Keep your hand away from your sword when they come," he murmured to Arslan.

The swordsmith suppressed a grimace at the unnec-essary advice, sitting like stone.

Temujin's pony tried to munch a patch of brown grass, and he slapped it on the neck, keeping the reins tight. He remembered his father as clearly as if he were there with him and he kept a tight hold on his emotion, showing a cold face of which Yesugei would have approved.

Arslan felt the change in the younger man, seeing the tension in his shoulders and the way he sat his horse. A man's past was always full of pain, he thought, delib-erately relaxing as he waited for the yelling warriors to finish their display of bravery.

"What if they refuse to give her up?" Arslan asked.

Temujin turned his yellow eyes on the swordsmith, and Arslan felt a strange emotion under that cold stare. Who was the boy to disturb him in such a way?

"I will not leave without her," Temujin said. "I will not be turned away without a death."

Arslan nodded, troubled. He could still remember being eighteen, but the recklessness of those years was long behind him. He had grown in skill since his youth, and he had yet to meet a man who could beat him with a sword or a bow, though he assumed such a man existed. What he could not do was follow Temujin into his coldness, to the sheer indifference to death that was only possible for the very young. He had a son, after all.

Arslan showed nothing of his internal struggle, but by the time the Olkhun'ut warriors were on them, he had emptied his mind and was perfectly still.

The riders screamed and whooped as they galloped close with bows drawn and arrows fitted to the strings. The display was meant to impress, but neither Arslan nor Temujin paid it any heed. Arslan saw one of the riders check and yank on the reins as he caught sight of Temujin's face. The sharp movement almost brought his pony to its knees, and the warrior's face grew tight with astonishment.

"It is you," the rider said.

Temujin nodded. "I have come for my wife, Koke. I told you I would."

Arslan watched as the Olkhun'ut warrior hawked his throat clear of phlegm and spat on the ground. Pressure from his heels brought his gelding close enough for him to reach out. Temujin looked on impassively as Koke raised his arm as if to strike him, his face working in pale rage.

Arslan moved, kicking his pony into range. His sword licked out so that its razor tip sat snugly under Koke's throat, resting there. The other warriors roared in anger, milling around them. They bent their bows ready to fire and Arslan ignored them as if they were not there. He waited until Koke's eyes flickered toward him, seeing the sick fear there.

"You do not touch the khan," Arslan said softly. He

used his peripheral vision to watch the other men, see-ing how one bow bent farther than the others. Death was close enough to feel on the breeze, and the day seemed to grow still.

"Speak carefully, Koke," Temujin said, smiling. "If your men shoot, you will be dead before we are."

Arslan saw that Temujin had noted the bending bow, and wondered again at his calm.

Koke was like a statue, though his gelding shifted nervously. He took a tighter grip on the reins rather than have his throat cut by a sudden jerk of his mount.

"If you kill me, you will be cut to pieces," he said in a whisper.

Temujin grinned at him. "That is true," he replied, offering no further help. Though he smiled, he felt a cold lump of anger surface deep inside. He had no pa-tience for the ritual humiliation of strangers, not from these people.

"Remove the sword," Koke said.

To his credit, his voice was calm, but Temujin could see sweat appear on his forehead, despite the wind. Coming close to death would do that for a man, he thought. He wondered why he felt no fear himself, but there was not a trace of it in him. A vague memory of wings beating his face came back to him, and he had a sense of being detached from the moment, untouched by danger. Perhaps his father's spirit watched him still, he thought.

"Welcome me to your camp," Temujin said.

Koke's gaze jumped back from Arslan to the young man he had known from so long before. He was in an impossible position, Temujin knew. Either he had to back down and be humiliated, or he would die.

Temujin waited, uncaring. He glanced around him at the other men, spending a long moment looking at the warrior who had drawn an arrow back to his ear. The man was ready to loose and Temujin raised his chin in a small jerk, showing he knew.

"You are welcome in the camp," Koke whispered.

"Louder," Temujin said.

"You are *welcome*," Koke said again, through gritted teeth.

"Excellent," Temujin replied. He turned in the saddle to the man who still waited with a drawn bow.

"If you loose that arrow, I will pull it out and shove it down your throat," he told him. The man blinked and Temujin stared until the needle-sharp point was lowered almost sheepishly. He heard Koke's gasp behind him as Arslan removed the blade, and he took a deep breath, finding to his surprise that he was enjoying himself.

"Ride in with us then, Koke," he said, clapping his cousin on the back. "I have come for my wife."

There was no question of entering the camp without visiting the khan of the Olkhun'ut. With a pang of memory, Temujin remembered Yesugei's games of status with Sansar, as one khan to another. He kept his head high, but he felt no shame as Koke led him to Sansar's ger in the center of the camp. Despite his successes against the Tartars, he was not Sansar's equal, as his father had been. At best, he was a war leader, a raider barely approaching the level where he could be received. If he had lacked even that status, Temujin knew that only his father's memory would have granted him an audience and perhaps not even then.

He and Arslan dismounted and allowed their ponies to be taken away, their bows with them. Koke had grown into a man in the years since they had last met, and Temujin was interested to see how the khan's bondsmen accepted his cousin's right to enter the ger after just a few murmured words. Koke had come up in the world, Temujin realized. He wondered what service he had performed for the khan of the Olkhun'ut.

When Koke did not return, Temujin was struck by a memory and chuckled suddenly, startling Arslan from his silent tension.

"They always make me wait, these people," Temujin said. "But I have patience, do I not, Arslan? I bear their insults with great humility." His eyes glittered with something other than amusement, and Arslan only bowed his head. The cool control he had seen in Temujin was under strain in that camp. Though he showed no sign if it, Arslan considered there was a chance of them both being killed through a rash word.

"You honor your father with your restraint," he said softly. "Knowing it is not from weakness, but from strength."

Temujin glanced sharply at him, but the words seemed to settle his nerves. Arslan kept his face clear of any relief. For all his ability, Temujin was only eighteen. Wryly, Arslan admitted that Temujin had chosen his companion well for the trip south. They had ridden into terrible danger and Temujin was as prickly as any other young man with his new status and pride. Arslan readied himself to be the calming force Temujin had known he needed when his judgment was clear.

Koke returned after an age, stiff disdain in every movement.

"My lord Sansar will see you," he said, "but you will give up your weapons."

Temujin opened his mouth to object, but Arslan untied his scabbard with a flick of his fingers and slapped the hilt of his sword into Koke's open hand.

"Guard the blade well, boy," Arslan told him. "You will not see another of that quality in your lifetime."

Koke could not resist feeling the balance of the sword, but Temujin spoiled his attempt by pressing the second of Arslan's blades into his arms, so that he had to take it or drop them both. Temujin's hand felt empty as he let it go, and his gaze remained fixed on the weapons as Koke stepped back.

It was Arslan who faced one of the khan's bondsmen at the door, opening his arms wide and inviting a search. There was nothing passive in the way he stood there, and Temujin was reminded of the deadly stillness of a snake about to strike. The guard sensed it too and patted down every inch of the swordsmith, including the cuffs of his deel and his ankles.

Temujin could do no less and he endured the search without expression, though inwardly he began to simmer. He could not like these people, for all he dreamed of forming a great tribe of tribes across the land. When he did, the Olkhun'ut would not be part of it until they had been bled clean.

When the bondsmen were satisfied, they ducked into the ger and, in an instant, Temujin was back on the night he had learned of his father's injury. The polished wooden floor was the same and Sansar himself seemed unmarked by the passage of years.

The khan of the Olkhun'ut remained seated as they

approached, his dark eyes watching them with a hint of jaded amusement.

"I am honored to be in your presence, lord," Temujin said clearly.

Sansar smiled, his skin crinkling like parchment. "I had not thought to see you here again, Temujin. Your father's passing was a loss for all our people, all the tribes."

"There is a high price still to pay for those who betrayed him," Temujin replied. He sensed a subtle tension in the air then as Sansar leaned forward in his great chair, as if expecting something more. When the silence had become painful, Sansar smiled.

"I have heard of your attacks in the north," the khan said, his voice sibilant in the gloom. "You are making a name for yourself. I think, yes, I think your father would be proud of you."

Temujin lowered his gaze, unsure how to respond.

"But you have not come to me to boast of little battles against a few raiders, I am sure," Sansar went on.

His voice held a malice that set Temujin on edge, but he replied with calm.

"I have come for what I was promised," he said, looking Sansar squarely in the eye.

Sansar pretended to be confused for a moment.

"The girl? But you came to us then as the son of a khan, one who might well inherit the Wolves. That story has been told and ended."

"Not all of it," Temujin replied, watching as Sansar blinked slowly, his inner amusement sparkling in his gaze. The man was enjoying himself and Temujin wondered if he would be allowed to leave alive. There were two bondsmen in the ger with their khan, both armed with swords. Koke stood to one side with his head bowed. In a glance, Temujin saw that the swords he held could be snatched from his grip. His cousin was still a fool.

Temujin forced himself to relax. He had not come to die in that ger. He had seen Arslan kill with blows from his hands, and he thought they might survive the first strikes of the bondsmen. Once the warriors gathered in his defense, it would be the end. Temujin dismissed the idea. Sansar was not worth his life; not then, or ever.

"Is the word of the Olkhun'ut not good, then?" he said softly.

Sansar drew in a long breath, letting it hiss over his teeth. His bondsmen shifted, allowing their hands to touch the hilts of their swords.

"Only the young can be so careless with their lives," Sansar said, "as to risk insulting me in my own home." His gaze dropped to Koke and sharpened at the sight of the twin swords.

"What can a mere raider offer me for one of the Olkhun'ut women?" he said.

He did not see Arslan close his eyes for a moment, struggling with indignation. The sword he carried had been with him for more than a decade, the best he had ever made. They had nothing else to offer. For an instant, he wondered if Temujin had guessed there would be a price and chosen not to warn him.

Temujin did not reply at first. The bondsmen at Sansar's side watched him as a man might watch a dangerous dog, waiting for it to bare its fangs and be killed.

Temujin took a deep breath. There was no choice, and he did not look at Arslan for approval.

"I offer you a perfect blade made by a man without equal in all the tribes," he said. "Not as a price, but as a gift of honor to my mother's people."

Sansar bowed his head graciously, gesturing at Koke to approach him. Temujin's cousin covered his smile and held out the two swords.

"It seems I have a choice of blades, Temujin," Sansar said, smiling.

Temujin watched in frustration as Sansar fingered the carved hilts, rubbing the balls of his thumbs over bone and brass. Even in the gloom of the ger, they were beautiful, and Temujin could not help but remember his father's sword, the first that had been taken from him. In the silence, he recalled the promise to his brothers and spoke again before Sansar could reply.

"As well as the woman I was promised, I need two more to be wives for my kin."

Sansar shrugged, then drew Arslan's blade and held it up to his eye to look along its length.

"If you will make me a gift of both blades, I will find your offer acceptable, Temujin. We have too many girls in the gers. You may take Sholoi's daughter if she will have you. She has been a thorn in our side for long enough, and no man can say the Olkhun'ut do not honor their promises."

"And two more, young and strong?" Temujin said, pressing.

Sansar looked at him for a long time, lowering the swords to his lap. At last, he nodded, grudgingly.

"In memory of your father, Temujin, I will give you two daughters of the Olkhun'ut. They will strengthen your line."

Temujin would have liked to reach out and grab the

khan by his skinny throat. He bowed his head and
Sansar smiled.

The khan's bony hands still fondled the weapons
and his gaze became distant, as he seemed almost to
have forgotten the men who stood in front of him. With
an idle gesture, he signaled the pair to be removed from
his presence. The bondsmen ushered them out into the
cold air, and Temujin took a deep draft of it, his heart
hammering in his chest.

Arslan's face was tight with anger and Temujin
reached out to touch him lightly on the wrist. The
swordsmith seemed to jump at the contact, and Temujin
remained still, sensing the inner force of the man as it
coiled and uncoiled within him.

"It was a greater gift than you know," Arslan said.

Temujin shook his head, seeing Koke come out behind them, his arms empty. "A sword is just a sword,"
he replied. Arslan turned a cold expression on him, but
Temujin did not flinch. "You will make a better one, for
both of us."

He turned to Koke then, who was watching the exchange with fascination.

"Take me to her, cousin."

Though the Olkhun'ut had traveled far in the years since
he had last stood in their camp, it seemed the status of
Sholoi and his family had remained the same. Koke led
Temujin and Arslan to the very edge of the gers, to the
same patched and mended home that he remembered.
He had spent just a few short days there, but they were
still fresh in his mind and it was with an effort that
Temujin shook off his past. He had been little more

than a child. As a man, he wondered if Borte would welcome his return. Surely Sansar would have said if she
had been married in his absence? Temujin thought
grimly that the khan of the Olkhun'ut might very well
enjoy gaining two fine swords for nothing.

As Koke approached, they saw Sholoi duck out
from the little door, stretching his back and hitching up
a belt of string. The old man saw them coming and
shaded his eyes against the morning sun to watch. The
years had left more of a mark on Sholoi than on the
khan. He was skinnier than Temujin remembered and
his shoulders sagged under an ancient, grubby deel.
When they were close, Temujin could see a web of blue
veins on his knotted hands, and the old man seemed to
start, as if he had only just recognized them. No doubt
his eyes were failing, though there was still a hint of
strength in those legs, like an old root that would stand
right up to the moment it broke.

"Thought you were dead," Sholoi said, wiping his
nose on the back of his hand.

Temujin shook his head. "Not yet. I said I would
come back."

Sholoi began to wheeze and it took a moment or
two before Temujin realized he was laughing. The
sound ended in choking and he watched as Sholoi
hawked and spat a lump of ugly-looking brown phlegm
onto the ground.

Koke cleared his own throat, irritably. "The khan
has given his permission, Sholoi," Koke said. "Fetch
your daughter."

Sholoi sneered at him. "I didn't see him here when
my seam split last winter. I didn't see old Sansar out in
the wind with me then, with a patch and some thread.

Now I think of it, I don't see him here now, so keep your tongue still while we talk."

Koke flushed, his eyes darting to Temujin and Arslan.

"Fetch the other girls, Koke, for my brothers," Temujin said. "I've paid a high price, so make sure they're strong and pretty."

Koke struggled with his temper, irritated at being dismissed. Neither Temujin nor Arslan looked at him as he strode away.

"How is your wife?" Temujin asked when his cousin had gone.

Sholoi shrugged. "Dead two winters back. She just lay down in the snow and went. Borte is all I have now, to look after me."

Temujin felt his heart thump at the mention of her name. Until that moment, he had not known for certain she was even alive. He had a flash of understanding for the old man's loneliness, but there was no help for it, nor for all the blows and hard words he had used with his children. It was too late to have regrets, though that seemed to be the way of the elderly.

"Where...?" Temujin began. Before he could go on, the door of the ger swung open and a woman stepped out onto the cold ground. As she straightened, Temujin saw Borte had grown tall, almost as tall as he was himself. She stood at her father's side and met his gaze with frank curiosity, finally dipping her head in greeting. Her gesture broke the spell and he saw she was dressed to travel, with a deel lined with fur and her black hair tied back.

"You were a long time coming," she said to Temujin.

He remembered her voice and his chest grew tight with memory. She was no longer the bony child he had known. Her face was strong, with dark eyes that seemed to look right into him. He could tell nothing else about her under the thick deel, but she stood well and her skin was unmarked by disease. Her hair gleamed as she bent and kissed her father on the cheek.

"The black colt has a hoof that needs lancing," she said. "I would have done it today."

Sholoi nodded miserably, but they did not embrace. Borte picked up a cloth bag from inside the door and slung it over her shoulder.

Temujin was mesmerized by her and hardly heard Koke returning with their ponies. Two young girls walked at his side, both red-faced and weeping. Temujin only glanced at them when one coughed and held a dirty cloth to her mouth.

"This one is sick," he said to Koke.

His cousin shrugged insolently and Temujin's hand dropped to where his blade should have been. Koke saw the fingers close on air and grinned.

"She is the one Sansar told me to fetch for you, with her sister," he replied.

Temujin set his mouth in a hard line and reached out to take the girl by her chin, raising her face to him. Her skin was very pale, he realized, his heart sinking. It was typical of Sansar to seek a bargain even after the terms had been sealed.

"How long have you been ill, little one?" Temujin asked her.

"Since spring, lord," she answered, clearly terrified of him. "It comes and goes, but I am strong."

Temujin let his gaze fall on Koke and held it until

his cousin lost his smile. Perhaps he was remembering the beating he'd had at Temujin's hands on a night long before. Temujin sighed. She would be lucky to survive the trip back to his camp in the north. If she died, one of his brothers would have to find a wife among the Tartar women they captured.

Arslan took the reins and Temujin mounted, looking down at Borte. The wooden saddle did not have room for two, so he held out an arm and she scrambled up to sit across his lap, clutching her bag to her. Arslan did the same with the girl who coughed. Her sister would have to walk behind them. Temujin realized he should have brought other ponies, but it was too late for regrets.

He nodded to Sholoi, knowing they would not meet again.

"Your word is good, old man," he said.

"Look after her," Sholoi replied, though his gaze did not leave his daughter.

Without replying, Temujin turned with Arslan and they made their way back through the camp, the girl of the Olkhun'ut trotting behind.

CHAPTER 22

ARSLAN HAD THE GOOD SENSE to leave them alone that first night. The swordsmith was still brooding about the loss of his blades and preferred to take a bow and hunt while Temujin came to know the woman of the Olkhun'ut. The sister who had walked was footsore and weary by the time they stopped that evening. Temujin learned that her name was Eluin and that she was used to tending to her sister, Makhda, when she was weak from her sickness. Temujin left the pair of them with the ponies after they had eaten, but he could still hear Makhda's barking cough come at intervals. They had the horse blankets to protect them against the cold, though neither sister seemed particularly hardy. If Makhda lived long enough to reach the north, Temujin thought his mother might be able to find herbs for her, but it was a slim hope.

Borte hardly spoke as Temujin unrolled a blanket on the ground by the crackling fire. He was used to sleeping with nothing but his deel to protect him from the frost, but it did not seem right to ask her to do the same. He did not know the life she was used to, nor how Sholoi had treated her after Temujin had gone. He had not grown up around sisters and was uncomfortable with her in a way he did not fully understand.

He had wanted to talk and listen to her as they rode, but she'd sat straight-backed and stiff, rocking with the motion and staring at the horizon. He had missed the chance to open a conversation naturally, and now there seemed to be a strain between them that he could not ease.

When Arslan returned from his hunt, he played the part of a manservant with his usual efficiency. He butchered a marmot he had caught, roasting the strips of flesh until they were brown and delicious. After that, he took himself off somewhere nearby, lost in the gathering gloom. Temujin waited for some sign of Arslan's acceptance of his trade for a wife, but there was nothing but grim silence from the older man.

As the stars turned around their northern point, Temujin began to fidget, unable to make himself comfortable. He had seen the smoothness of Borte's tanned skin as she washed her face and arms in a stream cold enough to make her teeth chatter. They were good teeth, he had noticed, strong and white. For a while, he considered complimenting her on them, but it seemed a little like admiring a new pony and the words wouldn't come. He could not pretend he didn't want her under a blanket with him, but the years apart sat between them like a wall. If she had asked, he would have told her everything he had done since the last time they met, but she did not, and he didn't know how to begin.

As he lay there under the stars, he hoped she would

hear the way he puffed air out in great sighs, but if she did, she made no sign she was even awake. He might have been alone in the world, and that was exactly how he felt. He imagined staying awake until dawn so that she would see his tiredness and feel sorry for ignoring him. It was an interesting idea, but he couldn't keep the sense of injured nobility for very long.

"Are you awake?" he said suddenly, without thinking. He saw her sit up under the stars.

"How could I sleep, with you huffing and blowing to yourself like that?" she replied.

He recalled the last time he had heard that voice in the dark and the touch of her hand on his cheek. The idea was exciting and he felt his body grow hot under his deel, despite the frozen air.

"I had an idea we would spend the first night under a blanket together," he said. Despite his best intentions, it came out as an irritable complaint, and he heard her snort before she replied.

"Who could resist such sweet words?" she replied.

He waited hopefully, but her continuing silence was enough of an answer. Apparently, she could. He sighed, catching himself in the sound as he heard her giggle, quickly stifled in the blanket. In the darkness, he smiled, suddenly amused.

"I have thought about you many times in the years away," he said. He saw her shape move then and guessed she had turned to him. He lay on his side facing her and scratched his nose where the damp grass tickled his skin.

"How many times?" she murmured.

He thought for a moment. "Eleven," he said. "Twelve, including tonight."

"You did not think of me," she told him. "What do you remember of who I was?"

"I remember you had a pleasant voice, and a lump of snot underneath your nose," he said, with such a ring of casual truth that it reduced her to stunned silence.

"I waited for you to come and take me away from my father for a long time," she said at last. "There were evenings when I dreamed of you riding up, full grown as a khan of the Wolves."

Temujin tensed in the darkness. Was that what it was? Had his new status made him less in her eyes? He raised himself on an elbow to reply, but she went on, unaware of his fast-changing moods.

"I turned down three young men of the Olkhun'ut," she said, "the last when my mother was ill and not likely to survive the winter. The women laughed at the girl who pined for a Wolf, and still I walked proudly amongst them."

"You knew I would come," Temujin said, with a touch of smugness.

She snorted. "I thought you were dead, but I did not want to be married off to some horse boy of the gers, to bear his children. They laughed at my pride, but it was all I had."

He stared into the gloom, trying to understand the struggle she had faced, perhaps as great in its way as his own. If he had learned anything in his life, it was that there are some who thrive on loneliness and take strength from it. They were vital, dangerous people and they cherished whatever kept them apart. Borte was one of those, it seemed. He was himself. He thought of his mother for a moment. She had told him to be kind.

"The first time I came to the Olkhun'ut, you were

given to me, accepted by my father," he said softly. "The second time, I came of my own will to find you."

"You wanted to put your seed in me," she said tightly.

He wished he could see her face in the darkness.

"I did," he said. "I want your spirit in my sons and daughters: the best of the Olkhun'ut. The best of the Wolves."

He heard a rustle and felt the warmth of her as she crept close and pulled her blanket over them both.

"Tell me I am beautiful," she whispered in his ear, exciting him.

"You are," he replied, his voice becoming hoarse. He moved his hands on her in the blackness, opening her deel and feeling the smoothness of her belly. "Your teeth are very white." He heard her chuckle into his ear at that, but her own hands moved on him and he had no more words, nor needed them.

The following day was strangely vivid as Temujin rode with Borte. His senses seemed heightened and almost painful. Every time their flesh touched, he thought of the night before and the nights to come, thrilled by the experiences and the closeness.

They did not make good progress, though Arslan took the reins and let both sisters ride together for most of the afternoon. They stopped to hunt and, between the two bows, they had enough meat to roast each night. Makhda's cough seemed to be growing worse away from the shelter of the Olkhun'ut gers, and her sister could be heard sobbing whenever she tended her. Arslan spoke kindly to them both, but as the first month ended, Makhda had to be tied into the saddle so that she would not fall from weakness. Though they did not speak of it, none of them expected her to live much longer.

The green of the land was fading as they rode north, and one morning, Temujin woke to see snow falling. He was wrapped in blankets with Borte and they had slept heavily, worn out by the cold and the endless plains. Seeing the snow brought a little ice back to Temujin's spirit, marking the end of a happy time, perhaps happier than he had ever known. He knew he was returning to hardship and fighting, to leading his brothers into a war with the Tartars. Borte sensed the new distance in him and retreated from it, so that they spent hours each day in weary silence, where before they had chattered like birds.

It was Arslan who saw the wanderers first in the distance, his voice snapping Temujin out of his reverie. Three men had gathered a small herd in the lee of a hill and pitched a grubby ger there against the winter cold. Ever since Sansar had taken their swords, Temujin had feared such a meeting. With Borte in his arms, he swore softly to himself. In the distance, the strangers mounted quickly, kicking their ponies into a gallop. Perhaps their intentions were peaceful, but the sight of three young women would excite them to violence. Temujin drew rein and lowered Borte to the ground. He removed his bow from its wrapping and fitted his best remaining string, pulling away the cap of his quiver. Arslan was ready, he saw. The swordsmith had cut the rope holding Makhda in the saddle, leaving her to sit on the frozen ground with her sister. As he mounted in her place, he and Temujin exchanged a glance.

"Do we wait?" Arslan called.

Temujin watched the galloping warriors and wished he had a sword. Three poor wanderers would not own a long blade between them and it would have been enough to make the outcome certain. As it was, he and Arslan could be left for the birds in just a few bloody moments. It was less of a risk to attack.

"No," he shouted back over the wind. "We kill them."

He heard the sisters moaning in fear behind as he kicked in his heels and readied his bow. Despite himself, there was an exhilaration in riding with only his knees, perfectly balanced to send death from his bow.

The distance between them seemed long as they raced along the plain, then suddenly they were close and the wind was roaring in their ears. Temujin listened to the sound of his pony's hooves striking the ground, feeling the rhythm. There was a point in the galloping stride where all four hooves left the ground for just a heartbeat. Yesugei had taught him to loose on that instant, so that his aim was always perfect.

The men they faced had not suffered through years of such training. They misjudged the distance in their excitement and the first shafts whined overhead before Temujin and Arslan reached them. The hooves thundered and again and again there was that moment of freedom when the ponies flew. Temujin and Arslan loosed together, the shafts vanishing away.

The warrior Arslan had marked fell hard from the saddle, punched off it by an arrow through his chest. His mount whinnied wildly, kicking out and bucking. Temujin's strike was as clean, and the second man spun free to thump unmoving onto the frozen ground.

Temujin saw the third release his arrow as they passed by each other at full speed, aimed right at Temujin's chest.

He threw himself sideways. The shaft passed above him, but he had fallen too far and could not pull himself up. He cried out in anger as his foot slipped from the stirrup and he found himself clinging almost under his pony's heaving neck at full gallop. The ground sped by underneath him as he yanked cruelly on the reins, his full weight pulling the bit free of his pony's mouth so that he dropped another foot. For a few moments he was dragged along the icy earth, then with a huge effort of will he opened his hand on the reins and fell, trying desperately to roll out of the way of the crushing hooves.

The pony raced on without him, the sound dwindling to the silence of snow. Temujin lay on his back, listening to his own shuddering breath and gathering his wits. Everything ached and his hands were shaking. He blinked groggily as he sat up, looking back to see what had become of Arslan.

The swordsmith had put his second shaft into the chest of the warrior's pony, sending him tumbling over the ground. As Temujin watched, the stranger staggered to his feet, obviously dazed.

Arslan drew a knife from his deel and walked unhurriedly to finish the killing. Temujin tried to shout, but as he took a breath, his chest stabbed at him and he realized he had broken a rib in the fall. With an effort, he stood and filled his lungs.

"Hold, Arslan!" he called, wincing at the sharpness. The swordsmith heard and stood still, watching the man he had brought down. Temujin pressed a hand into his ribs, hunching over the pain as he walked back.

The wanderer watched him come with resignation. His companions lay in heaps, their ponies cropping at the ground with their reins tangled and loose. His own mount lay dying on the frost. As Temujin came closer he saw the wanderer walk to the kicking animal and plunge a knife into its throat. The flailing legs grew limp and blood came out in a red flood, steaming.

The stranger was short and powerfully muscled, Temujin saw, with very dark, reddish skin and eyes set back under a heavy brow. He was bundled in many layers against the cold and wore a square hat that came to a point. With a sigh, he stepped away from his dead pony and beckoned to Arslan with his bloody knife.

"Come and kill me, then," he said. "See what I have for you."

Arslan did not respond, though he turned to Temujin.

"What do you see happening here?" Temujin shouted to the man, closing the distance between them. He took his hand away from his side as he spoke and tried to straighten, though every breath sent a jolt of pain through him. The man looked at him as if he were insane.

"I expect to be killed as you killed my friends," he said. "Unless you are going to give me a pony and one of your women?"

Temujin chuckled, gazing over to where Borte sat with Eluin and Makhda. He thought he could hear the coughing even from far away.

"That can wait until after we have eaten," he said. "I grant you guest rights."

The man's face creased in amazement. "Guest rights?"

"Why not? It's your horse we'll be eating."

When they rode out the following morning, the sisters were mounted on the ponies and they had another warrior for the raids against the Tartars. The newcomer did not trust Temujin at all, but with luck, his doubt and confusion would last long enough to reach the camp in the snows. If it did not, he would be given a quick death.

The wind tore viciously at them, snow stinging as it was hurled into their eyes and against any exposed skin. Eluin sat on her knees in the snow, wailing at the side of her sister's body. Makhda had not had an easy death. The constant cold had worsened the thickness in her lungs. For the previous moon, every morning had begun with Eluin thumping at her back and chest until great red clots of blood and phlegm were torn loose enough for her to spit. When she was too weak, Eluin had used her fingers to clear her sister's mouth and throat, while Makhda watched in terror and choked, desperate for another sip of the frozen air. Her skin had grown waxlike, and on the last day, they could hear her straining, as if she breathed through a whistling reed. Temujin had marveled at her endurance and more than once considered giving her a quick end with a knife across her throat. Arslan had pressed him to do it, but Makhda shook her head wearily every time he offered, right to the end.

They had been traveling for almost three months away from the Olkhun'ut when she slumped in the saddle, leaning to the side against the ropes, so that Eluin could not pull her upright. Arslan had lowered her down then and Eluin had begun to sob, the sound almost lost in the face of the howling wind.

"We must go on," Borte told Eluin, laying a hand on her shoulder. "Your sister is gone from here now."

Eluin nodded, red-eyed and silent. She arranged her sister's body with the hands crossed on her chest. The snow would cover her, perhaps before the wild animals found another meal, in their own struggle to survive.

Still weeping, Eluin allowed Arslan to lift her into the saddle. She looked back at the tiny figure for a long time before distance hid her from sight. Temujin saw Arslan had given her a spare shirt that she wore under her deel. They were all cold despite the layers and the furs. Exhaustion was close, but Temujin knew his camp could not be far away. The Pole Star had risen as they traveled north, and he judged that they had come into Tartar lands. At least the snow hid them from their enemies, as well as it hid them from his brothers and Jelme.

As they rested the ponies and trudged through the snow on frozen feet, Borte walked with Temujin, their arms entwined in each other's wide sleeves, so that at least one part of them felt warm.

"You will have to find a shaman to marry us," Borte said without looking at him.

They walked with their heads bowed against the wind and snow crusted on their eyebrows like winter demons. He grunted assent and she felt his grip tighten briefly on her arm.

"My blood has not come this month," she said.

He nodded vaguely, putting one foot in front of the other. The horses were skeletal without good grass and they too would be falling soon. Surely it was time to ride them again for a few hours? His legs ached and his broken rib still pained him with every jerk of the reins.

He drew up short in the snow and turned to her.

"You are pregnant?" he said incredulously.

Borte leaned forward and rubbed her nose against his.

"Perhaps. There has been so little food, and sometimes the blood doesn't come because of that. I think I am, though." She saw him surface from his walking trance and a smile come to his eyes.

"It will be a strong son to have had his beginnings on such a journey," he said. The wind roared in a great gust as he spoke, so that they had to turn away. They could not see the sun, but the day was fading and he shouted to Arslan to look for shelter.

As Arslan began to scout around them for somewhere out of the wind, Temujin caught a glimpse of movement through the sheets of snow. He felt a prickle of danger at his neck and gave a low whistle for Arslan to come back. The wanderer looked quizzically at him and drew his knife in silence, staring into the snow.

The three of them waited in tense silence for Arslan to return while the snow whipped and flailed around them. They were almost blind in its midst, but again Temujin thought he saw the shape of a mounted man, a shadow. Borte asked him a question, but he did not hear it as he shook ice from the wrappings around his bow and attached the horsehide string to one end. With a grunt of effort, he realized the string had grown damp despite the oilcloth. He managed to fit the loop over the nocked end, but it creaked ominously and he thought it could easily snap on the first pull. Where was Arslan? He could hear the rumble of horses galloping nearby, the sound echoing in the whiteness until he could not be sure which way they were coming. With an arrow on the string, he spun, listening. They were closer. He heard the wanderer give a hiss of breath through his teeth, readying himself for an attack. Temujin noted how the man held his ground, and he gave thanks that there was one more with courage to stand at his side. Temujin raised the creaking bow. He saw dark shapes and heard shouting voices, and for a heartbeat, he imagined the Tartars coming for his head.

"Here!" he heard a voice. "They are here!"

Temujin almost dropped the bow in relief as he recognized Kachiun and knew he was back amongst his people. He stood numbly as Kachiun leapt from his saddle into the snow and thumped into him, embracing his brother.

"It has been a good winter, Temujin," Kachiun said, hammering him excitedly on the back with his gloved hand. "Come and see."

CHAPTER 23

TEMUJIN AND THE OTHERS MOUNTED for the last mile, though their ponies were dropping in exhaustion. The camp they came to was set against the dark face of an ancient landslip, sheltered from the worst of the wind by an overhang above and the hill at their back. Two dozen gers clustered there like lichen, with wild dogs and tethered ponies in every available spot out of the wind. Despite aching for rest and hot food, Temujin could not help glancing around at the bustling place hidden away in the snow. He could see Jelme kept the camp on a war footing. Warriors on their way to a long watch strode by with their heads down against the wind. There were far more men than women and children, Temujin noticed, seeing the camp with the fresh eyes of a stranger. That was a blessing when they were ready to ride and fight at a moment's notice, but it could not go on forever. Men followed their leaders to war, but they wanted a home to return to, with a woman's touch in the dark and children round their feet like puppies.

Those who had known hunger and fear as wanderers might be satisfied with the fledgling tribe in the snow, though even then they were as wary of each other as wild dogs. Temujin repressed his impatience. The wanderers would learn to see a brother where once had stood an enemy. They would learn the sky father knew only one people and saw *no* tribes. It would come in time, he promised himself.

As he walked through the camp, he became more alert, shrugging off his weariness as the details caught his interest. He saw watchers high on the cliff above his head, bundled against the wind. He did not envy them and he thought they would see little in the constant snow. Still, it showed Jelme's thoroughness and Temujin was pleased. The camp had a sense of urgency in every movement, rather than the usual winter lethargy that affected the tribes. He felt the suppressed excitement as soon as he was amongst them.

There were new faces there, men and women who looked at him as if he were a stranger. He imagined they saw his ragged group as another wanderer family brought into the fold. Temujin looked at Borte to see how she was taking her first sight of his little tribe in the north. She too was pale with tiredness, but she rode close to his side and her sharp eyes took it all in. He could not tell if she approved. They passed a ger where Arslan had built a brick forge months before, and Temujin saw the glow from its flame, a tongue of light on the snow. There were men and women in there for the warmth, and he heard laughter as he trotted by. He turned to the swordsmith to see if he had noticed, but Arslan was oblivious. His gaze searched ceaselessly among the tribe, looking for his son.

Jelme came out to meet them as soon as he heard Kachiun shout. Khasar too came skidding from a different ger, beaming in delight at the sight of the small party who had been gone half a year. As they dismounted, grinning boys ran to take their ponies without having to be summoned. Temujin cuffed at one, making him duck. He was pleased with Jelme's stewardship of the tribe. They had not grown fat and slow in his absence.

Arslan's pride in his son was obvious and Temujin saw Jelme nod to his father. To Temujin's surprise, Jelme went down on one knee and reached out for Temujin's hand.

"No, Jelme, stand up," Temujin said, half irritably. "I want to get out of the wind."

Jelme remained where he was, though he raised his head.

"Let the new men see, my lord khan. They do not know you yet."

Temujin understood and his appreciation of Jelme went up a degree. Some of the wanderer families would have known Jelme as the closest thing to a khan for the months Temujin had been away. It was important to show them the true leader had returned. He did not argue again, and allowed Jelme to place his hand on his head before lifting him up and embracing him.

"Did you find a shaman amongst these new arrivals?" Temujin asked.

Jelme winced at the question as he rose. "There is one, though he stole the supply of airag and bargains his ration for more whenever he can."

"Keep him sober for a few days, then," Temujin said. "As long as he can dedicate my marriage to the sky father and earth mother, I'll keep him drunk for a month afterwards."

He looked around him once more, seeing how many faces had stopped in the snow and wind to watch the scene. As he caught the eyes of those he knew, they bowed their heads in acknowledgment. Jelme's gaze fell on Borte and Eluin and he bowed low at the waist.

"We are honored to have you with us, daughters of the Olkhun'ut," he said.

Borte did not know what to make of the confident stranger. She dipped her head jerkily in return, flushing as she looked away. Nothing in her life had prepared her to be treated with respect, and for a moment, she had to blink back tears.

Released from the formalities of his welcome, Jelme was finally free to take his father's arm and embrace him. "I have bled the Tartars," he told Arslan, struggling not to seem too proud. His father chuckled and slapped his son on the back. Perhaps in time, he too would become comfortable with the easy manner Temujin encouraged amongst his men.

"I am home," Temujin said, under his breath and unheard by the others. It was little more than a raiding camp on frozen ground, with barely enough food or shelter for any of them, but there was no question. He had brought Borte home.

"Take me to my mother, Jelme," he said, shivering in the wind. "She will be hungry for news of the Olkhun'ut." He caught a glimpse of Borte's nervousness at his words and sought to reassure her.

"She will welcome you, Borte, as if you were her own daughter."

As Jelme began to lead the way, Temujin saw the

raider he had taken under his wing standing uncomfortably on the outskirts of their little group. His mind swam with a hundred things to remember, but he could not leave the man standing amongst strangers.

"Kachiun? This is Barakh, a fine warrior. He needs work with the bow and he has never used a sword. He is brave and strong, however. See what you can make of him." He frowned to himself as he spoke, remembering yet another debt.

"Make sure that Arslan is given everything he needs to forge new swords. Have men sent out to dig for ore."

Kachiun nodded. "There is a seam in this hill. We have the gray stones piled ready for him. Jelme wouldn't let anyone touch it until his father returned."

Temujin saw that Arslan and his son were both listening.

"That was right," he said immediately. "Arslan will make two swords as great as any we have ever seen, is that not so?"

Arslan was still reeling from the pleasure of seeing his son alive and strong, a leader of men. He bowed his head.

"I will make them," he said.

"Now, by the sky father, let us get out of this wind," Temujin said. "I thought it would be spring by now."

Khasar shrugged. "We think this is the spring, as far north as we are. I am enjoying the milder weather, myself."

Temujin looked around at Khasar, Kachiun, Jelme, and Arslan. They were fine warriors and his heart soared at the thought of what they might accomplish together. He was home.

Hoelun had a ger to herself, with a young girl from the wanderer families to help her. She was in the process of rubbing clean mutton fat into her skin when she heard the commotion. Her servant went out into the snow for news, returning red-faced and gasping from the cold.

"Your son is in the camp, mistress," she said.

Hoelun let the pot of grease fall from her hands and wiped them on an old cloth. She made a clicking sound in her throat to hurry the girl along as she held out her arms and shrugged herself into the deel. The strength of her emotions surprised her, but her heart had leapt at the news. Temujin had survived again. Though she could not forget what he had done in the darkest times, he was still her son. Love was a strange and twisted thing for any mother, beyond all reason.

By the time she heard his voice outside, Hoelun had composed herself, taking little Temulun on her lap and combing her hair to calm her shaking hands. The girl seemed to sense her mother's strange mood and looked around wide-eyed when the door opened. Temujin brought the winter in with him in a gust of snow and bitter air that made Hoelun shiver and Temulun cry out with happiness at the older brother she had not seen for such a long time.

Hoelun watched as Temujin embraced his sister, complimenting her on her beautiful hair, as he always did. The girl chattered while Hoelun drank in every detail of the young man who inspired such mixed feelings in her. Whether he knew it or not, he was very much the son Yesugei would have wanted. In her darkest moments, she knew Yesugei would have approved the death of Bekter when they were close to starving. Her sons had inherited their father's ruthlessness, or perhaps had it hammered into them by the lives they had led.

"It is good to see you, my son," Hoelun said formally. Temujin only smiled, turning aside to bring in a tall young woman and another behind her. Hoelun's eyes widened as she took in the delicate features of her own people. It brought a pang of homesickness, surprising after so many years. She rose and took the two younger women by their hands, bringing them into the warmth. Temulun came to join them, snuggling in between and demanding to know who they were.

"More wood on the fire there," Hoelun told her girl. "You must both be freezing. Which of you is Borte?"

"I am, Mother," Borte responded shyly. "Of the Olkhun'ut."

"I knew that from your face and the markings on your deel," Hoelun said as she turned to the other. "And you, daughter, what is your name?"

Eluin was still stunned with grief, but she did her best to reply. Hoelun sensed her misery and embraced her on an impulse. She brought them both to where they could sit, calling for bowls of hot tea to warm them. Temulun was kept quiet with a bag of sweet yoghurt curds and sat in the corner, digging deeply into it. Temujin watched as the women of the Olkhun'ut talked together and was pleased to see Borte begin to smile at his mother's recollections. Hoelun understood their fears amongst the strangeness. She had felt the same way herself, once. While they thawed, she questioned them endlessly, her voice slipping into an old accent Temujin recognized from the Olkhun'ut. It was strange to hear it from his mother, and he was reminded again of the life she had led before Yesugei or her children.

"Is Sansar still the khan? What of my nephew, Koke, and his father, Enq?"

Borte answered Hoelun easily, responding to her motherly ways without embarrassment. Temujin looked on with pride, as if he were responsible. His mother seemed to have forgotten him, so he seated himself and nodded to the servant girl for a bowl of tea, accepting it gratefully and closing his eyes in pleasure as its warmth worked through him. Eluin too began to join the conversation and he allowed himself to relax at last and close his eyes

"...this cannot go on much longer, this storm," he heard his mother saying. "The thaw has already begun and the hill passes have begun to clear."

"I don't think I've ever been so cold," Borte replied, rubbing her hands together. The women seemed to like each other and Temujin settled back gratefully.

"I brought Eluin to be a wife to Khasar or Kachiun. Her sister died on the trip," he said, opening his eyes a fraction. Both women looked at him, then the conversation began again as if he had not spoken. He snorted softly to himself. No man could be a khan to his mother. The warmth made him drowsy and, with their soft voices in his ears, he dropped off to sleep.

Kachiun and Khasar sat in a neighboring ger, chewing on hot mutton that had been simmering in broth for the best part of a day. With the cold, it was necessary to keep a stew on the fire the whole time so that there was always a bowl to warm them before they went out again.

There had been little chance to relax while Temujin was away. The brothers tolerated Jelme's orders with good nature, knowing it was what Temujin would have wanted. In private, though, they dropped all masks and pretenses, talking long into the night.

"I liked the look of that Eluin," Khasar said.

Kachiun rose to the bait immediately, as his brother had known he would. "*Your* girl died, Khasar. Eluin was promised to me and you know it."

"I don't know anything like it, little brother. The eldest gets his tea and stew first, have you noticed? It is the same with wives."

Kachiun snorted, half in amusement. He had seen Eluin first, when he rode out to answer the scout's call. He had hardly noticed her then, bundled up against the cold, but he felt it gave him some sort of finder's rights. It was certainly a stronger claim than Khasar's, who had just stumbled out of a ger and met her.

"Temujin will decide," he said.

Khasar nodded, beaming. "I am glad we will not argue. I am the eldest, after all."

"I said he will decide, not choose you," Kachiun replied, sourly.

"She was pretty, I thought. With long legs."

"What could you see of her legs? She looked like a yak in all those layers."

Khasar looked off into the distance. "She was tall, Kachiun, didn't you notice? Unless you think her feet don't reach to the ground, there must be long legs in there somewhere. Strong legs to wrap around a man, if you know what I mean."

"Temujin could marry her to Jelme," Kachiun replied, more to sting his brother than because he believed it.

Khasar shook his head. "Blood comes first," he said. "Temujin knows that better than anyone."

"If you took a moment to listen to him, you'd hear he claims a blood tie to every man and woman in camp, regardless of tribe or family," Kachiun said. "By the spirits, Khasar, you think more of your stomach and loins than of what he's trying to do here."

The two brothers stared balefully at each other.

"If you mean I don't follow him around like a lost dog, then you're right," Khasar said. "Between you and Jelme, he has his own adoring little pack these days."

"You are an idiot," Kachiun told him, slowly and deliberately.

Khasar flushed. He knew he lacked the keen intelligence of Temujin and perhaps even Kachiun, but the world would freeze solid before he would admit it.

"Perhaps you should go and lie at the door of our mother's ger in the snow," he said. "You could press your nose up against it, or something."

Both of them had killed men, with Temujin and with Jelme, yet when they came together, it was with the roaring energy of two boys, all elbows and red-faced struggle. Neither one reached for their knives and Khasar quickly had Kachiun's head locked under his arm and was shaking him.

"Say you are his dog," Khasar said, breathing heavily with the exertion. "Quickly, I'm on watch next."

"I saw Eluin first and she's mine," Kachiun said as he choked.

Khasar squeezed even tighter. "Say you would

prefer her to bed your handsome older brother," he demanded.

Kachiun struggled violently and they fell together against a bed, breaking Khasar's grip. Both of them lay panting, watching each other warily.

"I don't care if I am his dog," Kachiun said. "Neither does Jelme." He took a deep breath in case his brother launched himself at him again. "Neither do you."

Khasar shrugged.

"I like killing Tartars, but if they keep sending old women out with their raiders, I don't know what I'm going to do. Even Arslan managed to find himself a pretty young thing before he left."

"Is she still refusing you?" Kachiun asked.

Khasar frowned. "She said Arslan would kill me if I touched her, and I think she could be right. There's one I don't want to cross."

Arslan stood in the ger he had constructed around his forge, letting the warmth seep into his bones. His precious tools had been oiled and wrapped against rust, and he found nothing to complain about as he faced Jelme.

"You have done well here, my son. I saw how the other men looked to you. Perhaps it was the sky father who guided us to the Wolves."

Jelme shrugged. "That is in the past. I have found a purpose here, Father, a place. I am concerned with the future now, if this winter ever comes to an end. I've never seen one like it."

"In all your many years," Arslan replied, smiling. Jelme seemed to have grown in confidence away from him, and he did not know quite how to take the strong young warrior who faced him so calmly. Perhaps he had needed the absence of his father to become a man. It was a sobering thought, and Arslan did not want to be sober.

"Can you find me a skin or two of airag while we talk?" he said. "I want to hear about the raids."

Jelme reached inside his ger and produced a fat skin of the potent liquid.

"I have arranged for hot stew to be brought to us," he said. "It's thin, but we still have a little meat dried and salted."

Both men stood against the forge, relaxing in the heat. Arslan untied his deel to let the warmth get through.

"I saw your swords had gone," Jelme said.

Arslan grunted irritably. "They were the price for the women Temujin brought back."

"I'm sorry," Jelme said. "You will make others just as fine, or better."

Arslan frowned. "Each one is a month of solid work, and that doesn't include the time digging ore or making the ingots of iron. How many more do I have left in me, do you think? I won't live forever. How many times can I get just the right steel and work it without flaws?" He spat on the forge and watched it bubble gently, not yet hot enough to skitter away. "I thought you would inherit the blade I carried."

"Perhaps I will yet, if we grow strong enough to take it from the Olkhun'ut," Jelme replied.

His father turned away from the forge and stared at him.

"Is that what you think? That this small group of raiders will sweep across the land in the spring?"

Jelme met his gaze stubbornly, but did not reply. Arslan snorted.

"I brought you up to have more sense than that. Think tactically, Jelme, as I taught you. We have, what, thirty warriors at most? How many have been trained from their earliest years as you were, as Temujin and his brothers were?"

"None of them, but—" Jelme began.

His father brought his hand down in a chopping gesture, his anger growing.

"The smallest tribes can field sixty to eighty men of good quality, Jelme, men who can take a bird on the wing with their bows, men with good swords and knowledge enough to form horns in the attack, or to retreat in good order. I would not trust this camp to stage an attack on a fifth of the Olkhun'ut warriors. Do not be deceived! This frozen little place will need the sky father's blessing to survive a single season after the thaw. The Tartars will come howling, looking for revenge for whatever petty damage they have suffered in the winter."

Jelme set his jaw tight at that and glared at his father.

"We have taken horses, weapons, food, even swords—"

Once again, his father silenced him.

"Blades I could bend in my hands! I know the quality of Tartar weapons, boy."

"Stop it!" Jelme suddenly roared at his father. "You know nothing of what we have done. You haven't even given me the chance to tell you before you are away with your warnings and prophecies of doom. Yes, we may be destroyed in the spring. I have done what I could to build them and train them while you were away. How many men have you taken on to work the forge and learn your skill? I have not heard of a single one."

Arslan opened his mouth, but Jelme had worked himself into a fury and there was no stopping him.

"Would you have me give up and lie in the snow? This is the path I have chosen. I have found a man to follow and I gave my oath. My word is iron, Father, as you told me it must be. Did you mean that it was strong only while the odds were on your side? No. You've taught me too well, if you expect me to give up on these people. I have a place, I told you, no matter how it comes out." He paused, taking deep breaths from the force of his emotion. "I have made the Tartars fear us, just as I said I would. I hoped you would be proud of me and instead you blow like a windy old man with your fears."

Arslan did not mean to strike him. His son was standing too close and when he moved his hands, Arslan reacted from instinct, snapping out an iron-hard fist to crack against his son's jaw. Jelme fell, dazed, his shoulder striking the edge of the forge.

Arslan watched, appalled, as Jelme took a moment and rose with icy calm. His son rubbed at his jaw and his face was very pale.

"Do not do that again," Jelme said softly, his eyes hard.

"It was a mistake, my son," Arslan replied. "It was worry and weariness, nothing more." He looked as if he felt the pain himself.

Jelme nodded. He had suffered worse in their practice bouts together, but there was still anger running through him and it was hard to shake it off.

"Train men to make swords," Jelme said, making it an order. "We will need every last one of them, and as you say, you will not live forever. None of us does." He rubbed his jaw again, wincing as it clicked.

"I have found something of worth here," he said, trying hard to make his father understand. "The tribes fight amongst themselves and waste their strength. Here, we have shown a man can begin again and it does not matter whether he was once a Naiman or a Wolf."

Arslan saw a strange light in his son's eyes and was worried by it. "He gives them food in their bellies and, for a little while, they forget old feuds and hatreds. That is what I am seeing here!" he snapped at his son. "The tribes have fought for a thousand years. You think one man can cut through all that history, that hatred?"

"What is the alternative?" Temujin said from the door.

Both men spun to face him and he glanced at the dark bruise on Jelme's jaw, understanding it in an instant.

He looked exhausted as he came to stand by the forge.

"I could not sleep with three women and my sister chattering like birds, so I came here."

Neither son nor father replied and Temujin went on, closing his eyes as the warmth reached him.

"I do not ask for blind followers, Arslan," he said. "You are right to question our purpose here. You see a ragged group with barely enough food to get through to the thaw. Perhaps we could find ourselves a valley somewhere and raise herds and children while the tribes continue to roam and butcher each other."

"You won't tell me you care how many strangers die in those battles," Arslan said with certainty.

Temujin fixed his yellow eyes on the swordsmith, seeming to fill the small space of the ger.

"We feed the soil with our blood, our endless feuding," he said after a time. "We always have, but that does not mean we always should. I have shown that a tribe can come from the Quirai, the Wolves, the Woyela, the Naimans. We are one people, Arslan. When we are strong enough, I will *make* them come to me, or I will break them one at a time. I tell you we are one people. We are *Mongols,* Arslan. We are the silver people and one khan can lead us all."

"You are drunk, or dreaming," Arslan replied, ignoring his son's discomfort. "What makes you think they would ever accept you?"

"I am the land," Temujin replied. "And the land sees no difference in the families of our people." He looked from one to the other. "I do not ask for your loyalty. You gave me that with your oath and it binds you until death. It may be that we will all be killed in the attempt, but you are not the men I think you are if that will stop you." He chuckled to himself for a moment, knuckling his eyes against the weariness made worse by the warmth.

"I climbed for an eagle chick once. I could have stayed on the ground, but the prize was worth the risk. It turned out that there were two of them, so I was luckier than I had hoped to be." His chuckle seemed bitter, though he did not explain. He clapped father and son on the shoulder.

"Now stop this bickering and *climb* with me," he said. He paused for a moment to see how they took his words, then went back out into the cold snow to find somewhere to sleep.

CHAPTER 24

WEN CHAO KEPT A CLOSE EYE on his servants through the hangings of the litter as they struggled under its weight. With three men to each wooden handle, the labor should have been just enough to keep them warm, but when he glanced out of the silk awning, he noticed more than one was growing blue around the lips. He had not moved before the winter snow had begun to melt, but there was still crunching ice underfoot and the wind was cruel. He suspected he would lose another slave before they reached the Mongol camp, if not two. He pulled his furs around him and wondered peevishly if they would find the camp at all.

He amused himself for a time by cursing Togrul, the khan of the Kerait, who had claimed to know where the raiding band were waiting out the winter. With a little more heat and imagination, he practiced even more complicated insults for the members of the Chin court in Kaifeng.

He had known he had been outmaneuvered from

the moment he laid eyes on the expressions of the eunuchs. They were as bad as gossipy old women, and there was little that went on in the court that they did not hear. Wen remembered the acid delight in little Zhang, the first amongst them, as he had ushered him into the presence of the first minister.

Wen pursed his lips in irritation at the memory. He prided himself on his expertise in the games of power, but there it was. He had been lulled by a woman of the best Willow house in Kaifeng and missed just one important meeting. He sighed at the thought of her skill, remembering every wanton touch and the peculiar thing she had tried to do with a feather. He hoped her services had cost his enemies dearly, at least. When he had been summoned from her bed in the middle of the night, he had known immediately that he would pay for his pleasures. Ten years of cleverness had been wasted by one drunken night of poetry and love. It hadn't been good poetry, either, he reflected. The minister had announced a diplomatic mission to the barbarous tribes as if it were a great honor, and of course, Wen had been forced to smile and knock his head on the floor as if he had been given his heart's desire.

Two years later, he was still waiting to be recalled. Away from the machinations and games of the Chin court, no doubt he had been forgotten. He addressed copies of his reports to trusted friends with instructions to send them on, but it was likely none of them was ever read. It was no great chore to lose them amongst the thousands of scribes who tended the court of the Middle Kingdom, not for one as devious as Zhang, at least.

Although Wen refused to despair, there was a

chance he would end his days among the ugly Mongol tribes, frozen to death or poisoned by their endless rancid mutton and sour milk. It was really too much for a man of his position and advanced years. He had taken barely a dozen servants, as well as his guards and litter-bearers, but the winter had proved too much for the weaker ones, passing them back into the wheel of life for their next reincarnation. Remembering the way his personal scribe had caught a fever and died still made him furious. The man had sat down in the snow and refused to go on. One of the guards had kicked him, on Wen's instructions, but the little fellow gave up the spirit with every sign of spiteful pleasure as he died.

Wen hoped fervently that he would return as a scrubber of floors, or a pony that would be beaten regularly and with much enthusiasm. Now that the man was gone, Wen could only regret the beatings he had not inflicted himself. There was never enough time, even for the most conscientious of masters.

He heard the thumping rhythm of hoofbeats and considered twitching back the hanging that kept out the wind from his litter, before thinking better of it. No doubt it would be the guards reporting a complete lack of sign, as they had done for the previous twelve days. When he heard them shout, his old heart thumped with relief, though it was beneath him to show it. Was he not the fifth cousin of the Emperor's second wife? He was. Instead, he reached for one of his most annotated scrolls and read the words of philosophy, finding calm in their simple thoughts. He had never been comfortable with the high moral tone of Confucius himself, but his disciple Xun Zi was a man Wen would have liked to take for a drink. It was his words he turned to most often when his mood was low.

Wen ignored the excited chatter of his guards as they decided who should disturb him in his solitary splendor. Xun Zi believed the path to excellence was the path of enlightenment, and Wen was considering a delicious parallel in his own life. He was just reaching for his writing tools when the litter was laid down and he heard a nervous throat being cleared near his ear. He sighed. The travel had been dull, but the thought of mingling once more with unwashed tribesmen would try his patience to the limit. All this for one night of debauchery, he thought, as he moved the hanging aside and stared into the face of his most trusted guard.

"Well, Yuan, we seem to have stopped," he said, letting his long fingernails click on the parchment in his hand to show his displeasure. Yuan was crouching by the litter and dropped flat as soon as Wen spoke, pressing his forehead against the icy ground. Wen sighed audibly.

"You may speak, Yuan. If you do not, we will be here all day." In the distance, he heard the mournful note of warning horns on the wind. Yuan glanced back in the direction he'd ridden from.

"We found them, master. They are coming."

Wen nodded. "You are first among my guards, Yuan. When they have finished blustering and yelping, let me know."

He let the silk hanging fall back into place and began tying his scrolls in their scarlet ribbons. He heard the rumble of approaching horses and felt the tickle of curiosity become overwhelming. With a sigh at his own weakness, Wen slid back the spyhole in the wooden edge of the litter, peering through it. Only Yuan knew it was there and he would say nothing. To the slaves, it would seem as if their master scorned the danger. It was important to present the right image for slaves, he thought, wondering if there was time to add a note to his own small thoughts on philosophy. He would have his work bound and sent back to be published, he promised himself. It was particularly critical of the role of eunuchs in the court of Kaifeng. As he squinted through the tiny hole, he thought it would be best to publish it anonymously.

Temujin rode with Arslan and Jelme on his flanks. Ten of his best men came with them, while Khasar and Kachiun had split smaller forces around the camp to look for a second attack.

From the first sighting, Temujin knew something was wrong with the little scene. He wondered why so many armed men seemed to be guarding a box. The men themselves were strange, though he recognized seasoned warriors when he saw them. Instead of attacking, they had formed a defensive square around the box to wait for his arrival. Temujin glanced at Arslan, with his eyebrows raised. Over the sound of the galloping hooves, Arslan was forced to shout.

"Tread carefully, my lord. It can only be a representative of the Chin, someone of rank."

Temujin looked back at the strange scene with renewed interest. He had heard of the great cities in the east, but never seen one of their people. They were said to swarm like flies and use gold as a building material, it was so common. Whoever it was, they were important enough to travel with a dozen guards and enough slaves to carry the lacquered box. In itself, that was a strange thing to see in the wilderness. It shone blackly and at its sides were draped hangings the color of the sun.

Temujin had an arrow on the string and was guiding his pony with his knees. He lowered the bow, giving a short call to those around him to do the same. If it was a trap, the Chin warriors would find they had made an error coming into those lands.

He reined in. For those with an eye to see it, his men kept their formation perfectly as they matched him. Temujin tied his bow neatly to the thong on his saddle, touched the hilt of his sword for luck, and rode up to the man at the center of the strange party.

He did not speak. Those lands were Temujin's by right and he did not have to explain his presence in them. His yellow gaze was steady on the warrior, and Temujin noted the overlapping armor with interest. Like the box itself, the panels were lacquered in a substance that shone like black water, the fastenings hidden by the design. It looked as if it would stop an arrow, and Temujin wondered how he could obtain a set to test.

The warrior watched Temujin from beneath the rim of a padded helmet, his face half covered by cheekpieces of iron. He looked ill to Temujin, a ghastly yellow color that spoke of too many evenings drinking. Yet the whites of his eyes were clear and he did not flinch from the sight of so many armed men as they waited for orders.

The silence stretched and Temujin waited. At last, the officer frowned and spoke.

"My master of the Jade Court wishes to speak with you," Yuan said stiffly, his accent strange to Temujin's ears. Like his master, Yuan disliked the warriors of the tribes. They had no discipline of the sort he understood, for all their ferocity. He saw them as ill-tempered hounds and it was undignified to have to converse with them like human beings.

"Is he hiding in that box?" Temujin asked.

The officer tensed and Temujin dropped his hand near the hilt of his sword. He had spent hundreds of evenings training with Arslan, and he did not fear a sudden clash of blades. Perhaps his amusement showed in his eyes, for Yuan restrained himself and sat like stone.

"I am to say a message from Togrul of the Kerait," Yuan continued.

Temujin reacted to the name with intense curiosity. He had heard it before and his camp contained three wanderers who had been banished from that tribe.

"Say your message then," Temujin replied.

The warrior spoke as if he were reciting, looking off into the far distance. "Trust these men and offer them guest rights in my name," Yuan said.

Temujin grinned suddenly, surprising the Chin soldier. "Perhaps that would be wise. Have you considered the alternative?"

Yuan looked back at Temujin, irritated. "There is no alternative. You have been given your orders."

Temujin laughed aloud at that, though he never lost his awareness of the soldier in reach of a sword.

"Togrul of the Kerait is not my khan," he said. "He does not give orders here." Still, his interest had grown in the party who had come into the lands around his war camp. The officer said nothing more, though he radiated tension.

"I might just have you all killed and take whatever is

in that fine box you are protecting," Temujin said, more to sting the man than anything else. To his surprise, the officer did not grow angry as he had before. Instead, a grim smile appeared on his face.

"You do not have enough men," Yuan replied with certainty.

As Temujin was about to respond, a voice from the box snapped an order in a language he could not understand. It sounded like the honking of geese, but the officer bowed his head immediately.

Temujin could not resist his curiosity any longer.

"Very well. I grant you guest rights in my home," he said. "Ride in with me so that my guards do not send arrows down your throat as you come." He saw that Yuan was frowning and spoke again. "Ride slowly and make no sudden gestures. There are men in my camp who do not like strangers."

Yuan raised a fist and the twelve bearers gripped the long handles and stood as one, gazing impassively forward. Temujin did not know what to make of any of it. He snapped orders to his men and took the lead with Arslan, while Jelme and the others trotted their ponies around the little group to bring up the rear.

As he came abreast with Arslan, Temujin leaned over in the saddle, his voice a murmur.

"You know these people?"

Arslan nodded. "I have met them before."

"Are they a threat to us?" Temujin watched as Arslan considered.

"They could be. They have great wealth and it is said their cities are vast. I do not know what they want with us, in this place."

"Or what game Togrul is playing," Temujin added.

Arslan nodded and they did not speak again as they rode.

Wen Chao waited until his litter had been placed on the ground and Yuan had come to the side. He had watched their arrival in the camp with interest and suppressed groans at the sight of the familiar gers and scrawny sheep. The winter had been hard and the people he saw had a pinched look to their faces. He could smell the mutton fat on the breeze long before he came to the camp, and he knew the odor would stay in his robes until they were washed and washed again. As Yuan drew back the silk hangings, Wen stepped out amongst them, breathing as shallowly as he possibly could. From experience, he knew he would get used to it, but he had yet to meet a tribesman who troubled to wash more than once or twice a year, and then only if he fell in a river. Nonetheless, he had a task to perform and, though he cursed little Zhang under his breath, he stepped out into the cold wind with as much dignity as he could muster.

Even if he had not seen how the other men deferred to the young one with the yellow eyes, Wen would have known him for the leader. In the court of Kaifeng, they knew of those who were "tigers in the reeds," those who had the warrior's blood running in them. This Temujin was one of those tigers, Wen decided, as soon as he faced those eyes. Such eyes they were! Wen had seen nothing like them.

The wind was bitter for one dressed in thin robes, but Wen showed no discomfort as he faced Temujin and bowed. Only Yuan would know the gesture was far short of the angle courtesy dictated, but it amused Wen to insult the barbarians. To his surprise, the raider merely watched the movement and Wen found himself prickling.

"My name is Wen Chao, ambassador of the Chin court of the Northern Sung. I am honored to be in your camp," he said. "Word of your battles with the Tartars has spread far across the land."

"And that brought you here in your little box, did it?" Temujin replied. He was fascinated by every aspect of the strange man waited upon by so many servants. He too had the yellow skin that looked ill to Temujin's eyes, but he bore himself well in the wind as it plucked at his robes. Temujin estimated his age as more than forty, though the skin was unlined. The Chin diplomat was a strange vision for those who had grown up in the tribes. He wore a green robe that seemed to shimmer. His hair was as black as their own, but scraped back on his head and held in a tail with a clasp of silver. To Temujin's astonishment, he saw that the man's hands ended in nails like claws that caught the light. Temujin wondered how long the man could stand the cold. He seemed not to notice it, but his lips were growing blue even as Temujin watched.

Wen bowed again before speaking.

"I bring greetings of the Jade Court. We have heard much of your success here, and there are many things to discuss. Your brother in the Kerait sends his greetings."

"What does Togrul want with me?" Temujin replied.

Wen fumed, feeling the cold bite at him. Would he not be invited into the warm gers? He decided to push a little.

"Have I not been granted guest rights, my lord? It is

not fitting to talk of great issues with so many ears around us."

Temujin shrugged. The man was clearly freezing and he wanted to hear what had brought him across a hostile plain before he passed out.

"You are welcome here"—he tasted the name on his tongue before mangling it horribly—"Wencho?"

The old man controlled a wince and Temujin smiled at his pride.

"Wen *Chao,* my lord," the diplomat replied. "The tongue must touch the roof of the mouth."

Temujin nodded. "Come in to the warmth then, Wen. I will have hot salt tea brought to you."

"Ah, the tea," Wen Chao murmured, as he followed Temujin into a ragged ger. "How I have missed it."

In the gloom, Wen seated himself and waited patiently until a bowl of hot tea was pressed into his hands by Temujin himself. The ger filled with men who stared at him uneasily, and Wen forced himself to breathe shallowly until he became used to the sweaty closeness of them. He longed for a bath, but such pleasures were long behind.

Temujin watched as Wen tasted the tea through pursed lips, clearly pretending to enjoy it.

"Tell me of your people," Temujin said. "I have heard they are very numerous."

Wen nodded, grateful for the chance to speak rather than sip.

"We are a divided kingdom. The southern borders hold more than sixty thousand souls under the Sung emperor," he said. "The northern Chin, perhaps the same."

Temujin blinked. The numbers were larger than he could imagine.

"I think you are exaggerating, Wen Chao," he replied, pronouncing the name correctly in his surprise.

Wen shrugged. "Who can be sure? The peasants breed worse than lice. There are more than a thousand officials in the Kaifeng court alone, and the official count took many months. I do not have the exact figure." Wen enjoyed the looks of astonishment that passed between the warriors.

"And you? Are you a khan amongst them?" Temujin persisted.

Wen shook his head. "I passed my . . ." He searched his vocabulary and found there was no word. "Struggles? No." He said a strange word. "It means sitting at a desk and answering questions with hundreds of others, first in a district, then in Kaifeng itself for the emperor's officials. I came first among all those who were tested that year." He looked into the depths of his memory and raised his bowl to his mouth. "It was a long time ago."

"Whose man are you, then?" Temujin said, trying to understand.

Wen smiled. "Perhaps the first minister of the civil service, but I think you mean the Sung emperors. They rule the north and south. Perhaps I will live to see both halves of the Middle Kingdom rejoined."

Temujin struggled to understand. As they stared at him, Wen placed his bowl down and reached inside his robe for a pouch. A collective tension stopped him.

"I am reaching for a picture, my lord, that is all."

Temujin gestured for him to continue, fascinated at the idea. He watched as Wen removed a packet of brightly colored papers and passed one to him. There were strange symbols on it, but in the middle was the face of a young man, glaring out. Temujin held the paper at different angles, astonished that the little face seemed to watch him.

"You have painters of skill," he admitted grudgingly.

"That is true, my lord, but the paper you hold was printed on a great machine. It has a value and is given in exchange for goods. With a few more like it, I could buy a good horse in the capital, or a young woman for the passage of a night."

He saw Temujin pass it around to the others and watched their expressions with interest. They were like children, he thought. Perhaps he should give them each a note as a gift before he left.

"You use words I do not know," Temujin said. "What is the printing you mentioned? A great machine? Perhaps you have decided to fool us in our gers."

He did not speak lightly, and Wen reminded himself that the tribesmen could be ruthless even with their friends. If they thought for a moment that he was mocking them, he would not survive. If they were children, it was best to remember they were deadly as well.

"It is just a way of painting faster than one man alone," Wen said soothingly. "Perhaps you will visit Chin territory one day and see for yourself. I know that the khan of the Kerait is much taken with my culture. He has spoken many times of his desire for land in the Middle Kingdom."

"Togrul said that?" Temujin asked.

Wen nodded, taking the note back from the last

man to hold it. He folded it carefully and replaced the pouch while all their eyes watched.

"It is his dearest wish. There is soil there so rich and black that anything can be grown, herds of wild horses beyond counting and better hunting than anywhere in the world. Our lords live in great houses of stone and have a thousand servants to indulge their every whim. Togrul of the Kerait would wish such a life for himself and his heirs."

"How can you move a house of stone?" one of the other men asked suddenly.

Wen nodded to him in greeting. "It cannot be moved, as you move your gers. There are some the size of mountains."

Temujin laughed at that, knowing at last that the strange little man was playing games with them.

"Then it would not suit me, Wen," he said. "The tribes must move when the hunting is poor. I would starve to death in that stone mountain, I think."

"You would not, my lord, because your servants would buy food in the markets. They would raise animals to eat and grow crops to make bread and rice for you. You could have a thousand wives and never know hunger."

"And that appeals to Togrul," Temujin said softly. "I see how it could." His mind was whirling with so many strange new ideas, but he still had not heard the reason for Wen to seek him out in the wilderness, so far from his home. He offered Wen a cup and filled it with airag. When he saw the man was setting his jaw to stop his teeth from chattering, Temujin grunted.

"Rub it on your hands and face and I will refill the cup," he said.

Wen inclined his head in thanks before doing as Temujin suggested. The clear liquid brought a flush to his yellow skin, making it bloom with sudden heat. He drained the rest down his throat and emptied the second as soon as Temujin had poured it, holding the cup out for a third.

"Perhaps I will journey east someday," Temujin said, "and see these strange things with my own eyes. Yet I wonder why you would leave all that behind, to travel where my people rule with sword and bow. We do not think of your emperor here."

"Though he is father to us all," Wen said automatically. Temujin stared at him and Wen regretted drinking so quickly on an empty stomach.

"I have been among the tribes for two years, my lord. There are times when I miss my people very much. I was sent here to gather allies against the Tartars in the north. Togrul of the Kerait believes you are one who shares our dislike for those pale-skinned dogs."

"Togrul is well informed, it seems," Temujin replied. "How does he know so much of my business?" He refilled Wen's cup a fourth time and watched as it too went the way of the others. It pleased him to see the man drink, and he filled a cup of his own, sipping carefully to keep his head clear.

"The khan of the Kerait is a man of wisdom," Wen Chao replied. "He has fought the Tartars for years in the north and received much gold as tribute from my masters. It is a balance, you understand? If I send an order to Kaifeng for a hundred ponies to be driven west, they come in a season and, in return, the Kerait spill Tartar blood and keep them away from our borders. We do not want them straying into our land."

One of the listening tribesmen shifted uncomfortably and Temujin glanced at him.

"I will want your advice on this, Arslan, when we talk alone," Temujin said.

The man settled himself, satisfied. Wen looked around at them all.

"I am here to offer you the same arrangement. I can give you gold, or horses..."

"Swords," Temujin said. "And bows. If I agree, I would want a dozen sets of the armor your men are wearing outside, as well as a hundred ponies, mares and stallions both. I have no more use for gold than I have for a house of stone I cannot move."

"I did not see a hundred men in the camp," Wen protested. Inside, he rejoiced. The bargaining had begun with more ease than he could have imagined.

"You did not see them all," Temujin said, with a snort. "And I have not said I agree. What part does Togrul play in this? I have never met the man, though I know of the Kerait. Will he come after you to beg me for my help?"

Wen colored, putting down the cup of airag he had raised.

"The Kerait are a strong tribe, with more than three hundred men under arms, my lord. They heard from Tartar prisoners that you were raiding farther and farther north." He paused, choosing his words. "Togrul is a man of vision and he sent me, not to beg, but rather to have you join your force to his. Together, you will drive the Tartars back for a dozen generations, perhaps."

The man Temujin had called Arslan seemed to bristle again, and Wen saw Temujin drop a hand to his arm.

"Here I am khan, responsible for my people," he

said. "You would have me bend the knee to Togrul in return for a few ponies?" A subtle menace had come into the crowded ger, and Wen found himself wishing Yuan had been allowed to accompany him.

"You have merely to refuse and I will leave," he said. "Togrul does not need a bondsman. He needs a war leader with ruthlessness and strength. He needs every man you can bring."

Temujin glanced at Jelme. After the endless winter, he knew as well as anyone that the Tartars would be thirsting for revenge. The idea of joining forces with a greater tribe was tempting, but he needed time to think.

"You have said much of interest, Wen Chao," Temujin said, after a time. "Leave me now to make my decision. Kachiun? Find warm beds for his men and have some stew brought to ease their hunger." He saw Wen's gaze drop to the half-empty skin of airag by his feet. "And some airag to warm him tonight, as well," he added, carried away by his own generosity.

They all stood as Wen rose to his feet, not quite as steady as when he had come in. The man bowed once more, and Temujin noticed how it was a fraction deeper than the first attempt. Perhaps he had been stiff from traveling.

When they were alone, Temujin turned his bright gaze on his most trusted men.

"I want this," he said. "I want to learn as much as I can about these people. Houses of stone! Slaves by the thousand! Did it not make you itch?"

"You do not know this Togrul," Arslan said. "Are the silver people for sale, then?" He snorted. "These Chin think we can be bought with promises, awed with talk of the teeming millions in their cities. What are they to us?"

"Let us find out," Temujin said. "With the men of the Kerait, I can drive a spike into the Tartars. Let the rivers run red with what we will do."

"My oath is to you, not to Togrul," Arslan said.

Temujin faced him. "I know it. I will not be bondsman to any other. Yet if he will join his strength with us, I will have the greater part of the bargain. Think of Jelme, Arslan. Think of his future. We are too full of life to build our tribe in ones and twos. Let us leap upwards in great bounds and risk it all each time. Would you sit and wait for the Tartars?"

"You know I would not," Arslan said.

"Then my decision is made," Temujin said, filled with excitement.

CHAPTER 25

WEN CHAO STAYED for three days in the camp, discussing terms. He allowed them to press skins of airag on him before he lowered the gold curtains of his litter and Yuan gave the signal for him to be lifted.

Behind the silk hangings, Wen scratched himself, convinced he had picked up lice from the gers. It had been a trial, as he had expected, but they seemed as keen on war with the Tartars as Togrul had hoped. It was no surprise, Wen thought to himself, as he was borne over the plains. The tribes raided each other even in winter. Now that the spring had brought the first grass through the frozen ground, they would be at their business in earnest. It had always been their way. Wen smiled to himself as he read the works of Xun Zi and drowsed, occasionally making notes in the margins. The minister had been right to send someone with his diplomatic skills, he thought. Little Zhang could not have brokered such a deal, even with the promises of ponies and armor. The lisping eunuch would certainly have shown his disgust at the wedding ceremony Wen Chao had witnessed the previous day. He shuddered at the thought of the hot drink of milk and blood he had been given. Xun Zi would have applauded his discipline then. The woman Borte had been as stringy and hard as her husband, Wen reflected. Not his taste at all, though the young raider seemed to find her pleasing. What Wen would have given for a night with one of the Willow women! There was no place for sleek, powdered thighs in that hard land, and Wen cursed his work yet again, miserably.

On the fourth day out, he was ready to give the order to stop for a meal, when Yuan galloped back from his scouting. Wen listened impatiently from inside the litter as Yuan snapped orders. It was frustrating to play the part of the noble when interesting things were going on around him. He sighed to himself. His curiosity had landed him in trouble more than once before.

When Yuan finally approached the litter, Wen had stowed his scrolls and warmed himself with a draft of the clear fluid the tribes brewed. That, at least, was useful, though it paled in comparison with the rice wine he knew at home.

"Why do you disturb me this time, Yuan?" he asked. "I was going to take a nap before the meal." In fact, one glance at his first guard's flushed face had set his pulses throbbing. He needed rebalancing, he was sure of it. Too much time amongst the tribes and he would be thinking of taking up a sword himself like a common soldier. They had that effect on even the most cultured of men.

"Riders, my lord. Tartars," Yuan said, touching his forehead to the icy grass.

"Well? We are in Tartar lands, are we not? It is no surprise to meet a few of them while we travel south to the Kerait. Let them pass, Yuan. If they stand in our way, kill them. You have disturbed me for nothing."

Yuan bowed his head and Wen spoke quickly to avoid shaming his first guard. The man was as prickly as a eunuch over matters of honor.

"I spoke rashly, Yuan. You were right to bring it to my attention."

"My lord, there are thirty warriors, all of them well armed and riding fresh ponies. They can only be from a larger camp."

Wen spoke slowly, trying to restrain his patience. "I do not see how that affects us, Yuan. They know better than to interfere with a representative of the Chin. Tell them to go around us."

"I thought..." Yuan began. "I wondered if you might send a rider back to the camp we left, my lord. To warn them. The Tartars could well be looking for them."

Wen blinked at his first guard in surprise. "You have grown affectionate toward our hosts, I see. It is a weakness in you, Yuan. What do I care if the Tartars and Mongols kill each other? Is that not my task, handed down from the first minister himself? Honestly, I think you forget yourself."

A warning shout came from one of the other guards, and both Wen and Yuan heard the approach of riders. Yuan remained where he was.

Wen closed his eyes for a moment. There was no peace to be had in this land, no silence. Whenever he thought he had found it, someone would go riding past, looking for enemies to kill. He felt a wave of homesick-ness strike him like a physical force, but crushed it down. Until he was recalled, this was his fate.

"If it please you, Yuan, tell them we have not seen the raiders. Tell them I am exercising my men ready for spring."

"Your will, master."

Wen watched as the Tartar warriors rode up. They did look as if they were armed for war, he acknowl-edged, though he cared nothing for Temujin or his ragged gers. He would not have shed a tear if the entire Tartar nation was destroyed, and the Mongol tribes with them. Perhaps then he would be called home at last.

He saw Yuan speak with the leader, a heavyset man wrapped in thick furs. It made Wen shudder to see such a filthy warrior, and he would certainly not lower him-self to address him in person. The Tartar seemed angry, but Wen cared nothing for that. His men were chosen from the personal guard of the first minister, and any one of them was worth half a dozen screaming tribes-men. Yuan himself had won his sword in a tournament of all the army, standing first amongst his division. In that, at least, Wen had been well served.

With furious glances at the litter, the Tartars blus-tered and pointed their swords, while Yuan sat his horse impassively, shaking his head. Only their youthful pride prevented them from riding away, and Wen wondered if he would indeed be called out to remind them of his sta-tus. Even unwashed Tartars knew the Chin representa-tive was not to be touched, and he was relieved when the warriors finished their display and rode on without look-ing back. A small part of him was disappointed that they had not decided to draw swords. Yuan would have butchered them. Idly, Wen wondered if Temujin was ready for such a force. He decided he did not care. If they found the Mongol camp, one or the other would prevail. Either way, there would be fewer tribesmen to trouble his sleep.

When they were gone, Wen found his digestion had become disturbed. Blowing air from his lips in irritation, he called for Yuan to set up the small pavilion he used to empty his bowels away from prying eyes. He did all he could to make himself comfortable, but the pleasures of the court haunted his dreams and he had not had a woman in a long, long time. Perhaps if he wrote humbly to little Zhang, he could arrange his recall. No. He could not bear the thought.

The Tartar raiders came in hard and fast as soon as they heard the warning horns sound. They kicked their ponies into a gallop and each man rode with a bow ready to send death down the throat of anyone standing in the way.

Temujin and his brothers came skidding out of their gers while the first horn notes still echoed. The warriors moved to their positions without panic. Those on the main path pulled wooden barriers up from the ground, jamming staffs under them to keep them solid. Riders would not be able to gallop right between the gers. They would have to jink around the obstacles, and be forced to slow down.

Temujin saw his men ready their arrows, laying them down on the frozen ground. They were finished moments before they sighted the first enemy in his stinking furs.

The Tartars rode three abreast, high in the saddle as they searched for targets. Temujin saw they were relying on fear and confusion, and he showed his teeth as he watched them come. He felt the ground shudder underneath his feet, and he wished he had the sword Arslan had made for him. In its place was a Tartar blade of poor quality. It would have to serve.

The first riders saw the barrier in their path. Two swung their mounts around it, interfering with the third. They saw the men in its shadow and released their shafts from instinct, hammering them uselessly into wood. As soon as they struck, Kachiun and Khasar rose above the edge and loosed, the bowstrings humming. The arrows punched through the riders, slamming two of the Tartars into the hard ground at full gallop. They did not rise again.

At first, it was a massacre. The Tartars who galloped behind their fellows found their way blocked by riderless ponies and the dead. Two of them leapt the barricade before Kachiun and Khasar could set another arrow. The riders found themselves in an open space, with drawn bows all around. They had barely time to shout before dark shafts impaled them, cutting off their war cries and sending them spinning out of the saddles.

Another of the Tartars tried to leap the first barrier. His pony missed the jump and crushed it flat, snapping the staff that held it upright. Khasar rolled away, but Kachiun's leg was caught and he swore in pain. He lay helpless on his back as more galloped in, knowing he could measure his life in moments.

A rider saw Kachiun struggling and drew back on his bow to pin him to the ground. Before he could loose, Arslan stepped out from one side and ripped a sword

across his throat. The Tartar collapsed, his pony veering
wildly. Arrows whined around them as Arslan yanked
Kachiun free. Khasar was on one knee, sending shaft after shaft into the Tartars, but he had lost his calm and six
men broke through, untouched by any of them.

Temujin saw them coming. Without the first barrier, the men could ride straight down the left of the
main path. He saw two of his men face them and fall
with Tartar arrowheads sticking out of their backs. The
second barrier group turned to send arrows after them
and, behind, another group of six broke past his brothers. The raid was hanging in the balance, despite his
preparations.

He waited until a Tartar had loosed his shaft before
stepping out and chopping his blade into the man's
thigh. Blood spattered him as the man screamed, yanking wildly on his reins. Out of control, the Tartar turned
his pony into a ger, which collapsed with a crackle of
broken wood, catapulting him over the pony's head.

The first group of six turned their bows on Temujin,
forcing him to leap for cover. A snarling warrior rode at
him, his bow bent to send the spiked arrow down into
his chest. Temujin rolled, coming up with his sword outstretched. The man yelled as the blade buried itself in his
gut and the arrow buzzed over Temujin's head. The
shoulder of the pony hit Temujin as it passed, knocking
him flat. He rose groggily and looked around him.

The camp was in chaos. The Tartars had lost a lot of
men, but those who lived were riding around in triumph, looking for targets. Many of them had dropped
their bows and drawn swords for the close work.
Temujin saw two kick their mounts at Arslan while he
himself scrabbled for his own bow to send a shaft after

them. The first arrow he touched was broken and the rest were scattered. He found one that would do, after a moment's frenzied search. He could hear his mother yelling and, as he turned to see, Borte darted out from a ger, rushing after little Temulun. His young sister was running in panic and neither of them saw the Tartar bearing down on them. Temujin held his breath, but Arslan was armed and ready for his attackers. He made his choice.

Temujin heaved back on the string, aiming at the lone warrior bearing down on Borte. He heard a sudden thunder and another Tartar was riding at him, sword already swinging to take off his head. There was no time to dodge, but Temujin dropped to his knees as he let go, struggling to adjust his aim. The arrow went skipping over the ground, wasted. Then something hit him hard enough to shake the world and he fell.

Jelme stepped up to his father's side as the two Tartars bore down on them.

"Go left," Arslan snapped at his son, even as he stepped to the right.

The Tartars saw them move, but the father and son had left it to the very last moment and they could not adjust. Arslan's blade tip found the neck of one man as Jelme cut the other, almost taking his head off. Both Tartars were dead in a heartbeat, their ponies hammering past without direction.

The Tartar leader had not survived the first attack on the barricades, and there were barely a dozen left of the original force. With the hill backing onto the camp, there was no chance to ride through and away, so those that still lived shouted and wheeled, cutting at anything against them. Arslan saw two pulled out of their saddles and knifed as they writhed, screaming. It was a bloody business, but the main Tartar force had been destroyed. The few survivors lay low on the saddles as they galloped back the way they had come, shafts whistling after them.

Arslan saw one coming back from the other side of the camp, and he readied himself to kill again, standing perfectly still in the pony's path. In the last moment, he saw the kicking legs of a captive across the saddle and spoiled his own blow. His left hand snapped out to yank Borte free, but his fingers caught only an edge of cloth and then the man was past. Arslan saw Khasar was following the rider with an arrow on the string, and he shouted.

"Hold, Khasar. Hold!"

The order rang across a camp that was suddenly quiet after the roaring Tartars. Not more than six made it away and Arslan was already running for the ponies.

"Mount up!" he roared. "They have one of the women. Mount!"

He looked for Temujin as he ran, then saw a limp figure and skidded to a stop in horror. Temujin lay surrounded by dead men. A pony with a broken leg stood shivering next to him, its sides streaked with whitish sweat. Arslan ignored the animal, pushing it away as he knelt beside the young man he had rescued from the Wolves.

There was a lot of blood and Arslan felt his heart contract in a painful spasm. He reached down and touched the flap of flesh that had been torn free from Temujin's scalp. With a shout of joy, he saw it still bled into the pool that lay around his head. Arslan lifted Temujin free of the blood that covered half his face.

"He is alive," Arslan whispered.

Temujin remained unconscious as Arslan carried him to a tent. His brothers galloped out after the raiders, sparing only a glance for the figure in Arslan's arms. They were grim-faced and angry as they passed him, and Arslan did not pity any Tartars they caught that day.

Arslan laid Temujin down in his mother's ger, surrendering him to her. Temulun was crying bitterly in a corner, the sound almost painful. Hoelun looked up from her son as she reached for her needle and thread.

"Comfort my daughter, Arslan," she said, concentrating on her task.

Arslan ducked his head in acknowledgment, going over to the little girl.

"Would you like to be picked up?" he asked her.

Temulun nodded through her tears and he jerked her into the air. She looked up at him and he forced himself to smile. The reaction to killing was setting in and he felt himself grow light-headed as his pounding heart beat too fast for stillness and quiet. Hoelun pushed the bone needle through the first piece of Temujin's scalp and Arslan saw the little girl wince and her mouth open to resume crying.

"It's all right, little one, I'll take you to Eluin. She has been looking for you," he said. He did not want the girl to see the bodies outside but, equally, he could not stay in the ger and do nothing. He hoped Eluin was still alive.

As he turned to leave, he heard Temujin give a shuddering gasp. When Arslan looked, he saw Temujin's eyes were open and clear, watching Hoelun as she stitched with quick, neat hands.

"Lie still," Hoelun said, when her son tried to get up. "I need to do this well."

Temujin subsided, his gaze finding Arslan at the door. "Tell me," he ordered.

"We broke the attack. They have Borte," Arslan replied.

As he spoke, Hoelun tugged at the thread and a whole section of Temujin's scalp wrinkled. Arslan bounced Temulun in his arms, but she had quieted again and seemed content to play with a silver button on his deel.

Hoelun used a cloth to dab blood out of her son's eyes. The scalp wound was still bleeding heavily, but the stitching helped. She pushed the needle through another bit of flesh and felt Temujin tense.

"I need to be up, Mother," he murmured. "Are you nearly finished?"

"Your brothers have gone after the last of them," Arslan said quickly. "With such a wound, there is no point in following them, not yet. You have lost a lot of blood and there's no point in risking a fall."

"She is my wife," Temujin replied, his eyes growing cold. His mother bent forward as if to kiss him, instead biting off the end of the thread in his skin. He sat up as soon as she moved away, raising his fingers to the line of stitches.

"Thank you," he said. His eyes lost their hard focus then and Hoelun nodded as she rubbed at the dried blood on his cheek.

Arslan heard Eluin's voice outside the ger and stepped through the door to pass Temulun into her care. He returned, looking grim, as Temujin tried to stand. The young khan swayed, taking hold of the central spar of the ger to keep himself upright.

"You cannot ride today," Arslan told him. "All you could do is follow the tracks of your brothers. Let them find her."

"Would you?" Temujin demanded. He had closed his eyes against the dizziness, and Arslan's heart swelled to see his determination. He sighed.

"No, I would go after them. I will bring your pony and fetch my own."

He ducked out of the ger and Hoelun stood and took Temujin's free hand in her own.

"You will not want to hear what I have to say," she murmured.

Temujin opened his eyes, blinking against a fresh trail of blood.

"Say whatever you have to," he replied.

"If your brothers cannot run them down before night, they will hurt her."

"They will rape her, Mother. I know. She is strong."

Hoelun shook her head. "You do not know. She will be ashamed." She paused for a moment, wanting him to understand. "If they have hurt her, you will have to be very strong. You cannot expect her to be the same, with you or any man."

"I will kill them," Temujin promised, rage kindling in him. "I will burn them and eat their flesh if they do."

"That will bring you peace, but it will not change anything for Borte," Hoelun said.

"What else can I do? She cannot kill them as I could, or force them to kill her, even. Nothing that happens is her fault." He found himself crying and wiped angrily at bloody tears on his cheeks. "She trusted me."

"You cannot make this right, my son. Not if they escape your brothers. If you find her alive, you will have to be patient and kind."

"I know that! I love her; that is enough."

"It was," Hoelun persisted. "It may not be enough any longer."

Temujin stood in the cold wind, his head throbbing. As Arslan brought the ponies, he looked around, smelling blood on the breeze. The camp was littered with broken bodies. Some still moved. One Tartar lay on his back as if dead, but his fingers plucked at two arrow shafts in his chest, twitching like pale spiders. Temujin drew a knife from his belt and staggered over to him. The man could only have been moments from death, but Temujin still knelt at his side and placed the point of his blade onto the pulsing throat. The touch of it stilled the scrabbling fingers, and the Tartar turned his eyes mutely onto Temujin. As he met them, Temujin pushed slowly downwards, cutting the windpipe and breathing in a gust of bloody air.

When he rose, Temujin was still unsteady. The sun seemed too bright and, without warning, he turned and vomited. He heard Hoelun speaking to him, but it was through a roaring sound that he could not clear. She and Arslan were arguing about him going out, and Temujin could see Arslan's face frowning in doubt.

"I will not fall," Temujin said to both of them, taking hold of his saddle horn. "Help me up, here. I have to follow them."

It took both of them to heave him into the saddle, but once there, Temujin felt a little more secure. He shook his head, wincing at the pain crashing behind his eyes.

"Jelme?" he called. "Where are you?"

Arslan's son was spattered with drying blood, his sword still bare as he walked around corpses to reach them. Temujin watched him come, dimly aware that he had never seen Jelme angry before.

"While we are gone, you must move the camp," Temujin said, slurring his words. His head felt too large, lolling on his shoulders. He did not hear what Jelme said in reply.

"Travel by night. Take them into the hills, but move south toward the Kerait. If Togrul has the men to match us, I will burn the Tartars from the face of the world. I will look for you when I have found my wife."

"Your will, my lord," Jelme said. "But if you do not come back?" It had to be said, but Temujin winced again as the pain became overwhelming.

"Then find that valley we talked about and raise sons and sheep," he said at last.

He had done his duty as khan. Jelme was a fine leader and those who looked to Temujin for leadership would be safe. He took a firm grip on the reins. He could not be far behind his brothers. All that was left was vengeance.

CHAPTER 26

AS THE SUN SANK in the west and bathed the plains in gold, Khasar and Kachiun came across the body of one of the men they were following. Wary of a trap, Kachiun remained in the saddle with his bow drawn back while Khasar approached, flipping the corpse over with the toe of his boot.

The Tartar had a broken shaft protruding from his stomach where he'd snapped it off. His entire lower body was black with blood and his face was chalk white and stiff. His companions had taken his pony with them, its lighter hoof marks still visible in the turf. Khasar searched the body quickly, but if there had been anything of use, the Tartars had already taken it.

The brothers rode as long as they could see tracks, but in the end, the growing gloom forced them to stop or risk losing the men they were chasing. Neither of them spoke as they mixed a draft of milk and blood tapped from a vein in Kachiun's mare. They had both seen Temujin unconscious in Arslan's arms, and they were desperate not to let the raiders get away.

They slept uncomfortably and woke before dawn, moving on as soon as the first light revealed the tracks of the raiders once more. With just a glance at each other, they kicked their mounts into a gallop. They were both fit and hardened. They would not let them escape through weakness.

Throughout the second day, the hoofprints grew fresher and easier to see. Kachiun was a better tracker than his brother, who never had the patience to learn the subtleties. It was Kachiun who leapt from the saddle to press his hand into the lumps of dung, looking for a trace of warmth. On the evening of the second day, he grinned as he dug his fingers into a dark ball.

"Fresher than the last. We are gaining on them, brother," he told Khasar.

The Tartars had made little attempt to confuse their trail. They had tried to lose their pursuers at first, but the tracks of the second morning were almost straight, running fast toward some destination. If the Tartars knew they were still being followed, they no longer tried to throw them off.

"I hope we catch them before they reach wherever they're going," Khasar said, gloomily. "If they're heading for a large camp, we'll lose them and Borte."

Kachiun mounted again, his face drawn into a grimace as his tired muscles protested.

"They must have come from somewhere," he said. "If they get to safety, one of us will go back and gather the others. Maybe even ride with Temujin to the Kerait and join forces. They will not escape us, Khasar. One way or the other we'll hunt them down."

"If Temujin is alive," Khasar muttered.

Kachiun shook his head. "He is. The Wolves themselves couldn't stop him. You think a wound from the Tartars will?"

"It did for our father," Khasar said.

"That is still a debt to be paid," Kachiun replied savagely.

As the brothers slept on the third night, both were stiff and tired from the hard riding. The mixture of blood and milk could sustain them indefinitely, but they had no remounts, and the mare was showing signs of soreness, much as they were themselves. Both men had taken bruising impacts in the raid, and Kachiun's ankle was swollen and painful to the touch. He did not speak of it to his brother, but he could not hide his limping gait whenever they dismounted. They slept soundly and Kachiun woke with a start when a cold blade touched his throat.

It was pitch dark under the stars as his eyes jerked open. He tried to roll away, but relief flooded him on hearing a voice he knew.

"Arslan could show you a thing or two about tracking, Kachiun," Temujin said by his ear. "It is almost dawn; are you ready for another day?"

Kachiun sprang to his feet and embraced Temujin and then Arslan, surprising the older man. "We cannot be far behind them," he said.

A few paces away, Khasar had stopped snoring and turned over. Kachiun strode to him and booted him in the ribs.

"Up, Khasar, we have visitors."

They heard Khasar scramble to his feet and the

creak of a bow being drawn. Though he slept like the dead, there was nothing wrong with his reflexes.

"I am with you, my brother," Temujin said softly into the darkness. The bow creaked again as Khasar eased the string back.

"How is your head?" Khasar asked.

"It aches, but the stitches hold," Temujin replied. He glanced toward the east and saw the wolf dawn, the first gray light before the sun rose. He held a skin of black airag out to them.

"Drink quickly and be ready to ride," he said. "We have been too long on the chase already."

His voice held a quiet pain they all understood. Borte had spent three nights with the raiding party. They did not speak of it. The airag warmed their empty stomachs and gave them a rush of energy they sorely needed. Milk and blood would follow later in the day. It would be enough.

The three brothers and Arslan were dusty and tired by the time they caught a glimpse of their prey. The trail had wound up through a range of hills, and the broken ground had slowed their headlong pace. Temujin had not spoken a word to any of them, his gaze constantly on the horizon as he searched for the last of the Tartars.

The sun was low on the horizon when they reached a crest and saw the ragged group at the far end of the valley. All four of them slid out of the saddles and pulled their ponies down with them, so that they would not be easy to see. Temujin lay with his arm over the neck of his mount, pressing it into the grass.

"It will be tonight, then," he said. "We'll take them when they make camp."

"I have three arrows," Kachiun said. "All that were left in the quiver when I rode out."

Temujin turned to his younger brother, his face like stone. "If you can, I want them down but not dead. I do not want it to be quick, for these."

"You make it harder, Temujin," Arslan said, peering at the small group in the far distance. "Better to spring an attack and kill as many as we can. They too have bows and swords, remember."

Temujin ignored the older man, holding Kachiun's eyes. "If you *can*," he repeated. "If Borte is alive, I want her to see them die, perhaps with her own knife."

"I understand," Kachiun murmured, remembering when they had killed Bekter. Temujin had worn the same expression, though it was made worse by the ugly line of stitches seaming his forehead. Kachiun was not able to hold the fierce gaze, and he too looked over the valley. The Tartars had reached the end and passed into thick trees.

"Time to move," Temujin said, rising. "We must close the gap before they make camp for the night. I do not want to lose them in the dark." He did not look to see if they followed as he forced his pony to gallop once more. He knew they would.

Borte lay on her side on a damp layer of old leaves and pine needles. Her hands and feet had been expertly tied by the Tartar tribesmen as they made their camp in the woods. She watched them fearfully as they used a hatchet to hack out the dry wood from a dead tree and built a small fire. They were all starving and the stunned despair of the first few nights was only just beginning to fade. She listened to their guttural voices and tried not to be afraid. It was hard. They had ridden into Temujin's camp with every expectation of a successful raid. Instead, they had been smashed and broken, losing brothers and friends and almost their own lives. Two of them in particular were still seething at the shame of their retreat. It was those two who had come for her on the first night, taking out their frustration and anger in the only way they had left. Borte shuddered as she lay there, feeling again their rough hands on her. The youngest of them was little more than a boy, but he had been the cruellest and smacked his closed fist across her face until she was dazed and bleeding. Then he had raped her with the others.

Borte made a small sound in her throat, an animal sound of fear that she could not control. She told herself to be strong, but as the young one stood up from the fire and walked over to her, she felt her bladder give way in a sudden hot rush, steaming in the cold air. Though it was growing dark, he saw it and showed his teeth.

"I thought about you all day when we were riding," he told her, crouching at her side.

She began to shiver and hated herself for the signs of weakness. Temujin had told her she was a wolf, as he was; that she could endure anything. She did not cry out as the young Tartar took her by a foot and dragged her behind him to the men around the fire. Instead, she tried to think of her childhood and running amongst the gers. Even then, the memories were all of her father hitting her, or her mother's indifference to her misery. The only memory that stayed was the day Temujin had come for her at last, so tall and handsome in his furs that the Olkhun'ut could not even look at him.

The Tartars around the fire watched with interest as the youngest untied her feet. She could see the lust in their eyes and she gathered herself to fight them again. It would not stop them, but it was all she had left and she would not give them that last piece of her pride. As soon as her legs were free, she kicked out, her bare foot thumping uselessly into the young Tartar's chest. He slapped it away with a grim chuckle.

"You are all dead men," she snapped. "He will kill you all."

The youngest was flushed and excited and he did not respond as he yanked at her deel and exposed her breasts to the evening cold. She struggled wildly and he nodded to one of the others to help him hold her down. The one who rose was thick-bodied and stank. She had smelled his foul breath close to her face the night before, and the memory made her gag, her empty stomach heaving uselessly. She kicked out with all her strength and the young one cursed.

"Take her legs, Aelic," he ordered, pulling at his furs to expose himself.

The older man reached down to do as he was told, and then they all heard the crunch of footsteps on the leaves.

Four men strode out from between the trees. Three carried swords ready in their hands and the fourth had a bow drawn right back to his ear.

The Tartars reacted quickly, leaping up and grabbing their weapons. Borte was dropped back onto the wet ground and scrambled to her knees. Her heart thumped painfully in her chest as she saw Temujin and his brothers, with the swordsmith Arslan in their midst.

They ran forward on light feet, perfectly balanced for the first strikes.

The Tartars roared in alarm, but the newcomers were silent as they darted in. Temujin swayed aside from a sweeping blade, then used his hilt to punch a man from his feet. He kicked down hard as he went over his enemy, feeling the nose bone snap under his heel. The next was rising from Borte and Temujin did not dare look at her as the man threw himself forward, armed only with a knife. Temujin let him come in, shifting just a little so that the blow was lost in his deel. He punched out hard with his left hand, rocking the Tartar backwards, then ripped his sword across the man's thighs, shoving him onto his back as he yelled in pain. The knife fell in the leaves as Temujin turned away panting, looking for another target. It came to rest by Borte and she picked it up in her bound hands.

The young Tartar lay howling on the ground, his limbs flailing as he tried to rise. Temujin had moved away to attack a third with Kachiun, and the Tartar did not see Borte at first as she crept toward him on her knees. When his gaze fell on her, he shook his head, desperately. He raised his fists, but Borte jammed a knee onto his right arm and struggled to bring the blade down. His free hand found her throat and his strength was still frightening. She felt her vision blur as he squeezed desperately, but she would not be denied. Her head was shoved up high by his locked arm as she found his pulsing throat under her fingers. She could have pushed the knife in there, but she eased her hand higher, holding his straining head still as best she could. He struggled, but blood was pouring from his legs and she could feel him growing weaker as she grew strong.

She found his eyes and dug her nails into them, listening to him scream. The knife point scraped along his face, laying his cheek open before she was able to press her full weight down. Suddenly there was no resistance, as she found the eye socket and shoved. The arm at her throat fell away limply and she slumped, gasping. She could still smell the men on her skin, and she mouthed wordless rage as she twisted the blade in the socket, digging deeper.

"He is dead," Arslan said at her side, laying a hand on her shoulder. She jerked away from the touch as if it had scalded her, and when she looked up, the older man's eyes were full of sorrow. "You are safe now."

Borte did not speak, though her eyes filled with tears. In a rush, the sounds of the camp came back to her from where she had lost herself. The rest of the Tartars were crying out in agony and fear all around. It was no more than she would have wanted.

Borte sat back on her haunches, looking dazedly at the blood that covered her hands. She let the knife fall once more and looked into the far distance.

"Temujin," she heard Arslan call. "Come and tend her." She saw the swordsmith pick up the knife and toss it into the trees. She did not understand why he would waste a good blade, and she raised her head to ask him.

Temujin strode across the camp, scattering the small fire without noticing or caring. He took her by the shoulders and pulled her into his arms. She struggled then, bursting into sobs as she tried to get away from him.

"Be still!" he ordered, as she raised her fists to hammer at his face. The first blows made him duck his head and hold her tighter. "It is over, Borte. Be still!"

The fight went out of her in an instant and she sagged in his embrace, weeping.

"I have you now," he whispered. "You are safe and it is over." He repeated the words in a mumble, his emotions whirling painfully. He was relieved to find her alive, but still there was a red core to him that wanted to hurt the men who had taken her. He glanced to where his brothers were tying the Tartars. Two of them were yelling like children, with Kachiun's arrows in their legs and arms. A third would probably die from where Arslan had opened his gut, but the others would live long enough.

"Build up the fire," Temujin said to his brothers. "I want them to feel the heat and know what is coming."

Khasar and Kachiun set about gathering the embers he had kicked apart, dragging an old log onto the rest. Flames soon licked around the dry wood, catching quickly.

Arslan watched as husband and wife stood together. Borte's face was blank, almost as if she had fainted. The swordsmith shook his head.

"Let us kill them and go back to the others," Arslan said. "There is no honor in what you are planning."

Temujin turned to him, his eyes wild.

"Leave if you want to," he snapped. "This is a blood debt."

Arslan stood very still.

"I will take no part in it," he said at last.

Temujin nodded. Khasar and Kachiun had come to stand by his side. All three brothers looked at the swordsmith and he felt cold. There was no pity in any of their eyes. Behind them, the Tartars moaned in terror and the fire crackled as it grew.

Temujin stood bare-chested, sweat gleaming on his skin. His brothers had piled wood on the fire until it was an inferno and they could not approach the roaring yellow heat.

"I give these lives to the sky and earth, scattering their souls in fire," Temujin said, raising his head to the cold stars. His mouth and chest were bloody in a great black streak that reached down to his waist. He held the last Tartar by the throat. The man was weak from his wounds, but he still struggled feebly, his legs scratching marks in the ground. Temujin did not seem to feel the weight. He stood so close to the fire that the fine hair on his arms had vanished, but he was lost in the trance of death and felt no pain.

Kachiun and Khasar watched in grim silence from a few paces farther back. They too had been marked with the blood of the Tartars and tasted flesh burnt in the flames. Three bodies lay naked to one side of the fire, two of them with black holes in their chests and enough blood to wash away grief and anger. They had not cut the man Borte had killed. The fire was only for the living.

Unaware of them all, Temujin began to chant words he had not heard since old Chagatai had whispered them on a frozen night long before. The shaman's chant spoke of loss and revenge, of winter, ice, and blood. He did not have to struggle to recall the words; they were ready on his tongue as if he had always known them.

The last Tartar moaned in terror, his hands clawing at Temujin's arm and scratching the skin with broken nails. Temujin looked down at him.

"Come closer, Borte," he said, holding the man's gaze.

Borte stepped into the firelight, the shadows of the flames playing on her skin. Her eyes caught the flickering light, so that she seemed to have flames within her.

Temujin looked up at his wife and drew his knife again from his belt, already slick with dark life. In a sharp jerk, he opened a gash in the Tartar's chest, ripping the weapon back and forth to slice through muscle. The Tartar's mouth opened, but no sound came out. Shining organs pulsed as Temujin reached in, gripping and sawing. Between two fingers, he pulled out a piece of streaming flesh from the heart. He pressed it onto the tip of his blade and held it into the flames, so that his own skin blistered as the meat sizzled and spat. He grunted at the pain, aware of it but uncaring. He let the Tartar fall onto the crisping leaves, his eyes still open. Without a word, Temujin pulled the seared flesh from the blade and held it out to Borte, watching as she held it to her lips.

It was still almost raw and she chewed hard to swallow it, feeling hot blood dribble over her lips. She had not known what to expect. This was the oldest magic: the eating of souls. She felt the meat slide down her throat and with it came a sense of great lightness, and of strength. Her lips slid back to show her teeth and Temujin seemed to slump as if something had gone out of him. Before, he had been a worker of dark incantations, a bringer of retribution. In an instant, he was no more than a tired man, worn out by grief and pain.

Borte raised her hand to her husband's face, touching his cheek and leaving a smear of blood there.

"It is enough," she said over the crackle of flame. "You can sleep now."

He nodded wearily, stepping away from the flames at last to join his brothers. Arslan stood farther back, his expression dark. He had not joined in the bloodletting, or eaten the slivers of flesh cut from live men. He had not felt the rush of life that came with it, nor the exhaustion that followed. He did not look at the mutilated bodies of the Tartars as he settled himself on the ground and drew his arms into the deel. He knew his dreams would be terrible.

CHAPTER 27

TOGRUL OF THE KERAIT was roused from sleep by the hand of his first wife, shaking him roughly.

"Up, lazy!" she said, her hard voice splitting apart a happy dream with its usual force.

Togrul groaned as he opened his eyes. Six daughters she had given him and not a single son. He regarded her irritably as he rubbed his face.

"Why do you disturb me, woman? I was dreaming of when you were young and attractive."

Her response was to poke him hard in the ribs.

"This new man you summoned has arrived with his ragged followers. They look no better than dirty wanderers, from what I can see. Will you stay all day in your fat slumber while they inspect your gers?"

Togrul frowned, stifling a yawn as he scratched himself. He swung his legs onto the cold floor and looked around.

"I do not see food to give me strength," he said,

frowning. "Must I go out to them on an empty stomach?"

"That stomach is never empty," she retorted. "It is not fitting to keep them waiting while you force another sheep down your throat."

"Woman, tell me again why I keep you on," he said, standing. "I have forgotten."

She snorted as he dressed, moving surprisingly quickly for such a large man. As he splashed water on his face, she pressed a warm pouch of mutton and bread into his hands, thick with grease. He smiled at last on seeing it, taking half in a great bite and belching softly as he chewed. Sitting down once more, he worked on finishing it as his wife tied his boots. He loved her very much.

"You look like a sheepherder," she told him, as he moved toward the door. "If they ask where the real khan of the Kerait is hiding, tell them you ate him."

"Woman, you are the light of my heart," he said, dipping his head to pass out into the dawn light. He chuckled as she threw something that clattered against the closing door.

His mood changed as he saw the warriors who had come into the gers of the Kerait. They had dismounted and were surrounded by his foolish families, already looking irritated by the close press of the crowd. Togrul blew air from his lips, wishing he had brought another of the pouches with him. His stomach growled and he thought the newcomers would welcome a feast in their honor. His wife could hardly complain about that.

The crowd of Kerait children parted and he saw his bondsmen were there before him. He looked around for Wen Chao, but the Chin ambassador had not yet stirred from his sleep. As Togrul approached the group, his heart sank at the small number of them. Where was the horde Wen had promised?

Many of the newcomers stared around them with fascination and nervousness. In the center, Togrul saw five men standing by thin ponies, their faces hard and strained. He beamed at them as he came forward, his bondsmen falling in behind.

"I grant you guest rights in my home," he said. "Which one of you is Temujin of the Wolves? I have heard much about you."

The tallest stepped forward, bowing his head stiffly, as if the gesture were unfamiliar.

"No longer of the Wolves, my lord. I owe no loyalty to the tribe of my father. These are my only people now."

Temujin had never seen a man quite as fat as Togrul before. He tried to keep the surprise from his face as Togrul greeted his brothers, as well as Jelme and Arslan. The khan could not have been more than thirty and his grip was strong, but flesh cloaked him, so that his deel strained under a wide belt. His face was round, with thick rolls of fat over his collar. Even stranger was the fact that he wore a robe very similar to the one Wen had worn on his visit. Togrul's hair was tied back in the manner of the Chin, and Temujin did not know what to make of such a man. He looked like no khan he had ever seen, and only the familiar features and reddish skin marked him as one of their own people.

Temujin exchanged a glance with Kachiun as Togrul finished his welcome and placed heavy hands on his belly.

"The beast has woken, my friends. You must be hungry after your journey, yes?"

He clapped his hands together and called for food to be brought. Temujin watched as the crowd moved away to the gers, no doubt looking for enough food to ease the khan's appetite. They seemed long familiar with the task.

"I do not see more than thirty warriors with you," Togrul said, counting under his breath. "Wen Chao told me there could be as many as a hundred."

"I will find more," Temujin told him, instantly defensive.

Togrul raised an eyebrow in surprise. "It is true, then, that you welcome wanderers in your camp? Do they not steal?"

"Not from me," Temujin replied. "And they fight well. I was told you needed a war leader. If you do not, I will take them back into the north."

Togrul blinked at this sharp response. For a moment, he wished he had a single son instead of the daughters his wife had given him. Perhaps then he would not need to be courting savages fresh in from the hills.

"Wen Chao spoke highly of you and I trust his recommendation," he said. "However, we will talk of that when we have eaten." He smiled again in anticipation, already able to smell mutton sizzling in the gers.

"There is a Tartar camp a month's ride to the north," Temujin said, ignoring the offer. "There are perhaps a hundred warriors there. If you will match my men with thirty more, I will bring you Tartar heads and show you what we can achieve."

Togrul blinked at him. The young warrior was surrounded by a huge camp and many armed men. He was addressing a man he needed to persuade to his side, but he spoke as if Togrul were the one who should be bowing his head. He wondered briefly if he should remind the man of his position, but thought better of it.

"We will talk of that, also," he said. "But if you do not eat with me, I will be insulted."

He watched as Temujin nodded. Togrul relaxed as platters of steaming meat were brought out into the cold air. He saw the eyes of the newcomers dart toward them. No doubt they had been half starved all winter. A fire had been laid in the center of the camp, and Togrul nodded toward it as the flames caught. Temujin shared a wary glance with his companions, and Togrul saw his brothers shrug, one of them smiling in anticipation.

"Very well, my lord," Temujin said, reluctantly. "We will eat first."

"I am honored," Togrul said, unable to keep a sharp tone from his voice. He told himself to remember the estates Wen had promised. Perhaps this raider would bring them a little closer.

Wen Chao joined them at the fire when the sun had cleared the horizon. His servants disdained the blankets provided to keep off the chill of the ground. Instead, they brought out a small bench for their master. Temujin watched in interest as the servants spiced the meat with powders from tiny bottles before handing it over. Togrul snapped his fingers to have his own meat treated, and the servants moved quickly to do his bidding. It was obviously not a new request from the khan of the Kerait.

Wen Chao's soldiers did not join in the feasting. Temujin saw the first among them, Yuan, direct the others to defensive positions around the camp while his master ate, apparently oblivious.

Togrul would not allow conversation until he had sated his appetite. Twice Temujin began to speak but, both times, Togrul merely gestured to the food, too busy with his own. It was frustrating and Temujin was sure Wen Chao had a sparkle of amusement in his eyes. No doubt he was recalling his own surprise at Togrul's prodigious ability to eat and drink. The fat khan seemed to have no limit to the amount he could take in, and Temujin and his brothers had all finished long before him and only just after Wen, who ate as little as a bird.

At last, Togrul announced himself satisfied and hid a belch with his hand.

"You can see we have not gone hungry in the winter," he said cheerfully, patting his belly. "The spirits have been good to the Kerait."

"And they will be generous in the future," Wen Chao added, watching Temujin. "I am glad to see you have accepted the offer I brought you, my lord."

The last words sounded oddly false in his throat, but Temujin accepted them as his due.

"Why am I needed here?" he asked Togrul. "You have enough men and weapons to smash the Tartars on your own. Why call on my men?"

Togrul reached up to wipe his greasy lips with the back of a hand. He seemed to feel Wen Chao's gaze fall on him and instead took a cloth from his deel for the task.

"Your name is known, Temujin. It is true that the Kerait are strong, too strong for another tribe to attack, but Wen has convinced me of the need to carry the fight farther into the north, as you have done."

Temujin said nothing. From his first glance at the enormous man, he had no need to ask why Togrul did not lead them himself. He wondered if the man could even sit a pony for more than a few miles. Yet he could see hundreds of the Kerait around the feast, as well as the fifty or so who had joined them at the fire. The tribe was larger than the Wolves or even the Olkhun'ut. Surely there was someone amongst them who could lead a raiding party? He did not voice the thought aloud, but Togrul saw his expression and chuckled.

"I could have one of my bondsmen attack the Tartars, could I not? How long would it be before he came to me with a knife hidden in a sleeve of his deel? I am not a fool, Temujin, do not think it. The Kerait have grown because I kept them strong and because Wen Chao has brought us horses, food, and gold from the east. Perhaps one day I will look out on lands of my own in that country. The Kerait will know peace and plenty in my lifetime if I can drive back the Tartars."

"You would take the entire Kerait tribe into Chin territory?" Temujin said incredulously.

Togrul shrugged. "Why not? Is it too much to imagine living without a dozen baying tribes all around, watching for weakness? Wen has promised us the land, and the Kerait will thrive there."

Temujin darted a sharp look at the Chin representative.

"I have heard much of promises," he said. "But I have seen nothing real yet, except for pictures on paper.

Where are the ponies I was promised, the armor and weapons?"

"If we agree on a course today, I will send a messenger to the city of Kaifeng. You will have them in less than a year," Wen replied.

Temujin shook his head. "More promises," he said. "Let us talk of things I can touch." He looked at Togrul, his yellow eyes seeming gold in the morning light.

"I told you there is a Tartar camp in the north. My brothers and I scouted it thoroughly, seeing how they placed their men. We followed a smaller group right up to a day's ride away and we were not spotted. If you want me to lead your men on raids, give me ones who have been blooded and I will destroy the Tartars. Let that be what seals our bargain, not gifts which may never arrive."

Wen Chao was angry at having his word doubted. His face showed no sign of it as he spoke.

"You were lucky not to meet the outriders of that camp, my lord. I came across them as I returned to the Kerait."

Temujin turned his pale gaze on the Chin diplomat. "They are all dead," he said. Wen sat like stone as he digested the news. "We tracked the last of them as they ran back to their main camp."

"Perhaps that is why you brought so few men to the Kerait," Wen said, nodding. "I understand."

Temujin frowned. He had exaggerated his numbers and been caught, but he could not let it pass.

"We lost four men in the raid and killed thirty. We have their horses and weapons, but not the men to ride them, unless I find them here."

Togrul looked at Wen Chao, watching his reaction with interest.

"They have done well, Wen, is it not so? He deserves the reputation he has gathered for himself. At least you have brought the right man to the Kerait." The khan's gaze fell on a few greasy scraps of meat left on a platter. He reached for them, scooping up the rich fat in his hand.

"You will have your thirty men, Temujin, the best of the Kerait. Bring me a hundred heads and I will have your name written into the songs of my people."

Temujin smiled tightly. "You honor me, my lord, but if I bring you a hundred heads, I will want a hundred warriors for summer."

He watched as Togrul wiped his hands with a cloth, thinking. The man was obscenely large, but Temujin did not doubt the fierce intelligence that lurked in those dark eyes. Togrul had already voiced his fear of being betrayed. How could he trust a stranger better than a man from his own tribe? Temujin wondered if Togrul believed the Kerait warriors would return to his gers unchanged after a battle with the Tartars. Temujin remembered the words of his father long ago. There was no bond stronger than that between those who have risked their lives in each other's company. It could be greater than tribe or family, and Temujin meant to have those warriors of the Kerait as his own.

Wen Chao was the one to break the silence, perhaps guessing at Togrul's misgivings.

"Give just a year to war, my lord," he said to Togrul, "and you will have another thirty at peace. You will rule lands of beauty."

He spoke almost in a whisper and Temujin watched

him with growing dislike. Togrul did not move as the words reached his ear, but after a time, he nodded, satisfied.

"I will give you my best men to crush the Tartar camp," he said. "If you succeed, perhaps I will trust you with more. I will not burden you with other promises, as you seem to scorn them. We can aid each other and each man will get what he wants. If there is betrayal, I will deal with that as it comes."

Temujin maintained the cold face as he replied, showing nothing of the hunger that ate at him. "We are agreed, then. I will want your warrior with me, also, Wen Chao. The one called Yuan."

Wen sat very still, considering. In fact, he had been going to suggest the same thing and wondered at his luck. He made himself look reluctant.

"For this first attack, you may take him. He is a fine soldier, though I would prefer him not to know I said that."

Temujin put out his hand and Togrul took it first in his fleshy fingers, before Wen pressed his own bonier fingers in a grip.

"I will make them *reel*," Temujin said. "Have this Yuan brought to me, Wen Chao. I want to test his armor and see if we can make more."

"I will have a hundred sets sent within a year," Wen protested.

Temujin shrugged. "I could be dead within a year. Summon your man."

Wen nodded to one of his ever-present servants, sending him scurrying away to return with Yuan in a few moments. The soldier's face was utterly blank of emotion as he bowed first to Togrul and Wen Chao, then to

Temujin himself. Temujin approached him as Wen barked orders in his own language. Whatever he had said, Yuan stood like a statue while Temujin examined his armor closely, seeing how the overlapping plates were joined and sewn into heavy, rigid cloth underneath.

"Will it stop an arrow?" Temujin asked.

Yuan dropped his gaze and nodded. "One of yours, yes," he replied.

Temujin smiled tightly. "Stand very still, Yuan," he said, striding away.

Wen Chao watched with interest as Temujin picked up his bow and strung it, fitting an arrow to the string. Yuan showed no fear and Wen was proud of his apparent calm as Temujin pulled back to his ear, holding the bow in perfect stillness for a moment as he sighted down it.

"Let us find out," Temujin said, releasing in a snap.

The arrow struck hard enough to send Yuan backwards, hammering him off his feet. He lay stunned for a moment, then just as Temujin thought he was dead, Yuan raised his head and struggled upright. His face was impassive, but Temujin saw a glint in his eyes that suggested there was life somewhere deep.

Temujin ignored the shocked cries of the Kerait around him. Togrul was on his feet, and his bondsmen had moved quickly to put themselves between their khan and the stranger. Carefully, so as not to excite them, Temujin put his bow down and loosened the string before crossing the distance to Yuan.

The arrow had broken through the first plate of lacquered iron, the head catching in the thick cloth underneath so that it stuck out and vibrated with Yuan's breath. Temujin undid the ties at Yuan's throat and waist, pulling aside a silk under-tunic until the bare chest was exposed.

There was a flowering bruise on Yuan's skin, around an oval gash. A thin line of blood trickled down the muscles to his stomach.

"You can still fight?" Temujin asked.

Yuan's voice was strained as he spat a reply. "Try me."

Temujin chuckled at the anger he saw. The man had great courage and Temujin clapped him on the back. He peered closer at the hole left by the arrow.

"The tunic of silk has not torn," he said, fingering the spot of blood.

"It is a very strong weave," Yuan replied. "I have seen wounds where the silk was carried deep into the body without being holed."

"Where can I find shirts of it?" Temujin murmured.

Yuan looked at him. "Only in the Chin cities."

"Perhaps I will send for some," Temujin said. "Our own boiled leather does not stop arrows as well as this. We can make use of your armor." He turned to Togrul, who still stood in shock at what he had witnessed. "The Kerait have a forge? Iron?"

Togrul nodded mutely and Temujin looked at Arslan.

"Can you make this armor?"

Arslan stood to inspect Yuan as Temujin had, pulling the arrow from where it had lodged and examining the torn square of gray metal. The lacquer had fallen away in flakes and the metal had buckled before allowing the arrow through. Under the pressure of Arslan's fingers, the last of the stitching fell away and it came free in his hand.

"We could carry replacements," Arslan said. "This one cannot be used again." Yuan's eyes followed the broken piece of iron as Arslan moved it. His breathing had steadied and Temujin could not help but be impressed by the man's personal discipline.

"If we stay with the Kerait for five days, how many sets can I have?" Temujin said, pressing him.

Arslan shook his head as he thought. "These thin iron plates are not difficult to forge, though each one must be finished by hand. If I leave them rough and have helpers in the forge and women to sew them..." He paused to think it through. "Perhaps three, maybe more."

"Then that is your task," Temujin said. "If Wen Chao will lend us more from his guards, we will have a force of men the Tartars cannot kill. We will make them fear us."

Wen pursed his mouth as he considered. It was true that the first minister would send gold and horses if he asked. The court did not stint on the materials to bribe the tribes. He was not certain they would be so generous with weapons and armor. Only a fool gave away his advantages in war, for all the promises Wen had made to the young raider. If he allowed Temujin to take his men's armor, he did not doubt it would raise an eyebrow in the court if they ever heard of it, but what choice did he have? He inclined his head, forcing a smile.

"They are yours, my lord. I will have them brought to you tonight." He repressed a shudder at the thought of Temujin's men going as well armored as any soldier of the Chin. Perhaps in time he would have to court the Tartars to have them curb the Mongol tribes. He wondered if he might have extended his stay in the plains, his heart sinking at the thought.

In the gers of the Kerait the following night, Khasar cuffed his youngest brother, sending Temuge spinning. At thirteen years of age, the boy had none of the fire of his older brethren and tears sparkled in his eyes as he steadied himself.

"What was that for?" Temuge demanded.

Khasar sighed. "How is it that you are our father's son, little man?" he demanded. "Kachiun would have taken my head off if I tried to hit him like that, and he is only a couple of years older than you."

With a shout, Temuge launched himself at Khasar, only to be knocked flat as his brother cuffed him again.

"That was a little better," Khasar admitted grudgingly. "I had killed a man by the time I was your age..." He stopped, shocked to see that Temuge was sniveling, tears running down his cheeks. "You're not *crying*? Kachiun, can you believe this little scrap?"

Kachiun lay on a bed in the corner of the ger, ignoring them as he applied a layer of oil to his bow. He paused at the question, looking over to where Temuge was rubbing at his nose and eyes.

"He's just a child, still," he said, returning to his task.

"I am not!" Temuge shouted, red in the face.

Khasar grinned at him. "You cry like one," he said, taunting. "If Temujin saw you like that, he'd leave you for the dogs."

"He would not," Temuge said, tears appearing in his eyes again.

"He would, you know. He'd strip you naked and leave you on a hill for the wolves to bite," Khasar continued, looking sad. "They like the young ones, for the tender meat."

Temuge snorted in disdain. "He said I could ride with him against the Tartars, if I wanted," he announced.

Khasar knew Temujin had made the offer, but he feigned amazement. "What, a little scrap like you? Against those great hairy Tartars? They're worse than wolves, boy, those warriors. Taller than us and white-skinned, like ghosts. Some people say they are ghosts and they come for you when you fall asleep."

"Leave him alone," Kachiun murmured.

Khasar considered, subsiding reluctantly. Kachiun took his silence for assent and sat up on the bed.

"They are not ghosts, Temuge, but they are hard men and good with the bow and the sword. You are not strong enough yet to stand against them."

"You were, at my age," Temuge said.

There was a line of shining mucus under his nose, and Khasar wondered if it would drip down to the boy's mouth. He watched it with interest as Kachiun swung his legs to the floor to address Temuge.

"I could fire a bow better than you at your age, yes. I practiced every day until my hands were cramped and my fingers bled." He patted his right shoulder with his left hand, indicating the compact muscle there. It was larger than his left and writhed whenever he moved.

"It built my strength, Temuge. Have you done the same? Whenever I see you, you are playing with the children, or talking to our mother."

"I have practiced," Temuge said sullenly, though

they both knew he was lying, or at least skirting the truth. Even with a bone ring to protect his fingers, he was a hopeless archer. Kachiun had taken him out many times and run with him, building his stamina. It did not seem to make the boy's wind any better. At the end of only a mile, he would be puffing and gasping.

Khasar shook his head, as if weary. "If you cannot fire a bow and you are not strong enough to use a sword, will you kick them to death?" he said. He thought the little boy might leap at him again, but Temuge had given up.

"I hate you," he said. "I hope the Tartars kill you both." He would have stormed out of the ger, but Khasar deliberately tripped him as he passed, so that he fell flat in the doorway. Temuge ran off without looking back.

"You are too hard on him," Kachiun said, reaching for his bow again.

"No. If I hear one more time that he is such a 'sensitive boy,' I think I will lose my dinner. Do you know who he was talking to today? The Chin, Wen Chao. I heard them chattering about birds or something as I went by. You tell me what that was about."

"I can't, but he is my baby brother and I want you to stop nagging at him like an old woman; is that too much to ask?"

Kachiun's voice contained a little heat and Khasar considered his response. He could still win their fights, but the last few had resulted in so many painful bruises that he did not provoke one lightly.

"We all treat him differently, and what sort of a warrior is he as a result?" Khasar said.

Kachiun looked up. "Perhaps he will be a shaman, or a storyteller like old Chagatai."

Khasar snorted. "Chagatai was a warrior when he was young, or so he always said. It's no task for a young man."

"Let him find his own path, Khasar," Kachiun said. "It may not be where we lead him."

Borte and Temujin lay together without touching. With blood fresh on their mouths, they had made love on the first night of the punishment raid against the Tartars, though she had cried out in grief and pain as his weight came down on her. He might have stopped then, but she had gripped his buttocks, holding him in her while tears streamed down her face.

It had been the only time. Since that day, she could not bring herself to let him touch her again. Whenever he came to the furs, she would kiss him and curl into his arms, but nothing more. Her monthly blood had not come since leaving the Olkhun'ut, but now she feared for the child. It had to be his, she was almost certain. She had seen the way many dogs would mount a bitch in the camp of the Olkhun'ut. Sometimes the puppies would show the colors of more than one of the fathers. She did not know if the same could apply to her, and she did not dare ask Hoelun.

In the darkness of an unfamiliar ger, she wept again while her husband slept, and did not know why.

CHAPTER 28

TEMUJIN RUBBED ANGRILY at the sweat in his eyes. The armored cloth Arslan had made was far heavier than he had realized. It felt as if he were rolled in a carpet, and his sword arm seemed to have lost half its speed. He faced Yuan as the sun rose, seeing to his irritation how the man wore the same armor without even a trace of perspiration on his forehead.

"Again," Temujin snapped.

Yuan's eyes sparkled with amusement and he bowed before bringing his sword up. He had told them to wear the armor at all times, until it became a second skin. Even after a week on the route back to the Tartar camp, they were still too slow. Temujin forced his men to practice for two hours at dawn and dusk, whether they wore the armor or not. It slowed the progress of the sixty who had ridden out from the Kerait, but Yuan approved of the effort. Without it, the armored men would be like the turtles he remembered from home.

They might survive the first arrows of the Tartars, but on the ground, they would be easy prey.

With the help of the Kerait swordsmiths, Arslan had made five sets of the plated robes. In addition, Wen had made good his promise and delivered ten more, keeping only one back for his new personal guard. Yuan had chosen the man himself, making sure he understood his responsibilities before he left.

Temujin wore one of the new sets, with the plating on a long chest piece as well as another to cover his groin and two more on his thighs. Shoulder guards reached from his neck to his elbow, and it was those that caused him the most difficulty. Time and again, Yuan simply stepped aside from blows, dodging their slow speed easily.

He watched Temujin move toward him, reading his intentions from the way he stepped. The young khan's weight was more strongly on the left foot, and Yuan suspected he would begin the blow from the low left, rising upwards. They used sharp steel blades, but so far there had been little real danger for either of them. Yuan was too much a perfectionist to cut the man in a practice bout, and Temujin never came close.

At the last second, Temujin shifted his weight again, turning the sweep into a lunge. Yuan dropped his right leg back to shift out of the way, letting the blade rasp along the scales of his own armor. He did not fear a cut without force behind it, and that too Temujin was having to learn. Many more blows could be ignored or merely turned with a little delicacy.

As the sword slid past, Yuan stepped forward briskly and brought his hilt up to touch Temujin lightly on the nose. At the same time, he let air explode from his lungs, calling "Hei!" before stepping back.

"Again," Temujin said irritably, moving before Yuan had taken position. This time he held the blade above his head, bringing it down in a chopping motion. Yuan caught the blade on his own and they came chest to chest in a clash of armor. Temujin had placed his leading foot behind Yuan's, and the soldier found himself falling backwards.

He regarded Temujin from the ground, waiting for the next strike.

"Well?"

"Well, what?" Temujin said. "Now I would plunge the sword through your chest."

Yuan did not move. "You would not. I have been trained to fight from any position." As he spoke, he kicked out with one leg, dropping Temujin neatly.

Temujin leapt up, his face strained.

"If I were not wearing this heavy armor, you would not find this so easy," he said.

"I would shoot you from far away," Yuan replied. "Or shoot your horse, if I saw that you were armored."

Temujin was in the process of raising his sword again. His wrists burned with fatigue, but he was determined to get in one solid blow before mounting up for the day's ride. Instead, he paused.

"We must armor the ponies, then, just the heads and chest."

Yuan nodded. "I have seen it done. The iron plates can be sewn into a leather harness just as easily as your armor."

"You are a skilled teacher, Yuan, have I told you?" Temujin said.

Yuan watched him carefully, knowing a sudden strike was possible. In truth, he was still amazed that Temujin did not appear to mind being beaten time and time again in front of his men. Yuan could not imagine his old officers ever allowing such a display. The humiliation would have been too much for them, but Temujin seemed unaware, or uncaring. The tribesmen were a strange breed, but they soaked up whatever Yuan could tell them about their new armor. He had even taken to discussing tactics with Temujin and his brothers. It was a new experience for Yuan to have younger men listening so intently. When he was guarding Wen Chao, he knew he existed to give his life for the ambassador, or at least to kill as many enemies as he could before falling. The men who had come into the plains with him all knew their work, and rarely did Yuan have to correct them. He had found that he enjoyed the teaching.

"Once more," he heard Temujin say. "I am going to come from your left."

Yuan smiled. The last two times Temujin had thought to warn him, the attack had come from the right. It did not matter particularly, but he was amused at the attempts to cloud his judgment.

Temujin came in fast, his sword darting with greater speed than Yuan had seen before. He saw the right shoulder dip and brought his blade up. Too late to correct, he saw Temujin had followed through on the left, deliberately. Yuan could still have spoiled the blow, but he chose not to, letting the blade tip touch his throat as Temujin stood panting and exhilarated.

"That was better," Yuan said. "You are getting faster in the armor."

Temujin nodded. "You let the blade through, didn't you?"

Yuan allowed a smile to show. "When you are better still, you will know," he said.

At full gallop, Yuan looked right and left, seeing how Temujin's brothers kept the line solid. The exercises went on all day and Yuan found himself involved in solving the problems of a massed attack. He rode with his bow strapped on his saddle, but the archery of the sixty men was not in question. Togrul had given twenty of his personal bondsmen to the group. They were fit and skilled, but they were not experienced in war and Temujin was scathing at first with them. His own raiders followed his orders with instant obedience, but the new men were always slow.

Yuan had been surprised to be given command of the left wing. The position called for a senior officer and he had expected it to go to Khasar. Certainly Khasar had thought so. Yuan had not missed the glowering looks coming his way from Temujin's brother as he rode with his own ten just inside. After the training bouts each evening, Temujin would gather them around a small fire and give his orders for the following day. It was a small thing perhaps, but he included Yuan in his council, along with Jelme and Arslan, asking a thousand questions. When Yuan could answer from experience, they listened intently. Sometimes Temujin would shake his head halfway through, and Yuan understood his reasoning. The men Temujin commanded had not fought together for years. There was a limit to what could be taught in a short time, even with ruthless discipline.

Yuan heard Temujin's horn sound two short blasts. It meant the left wing was to ride ahead of the rest of them, skewing the line. Over the pounding of hooves, Yuan shared a glance with Khasar and both groups of ten accelerated to their new position.

Yuan looked around him. It had been neatly done, and this time even Togrul's bondsmen had heard the call and responded. They were improving and Yuan felt a spark of pride in his heart. If his old officers could see him, they would laugh themselves sick. First sword in Kaifeng and here he was riding with wild savages. He tried to mock himself as the soldiers at home would have done, but somehow his heart wasn't in it.

Temujin blew a single note and the right wing moved up alongside, leaving the center behind. Yuan looked across at Kachiun and Jelme riding there, grim-faced in their armor. The riders around Temujin's brother were a little more ragged, but they dressed the line as Yuan watched, thundering forward as one. He nodded to himself, beginning to relish the battle to come.

From behind, Temujin blew a long note, falling. They slowed together, each of the officers shouting orders at the men in their groups of ten. The rugged ponies slowed to a canter, then a trot, and Temujin moved up the center group with Arslan.

Temujin rode ahead as the line re-formed, swinging his mount across to the left wing. He allowed them to catch him and Yuan saw his face was flushed with excitement, his eyes bright.

"Send the scouts on ahead, Yuan," Temujin called. "We will rest the ponies while they search."

"Your will, my lord," Yuan replied automatically.

He caught himself as he turned in the saddle to two young warriors, then shrugged. He had been a soldier too long to change his habits, and in truth, he was enjoying the task of shaping the tribesmen into a battle group.

"Tayan, Rulakh, move ahead until sunset. If you see anything more than a few wanderers, ride back." By now, he knew all sixty names, forcing them to memory, a matter of personal habit. Both of the men were from Temujin's raiders. They bowed their heads as they passed him, kicking their mounts forward. Yuan showed nothing of his hidden satisfaction, though Temujin seemed to sense it from the grin that came to his face.

"I think you have missed this, Teacher," Temujin called. "The spring is rising in your blood."

Yuan did not respond as Temujin rejoined the line. He had been two years with Wen Chao on guard duty. The oath he had given to the emperor bound him to follow any order given by a lawful authority. In his deepest heart, he acknowledged the truth of Temujin's words. He had missed the comradeship of a campaign, though the tribesmen were nothing like the men he had known. He hoped the brothers would live past the first clash of arms.

The moon was full again a month out from the Kerait. The exuberance of the first weeks had been replaced by a grim purpose. There was not so much chatter round the fires as there had been, and the scouts were on edge. They had found the site where Temujin and his brothers had seen the large group of Tartars. The blackened circles of grass brought back dark memories for the men who had been there. Kachiun and Khasar were particularly quiet as they remounted. The night they had rescued Borte had been burnt into them, too deep to forget Temujin's chant, or the burst of light they had felt as they swallowed the flesh of their enemies. They did not speak of what they had done. That night had seemed endless, but when the dawn had finally come, they had scouted the area, trying to see where the small group had been taking her. The main Tartar camp had not been far away. The last of the raiders could have reached it in a morning's ride, and Borte would have been lost for months, if not forever.

Temujin pressed his hand into the ashes of a fire and grimaced. It was cold.

"Send the scouts out wider," he said to his brothers. "If we catch them on the move, it will be quick."

The Tartar camp had come prepared for a season, perhaps with the intention of hunting the raiders who had troubled them all winter. They moved with carts laden with gers and large herds whose droppings could be read and counted. Temujin wondered how close they were. He remembered his frustration as he lay with Tartar blood on his mouth and watched a peaceful camp too large to attack. There was no question of letting them escape. He had gone to Togrul as one having no other choice.

"There were many people in this place," Yuan noted at his shoulder. The Chin warrior had counted the black circles and noted the tracks. "More than the hundred you told Togrul."

Temujin looked at him. "Perhaps. I could not say for sure."

Yuan watched the man who had brought them to kill across a wilderness. It occurred to him that fifty of Togrul's best men would have been better than thirty. The newcomers would have outnumbered Temujin's people, and perhaps that was not to the young man's liking. Yuan had noticed how Temujin had mixed the groups, making them work together. His reputation for ferocity was known—and for success. Already, they looked on him as a khan. Yuan wondered if Togrul knew the risk he had taken. He sighed to himself as Temujin moved away to talk with his brothers. Gold and land would buy great risks, if used well. Wen Chao had shown the truth of that.

Temujin nodded to his brothers, including Temuge in the gesture. His youngest brother had been given the smallest set of armor. Wen Chao's men were given to lightness of frame, but it was still too big for him, and Temujin repressed a smile as he saw Temuge turn stiffly to his pony, testing the straps and reins.

"You have done well, little brother," Temujin said as he passed him. He heard Khasar snort nearby, but ignored it. "We will find them soon, Temuge. Will you be ready when we ride to the attack?"

Temuge looked up at the brother he revered. He did not speak of the cold fear in his stomach, nor of the way the riding had exhausted him until he thought he would drop from the saddle and shame them all. Every time he dismounted, his legs had stiffened to the point where he had to hold the pony tightly or drop to his knees.

"I will be ready, Temujin," he said, forcing a cheerful tone. Inside, he despaired. He knew his own archery was barely worth the name, and the Tartar sword

Temujin had given him was too heavy for his hand. He had a smaller blade hidden inside his deel, and he hoped to use that. Even then, the thought of actually cutting skin and muscle, of feeling blood pour over his hands, was something he dreaded. He could not be as strong and ruthless as the others. He did not yet know what use he could be to any of them, but he could not bear the scorn in Khasar's eyes. Kachiun had come to him the night before they left, saying that Borte and Hoelun would need support in the camp of the Kerait. It had been a transparent attempt to let him out of the fighting to come, but Temuge had refused it. If they needed help at all, fifty warriors could not save them in the heart of the Kerait. Their presence was a surety that Temujin would return with the heads he had promised.

Of all the brothers, only Temuge had not been made an officer. With Jelme, Arslan, and Yuan as well as his brothers, Temujin had the five he needed, and Temuge knew he was still too young, too inexperienced in war. He touched the blade of his long knife as he mounted, feeling its sharpness. He dreamed of saving their lives, over and over, so that they would look at him with astonishment and realize he was truly Yesugei's son. He did not like to wake from those dreams. He shivered as they rode out once again, feeling the cold more than the other men seemed to. He looked inside himself for the easy courage they displayed and found nothing but terror.

The scouts found the main force of the Tartars only two days after Temujin had visited the old camp. The men rode in at full gallop, leaping from their horses to report to Temujin.

"They are moving, my lord," the first blurted out. "They have outriders in all directions, but the army is moving slowly through the next valley, coming this way."

Temujin showed his teeth. "They sent out thirty men to find us and not a single one made it back alive. They must suspect a large tribe is in the area. Good. If they are cautious, they will hesitate."

He raised his arm to bring his officers in close. They had all watched the excited actions of the scouts, and they came in fast, expecting the news.

"Tell your men to follow their orders," Temujin said as he mounted. "We ride as one, taking your speed from me. If any man breaks formation, I will leave him for the hawks."

He saw Khasar grinning and glowered at him.

"Even if he is my own brother, Khasar, even then. Loose your arrows on my call, then draw swords. We will hit them as one line. If you are unhorsed, stay alive long enough for the rest of us to finish the killing."

"You will not take prisoners?" Arslan asked.

Temujin did not hesitate. "If any survive our attack, I will question their leaders to learn more. After that I have no use for them. I will not swell our ranks with blood enemies."

The word spread quickly through the warriors as their officers returned to them. They walked their ponies forward in a single rank. As they passed a ridge, each man could see the Tartar formation, with riders and carts moving slowly across the plain.

As one, they began to trot toward the enemy.

Temujin heard distant alarm horns sound and he untied his bow, fitting a string and testing it. He reached back to open the quiver strapped to his saddle, raising the first arrow and testing the feathers with his thumb. It would fly straight and true, as they would.

CHAPTER 29

THE TARTARS did not lack for courage. As their warning horns moaned across the plain, every warrior ran for his horse, mounting with shrill yells that carried to the ears of Temujin's warriors. His sixty rode together as they increased their pace to a gallop. His officers snarled orders at any man who proved too eager, watching Temujin himself as he drew his first arrow in perfect balance.

Yuan had discussed the advantage of hitting the enemy as a line, and it showed in the first bloody contacts with the Tartar outriders. As Temujin's men reached them the Tartar scouts were spitted on long shafts, their bodies falling with their horses. Temujin could see the Tartars had split their force to leave some to defend their carts, but there were still more than he had guessed, boiling out across the plains like wasps.

Temujin's charge swept through them, crashing over dying horses and men as they were met in twos, in fives, a dozen at a time. The bows snapped quick death at the gallop and brought too great a force to resist on the loose Tartar formations. It seemed to Temujin as if just heartbeats passed before they had left a trail of dead men and riderless horses behind them and the carts were approaching at dizzying speed. He glanced left and right before blowing three quick blasts, calling for the horns formation. He had almost left it too late, but Yuan's men moved up, matching Kachiun and Jelme on the right. They hit the carts in a crescent, enveloping the herds and Tartars with a roar.

Temujin's grasping fingers found his quiver was empty, and he threw his bow to the ground, drawing his sword. At the center of the crescent, he found his way blocked by a heavy cart laden with felt and leather. He barely saw the first man to step into his path, taking his head with a single swing of his blade before kicking in his heels and charging into a mass of Tartar warriors. Arslan and ten more went with him into the center, killing as they went. Women and children threw themselves under the carts in terror as the riders swept through, and their wailing was like the keening of hawks on the wind.

The change came without warning. One of the Tartars dropped his sword, and even then he would have been killed if he had not thrown himself flat as Khasar passed by. Others did the same, lying prostrate as Temujin and his officers galloped around the camp, looking for resistance. It took time for the bloodlust to ease in them, and it was Temujin himself who reached for his horn and blew the falling note that meant a slower pace. His men were spattered with fresh blood, but they heard him and ran their fingers along their blades, cleaning away the sheen of life.

There was a moment of utter stillness. Where, before, their ears had rung with pounding hooves and bellowing orders, the quiet now swelled around them. Temujin listened in wonder to a silence that lasted long enough for his brothers to come to his side. Somewhere a woman began to wail and the bleating of sheep and goats began again. Perhaps they had always been there, but Temujin had not heard them over the pulse of blood that stopped his ears and made his heart throb in his chest.

He tightened his reins, turning his horse around as he surveyed the scene. The camp had been shattered. Those Tartars who still lived were on their faces in the grass, silent and despairing. He looked back over the path of the attack and saw one rider who had somehow survived the charge. The man was slack-jawed at what he had witnessed, too stunned even to ride for his life.

Temujin squinted at the lone rider, nodding to Kachiun.

"Bring him in, or kill him," he said.

Kachiun gave a brisk nod and tapped Khasar on the shoulder for more arrows. Khasar had only two, but he handed them over and Kachiun took up his bow from where it was neatly strapped to his saddle. He had not thrown the valuable weapon down, Temujin noticed, with wry amusement.

Temujin and Khasar watched as Kachiun galloped out after the Tartar rider. The sight of him coming seemed to jerk the man out of a trance, and he turned his mount to escape at last. Kachiun closed the gap before the Tartar could hit full gallop, then fired an arrow that took him high in the back. The man rode on for a few moments before he fell, and Kachiun left him there, turning back to the camp and raising his bow to signal the kill.

Temujin started as his men roared. They had all been watching and the gesture released their excitement. Those who had bows raised them up, jerking their arms in triumph. It had happened so fast that they had been caught somehow at the finish, unsure. Now the great rush of joy that comes from facing death and living filled them all, and they dismounted. Some of Togrul's bondsmen moved excitedly to the carts, pulling aside hides and felt to see what they had won for themselves.

Arslan's men tied the prisoners, taking away their weapons. Some of them were unmarked and they were treated roughly, with contempt. They had no right to be alive after such a battle, and Temujin cared nothing for them. He found his hands were shaking, and as he dismounted he led his horse to keep a grip on the reins that would hide the weakness.

He glanced up from his thoughts when he saw his brother Temuge ride in close and swing a leg down. The boy was milk-white and clearly shaken, but Temujin saw he carried a bloody blade as if he did not know how it came to be in his hand. Temujin tried to catch his brother's eye to congratulate him, but Temuge turned and vomited on the grass. Temujin walked away rather than shame him by noticing. When he had recovered, he would find a few words of praise for the boy.

Temujin stood in the center of the carts, feeling the eyes of his officers on him. They were waiting for something and he raised a hand to his eyes, pressing away the dark thoughts that slid and jostled for space in his mind. He cleared his throat and made his voice carry.

"Arslan! Find whatever skins of airag they had with them and put a guard on them, someone you can trust. Khasar, send out eight men as scouts around us. There may be more of them." He turned to Kachiun as he returned and leapt nimbly down from his pony. "Gather the prisoners, Kachiun, and have your ten set up three of their gers as quickly as you can. We will stop here for tonight."

It was not enough, he realized. They still watched him with gleaming eyes and the beginnings of smiles.

"You have done well," he called to them. "Whatever we have won is yours, to be split equally among you."

They cheered at that, stealing glances at the Tartar carts laden with valuables. The horses alone would mean instant wealth for many of them, but Temujin did not care for that. At the moment the battle was won, he had faced the prospect of returning to Togrul. The khan of the Kerait would claim his share, of course. That was his right, even if he had not been present. Temujin would not begrudge him a few dozen ponies and swords. Still, it nagged at him. He did not want to return. The thought of meekly handing back the bondsmen who had served him so well made his jaw clench in irritation. He needed them all, and Togrul was a man who saw only the lands of the Chin as a reward. On impulse, Temujin reached down and brushed the grass at his feet. Someone had been killed over that patch, he realized. Tiny droplets of blood clung to the blades and spotted his hand as he stood straight. He raised his voice again.

"Remember this, when you tell your children you fought with the sons of Yesugei. There is one tribe and one land that recognizes no borders. This is merely a beginning."

Perhaps they cheered because they were still filled with the excitement of victory; it did not matter.

The Tartars had come prepared for a long campaign. The carts contained oil for lamps, woven ropes, cloths from the thinnest silk to canvas so thick it would hardly bend. In addition, there was a leather bag of silver coins and enough black airag to warm the coldest throats on winter nights. Temujin had those last items brought to him and stacked against the inner wall of the first ger to be erected. More than twenty Tartars had survived the attack, and he had questioned them to find their leader. Most had merely looked at him, remaining silent. Temujin had drawn his sword and killed three before the fourth man swore and spat on the ground.

"There is no leader here," the Tartar had said in fury. "He died with the others."

Without a word, Temujin had yanked the man to his feet and handed him over to stand by Arslan. He looked down the line of men, his face cold.

"I have no love for your people, no need to keep you alive," he said. "Unless you can be useful to me, you will be killed here."

No one else responded and the Tartars did not meet his eyes.

"Very well," Temujin said into the silence. He turned to the closest of his warriors, one of the brothers he had brought into his camp in the north. "Kill the rest quickly, Batu," he said. The little man drew his knife without expression.

"Wait! I can be of use to you," another of the Tartars said suddenly.

Temujin paused, then shrugged and shook his head. "It is too late," he said.

In the ger, Arslan had bound the sole survivor of the Tartar force. The cries of the rest had been pitiful and the warrior looked at them with hatred.

"You have killed the others. You will kill me, no matter what I say," he said, straining at the ropes behind his back.

Temujin considered. He needed to know as much as possible about the Tartars.

"If you hold nothing back, I give you my oath you will live," he said.

The Tartar snorted. "How long would I live out here on my own without even a weapon?" he snapped. "Promise me a bow and a pony and I will tell you anything you like."

Temujin grinned suddenly. "You are bargaining with me?"

The Tartar did not reply and Temujin chuckled.

"You are braver than I expected. You have my oath that you will be given whatever you ask."

The Tartar slumped in relief, but Temujin spoke again before he could marshal his thoughts.

"Why have you come into the lands of my people?"

"You are Temujin of the Wolves?" the man asked.

Temujin did not trouble to correct him. It was the name that spread fear in the north, whether he was part of that tribe or not.

"I am."

"There is a blood price on your head. The khans of the north want you dead," the Tartar said with grim pleasure. "They will hunt you down wherever you go."

"You do not hunt a man who comes looking for you," Temujin reminded him softly.

The Tartar blinked, considering the events of the day. He had begun that morning in the midst of strong warriors, and ended it with piles of the dead. He shuddered at the thought and suddenly gave a barking laugh.

"So we hunt each other and only the crows and hawks grow fat," he said. The laughter turned bitter and Temujin waited patiently for the man to regain his control.

"Your people murdered the khan of the Wolves," Temujin reminded him. He did not speak of Borte. That pain was still too ragged and bloody to allow past his lips.

"I know of it," the Tartar replied. "I know who gave him to us, as well. It was not one of my people."

Temujin leaned forward, his yellow eyes fierce.

"You have sworn to tell me all you know," he murmured. "Speak and you will be safe."

The prisoner dropped his head as he thought. "Loose my bonds, first," he said.

Temujin drew his sword, still spattered with the blood of those he had killed. The Tartar began to turn away, holding out his hands to have the ropes cut. Instead, he felt the cold metal touch his throat as Temujin reached around him.

"Tell me," he said.

"The khan of the Olkhun'ut," the Tartar said, the words tumbling. "He took silver to send word to us."

Temujin stepped back. The Tartar turned to face him again, his eyes wild.

"That is where this blood feud started. How many have you killed by now?"

"For my father? Not enough," Temujin replied. "Not nearly enough." He thought again of his wife and the coldness between them. "I have not yet begun to repay my debts to your people."

Temujin held the Tartar with his eyes as the door opened. At first, neither of them looked to see who had come into the ger, then the Tartar's gaze flickered and he looked up. He took in a sharp breath as he saw Yuan standing there, his face grim.

"I know you!" the Tartar said, yanking at his bound wrists in desperation. He turned his face to Temujin in clear terror. "Please, I can—"

Yuan moved quickly, drawing and killing in a single stroke. His blade cut through the Tartar's neck in a spray of blood.

Temujin reacted with blinding speed, seizing Yuan's wrist and bearing him backwards until he came up against the wicker lattice wall and was pinned there. He held Yuan by the throat and hand, his face working in fury.

"I told him he would live," Temujin said. "Who are you to bring dishonor to my word?"

Yuan could not reply. The fingers on his throat were like iron and his face began to grow purple. Temujin ground the bones in his wrist until the sword fell from his fingers and then shook him in rage, cursing.

Without warning, Temujin let go and Yuan fell to his knees. Temujin kicked his sword away before he could recover.

"What secrets did he have, Yuan? How did he know you?"

When he spoke, Yuan's voice was a hoarse croak and bruising had already started on his throat.

"He knew nothing. Perhaps I have seen him before when my master traveled into the north. I thought he was attacking you."

Temujin sneered. "On his knees? With his hands bound? You are a liar."

Yuan looked up, his eyes blazing. "I will accept your challenge, if you wish. It does not change anything."

Temujin slapped him hard enough to rock his head to one side.

"What are you hiding from me?" he demanded.

Behind them, the door opened again and Arslan and Kachiun came inside in a rush, their weapons drawn. The gers were not private to anyone standing close by, and they had heard the struggle. Yuan ignored their blades, though his sullen gaze flickered over Arslan for a moment. As they watched, he took a deep breath and closed his eyes.

"I am ready for death, if you choose to take my life," he said, calmly. "I have brought dishonor to you, as you said."

Temujin drummed the fingers of one hand on the other as he watched Yuan kneeling on the ground.

"How long has Wen Chao been among my people, Yuan?" Temujin asked.

It seemed to take an effort of will for Yuan to answer, as if he had gone far away.

"Two years," he said.

"And before him, who did your first minister send?"

"I do not know," Yuan replied. "I was still with the army then."

"Your master has bargained with the Tartars," Temujin continued.

Yuan did not respond, gazing steadily at him.

"I have heard that the khan of the Olkhun'ut betrayed my father," Temujin said softly. "How could the Tartars approach a great tribe to arrange such a thing? It would take an intermediary, a neutral they both trusted, would it not?"

He heard Kachiun gasp behind him as the news sank in.

"Did you travel to the Olkhun'ut as well? Before the Kerait?" Temujin went on, pressing.

Yuan remained still, as if he were made of stone. "You are talking of a time before my master was even in this land," Yuan said. "You are looking for secrets where there are none."

"Before Wen Chao, I wonder who else came among us," Temujin said, murmuring. "I wonder how many times the Chin have sent their men into my lands, betraying my people. I wonder what *promises* they made."

The world that had seemed so solid that morning was crumbling all around him. It was too much to take in and Temujin found himself breathing hard, almost dizzy with the revelations.

"They would not want us to grow strong, would they, Yuan? They would want the Tartars and Mongols to tear each other to pieces. Is that not what Wen Chao said to me? That the Tartars had grown too strong, too close to their precious borders?"

Temujin closed his eyes, imagining the cold gaze of the Chin as they considered the tribes. For all he knew, they had been subtly influencing the tribes for centuries, keeping them at each other's throats.

"How many of my people have died because of yours, Yuan?" he said.

"I have told you all I know," Yuan said, raising his

head. "If you will not believe me, then take my life, or send me back to Wen Chao." His face hardened as he continued. "Or put a sword in my hand and let me defend myself against these accusations."

It was Arslan who spoke, his face pale at what he had heard. "Let me, my lord," he said to Temujin, never taking his eyes from Yuan. "Give him a sword and I will face him."

Yuan turned to look at the swordsmith, his mouth turning upwards at the edges. Without speaking, he bowed his head slightly, acknowledging the offer.

"I have heard too much. Bind him until dawn and I will decide then," Temujin said. He watched as Kachiun tied Yuan's hands expertly. He did not resist or struggle, even when Kachiun kicked him onto his side. He lay by the body of the Tartar he had killed, his face calm.

"Post a guard on him while we eat," Temujin ordered, shaking his head. "I need to think."

At the first light of dawn, Temujin paced up and down outside the cluster of small gers, his face troubled. He had not slept. The scouts he had sent away with Khasar had not yet returned, and his thoughts still writhed without answers. He had spent years of his life punishing the Tartars for what they had done, for the life of his father and the lives his sons should have led. If Yesugei had survived, Bekter or Temujin would have become khan to the Wolves and Eeluk would have remained a loyal bondsman. There was a trail of death and pain between the day he had been told and the current one that found him troubled and depressed, his life torn into tatters. What had he accomplished in those years? He thought of Bekter and, for a moment, wished he were alive. The path could have been very different if Yesugei had not been killed.

As Temujin stood alone he felt fresh anger kindle in his chest. The khan of the Olkhun'ut deserved some measure of the misery he had caused. Temujin remembered the revelation he had experienced as a captive of the Wolves. There was no justice in the world—unless he made it for himself. Unless he cut twice as deep as he had been cut and gave back blow for blow. He had the right.

In the dim distance, he saw two of his scouts racing back toward the gers. Temujin frowned at their headlong pace, feeling his heart thump faster. Their arrival had not gone unnoticed and he sensed the camp come alive around him as men pulled on deels and armor, saddling their horses with quick efficiency. He was proud of them all and he wondered again what to do about Yuan. He could not trust him any longer, but Temujin had conceived a liking for the man ever since he had fired an arrow at his chest in the camp of the Kerait. He did not want to kill him.

As the scouts came closer he saw that Khasar was one of them, riding like a maniac. His horse was blowing and lathered in sweat, and Temujin felt the alarm spread through the men who waited for news. Khasar was not one to panic easily, but he rode without thought for his own safety or that of his mount.

Temujin forced himself to remain still while Khasar rode up and jumped to the ground. The men had to see him as different, untouched by their own fears.

"What is it, my brother, to have made you ride so fast?" Temujin asked, keeping his voice steady.

"More Tartars than I have ever seen," Khasar replied, panting. "An army to make these ones we killed look like a raiding band." He paused for breath. "You said they might come in force in the spring, and they have."

"How many?" Temujin snapped.

"More than I could count, a day's ride at most, probably closer by now. The ones we have killed are just the trailbreakers. There are *hundreds* of carts coming, horses. Maybe a thousand men. I've never see anything like it, brother, never."

Temujin grimaced. "I have news of my own that you will not want to hear. It will wait for this. Water your horse before it drops dead. Have the men mount up and find a fresh pony yourself. I will want to see this army that can frighten my little brother."

Khasar snorted. "I didn't say they frightened me, but I thought you might like to know the entire Tartar nation is coming south for your head. That's all." He grinned at the idea. "By the spirits, Temujin. We stung them and stung them and now they are roaring." He looked around at the men who watched, listening to every word. "What are we going to do now?"

"Wait, Khasar. There is something I must do first," Temujin said. He strode to the ger where Yuan had spent the night, vanishing inside. Arslan and Kachiun went after him and the three men escorted Yuan out into the gray light, where he blinked and rubbed his wrists. His ropes had been cut and Khasar could only stand in amazement, wondering what had happened in his absence.

Temujin faced the Chin soldier.

"I have come to think of you as a friend, Yuan. I

cannot kill you today," he said. As Yuan stood in silence, Temujin brought a saddled pony to him and passed the reins into his hands.

"Return to your master," Temujin said.

Yuan mounted easily. He looked down at Temujin for a long moment.

"I wish you good fortune, my lord," Yuan said at last.

Temujin slapped his hand on the pony's rump, and Yuan went trotting away without looking back.

Khasar came up to his brothers, his gaze following theirs after the retreating soldier.

"I imagine this means I have the left wing," he said.

Temujin chuckled. "Find a fresh horse, Khasar, and you too, Kachiun. I want to see what you saw." He looked round to find Jelme already mounted and ready to go.

"Take the men back to the Kerait and tell them an army is gathered. Togrul will have to fight or run, as he pleases."

"What about us?" Khasar said, bewildered. "We need more than sixty warriors. We need more men than the Kerait can put in the field."

Temujin turned his face to the south, bitter with memories.

"When I have seen this invading army with my own eyes, we will come back to the lands around the red hill," he said. "I will find the men we need, but we have another enemy we must face first." He looked so grim that even Khasar did not speak, and Temujin spoke so quietly they barely heard him.

"My brothers and I have a debt to settle with the

Olkhun'ut, Arslan. We could all be killed. You do not have to come with us."

Arslan shook his head. He did not look at Jelme, though he felt his son's eyes on him.

"You are my khan," he replied.

"Is it enough?" Temujin said.

Arslan nodded slowly.

"It is everything."

CHAPTER 30

TEMUJIN STOOD with his arms outstretched as the bondsmen of the Olkhun'ut searched him thoroughly. Khasar and Arslan endured the same hands patting down every inch of them. The men who guarded Sansar's ger sensed the grim moods of the visitors and missed nothing. All three men wore Chin armor over summer deels and silk undertunics taken from the Tartars. Temujin glared as the bondsmen fingered the strange plates sewn into the heavy cloth. One of the men began to comment on them, but Temujin chose that moment to slap his hand away, as if irritated by the affront to his dignity. His heart beat a fast rhythm in his chest as he stood there, waiting to meet his oldest enemy.

Around them, the ever-curious Olkhun'ut had gathered, chattering to each other and pointing at the strangely garbed men who had disturbed their morning work. Temujin did not see old Sholoi among them, but his glowering uncle was there and Koke had taken possession of their swords once more, disappearing into the khan's ger to bring news of their arrival. The young warrior had accepted their blades with something like disappointment on his face. Even at a glance, he could tell they were not of the quality that Temujin had carried before. The Tartar workmanship was rough, and the blades had to be sharpened more often than Arslan's best steel.

"You may enter," one of the bondsmen said at last. "And you," he added, pointing to Khasar. "Your friend will have to wait out here."

Temujin hid his dismay. He was not certain he could trust Khasar to keep his temper under strain, but Kachiun had other tasks that morning. He did not bother to reply and dipped low to pass through the small door, his mind racing.

For once, Sansar was not sitting in the great seat that dominated the ger he used for formal meetings. He was talking in a low voice to two more of his bondsmen as Temujin entered. Koke stood to one side, watching them. The swords they had carried were carelessly piled against the wall, an indication of their value.

At the creak of the door, Sansar broke off his murmuring and stepped up to his seat. Temujin saw that he moved with care, as if age were making his bones brittle. The khan still had the look of an old snake, with his shaved head and sunken eyes that were never still. It was hard for Temujin to look at him without showing a trace of hatred, but he kept the cold face. The Olkhun'ut bondsmen took up positions on either side of their master, glaring at the new arrivals. Temujin forced himself to remember the courtesies owed to a khan of a powerful tribe.

"I am honored to be in your presence, my lord Sansar," he said.

"Yet again," Sansar replied. "I thought I had seen the last of you. Why do you trouble me in my home, Temujin? I seem to see more of you than my own wives. What more could you possibly want from me?"

Temujin saw Koke smile out of the corner of his eye, and he flushed at the tone. He sensed Khasar stirring irritably and flashed a warning glance at his brother before speaking.

"Perhaps you have heard of the Tartar army coming fast out of the wastes of the north. I have seen them with my own eyes and I have come to warn you."

Sansar gave a dry chuckle. "Every wanderer and herdsman for a thousand miles is talking of them. The Olkhun'ut have no quarrel with the Tartars. We have not traveled that far north for forty years, before my time as khan." His eyes gleamed as he leaned forward in the chair, looking down at the two men standing stiffly before him.

"You have stirred them to war, Temujin, with your raids. You must accept the consequences. I fear for you, I really do." His tone belied the words and Temujin hoped Khasar would keep silent as he had been ordered.

"They will not respect those tribes who claim no blood feud with them, my lord," Temujin continued. "I saw a thousand warriors, with as many women and children in their camp. They have come into our lands in greater force than anyone can remember."

"I am appalled," Sansar said, smiling. "What then do you propose to do?"

"Stand in their way," Temujin snapped, his own

temper fraying under the older man's evident amusement.

"With the Kerait? Oh, I have heard of your alliance, Temujin. The news spreads quickly when it is something so interesting. But will it be enough? I don't think Togrul can bring more than three hundred warriors to that particular feast."

Temujin took a slow breath, mastering himself. "The Olkhun'ut archers have a high reputation, my lord. With another three hundred of your men, I could—"

He broke off as Sansar chuckled, looking round at Koke and his two bondsmen. Sansar saw the angry expressions of Temujin and Khasar and made an attempt to be serious.

"I am sorry, but the idea was . . ." He shook his head. "You are here to beg warriors from me? You expect to have the entire strength of the Olkhun'ut ride back under your command? No."

"The Tartars will take us one tribe at a time," Temujin said, taking a step forward in his need to persuade the khan. The bondsmen saw the movement and tensed, but Temujin ignored them. "How long will you be safe, once the Kerait have been destroyed? How long will the Quirai survive, the Naimans, the Wolves? We have remained apart for so long, I think you forget we are one people."

Sansar grew very still, watching Temujin from the recesses of his dark eyes.

"I know no brothers in the Kerait," he said at last, his voice almost a whisper. "The Olkhun'ut have grown strong without their help. You must stand or run on your own, Temujin. You will not have my warriors with you. That is my answer. There will be no other from me."

For a moment, Temujin was silent. When he spoke, it was as if each word were wrung out of him.

"I have bags of silver ingots, captured from the Tartars. Give me a price per man and I will buy them from you."

Sansar threw his head back to laugh and Temujin moved. With a savage jerk, he snapped one of the iron plates from his armor and leapt forward, jamming it into Sansar's bare throat. Blood splashed his face as he ripped the metal edge back and forth, ignoring Sansar's hands as they clawed at him.

The bondsmen were not ready to deal with sudden death. As they broke from shock and drew their swords, Khasar was already there, his fist hammering into the nose of the closest man. He too held a piece of sharpened iron torn from where he and Temujin had weakened the threads in the armor. He used it to cut the throat of the second bondsman in a vicious swipe. The man staggered backwards, falling with a crash on the wooden floor. A bitter smell filled the air as the bondsman's bowels released, his legs still kicking in spasms.

Temujin pulled back from the broken body of the khan, panting and covered with blood. The bondsman Khasar had punched surged forward in mindless rage, but Khasar had taken the sword from his companion. As they met, Temujin leapt from the chair, hammering into Sansar's man and taking him to the polished floor. While Temujin held him, Khasar plunged his blade through the bondsman's heaving chest, working it back and forth until he too was still.

Only Koke stood then, his mouth open in speechless horror. As Temujin and Khasar turned their hard eyes on him, he backed away to the wall, his feet knocking against the Tartar swords. He grabbed at one in desperate fear, pulling the blade free of its scabbard with a jerk.

Temujin and Khasar met each other's gaze. Temujin picked up the second sword and both men stepped toward him with deliberate menace.

"I am your cousin," Koke said, his sword hand visibly shaking. "Let me live, for your mother, at least."

Outside, Temujin could hear shouts of alarm. The warriors of the Olkhun'ut would be gathering, and his life hung in the balance.

"Drop the sword and you will live," he said.

Khasar looked at his brother, but Temujin shook his head. Koke's blade clattered on the floor.

"Now get out," Temujin said. "Run if you want, I do not need you."

Koke almost broke the hinges in his hurry to get the door open. Temujin and Khasar stood for a moment in silence, looking at the gaping throat of the khan of the Olkhun'ut. Without a word, Khasar approached the chair and kicked the body, the force of the blow making it slide down to sprawl bonelessly at their feet.

"When you see my father, tell him how you died," Khasar muttered to the dead khan.

Temujin saw two swords he knew on the wall and he reached for them. They could both hear the shouts and clatter of assembling men outside. He looked at Khasar, his yellow eyes cold.

"Now, brother, are you ready to die?"

They stepped out into the spring sunshine, eyes shifting quickly to judge what waited for them. Arslan stood a pace away from the door, two bodies lying at his feet.

The night before, they had talked through every detail of the plan, but there was no way of knowing what would happen next. Temujin shrugged as he met Arslan's eyes. He did not expect to survive the next few moments. He had given them both a chance to ride away, but they had insisted on coming with him.

"Is he dead?" Arslan said.

"He is," Temujin replied.

He held Arslan's old swords and he pressed the one the swordsmith had carried into his hand. Arslan knew he might not hold it for long, but he nodded as he took it, dropping a Tartar blade to the ground. Temujin looked past the swordsmith to the chaos of the Olkhun'ut warriors. Many of them held drawn bows, but they hesitated without orders and Temujin took the chance before they could find calm and shoot them down.

"Stand still and be silent!" he roared at the crowd.

If anything, the noise of fear and shouting increased, but those who were close by paused and stood watching. Temujin was reminded of the way animals could freeze in the stare of a hunter until it was too late.

"I claim the Olkhun'ut by right of conquest," he bellowed, trying to reach as many of them as he could. "You will not be harmed, on my oath."

He looked around them, judging the level of their fear and rage. Some of the warriors seemed to be urging the others on, but no one was willing yet to rush the khan's ger and kill the men who stood so confidently before them.

On instinct, Temujin took two paces forward, moving toward a group of Sansar's bondsmen. They were seasoned warriors and he knew the risk was greatest there. A single missed word or hesitation and they would erupt into a spasm of violence, too late to save the man they were sworn to protect. Humiliation battled with anger in their faces as Temujin raised his voice again over their heads.

"I am Temujin of the Wolves. You know my name. My mother was Olkhun'ut. My wife is Olkhun'ut. My children will be. I claim the right of inheritance through blood. In time, I will bring all the other tribes under my banners."

Still the bondsmen did not respond. Temujin kept his blade low, by his feet, knowing that to raise it would trigger his death. He saw drawn bows sighted at him and forced calm onto his face. Where was Kachiun? His brother must have heard the disturbance.

"Do not fear when you hear the horns of the watchers," he said in a lower voice to the bondsmen. "It will be my men, but they have orders not to touch my people."

They had begun to lose the pale shock of the first moments and he did not know what they would do. The closest ones seemed to be listening.

"I know you are furious, but you will be honored as I take my people north against the Tartars," he told them. "You will revenge my father's death and we will be one tribe across the face of the plains, one people. As it should always have been. Let the Tartars fear us then. Let the Chin fear us."

He saw their tense hands begin to relax and struggled to keep his triumph from showing on his face. He heard the alarm horns sound and once more sought to reassure the crowd.

"Not one of the Olkhun'ut will be harmed, I swear it on my father's soul. Not by my men. Let them through and consider the oath I will ask you to take." He looked around at the crowd and found them staring back at him, every eye on his.

"You have heard I am a wild wolf to the Tartars, that I am a scourge to them. You have heard my word is iron. I tell you now, the Olkhun'ut are safe under my hand."

He watched as Kachiun and his ten men rode slowly through the crowd, relieved beyond words to see them. Some of the Olkhun'ut still stood rooted to the spot and had to be gently nudged out of the way by their ponies. The crowd held its silence as Kachiun and his men dismounted.

Kachiun did not know what he had expected, but he was amazed at the frozen Olkhun'ut staring at his brother. To his surprise, Temujin embraced him quickly, overcome with emotions that threatened to spoil what he had won.

"I will see the bondsmen privately and take their oath," Temujin said to the crowd. In the silence, they could all hear him. "At sunset, I will take yours. Do not be afraid. Tomorrow, the camp will move north to join the Kerait, our allies." He looked around, seeing that the drawn bows had been lowered at last. He nodded stiffly to the archers.

"I have heard the Olkhun'ut are feared in battle," he said. "We will show the Tartars that they may not come into our lands unpunished."

A heavyset man shouldered his way through the crowd from the rear. One boy was too slow to move and he smacked the back of his hand against the boy's head, knocking him down.

Temujin watched him come, his triumph evaporating. He had known Sansar had sons. The one who approached bore the same features as his father, though on a more powerful frame. Perhaps Sansar himself had once been as strong.

"Where is my father?" the man demanded as he came forward.

The bondsmen turned to see him and many of them bowed their heads automatically. Temujin set his jaw tight, ready for them to rush him. His brothers tensed at his side and every man there was suddenly holding a blade or an axe.

"Your father is dead," Temujin said. "I have claimed the tribe."

"Who are you to speak to me?" the man demanded. Before Temujin could reply, Sansar's son snapped a command at the bondsmen standing ready. "Kill them all."

No one moved and Temujin felt a spark of hope come back to his battered spirit.

"It is too late," he said softly. "I have claimed them by blood and conquest. There is no place for you here."

Sansar's son opened his mouth in amazement, looking round at the people he had known all his life. They would not meet his eyes and his face slowly became a cold mask. He did not lack courage, Temujin could see. His eyes were his father's, roving constantly as he weighed the new situation. At last, he grimaced.

"Then I claim the right to challenge you, in front of them all. If you would take my father's place, you will have to kill me, or I will kill you." He spoke with absolute certainty and Temujin felt a pang of admiration for the man.

"I accept," he said. "Though I do not know your name."

Sansar's son rolled his shoulders, loosening them. "My name is Paliakh, khan of the Olkhun'ut."

It was a brave statement and Temujin bowed his head rather than refute it. He walked back to Arslan and took the fine sword from his fingers.

"Kill him quickly," Arslan hissed under his breath. "If they start to cheer him, we are all dead."

Temujin met his eyes without replying, turning back to Paliakh and tossing him the sword. He watched to see how well Sansar's son caught it, and frowned to himself. All their lives depended now on his skill and the endless training bouts with Arslan and Yuan.

Paliakh swept the blade through the air, his teeth bared. He sneered as Temujin came to face him.

"With that armor? Why don't you just have me shot from a distance? Are you afraid to face me without it?"

Temujin would have ignored the words if the Olkhun'ut bondsmen had not murmured their approval. He held out his arms and waited as Arslan and Kachiun untied the panels. When they were gone, he wore only a light silk tunic and thick cotton trousers. He raised his blade under the eyes of every man and woman of the Olkhun'ut.

"Come at me," Temujin said.

Paliakh roared and darted forward, aiming in his fury to cut Temujin's head from his shoulders with a single downward strike. Temujin stepped left on the outside of the blow, chopping quickly at Paliakh's chest. He opened a gash on the man's side which he didn't seem to feel. The blade came round at blinding speed and Temujin was forced to parry it. They struggled face to face for a moment before Paliakh shoved him away with his free hand. In that instant, Temujin struck, bringing his edge sharply through the man's neck.

Sansar's son tried to spit the blood welling in his throat. Arslan's sword dropped from his fingers and he held both hands up to his neck with a grip of terrible force. Under Temujin's stare, he turned as if to walk away, then fell headlong and was still. A sigh went through the crowd and Temujin watched them coldly, wondering if they would tear him to pieces. He saw Koke there amongst them, his mouth open in horror. As Temujin met his eyes, his cousin turned and shoved through the crowd.

The rest of the Olkhun'ut stared like sheep and Temujin found his patience fraying. He strode through them to a cooking fire, taking a burning brand from under the pot. Turning his back on them all, he touched it to the khan's ger along the edges, watching grimly as the flames took hold and began to lick upwards on the dry felt. It would burn well, and he would not shame the bondsmen by making them see their khan in death.

"Leave us now, until sunset," he called to the crowd. "There is always work to be done and we will leave at dawn. Be ready."

He glared at them until the stunned crowd began to move away, breaking into smaller groups to discuss what had happened. They looked back many times at the figures around the burning ger, but Temujin did not move until only the bondsmen remained.

The men Sansar had chosen as his personal guard were fewer in number than Temujin had realized. The Olkhun'ut had not ridden to war in a generation, and even the Wolves kept more armed men around their khan. Still, they outnumbered the ones Kachiun had brought and there was an uneasy tension between the two groups as they were left alone.

"I will not disturb Sansar's wives and young children on this night," Temujin said to them. "Let them mourn his passing with dignity. They will not suffer by my hand, nor be abandoned as I once was."

Some of the bondsmen nodded their approval. The story of Yesugei's sons and wife was known to them all. It had passed around the tribes until it had become one with a thousand other tales and myths from the storytellers.

"You are welcome at my fire," Temujin told them. He spoke as if there were no possibility of being refused, and perhaps that was why they did not protest. He did not know, or care. A great weariness had descended on him and he found he was hungry and so thirsty he could barely speak.

"Have food brought to us while we discuss the war to come," he said. "I need sharp-witted men to be my officers, and I do not yet know which of you will command and which will be led."

He waited until Kachiun and Khasar had layered wood in a lattice on the cooking fire, building it high and fierce. At last, Temujin took a seat on the ground by the flames. His brothers and Arslan went with him, then the others followed, until they were all sitting on the cold ground, warily watching the new force in their lives.

CHAPTER 31

EXCEPT FOR WAR, there was no precedent for the Olkhun'ut to approach the Kerait on their own, and the warriors on each side showed their nervousness. Both tribes were on the move, as Togrul kept a gap between his own people and the Tartar invaders coming south.

Temujin had sent Kachiun ahead to warn Togrul, but the Kerait had still armed themselves and mounted, forming a defensive position around the center of their camp. Horns sounded their doleful note over and over on the still air. Temujin brought his mother's people closer until both groups could see each other, just half a mile away. He halted them then, riding out to a central point with Khasar, Arslan, and ten of Sansar's bondsmen. He left his own men with the carts, watching for a surprise attack from any direction. The tension was palpable and he did not need to warn them to stay alert. Even with the Kerait's retreat south, the Tartars could not have been more than two weeks' ride away and he was not yet ready for them.

He dismounted on the green grass, letting his pony's head drop to munch at it. In the distance, he could see Togrul and wondered vaguely how the man was going to find a horse to carry him. It was with a wry smile that he saw Togrul mount a cart drawn by two black geldings and whip the reins toward Temujin's party. Wen Chao came with him and the Kerait bondsmen formed a tight square around their lord, carrying bows and swords.

Temujin raised his hands as they came within shouting distance, showing they were empty. It was a pointless gesture considering he was surrounded by armed men, but he did not want to worry Togrul any more than he already had. He needed the support of the fat khan.

"You are welcome in my camp, Togrul of the Kerait," Temujin called. "I grant you guest rights in honor."

Togrul dismounted with elaborate care, his fleshy face set as if made of stone. When he came within arm's reach of Temujin, he looked past him to the ranks of warriors and the mass of the Olkhun'ut drawn up in formation. The assembly of warriors was almost as great as his own, and he gnawed his bottom lip before speaking.

"I accept, Temujin," he replied. Something in Temujin's eyes made him continue. "Are you now khan of the Olkhun'ut? I do not understand it."

Temujin chose his words carefully.

"I have claimed them, by right of my mother and my wife. Sansar is dead and they have come with me to fight the Tartars."

Knowing his man, Temujin had arranged for the cooking fires to be started as soon as the Olkhun'ut stopped on the green plain. As he spoke, enormous platters of roasted mutton and goat were brought forward and great white cloths of felt laid on the ground. As host, Temujin would normally have sat last, but he wanted to put Togrul at his ease. He seated himself on the felt, pulling his legs up under him. The khan of the Kerait had no choice after such a gesture and took a place opposite, gesturing to Wen Chao to join him. Temujin began to relax and did not look round as Khasar and Arslan took their positions with the others. Each of them was matched by a warrior from the Kerait until they were equal in strength. At Temujin's back, the people of the Olkhun'ut waited and watched their new khan in silence.

Yuan too was there and he bowed his head rather than look at Temujin as he lowered himself to the thick mat of felt. Wen Chao glanced at his first soldier and frowned to himself.

"If no one else will ask, Temujin," Togrul began, "how is it that you rode away with only a dozen men and returned with one of the great tribes at your bidding?"

Temujin gestured to the food before he replied, and Togrul began to eat almost automatically, his hands working independently of his sharp eyes.

"The sky father watches over me," Temujin said. "He rewards those of our people who respond to the threat to our land." He did not want to speak of how he had killed Sansar in his own ger, not in front of a man he needed as an ally. It would be too easy for Togrul to fear his war leader.

Togrul was clearly not satisfied with the answer and opened his mouth to speak again, revealing a mush of meat and sauce. Before he could continue, Temujin went on quickly.

"I have a claim on them through blood, Togrul, and

they did not refuse me. What matters is that we have enough men to break the Tartars when they come."

"How many have you brought?" Togrul said, chewing busily.

"Three hundred riders, well armed," Temujin replied. "You can match those numbers."

"The Tartars have more than a thousand, you told us," Wen Chao said suddenly.

Temujin turned his yellow eyes on the Chin ambassador without reply. He sensed Yuan watching him and wondered how much Wen Chao knew, how much Yuan had told him.

"It will not be easy," Temujin said to Togrul, as if Wen Chao had not spoken. "We will need many sets of the Chin armor. The Olkhun'ut have two men with forges and the skill for swords and plate. I have given them their orders. We will also need to armor our horses, with leather and iron on the neck and chest." He paused, watching as Togrul wrestled with a chewy piece of meat.

"I have shown the success of our tactics against the smaller groups," Temujin went on, "though we were outnumbered even then. The Tartars do not use our charging line, nor the horns formation to flank them." He flickered a glance at Wen Chao. "I do not fear their numbers."

"Still, you would have me risk everything," Togrul said, shaking his head.

It was Wen Chao who interrupted the silent communication between them.

"This army of Tartars must be broken, my lord khan," he said softly to Togrul. "My masters will remember your service in this. There are lands marked out for your people when the battle is over. You will be king there and never know hunger or war again."

Once more, Temujin saw the proof that Wen Chao had a peculiar hold over the fat khan, and his dislike for the Chin ambassador increased sharply. As much as their needs were the same, he did not enjoy seeing one of his own people in the thrall of the foreign diplomat.

To cover his irritation, Temujin began to eat, enjoying the taste of Olkhun'ut herbs. He noticed that it was only then that Wen Chao matched him and reached for the platters. The man was too used to intrigue, Temujin thought. It made him dangerous.

Togrul too had noticed the movement, considering the meat in his hand for a moment before popping it into his mouth with a shrug.

"You wish to lead the Kerait?" Togrul said.

"For this one battle, yes, as I have done before," Temujin replied. This was the heart of it and he could not blame Togrul for his fears. "I have my own tribe now, Togrul. Many look to me for safety and leadership. When the Tartars are crushed, I will go south into warmer lands for a year or so. I have had enough of the cold north. My father's death has been avenged and perhaps I will know peace and raise sons and daughters."

"Why else do we fight?" Togrul murmured. "Very well, Temujin. You will have the men you need. You will have my Kerait, but when we are done, they will come east with me to a new land. Do not expect them to remain where no enemy threatens us."

Temujin nodded and put out his hand. Togrul's greasy fingers closed over his and their eyes met, neither man trusting the other.

"Now I am sure my wife and mother would like to

be reunited with their people," Temujin said, gripping the hand tightly.

Togrul nodded. "I will have them sent to you," he said, and Temujin felt the last of his tension ease within him.

Hoelun walked through the camp of her childhood with Borte and Eluin. The three women were accompanied by Khasar and Kachiun, as well as Arslan. Temujin had warned them not to relax. The Olkhun'ut had apparently accepted him, carried along by the irresistible tide of events. It did not mean they were safe to stroll anywhere amongst the gers.

Borte's pregnancy was growing heavy, altering her gait so that she could barely keep up with Hoelun. She had leapt at the chance to visit the families of the Olkhun'ut. She had left them as the woman of a raider. To return as the wife of their khan was an exquisite pleasure. She strode with her head high, calling out to those she recognized. Eluin craned her neck in excitement, searching for a glimpse of her family. When she saw them, she darted past two sleeping dogs to embrace her mother. She had grown in confidence since coming to the camp. Khasar and Kachiun were both courting her and Temujin seemed content to let them settle it between themselves. Eluin had bloomed under the attention. Hoelun watched as she broke the news of her sister's death, her voice too low to be heard. Her father sat down heavily on a log by the door of their ger, bowing his head.

For herself, Hoelun felt only sadness as she looked around the camp. Everyone she knew had grown, or passed on to the birds and spirits. It was a strangely un-comfortable experience to see the gers and decorated deels of families she had known as a girl. In her mind, it had remained the same, but the reality was a place of un-known faces.

"Will you see your brother, Hoelun? Your nephew?" Borte murmured. She stood almost en-tranced as they watched Eluin's reunion. Hoelun could see a yearning in the young wife of her son. She had not mentioned a visit to her own home.

In the distance, they heard the pounding of hooves as Temujin and his officers drilled the Olkhun'ut and Kerait in their tactics for war. They had been out since dawn and Hoelun knew her son would run them to ex-haustion in the first few days. His new status did not af-fect the resentment many of the Kerait felt at having to fight alongside lesser families. Almost before the first evening was over, there had been two fights and one Kerait man had been gashed with a knife. Temujin had killed the victor without giving him a chance to speak. Hoelun shuddered as she pictured her son's face. Would Yesugei ever have been so ruthless? She thought he would, if he had ever had the chance to command so many. If the shamans spoke truly about one soul being left for the land as well as one to join the sky, he would be proud of his son's accomplishments.

Hoelun and Borte watched as Eluin kissed her fa-ther's face again and again, her own tears mingling with his. At last she stood to leave them and her mother took her head in the cradle of her shoulder, pressing her there. Borte looked away from the moment of affection, her expression unreadable.

Hoelun had not needed to ask what had happened

with the Tartars who had borne her away from her husband. It was all too clear in the way she resisted any touch, jerking back even as Hoelun reached for her arm. Hoelun's heart went out to her for what she had suffered, but she knew better than anyone that time would dull the blade of grief. Even the memories of Bekter seemed distant, somehow; no less vivid, but robbed of their pain.

The sun seemed chill on her skin and Hoelun found she was not enjoying the return to the Olkhun'ut as she had hoped. It was too different. She was no longer the little girl who had ridden out with her brothers and come across Yesugei. She remembered him on that day, handsome and fearless as he charged them. Enq had yelled as he took Yesugei's arrow in the hip, putting his heels to his horse and galloping away. She had hated the strange warrior then, but how could she have known Yesugei would be a man to love? How could she have known she would stand amongst her people again as the mother of a khan?

Through the gers, she saw an old man walking stiffly, leaning his weight on a stick. Borte gasped as she glanced at him and Hoelun guessed who he was from the way his daughter stood painfully straight, summoning her pride.

Sholoi hobbled to them, taking in every detail of the warriors for their protection. His eyes passed over Hoelun, then snapped back in sudden recognition.

"I remember you, girl," he said, "though it's a long time ago."

Hoelun narrowed her eyes, trying to recall him as he might have been when she was young. A vague memory came back to her, a man who had taught her to braid harness from rope and leather. He had been ancient then, at least to her young eyes. To her surprise, she felt tears brimming.

"I remember," she said, and he grinned at her, revealing brown gums. Borte had not spoken and he nodded to his daughter, his toothless smile widening.

"I hadn't thought to see you again in these gers," he said.

Borte seemed to stiffen and Hoelun wondered if she could hear the affection in her father's gruff tone. He laughed suddenly.

"Two wives to khans, two mothers to more. Yet only two women stand before me. I will win a skin or two of airag with such a fine riddle."

He reached out and touched the hem of Borte's deel, rubbing two fingers together to judge the cloth.

"You made the right choice, girl. I can see that. I thought there was something about that Wolf. Didn't I tell you that?"

"You said he was probably dead," Borte replied, her voice as cold as Hoelun had ever heard.

Sholoi shrugged. "Maybe I did," he said sadly.

The silence ached between them and Hoelun sighed.

"You adore her, old man," she said. "Why don't you tell her that?"

Sholoi colored, though whether with anger or embarrassment, they could not tell.

"She knows it," he muttered.

Borte paled as she stood there. She shook her head. "I did not," she replied. "How could I have known if you never said?"

"I thought I must have done," Sholoi replied, looking out across the camp. The maneuvers on the plain of massed warriors seemed to hold his attention, and he could not look at his daughter.

"I am proud of you, girl, you should know that," he said suddenly. "I would treat you more kindly if I could raise you again."

Borte shook her head. "You can't," she said. "And I have nothing to say to you now."

The old man seemed to shrivel under the words, and when Borte turned to Hoelun, there were tears in her eyes. Sholoi did not see them and he continued to stare out across the plains and gers.

"Let us go back," Borte said, her eyes pleading. "It was a mistake to come here."

Hoelun thought of leaving her there for a few hours with her father. Temujin had been firm, however. Borte carried his heir and could not be risked. Hoelun suppressed her irritation. Perhaps it was part of being a mother, but the complexities between the pair seemed foolish. If they left then, she knew Borte would never see her father again and would spend her later years regretting the loss. Temujin would simply have to wait.

"Make yourselves comfortable," Hoelun snapped to her sons and Arslan. At least Khasar and Kachiun were used to her authority. "We will stay here while Borte visits her father in his ger."

"The khan was very clear..." Arslan began.

Hoelun turned sharply to him. "Are we not one people?" she demanded. "There is nothing to fear from the Olkhun'ut. I would know if there were."

Arslan dropped his gaze, unsure how to respond.

"Kachiun," Hoelun said, "go and find my brother Enq and tell him his sister will eat with him." She waited while Kachiun ran swiftly away, his legs moving before he thought to ask where the ger in question might be. Hoelun watched him hesitate at a crossed path and smiled. He would ask directions rather than come sheepishly back, she was sure. Her sons could think for themselves.

"You will accompany me, Khasar, and you too, Arslan. You will eat and then we will find Borte and her father and take them back."

Arslan was torn, remembering Temujin's warnings. He did not relish being put in such a situation, but to argue further would shame Hoelun in front of the Olkhun'ut and he could not do that. In the end, he bowed his head.

Sholoi had turned back to watch the exchange. He flickered a glance at his daughter to see how she was taking it.

"I would like that," he said.

Borte nodded stiffly and his smile lit up his face. Together, they walked back through the gers of the Olkhun'ut, and Sholoi's pride was visible from far away. Hoelun watched them go with satisfaction.

"We are going to war," she murmured. "Would you deny them their last chance to talk as father and daughter?"

Arslan did not know if the question was aimed at him, so he did not respond. Hoelun seemed lost in memories, and then she shook herself.

"I am hungry," she announced. "If my brother's ger is where it used to be, I can find it still." She strode forward and Arslan and Khasar fell in behind, unable to look each other in the eye.

Four days after Temujin had brought the Olkhun'ut, warning horns sounded as the sun set across the plains. Though the warriors of both tribes had been run to exhaustion during the day, they leapt up from their meal, hunger forgotten as they gathered weapons.

Temujin mounted his pony to give him a better view. For a single sickening instant, he thought the Tartars had somehow marched around them, or split their forces to attack on two fronts. Then his hands tightened on the reins and he paled.

Kachiun's eyes were as sharp as they had ever been, and he too stiffened. Arslan looked at the reaction of the younger men, still unable to make out details in the growing gloom.

"Who are they?" he asked, squinting at the mass of dark riders galloping in.

Temujin spat furiously onto the ground by Arslan's feet. He saw how well the strangers rode in formation and his mouth remained bitter.

"They are my father's tribe, Arslan. They are the Wolves."

CHAPTER 32

IRON TORCHES FLICKERED and roared in the night wind as Eeluk entered the joint camp. Temujin had sent Arslan out to grant a meeting with the khan as soon as the Wolves halted. He would not go himself, and even as he saw Eeluk stride through the gers to where he sat with his brothers, he did not know if he could let him leave alive. To attack a guest was a crime that would hurt him with the Olkhun'ut and the Kerait, but he thought Eeluk could be goaded into breaking the protection and then Temujin would be free to kill him.

Eeluk had grown thicker in body in the years since Temujin had seen him last. His head was bare, shaved to the skull except for a single lock of braided hair that swung as he walked. He wore a heavy black deel, trimmed in dark fur, over a tunic and leggings. Temujin narrowed his eyes as he recognized the wolf's-head hilt of the sword on his hip. Eeluk padded through the gers without looking round, his gaze fixed on the figures by the central fire. Tolui walked at his shoulder, even larger and more powerful than Temujin remembered.

Temujin had wanted to remain seated, to show how little he cared about the man who had come to him, but he could not. As Eeluk and Tolui approached he rose to his feet, his brothers standing with him as if at a signal. Togrul saw how tense they were and, with a sigh, he too levered himself up. Yuan and a dozen of his best men stood at his back. Whatever Eeluk intended, his life would be forfeit at the slightest provocation.

Eeluk's gaze flickered from Temujin to Khasar and Kachiun, frowning as he saw Temuge there. He did not recognize the youngest son of Yesugei, though he saw the fear in his eyes.

There was no fear in the others. Each of them stood ready to attack, their faces pale as their muscles tightened and their hearts pounded. The khan of the Wolves had been in all their dreams, and they had killed him in a thousand ways before waking. Kachiun and Khasar had last seen him when he took the Wolves away, leaving them to die on the bleak plains with winter on its way. Everything they had suffered since that day could be laid at his feet. He had assumed the face of a monster in their imagination, and it was strange to see a man, grown older, but still strong. It was hard to keep the cold face.

Tolui's gaze was drawn to Temujin and captured there by the yellow eyes. He too had his memories, but he was far less confident than when he had captured Yesugei's son and taken him back to his khan. He had learned to bully those less powerful than himself and fawn on those who ruled him. He did not know how to respond to Temujin and looked away, troubled.

It was Togrul who spoke first, when the silence became uncomfortable.

"You are welcome in our camp," he said. "Will you eat with us?"

Eeluk nodded without looking away from the brothers. "I will," he said.

Hearing his voice brought a fresh spasm of hatred to Temujin, but he lowered himself to the mat of felt with the others, watching to see if Eeluk or Tolui reached for a weapon. His own sword was ready by his hand, and he did not relax. Sansar had believed himself safe in his own ger.

Eeluk took his bowl of salted tea in both hands, and only then did Temujin reach for his own, sipping without tasting any of it. He did not speak. As guest, Eeluk had to speak first and Temujin hid his impatience behind the bowl, showing him nothing.

"We have been enemies in the past," Eeluk said, when he had drained the bowl.

"We are enemies still," Temujin replied immediately, released.

Eeluk turned his flat face to him. With so many men ready to leap at his throat, he seemed calm, though his eyes were bloodshot, as if he had been drinking before the meeting.

"That may be true, though it is not why I have come here now," Eeluk said quietly. "The tribes are busy chattering about the Tartar army coming south, an army you provoked into existence with your raids."

"What of it?" Temujin snapped.

Eeluk smiled tightly, his temper rising. It had been many years since another man had dared to take such a harsh tone with him.

"The plains have emptied of wanderers," Eeluk continued. "They have come to join you against a common enemy."

Temujin suddenly understood why Eeluk had brought the Wolves. His mouth opened slightly, but he said nothing, letting Eeluk go on as he thought.

"I have heard many times about the young Wolf who raided the Tartars again and again," Eeluk said. "Your name is known on the plains now. Your father would be proud of you."

Temujin almost leapt at him then, fury rising in his throat like red bile. It took a huge effort to master himself, and Eeluk watched him carefully, sensing it.

"I did not know you had joined the Olkhun'ut with the Kerait warriors until I was already moving the Wolves. Still, I think you will need my men if you are to crush the Tartars and drive them back into the north."

"How many do you have?" Togrul asked.

Eeluk shrugged. "A hundred and forty." He looked at Temujin. "You know their quality."

"We do not need them," Temujin said. "I lead the Olkhun'ut now. We do not need you."

Eeluk smiled. "It is true that you are not as desperate as I thought you would be. Still, you need every rider you can find, if the numbers I heard are true. Having the Wolves with you will mean more of...your tribe are alive at the end. You know it."

"And in return? You are not here for nothing," Temujin said.

"The Tartars have silver and horses," Eeluk said. "They have women. This army is the movement of many tribes together. They will have things of value."

"So it is greed that has drawn you forth," Temujin said, sneering.

Eeluk colored slightly in anger and Tolui shifted at his shoulder, irritated at the insult.

"The Wolves could not face them alone," Eeluk replied. "We would have had to retreat south as they came. When I heard the Kerait would stand and that your raiders had joined them, I took the chance that you would be able to put aside our history. Nothing I have seen here changes that. You need the Wolves. You need me to stand with you."

"For a sixth of their riches," Togrul murmured.

Eeluk glanced at him, masking his distaste at the fleshy khan of the Kerait. "If three khans meet them, any spoils should be divided in thirds."

"I will not bargain like a merchant," Temujin said curtly, before Togrul could reply. "I have not yet said I will have you here."

"You cannot stop me from fighting against the Tartars if I choose to," Eeluk said softly. "There is no shame in discussing the split, for when they are beaten."

"I could stop you with a single order," Temujin said. "I could have the Wolves broken first." His temper had taken control of him and a small part knew he was raging like a fool, but his calm was a memory. Almost without noticing, he began to rise.

"You would not do that to the families," Eeluk said with certainty, stopping him. "Even if you could, it would be a waste of lives you need to fight the Tartars. Where is the sense in struggling amongst ourselves? I have been told you are a man of vision, Temujin. Show it now."

All the men present looked to Temujin to see how

he would respond. He felt their gaze and unclenched his cramped fists as he settled himself once more, taking his hand away from where it had fallen to his sword hilt. Eeluk had not moved in response. If he had, he would have died. His enemy's courage in coming there shamed Temujin, bringing back memories of being a boy amongst men. He knew he needed the warriors Eeluk had brought, if he could only stomach the alliance.

"Will they take my orders, these Wolves? Will you?" he said.

"There can be only one leader in battle," Eeluk said. "Give us a wing and let me command it. I will ride as hard as any man you have."

Temujin shook his head. "You will need to know the horn signals, the formations I have made with the others. There is more to this than riding in and killing as many as you can reach."

Eeluk looked away. He had not known exactly what he would find when he told the Wolves to pack their gers and ride. He had considered the chances of wresting spoils from the battered tribes who faced the Tartars, but in his most secret heart, he had smelled blood on the wind like a true wolf and he could not resist it. There had been nothing on the plains like the army of the Tartars in his lifetime. Yesugei would have ridden against them, and it had scalded Eeluk's soul to hear that the sons of the old khan were challenging the army coming south.

Still, he had expected to be welcomed by fearful men. Finding the Olkhun'ut already in alliance had changed the value of his warriors. He had been going to demand a full half of the spoils and, instead, he found the sons of Yesugei were coolly arrogant toward him.

Yet he had committed himself. He could not simply leave them on the plain and take the Wolves back. His control of the tribe would suffer after seeing him turned away. In the flickering torches, he could see dozens of gers stretching around him into darkness. Just the sight of so many warriors matched his dreams. What could a man achieve with so many at his back? If Yesugei's sons died in the battle, their men would be lost and frightened. They could swell the ranks of the Wolves.

"My men will follow your orders, through me," he said at last.

Temujin leaned forward. "But afterwards, when the Tartars have been gutted, we will settle an older debt between us. I claim the Wolves, as the oldest surviving son of Yesugei. Will you meet me with that sword you wear as if it were your own?"

"It *is* my own," Eeluk replied, his face tightening.

A hush fell on the camp around them. Togrul glanced at the two men, observing the hatred barely masked by civility. Eeluk forced himself to stillness as he pretended to consider. He had known Temujin would want him dead. He had considered the chance of absorbing surviving raiders into the Wolves, taken from Temujin's dead hands. Instead, he faced the khan of the Olkhun'ut and the prize was a hundred times greater. Perhaps the spirits were with him as they had not been before.

"When the Tartars are broken, I will meet you," he said, his eyes gleaming. "I will welcome the chance."

Temujin stood suddenly, causing many hands to reach for their swords. Eeluk sat like stone and looked up at him, but Temujin's gaze was elsewhere.

Hoelun walked slowly toward the gathering, as if in a trance. Eeluk turned to see who had captured Temujin's attention, and when he saw Yesugei's wife, he too rose with Tolui to face her.

Hoelun was pale and Eeluk saw how she ran the point of her tongue over her bottom lip, a sliver of red like a snake's warning. As he met her eyes, she rushed forward, holding up her arm to strike.

Kachiun stepped between them before she could reach the khan of the Wolves. He held his mother firmly as she swiped her hand out like a claw, straining for Eeluk's face. The nails did not touch him and Eeluk said nothing, sensing Temujin standing ready at his back. Hoelun struggled, her gaze finding her eldest son.

"How can you let him live after what he did to us?" she demanded, fighting Kachiun's grip.

Temujin shook his head. "He is a guest in my camp, Mother. When we have fought the Tartars, I will have the Wolves from him, or he will have the Olkhun'ut."

Eeluk turned to him then and Temujin smiled bitterly.

"Is that not what you want, Eeluk? I do not see more gers in your camp than when you left us on the plains to die. The sky father has abandoned the Wolves under your hand, but that will change."

Eeluk chuckled and flexed his shoulders. "I have said all I came to say. When we ride, you will know a better man holds your wing. After that, I will have a hard lesson for you and I will not let you live a second time."

"Go back to your gers, Eeluk," Temujin said. "I will begin training your men at dawn."

As the Tartars came south into the green plains, smaller tribes fled before their numbers. Some never paused as they sighted the host Temujin had assembled, skirting them so that they appeared as dark moving specks drifting across the hills far away. Others added their number to his warriors, so that the army grew daily in a trickle of furious riders. Temujin had sent messengers to the Naimans, the Oirats, any of the great tribes who could be found. Either they could not be reached or they would not come. He understood their reluctance, even as he scorned it. The tribes had never fought together in all their history. To have bound even three into a single force was astonishing. They had trained together until he thought they were as ready as they could ever be. Yet in the evenings he had been called time and again to forbid blood feuds, or punish fighting bands as they remembered grievances from generations before.

He had not visited the gers of the Wolves. Not one of the old families had spoken up for his mother when she was left to die with her children. There had been a time when he would have given anything to walk amongst the people he had known as a boy, but as Hoelun had discovered before him, they were not the same. While Eeluk ruled them, it would not bring him peace.

On the twentieth dawn after the arrival of the Olkhun'ut, the scouts came racing in to report the Tartar army on the horizon, less than a day's march away. With them came another family of wanderers, driven before them like goats. Temujin blew the signal to assemble and there was quiet in the camps as the warriors kissed their loved ones goodbye and mounted their horses. Many of them chewed packages of hot mutton and bread to give them strength, pressed into their hands by daughters and mothers. The wings formed, with Eeluk's Wolves taking the left and Kachiun and Khasar leading the Olkhun'ut on the right. Temujin held the Kerait in the center, and as he looked right and left along the line of horsemen, he was satisfied. Eight hundred warriors waited for his signal to ride against their enemies. The forges of the Kerait and Olkhun'ut had been fired night and day, and almost a third of them wore armor copied from the sets Wen Chao had given them. Their horses were protected by leather aprons studded with overlapping plates of iron. Temujin knew the Tartars had seen nothing like them. He waited while the women moved back, seeing Arslan reach down and kiss the young Tartar girl he had captured, then taken for a wife. Temujin looked around, but there was no sign of Borte. The birth was overdue and he had not expected her to come out of the gers. He remembered Hoelun telling him that Yesugei had ridden out on the night of his own birth, and he smiled wryly at the thought. The circle turned, but the stakes had grown. He had done everything he could and it was not hard to imagine his father watching his sons. Temujin caught the eye of Khasar and Kachiun, then found Temuge in the second rank to his left. He nodded to them and Khasar grinned. They had come a long way from the cleft in the hills where every day survived was a triumph.

When they were ready, the shaman of the Olkhun'ut rode to the front on a mare of pure white. He was thin and ancient, his hair turned the color of his mount. Every eye was on him as he chanted, raising his hands to the sky father. He held the fire-cracked shoulder blade of a sheep, and he gestured with it as if it were a weapon.

Temujin smiled to himself. The shaman of the Kerait had not been as thirsty for war, and Temujin had chosen the right man for the ritual.

As they watched, the shaman dismounted and pressed himself on the earth, embracing the mother who ruled them all. The chant was thin on the breeze, but the ranks of warriors sat in perfect stillness, waiting for the word. At last, the old man peered at the black lines on the bone, reading them as he ran his gnarled fingers along the fissures.

"The mother rejoices," he called. "She yearns for the Tartar blood we will release into her. The sky father calls us on in his name." He broke the shoulder blade in his hands, showing surprising strength.

Temujin filled his lungs and bellowed along the line. "The land knows only one people, my brothers," he shouted. "She remembers the weight of our steps. Fight well today and they will run before us."

They raised their bows in a great roar, and Temujin felt his pulses beat faster. The shaman mounted his mare and passed back through the ranks. Out of superstitious fear, none of the warriors would meet the eye of the old man, but Temujin nodded to him, bowing his head.

On the edges of the lines, riders carried small drums and they began to beat them, the noise matching his thumping heart. Temujin raised his arm and then dropped it to the right. He caught Khasar's eye as his brother trotted clear with a hundred of the best Olkhun'ut warriors. Every one of them wore the armored panels. At the charge, Temujin hoped they would be unstoppable. They rode away from the main force, and as he watched them Temujin prayed they would meet again.

When the line was silent and Khasar's hundred were almost a mile away, Temujin dug in his heels and the Kerait, Wolves, and Olkhun'ut went forward together, leaving the women and children, leaving the safety of the camp behind.

CHAPTER 33

THOUGH THEY HAD ALL KNOWN the enemy they faced, it was still a shock to see the vast expanse of the Tartar force. They moved like a slow stain across the land, a dark mass of riders, carts, and gers. Temujin and his brothers had scouted them five hundred miles to the north and still it was disturbing. Yet they did not falter. The men who rode with the sons of Yesugei knew they were ready for the battle. If there was fear in the ranks, it did not show as they kept the cold face. Only the constant checking of arrows revealed the strain as they heard the Tartar warning horns sound in the distance.

Temujin rode through a green valley, his mare made strong on good spring grass. Again and again, he bellowed orders to check the more impetuous of his leaders. Eeluk was the worst of them and his left wing crept ahead and had to be reined in until Temujin half believed it was a deliberate flouting of his orders. Ahead, they saw the Tartars boil around the gers, their thin shouts lost in the distance. The sun was bright and

Temujin could feel the warmth on his back like a blessing. He checked his own arrows yet again, finding them ready in the quiver as they had been before. He wanted to hit the Tartars at full gallop, and knew he must leave the acceleration until the last possible instant. The Tartars had been coming south for at least three moons, riding every day. He hoped they would not be as fresh as his own warriors, nor as hungry to kill.

At a mile away, he eased his weight forward, raising the beat of the hooves below him to a canter. His men followed perfectly, though once more Eeluk was straining to be first into the killing. Temujin blew on the signal horn and caught Eeluk's furious glance at him as they eased back into line. The noise of hooves filled his ears and Temujin could hear the excited cries of his warriors around him, their eyes tight against the increasing pressure of the wind. He fitted the first arrow to his string, knowing that the air would soon be full of them. Perhaps one would find his throat and send him dying to the ground below in a last embrace. His heart pounded and he lost his fear in the concentration. The first arrows came whining in from the Tartars, but he did not give the signal to gallop. It had to be perfect. As the armies grew closer, he chose his moment.

Temujin dug in his heels, calling "Chuh!" to his mount. The mare responded with a surge of speed, almost leaping forward. Perhaps she felt the excitement as they did. The line matched him and Temujin drew back on the bow with a heave of all his strength. For a few moments, it was as if he held the weight of a grown man by just three fingers, but he was steady. He felt the rhythm of the gallop coursing through him, and there was the moment of perfect stillness when the mare flew without touching the ground.

The Tartars were already in full gallop. Temujin risked a glance at his men. Two ranks pounded across the plain and all seven hundred were ready with their bows drawn. He showed his teeth against the strain in his shoulders and loosed his first shaft.

The noise that followed was a single snap of sound that echoed from the hills around them. Arrows flew into the blue sky and seemed to hang there for an instant before they plunged down into the Tartar ranks. Many were lost in the ground, disappearing right up to the feathers. Many more ripped into flesh and tore their riders from the world in a single blow.

Before Temujin could see what had happened, the reply came and arrows rose above him. He had never seen so many and felt a shadow pass over his line from the distant sun. The Tartar arrows moved slowly as he watched them, trying not to wince in anticipation. Then they seemed to move faster and he could hear them coming with an insectile buzzing. His fingers scrabbled for a second arrow and his men loosed again before the Tartar shafts struck their line in a hammer blow.

At full gallop, men vanished from the saddle, their cries lost far behind in an instant. Temujin felt something crash against his thigh and shoulder, ricocheting away. It had not pierced the armor and he yelled in triumph, almost standing in the stirrups as he sent arrow after arrow at his enemies. His eyes blurred in the wind, so that he could not see details, but he picked his men and killed with savage abandon.

It could only have been moments before they met the first of the Tartar riders, but it seemed to take forever. As they closed, Temujin dropped his bow onto a saddle hook so that it would be there for him. It was just one of the ideas he and his officers had devised. He drew the sword that Arslan had made for him, hearing the razor rasp as it cleared the scabbard. Every heartbeat was an age and he had time. He yanked at the horn on a cord around his neck and raised it to his lips, blowing three times. Out of the corner of his eyes, he saw the wings move forward and he took a two-handed grip on the sword as he galloped on, balanced and ready.

They hit the Tartars with a crash of sound. Horses came together at full speed, with neither rider giving way, so that they were spun out of the saddle in thunder. The armies hammered into one another, arrows fired into faces and necks at close range. Death came quickly and both armies lost dozens of men in a single instant. Temujin could see the armor was working and he roared again in challenge, calling the enemy to him. One Tartar warrior went past him in a blur, but Temujin had cut him before he was gone. Another fired a shaft at such close range that it punched through the armor, the tip cutting into Temujin's chest and making him cry out. He could feel the arrowhead moving, tearing his skin with every jerk. He brought his sword round in an arc and took the head of the archer.

Blood drenched him, dribbling between the iron plates of his armor. The charge had smashed the first line of Tartars, but there were so many of them that they did not break. The fighting lines had begun to falter into smaller groups of wildly hacking men, loosing arrows from numb fingers until their bows were useless and they turned to blades. Temujin looked for his brothers, but they were lost in the press of men. He killed again and again, his mare jerking forward with just the touch of his knees. A bellowing Tartar came at him, his open mouth already filled with blood. Temujin sank his blade into his chest, yanking viciously to free it. Another came from his side with a hatchet, chopping it against the armored layers. The blow did not penetrate, but Temujin was knocked sideways by the force. He felt muscles in his thighs tear as he struggled to stay mounted, but the man had gone on.

Eeluk's Wolves were smashing their way through on the left. Some of them had dismounted and walked together into the midst of the Tartars, firing arrow after arrow. They wore leather armor under their deels and many of them bristled with broken shafts. Some had red droplets around their mouths, but they still fought on, pressing closer and closer to the Tartar center. Temujin could see Eeluk riding with them, his face wet with blood as he chopped down with the sword that had once belonged to Yesugei.

Horses lay dying and kicking wildly, a danger to anyone who came too close. Temujin guided his mare around one, seeing an Olkhun'ut warrior trapped beneath. He met the man's eyes and cursed, leaping from the saddle to pull him clear. As he reached the ground, another arrow hammered into his chest, stopped by the iron. It sent him onto his back, but he scrambled up, heaving at the man until he was able to regain his feet. A quiver full of arrows lay on the ground nearby, and Temujin grabbed at it before mounting again, reaching for his bow. He kicked in his heels once more, putting all his strength into the draw. The Tartars seemed hardly to have noticed their losses, and still they did not break. He called to them, daring them to face him, and his warriors saw him remount. They took heart, cutting and killing with renewed energy. It could not last, he knew. He saw the Olkhun'ut pressing forward on his right, though they did not have the numbers to encircle the enemy. When their arrows were spent, they threw spinning hatchets into the press of the enemy, killing many before reaching for their swords.

Temujin heard the thunder of hooves before he saw Khasar coming in with his reserve. They had ridden around the battle site in a great circle, hidden by the hills. From the back of his mare, Temujin was able to see the solid line riding at reckless speed, with Khasar leading them. The Tartars in the flank tried to face them, but they were too tightly packed. Over the noise of galloping hooves, Temujin heard many of them scream, trapped amongst their own.

The armored horses and men hit the Tartar flank like a spear thrust, sinking deeply into them over a trail of bloody dead. Horses and men alike were hit by Tartar arrows, but they hardly slowed until they had cut right through to the center of the enemy, sending them reeling and crying out.

Temujin felt the Tartars give against him and he could not speak for the fierce excitement that filled his chest. He cantered into a mass of men, his mare shuddering in pain as arrows struck the leather and iron that protected her heaving chest. His quiver was empty once more and Temujin used Arslan's sword to hack any living thing he faced.

He looked for his officers and saw that they had gathered the lines and were moving on as one. Kachiun and Arslan had forced the Olkhun'ut to follow Khasar's wild rush into the center, yelling as they fought. Many had lost their mounts, but they kept together and took futile cuts on the armor while they killed with every strike. The Tartars heard their voices at their backs, and a ripple of panic went through them.

The battle slowed as men tired. Some of them had exhausted themselves with killing, so that they stood on both sides with their chests heaving and their breath ragged. Many of those fell easily to fresher men, their faces despairing as they felt their strength give way at last. The grass under their feet was red with wet flesh and littered with bodies, some still flailing weakly as they tried to ignore the coldness coming for them. The breeze blew through the fighting knots of men, taking the smell of the slaughterhouse into exhausted lungs. The Tartars began to falter at last, falling back step by step.

Eeluk threw himself against a cluster of them like one who had lost his mind. He was so covered in blood as to look like some wild-eyed death spirit. He used his great strength to smash men from their feet with his fists and elbows, trampling over them. His Wolves came with him and the Tartars barely raised their swords as terror took away their courage. Some of them ran, but others tried to rally the rest, pointing their swords back at the families around the gers behind.

Still mounted, Temujin could see the pale faces of women and children watching their men fight. He cared nothing for them. The sky father rewarded the strong with luck. The weak would fall.

"We have them!" he roared, and his men responded, seeing him ride with them. They were weary, but they took strength from his presence in their midst and the killing went on. Temujin's fingers were slippery with blood as he grasped the horn around his neck, sounding three times to encircle the enemy. He left a print of his palm on the polished surface, but did not see it as Eeluk and Kachiun moved forward. The quivers were all empty, but the swords still swung and the Tartars broke at last, running back for the gers before they could be completely hemmed in. They would make a last stand there, Temujin saw. He welcomed it.

He saw his men begin to rush after them and blew a falling note to slow the charge. They walked over the dead toward the Tartar gers. Those who had run numbered fewer than two hundred, all who remained alive. Temujin did not fear them now. To his irritation, he saw Eeluk's men were lost in the killing and had not heeded his call. For an instant, he considered letting them face the men at the gers alone, but he could not stand to see Eeluk slaughtered so easily. The Tartars would have bows there and shafts. Whoever faced them would have to come through a withering storm. Perhaps Eeluk had been right not to delay. Temujin set his jaw and blew a single blast for the advance. He rode over the breaking bones of the dead to lead them.

A ragged volley of arrows came from the gers. Some fell short as the women took up bows, but others had enough force to steal lives from men even as they rejoiced in their victory. Temujin heard his army pant as they ran and kicked their mounts on. They would not be stopped and the arrows whipped through them uselessly, making men stagger as they hit the iron plates of their armor. Temujin leaned into the wind as the gap closed, ready to finish what they had begun.

When it was over, the last stand of the Tartars could be read by the way the dead sprawled in clusters. They had held a line for a time before Khasar's horsemen had crashed through them. Temujin looked around as the three tribes searched for loot on the carts, for once acting with a single mind. They had fought and won together and he thought it would be hard to go back to their old distrust, at least of men they knew.

Wearily, Temujin dismounted and grimaced as he pulled at the ties that held his chest piece. A dozen of the iron plates had been torn away, and many that remained were buckled. Three broken shafts stood out from the layers. Two of them hung limply down, but the third stood straight and that was the one he wanted out of him. He found he could not pull the armored cloth clear. As he tried, something wrenched in his muscles, causing a wave of dizziness.

"Let me help you," Temuge said, at his shoulder.

Temujin glanced at his youngest brother and waved to be left alone. He did not feel like speaking and, as the battle fever passed, his body was revealing all the knocks and aches he had taken. As he stood there, he wanted nothing more than to cast off the heavy armor and sit down, but he could not even do that.

Temuge came closer and Temujin ignored him as his fingers probed the broken plate and the shaft sticking in him, rising and falling with his breath.

"It cannot be deep," Temuge murmured. "If you can stay still, I'll get it out of you."

"Do it then," Temujin replied, past caring. He ground his teeth as Temuge sawed through the shaft with his knife, then reached under the armored cloth to grip the other side. With a slow pull, he removed the chest protector and let it fall as he examined the wound. The silk had not torn, but it had been carried deep into Temujin's pectoral muscle. Blood seeped from around the tip, but Temuge looked pleased.

"A little farther and you would be dead. I can get this out, I think."

"You've seen this done?" Temujin said, looking down at him. "You have to twist the arrow as it comes."

To his surprise, Temuge grinned. "I know. The silk has trapped it. Just stand still."

Taking a deep breath, Temuge took a grip on the slippery wooden shaft, digging his nails into the wood to give him purchase. Temujin grunted in pain as the arrowhead tightened in him. His chest shuddered involuntarily, like a horse shrugging off flies.

"The other way," he said.

Temuge colored. "I have it now," he replied, and Temujin felt the twitching muscle relax as the arrow turned in his flesh. It had been spinning as it hit him. With Temuge's deft fingers twisting it the other way, it came out easily, followed by a dribble of clotted blood.

"Keep something pressed against it for a while," Temuge said. His voice was quietly triumphant and Temujin nodded to him, clapping him on the shoulder.

"You have a steady hand," he said.

Temuge shrugged. "It wasn't in me. If it had been, I would have cried like a child."

"No, you wouldn't," Temujin said. He reached out and gripped his brother behind the neck before turning away. Without warning, his expression changed so rapidly that Temuge spun to see what he had seen.

Eeluk was standing on top of one of the Tartar carts, holding a skin of airag in one hand and a bloody sword in the other. Even from a distance, he looked vital and dangerous. The sight of him brought life back to Temujin's limbs, banishing his exhaustion. Temuge watched as Eeluk shouted something to his Wolves.

"I don't remember him," Temuge murmured, as they stared across the bloody grass. "I try to, but it was a long time ago."

"Not to me," Temujin snapped. "I see his face whenever I sleep." He drew his sword slowly and Temuge turned to him, frightened at what he saw in his brother's face. They could hear the men laugh around the carts, and some of them cheered Eeluk as he shouted down to them.

"You should wait until you have rested," Temuge said. "The wound was shallow, but it will have weakened you."

"No. This is the time," Temujin replied, walking forward.

Temuge almost went with him, but he saw Kachiun and Khasar exchange glances and move to join their brother. Temuge did not want to see another death. He could not bear the thought that Temujin would be killed, and fear churned his stomach and made him light-headed. If Eeluk fought and won, everything they had achieved would be lost. Temuge watched Temujin walk steadily away and suddenly he knew he had to be there. They were the sons of Yesugei and it was time. He took one faltering step, and then he was hurrying after his brother.

Eeluk was roaring with laughter at something someone had called to him. It had been a glorious victory against the Tartar invader. He had fought with courage and the men had followed where he led them, right into the heart of the battle. He was not flattering himself when he accepted their cheering. He had played his part and more, and now the riches of the Tartars waited to be enjoyed. The women under the carts would be part of the celebration, and he would take many new girls back to the Wolves to bear sons for his bondsmen. The tribe would grow and word would spread that the Wolves had been part of the great battle. He was intoxicated by the pleasures of life as he stood there, letting the wind dry his sweat. Tolui was wrestling with a couple of the Wolf bondsmen, laughing as they tried to throw him. All three of them collapsed in a heap and Eeluk chuckled, feeling his skin tighten as dried blood cracked. He laid down his sword and rubbed both of his heavy hands over his face, scouring away the dried muck of battle. When he looked up, he saw Temujin and his brothers coming for him.

Eeluk grimaced before he bent and picked up his sword once again. The cart was high, but he leapt to the ground rather than clamber down with his back to them. He landed well and faced the sons of Yesugei with a smile twitching at his mouth. He and Temujin were the only khans to witness their victory. Though the Kerait had fought well, their fat leader was safe in his gers five miles to the south. Eeluk took a deep breath and steadied himself as he looked around. His Wolves had seen him jump down and they were drifting in, drawn to their khan. The Olkhun'ut too had broken off their looting with the Kerait and came in pairs and threes to stand close and watch what was to come. Word of the bad blood between their leaders had spread, and they did not want to miss the fight. The women under the carts wailed unheeded as the warriors walked over the grass to where Eeluk and Temujin stood in silence.

"It was a great victory," Eeluk said, looking around at the gathering men. A hundred of his Wolves had survived the battle, and they were no longer smiling as they saw the threat. Yet they were vastly outnumbered and Eeluk knew it could only be settled between the two men who had brought them to that place.

"This is an old debt," Eeluk shouted to them. "Let there be no reprisals." His eyes were bright as he looked at Temujin standing before him. "I did not ask for blood between us, but I am khan of the Wolves and I am not unwilling."

"I claim my father's people," Temujin said, his gaze passing over the ranks of warriors and bondsmen. "I see no khan where you stand."

Eeluk chuckled, raising his sword. "Then I will *make* you see," he said. He saw Temujin had removed part of his armor, and Eeluk held up a palm. Temujin stood ready, unmoving as Eeluk untied the boiled-leather shields that had kept him alive in the battle. Temujin raised his arms and his brothers did the same for him, so that both men stood in just tunics, leggings, and boots, with dark sweat patches drying in the breeze. Both of them hid their weariness and worried that the other seemed fresh.

Temujin raised his sword and eyed the blade Eeluk held as if the weight were nothing. He had seen Eeluk's face in a thousand training bouts with Arslan and Yuan. The reality was different and he could not summon the calm he desperately needed. Eeluk seemed somehow to have grown in height. The man who had abandoned the family of Yesugei to die was hugely strong, and without his armor, his frame was intimidating. Temujin shook his head, as if to clear it of fear.

"Come to me, carrion," he murmured, and Eeluk's eyes narrowed.

Both men exploded into movement from utter stillness, darting forward with quick steps. Temujin parried the first blow at his head, feeling his arms shudder under the impact. His chest ached where the arrow had torn his muscle, and he struggled to control a rage that would kill him with its wildness. Eeluk pressed him hard, swinging his blade like a cleaver with huge force so that Temujin either had to leap aside or bear a staggering blow. His right arm was growing numb as he caught and turned each impact. The men of three tribes gave them space in a great ring, but they did not call out or cheer. Temujin saw their faces as a blur as he circled his enemy, switching gaits to reverse back on himself as Eeluk swiped at air.

"You are slower than you used to be," Temujin told him.

Eeluk did not reply, his face growing hot. He lunged, but Temujin batted the blade aside and hammered his elbow against Eeluk's face. Eeluk struck back instantly, his fist thumping into Temujin's unprotected chest in a straight blow.

Pain soared through him and Temujin saw Eeluk had aimed for the bloody spot on his tunic. He growled aloud as he came in, his fury fed by the agony. Eeluk met his wild swing and punched again at the bloody muscle, starting a thin red stream that stained the tunic over older streaks. Temujin cried out and took a step back, but when Eeluk came with him, he stepped outside the line of his father's sword and chopped hard into Eeluk's arm below the elbow. With a less powerful man, he might have taken it off, but Eeluk's forearms writhed with muscle. Even then, the wound was terrible and blood spurted from it. Eeluk did not look down at his useless hand, though blood dripped through his knuckles and fell in fat drops.

Temujin nodded to him, showing his teeth. His enemy would weaken and he did not want it to be quick.

Eeluk came forward once more, his sword a blur. The clash of metal sent tremors right through Temujin each time they struck, but he exulted, feeling Eeluk's strength fade. As they fell back Temujin took a gash along his thigh that made his right leg buckle, so that he remained in place while Eeluk circled. Both men were panting by then, losing the last reserves of energy they had recovered after the battle. The tiredness was crushing their strength until it was only will and hate that kept them facing each other.

Eeluk used Temujin's bad leg against him, launching an attack, then stepping swiftly aside before Temujin could adjust. Twice the blades rang just clear of Temujin's neck, and Eeluk caught the replies with ease. Yet he was faltering. The wound on his arm had not ceased its bleeding, and as he stepped away, he suddenly staggered, his eyes losing focus. Temujin glanced down at Eeluk's arm to see the blood still pulsing out. He could hear it spattering on the dust whenever Eeluk was still, and now there was a paleness to his skin that had not been there before.

"You are dying, Eeluk," Temujin said.

Eeluk did not respond as he came in again, gasping with every breath. Temujin swayed aside from the first of his blows and let the second cut him along his side, so that Eeluk came in close. He struck back like a snake and Eeluk was sent staggering away, his legs weakening. A hole had appeared high in his chest and blood gouted from it. Eeluk bent over the wound, trying to brace himself on his knees. His left hand would not respond and he almost lost his sword as he struggled for breath.

"My father loved you," Temujin said, watching him. "If you had been loyal, you would have stood here with me now."

Eeluk's skin had gone a sick white as he heaved for air and strength.

"Instead, you dishonored his trust," Temujin continued. "Just *die,* Eeluk. I have no more use for you."

He watched as Eeluk tried to speak, but blood touched his lips and no sound came out. Eeluk went down onto one knee and Temujin sheathed his sword, waiting. It seemed to take a long time as Eeluk clung to life, but he slumped at last, sprawling sideways on the ground. His chest became still and Temujin saw one of the Wolves walk out from where they watched. Temujin tensed for another attack, but he saw it was the bondsman Basan, and he hesitated. The man who had saved Temujin from Eeluk once before came to stand over the body, looking down on it. Basan's expression was troubled, but without speaking, he reached down to pick up the wolf's-head sword and straightened. As Temujin and his brothers watched, Basan held out the blade hilt first and Temujin took it, welcoming its weight to his hand like an old friend. He thought for a moment that he might pass out himself before he felt his brothers hold him upright.

"I waited a long time to see that," Khasar murmured under his breath.

Temujin stirred from his apathy, remembering how his brother had kicked Sansar's corpse.

"Treat the body with dignity, brother. I need to win over the Wolves and they won't forgive us if we treat him badly. Let them take him up to the hills and lay him out for the hawks." He looked around at the silent ranks from three tribes. "Then I want to go back to the camp and claim what is mine. I am khan of the Wolves."

He tasted the words in a whisper and his brothers gripped him tighter on hearing them, their faces showing nothing to those who watched.

"I'll see to it," Khasar said. "You must have your wound bound before you bleed to death."

Temujin nodded, overcome with exhaustion. Basan had not moved and he thought he should speak to the Wolves as they stood stunned around them, but it would wait. They had nowhere else to go.

CHAPTER 34

MORE THAN TWO HUNDRED WARRIORS had been lost in the battle against the Tartars. Before Temujin's forces left the area, the skies were filled with circling hawks, vultures, and ravens, the hillsides writhing with wings as they stalked amongst the corpses, fighting and screeching. Temujin had given orders that no difference would be made between Kerait, Olkhun'ut, and Wolves. The shamans of three tribes overcame their dislike of each other and chanted the death rites while the warriors watched the birds of prey gliding overhead. Even before the chanting had finished, ragged black vultures had landed, their dark eyes watching the living as they hopped onto dead men.

They left the Tartars where they had fallen, but it was not until late in the day that the carts began to move back to their main camp. Temujin and his brothers rode in the lead, with the Wolf bondsmen at his back. If he had not been the son of the old khan, they could well have killed him as soon as Eeluk fell, but Basan had handed him his father's sword and they had not moved. Though they did not exult as the Olkhun'ut and Kerait did, they were steady and they were his. Tolui rode stiffly with them, his face showing the marks of a beating. Khasar and Kachiun had taken him quietly aside in the night, and he did not look at them as he rode.

As they reached Togrul's camp, the women came out to greet their husbands and sons, searching faces desperately until they saw their loved ones had survived. Voices cried out in pleasure and grief alike, and the plain was alive with cheering and noise.

Temujin trotted his battered mare to where Togrul had come out and was standing with Wen Chao. The khan of the Kerait had kept some guards to protect the families, and those men would not meet Temujin's gaze as it swept over them. They had not ridden with him.

Temujin dismounted.

"We have broken their back, Togrul. They will not come south again."

"Where is the khan of the Wolves?" Togrul asked, looking out across the milling warriors and their families.

Temujin shrugged. "He stands before you," he said. "I have claimed the tribe."

Wearily, Temujin turned away to give orders to his brothers, and he did not see Togrul's changing expression. They could all smell mutton sizzling on the breeze, and the returning warriors cheered at the scent. They were starving after the day before and nothing would be accomplished until they had fed and drunk their fill.

Wen Chao saw Yuan riding toward him, a bloody rag tied tightly round his shin. Temujin was heading toward the ger of his wife, and Wen Chao waited patiently until Yuan had dismounted and gone down on one knee.

"We have had no details of the battle, Yuan. You must tell us what you saw."

Yuan kept his gaze on the ground.

"Your will, master," he replied.

As the sun set, the hills were lit in bars of gold and shadow. The feasting had continued until the men were drunk and sated. Togrul had been part of it, though he had not cheered Temujin with the others, even when the bondsmen of the Wolves had brought their families out to take an oath of loyalty to the son of Yesugei. Togrul had seen Temujin's eyes fill with tears as they knelt before him, and he had felt a simmering resentment start. It was true he had not fought with them, but had he not played a part? It could not have been won without the Kerait, and it had been Togrul who had called Temujin out of the icy north. He had not been blind to the way his Kerait had mingled with the others until there was no telling them apart. They looked on the young khan with awe, a man who had gathered the tribes under his command and won a crushing victory against an ancient enemy. Togrul saw every glance and bowed head and felt fear worm its way into his gut. Eeluk had fallen and Sansar before him. It was not hard to imagine knives coming in the night for Togrul of the Kerait.

When the feasting was over, he sat in his ger with Wen Chao and Yuan, talking long into the night. As the moon rose he took a deep breath and felt the fumes of black airag hanging heavily in his lungs. He was drunk, but he needed to be.

"I have done everything I promised, Wen Chao," he reminded the ambassador.

Wen's voice was soothing. "You have. You will be a khan of vast estates and your Kerait will know peace. My masters will be pleased to hear of such a victory. When you have divided the spoils, I will come with you. There is nothing for me here, not anymore. Perhaps I will have the chance to enjoy my final years in Kaifeng."

"If I am allowed to leave," Togrul spat suddenly. His flesh shuddered with indignation and worry and Wen Chao tilted his head to look at him, like a listening bird.

"You fear the new khan," he murmured.

Togrul snorted. "Why would I not, with a trail of dead men behind him? I have guards around this ger, but in the morning who knows how long it will be before..." He trailed off, his fingers writhing together as he thought. "You saw them cheer him, my own Kerait among them."

Wen Chao was troubled. If Temujin killed the fat fool the following morning, any reprisal would fall on Wen as much as anyone. He considered what to do, very aware of Yuan's impassive face as they sat in the shadows.

When the silence became oppressive, Togrul drank a huge draft of airag, belching to himself.

"Who knows who I can trust any longer?" he said, his voice taking on a whining tone. "He will be drunk tonight and he will sleep heavily. If he dies in his ger, there will be no one to stop me leaving in the morning."

"His brothers would stop you," Wen Chao said. "They would react in fury."

Togrul felt his vision swimming and he pressed his knuckles into his eyes.

"My Kerait number half the army around us. They owe nothing to those brothers. If Temujin were dead, I would be able to take them clear. They cannot stop me."

"If you try and fail, all our lives would be forfeit," Wen Chao warned. He was worried Togrul would blunder around in the dark and get Wen killed just as the chance of returning to the Chin court had become real after his years in the wilderness. He realized his own safety was threatened either way, but it seemed a better chance to wait for the morning. Temujin owed him nothing, but the odds were good that Wen would be allowed to go home.

"You must not risk it, Togrul," he told the khan. "Guest rights protect you both and there will be only destruction if you risk it all from fear." Wen sat back, watching his words sink in.

"No," Togrul said, chopping a hand through the air. "You saw them cheering him. If he dies tonight, I will take my Kerait away before dawn. By sunrise, they will be long behind us and in chaos."

"It is an error..." Wen Chao began. To his utter astonishment, it was Yuan who interrupted him.

"I will lead men to his ger, my lord," Yuan said to Togrul. "He is no friend of mine."

Togrul turned to the Chin soldier and clasped his hand in both of his own fleshy palms.

"Do it, Yuan, swiftly. Take the guards around his ger and kill him. He and his brothers drank more than I did. They will not be ready for you, not tonight."

"And his wife?" Yuan asked. "She sleeps with him and she will wake and cry out."

Togrul shook his head against the fumes of airag.

"Not unless you must. I am not a monster, but I *will* live through tomorrow."

"Yuan?" Wen Chao snapped. "What foolishness is this?"

His first officer turned his face to him, dark and brooding in the shadows. "He has risen fast and far in a short time, this man. If he dies tonight, we will not see him at our borders in a few years."

Wen considered the future. It would still be better to let Temujin wake. If the young khan chose to kill Togrul, at least Wen would not have to bear the man's company back to the borders of his own lands. Surely Temujin would let the Chin ambassador leave? He was not certain, and as he hesitated, Yuan stood and bowed to both men, striding out the door. Caught in indecision, Wen Chao said nothing as he went. He faced Togrul with a worried frown, listening to Yuan talk to the guards outside. It did not take long before they went away into the darkness of the vast camp, too far to call back.

Wen decided to call for his bearers. No matter what happened, he wanted to be gone at sunrise. He could not shake the prickling feeling of danger and fear in his chest. He had done everything the first minister could have dreamed. The Tartars had been crushed and at last he would know the peace and sanctuary of the court once more. No longer would the smell of sweat and mutton be with him every waking hour. Togrul's drunken fear could still snatch it all away, and he frowned to himself as he sat with the khan, knowing he would get no rest that night.

Temujin was deep in sleep when the door to his ger creaked open. Borte lay at his side, troubled in her sleep. She was huge with the child inside her and so hot that she threw off the furs that kept out the winter chill. A dim glow from the stove gave an orange light to the ger. As Yuan entered with two other men, neither of the sleeping pair stirred.

The two guards carried drawn swords and they took a step past Yuan as he gazed down on Temujin and Borte. He reached out and pressed his forearms against his companions, halting them as if they had run into a wall.

"Wait," he hissed. "I will not kill a sleeping man."

They exchanged glances, unable to comprehend the strange soldier. They stood in silence as Yuan took a breath and whispered to the sleeping khan.

"Temujin?"

His own name called Temujin from troubled dreams. He opened his eyes blearily, finding his head throbbing. When he turned his head, he saw Yuan standing there, and for a moment, they merely looked at each other. Temujin's hands were hidden beneath the furs and, when he moved, Yuan saw he held his father's sword. The young man was naked, but he sprang out of the bed and threw the scabbard to one side. Borte opened her eyes at the movement and Yuan heard her gasp in fear.

"I could have killed you," Yuan said quietly to the naked man before him. "A life for a life, as you once granted me mine. There is no debt between us now."

"Who sent you? Wen Chao? Togrul? Who?" Temujin shook his head, but the room seemed to lurch. He struggled to clear his mind.

"My master had no part in this," Yuan continued. "We will leave in the morning and return home."

"It was Togrul, then," Temujin said. "Why does he turn on me now?"

Yuan shrugged. "He fears you. Perhaps he is right to. Remember that your life was mine to take tonight. I have dealt honorably with you."

Temujin sighed, his pounding heart beginning to ease. He felt dizzy and sick and wondered if he would vomit. Sour airag churned in his stomach and, despite the few hours of sleep, he was still exhausted. He did not doubt Yuan could have killed him cleanly if he had wished. For a moment, he considered calling his warriors from their gers and dragging Togrul out. Perhaps it was simple weariness, but he had seen too much of death and Eeluk's blood still itched on his skin.

"Before the sun is up, you will leave," he said. "Take Wen Chao and Togrul with you." Temujin looked at the two men who had entered with Yuan. They stood stunned at this development, unable to meet his eye. "His guards can accompany him. I do not want them here after what they tried to do."

"He will want the Kerait," Yuan said.

Temujin shook his head. "If he wishes, I can summon them all and tell them of this act of cowardice. They will not follow a fool. The tribes are mine, Yuan, the Kerait with them." He stood a little straighter as he spoke, and Yuan saw the wolf's-head sword glint in the dim light of the stove.

"Tell him I will not take his life if he leaves before dawn. If I find him here, I will challenge him in front of his warriors." His gaze was dark and hard as he regarded the Chin soldier.

"Every family riding on the sea of grass will acknowledge me as khan. Tell your master Wen Chao that, when you return to him. He is safe from me now, but I will see him again."

The Chin lands were a thousand miles away. Even the tribes gathered in Temujin's name were a tiny part of the armies Yuan had seen. He did not fear the man's ambition.

"The camp will wake as we leave," Yuan said.

Temujin looked at him, then clambered back into bed without bothering to respond. He saw Borte was wide-eyed in fear and reached out to smooth her hair back from her face. She allowed his touch, hardly seeming to feel it.

"Just go, Yuan," Temujin said softly. He was about to pull the furs over his body again when he paused. "And thank you."

Yuan ushered the two guards back into the chill night air. When they had left the ger behind, he stopped them again and sensed them turn to him questioningly in the darkness. They did not see the knife he drew from his belt, and even if they had, they were no match for a man who had been first sword in Kaifeng. Two quick blows left them on their knees, and he waited until they had fallen and were still. He had disobeyed his orders, but he felt lighthearted and now there were no witnesses to tell Wen Chao what he had done. The camp was silent, frozen under the stars. The only sound was his own crunching footsteps as he returned to his master to tell him that Temujin had been too well guarded. Yuan glanced back only once at the khan's ger as he walked away under the moonlight, fixing it in his mind. He had paid his debt.

When the moon was dipping down toward the hills, Temujin woke a second time as Khasar entered the ger. Before he was fully alert, Temujin had grabbed his father's sword and sprung up. Borte stirred, moaning in her sleep, and Temujin turned to her, reaching out to stroke her cheek.

"It is all right, it is just my brother," he murmured. Borte murmured something, but this time she did not come out of her sleep. Temujin sighed, looking down at her.

"I see you have been dreaming of attractive women," Khasar said, chuckling.

Temujin blushed, pulling the furs around his waist as he sat down on the bed.

"Keep your voice down before you wake her," he whispered. "What do you want?" He saw Kachiun enter behind Khasar and wondered if he would ever have peace that night.

"I thought you might like to know that there are two bodies outside on the ground."

Temujin nodded sleepily. He had expected it. Khasar frowned at his lack of reaction.

"Togrul and Wen Chao seem to be readying themselves to ride," Khasar said, still amused. "Their guards have gathered horses and that ridiculous box Wen Chao uses. Do you want me to stop them?"

Temujin placed his father's sword back on the furs, thinking.

"How many men are they taking with them?" he asked.

"Perhaps three dozen," Kachiun said from the doorway, "including Togrul's wife and daughters. With Yuan and the Chin guards, it makes a large group. Togrul has a cart for his bulk. Do you know something we don't?"

"Togrul sent men to kill me, but he chose Yuan," Temujin said.

Khasar let out a hiss of indignation. "I can get the Wolves out after him before he's gone a mile. They're closest and they have no allegiance to Togrul." He watched in surprise as Temujin shook his head.

"Let them go. We have the Kerait. I would have had to kill him anyway."

Kachiun whistled softly under his breath. "How many more will you bring in, brother? It was not that long ago that you were khan of a few raiders in the north."

Temujin did not reply for a long time. At last he raised his head, talking without looking at his brothers.

"I will be khan of them all. We are one people and one man can lead them. How else can we take the cities of the Chin?"

Khasar looked at his brother and a slow smile spread across his face.

"There are tribes who took no part in the battle against the Tartars," Kachiun reminded them both. "The Naimans, the Oirats..."

"They cannot stand alone against us," Temujin said. "We will take them one by one."

"Are we to be Wolves again, then?" Khasar asked, his eyes bright.

Temujin thought for a time.

"We are the silver people, the Mongols. When they ask, tell them there *are* no tribes. Tell them I am khan of the sea of grass, and they will know me by that name, as Genghis. Yes, tell them that. Tell them that I am Genghis and I will ride."

EPILOGUE

THE FORT AT THE BORDER of Chin lands was a massive construction of wood and stone. The few men of the Kerait who had come with their khan into exile looked nervous as they approached. They had seen nothing like the huge building, with its wings and courtyards. The entrance was a great gate of wood studded with iron into which a smaller door had been set. Two guards stood there, dressed in armor very like that worn by Wen Chao's men. They resembled statues in the morning sun, polished and perfect.

Togrul glanced up at the high walls, seeing more armed soldiers watching them. The border itself was no more than a simple track. On the journey, Wen Chao had boasted of a great wall across thousands of miles, but that was far to the south. He had made straight for the fort as soon as they sighted it, knowing that to do otherwise was to invite a quick death. The Chin lords did not welcome men who crept into their territory. Togrul felt out of his depth and in awe of the tallest building he had ever seen. He could not hide his excitement as Wen Chao's litter was placed on the ground and the ambassador stepped out.

"Wait here. I have papers I must show to them before we can pass," Wen Chao said. He too seemed animated, with his homeland in view. It would not be long before he was back in the heart of Kaifeng, and little Zhang would have to grind his teeth in private over his success.

Togrul stepped down from the cart, watching closely as Wen Chao approached the guards and spoke to them. They glanced back at the party of Mongols, soldiers, and slaves, but one of them bowed and opened the small door in the gate, vanishing inside. Wen Chao showed no impatience as he waited. He had survived years away from comfort, after all.

Yuan watched in silence as the commander of the fort came out and examined Wen Chao's papers. He could not hear what was said and he ignored the questioning glances Togrul sent his way. He too was tired of the tribesmen, and the sight of Chin lands reminded him of his family and friends.

At last, the commander seemed satisfied. He passed back the papers and Wen spoke to him again, as to a subordinate. The authority from the first minister demanded instant obedience, and the guards stood as stiffly as if they were being inspected. Yuan saw the door open again and the commander stepped inside it, taking his soldiers with him. Wen hesitated before following and turned to the watching group. His gaze found Yuan and rested there, troubled. He spoke in the Chin dialect of the court, in the most formal style.

"These men will not be allowed to enter, Yuan. Should I leave you with them?"

Yuan narrowed his eyes and Togrul took a step forward.

"What did he say? What is happening?"

Wen Chao's glance did not waver from Yuan.

"You failed me, Yuan, when you failed to kill the khan in his tent. What value is your life to me now?"

Yuan stood very still, showing no trace of fear. "Tell me to stand and I will stand. Tell me to come and I will come."

Wen Chao nodded slowly. "Then come to me, and live, knowing that your life was mine to take."

Yuan crossed the distance to the door and stepped inside. Togrul watched in growing panic.

"When do we cross over?" his wife asked.

Togrul turned to her and when she saw the terrible fear in his expression, her face crumpled. When the Chin ambassador spoke again, it was in the language of the tribes. He hoped it would be the last time the foul sounds crossed his lips.

"I am sorry," he said, turning away and passing through the door. It closed behind him.

"What is this?" Togrul shouted desperately. "Answer me! What is happening?" He froze at a movement on the high walls of the fort. A line of men stood there and, to Togrul's horror, he saw they were bending bows pointing down at him.

"No! I was promised!" Togrul roared.

Arrows spat through the air, hammering into them even as they turned in terror. Togrul fell to his knees with his arms outstretched, a dozen shafts in his flesh. His daughters screamed, the sounds cut off in thumping blows that hurt Togrul as much as his own agony. For a moment, he cursed the men who stole amongst the tribes as allies, ruling them with gold and promises. The thin grass under him was the dust of Mongol lands, filling his lungs and choking him. The anger faded and the morning was quiet once more.

AFTERWORD

The greatest joy a man can know is to conquer his
enemies and drive them before him. To ride their horses
and take away their possessions, to see the faces of those
who were dear to them bedewed with tears, and to clasp
their wives and daughters in his arms.

—Genghis Khan

The events of his youth that went to create Genghis
Khan make extraordinary reading. Very few contempo-
rary records survive and even the most famous of them,
The Secret History of the Mongols, was almost lost. The version in his own language commissioned by Genghis did
not survive the centuries. Fortunately, a version was
rendered phonetically in Chinese, and it is from that
writing that we have most of our knowledge of Temujin
of the Borjigin—the Blue Wolves. A translation into
English by Arthur Waley became my chief source for
this work.

Though the exact meaning of the name is disputed, Temujin-Uge was a Tartar killed by Yesugei, who then named his son after the warrior he had defeated. The name has similarities to the Mongolian word for "iron," and that is generally accepted as its meaning, though it could just be coincidence. Temujin was born holding a clot of blood in his hand, which would have frightened those who looked for such omens.

Temujin was tall for a Mongol, with "cat's eyes." Even amongst a hardy people, he was noted for his ability to endure heat and cold and was indifferent to wounds. He had complete mastery of his own body in terms of endurance. As a people, the Mongols have excellent teeth and eyesight, black hair, and reddish skin and believe themselves to be related to the Native American tribes who crossed the Bering Strait while it was frozen and so entered Alaska around fifteen thousand years ago. The similarities between the peoples are startling.

In modern Mongolia, the majority of the population still hunt with a bow or rifle, herd sheep and goats, and revere ponies. They practice shamanism, and any high place will be marked with lengths of blue cloth to honor the sky father. "Sky burial," that is, laying out bodies to be torn apart by wild birds in high places, is as I have described it.

The young Temujin was taken to his mother's old tribe, the Olkhun'ut, to find him a wife, though his mother, Hoelun, was taken in the *other* way of finding a woman—by Yesugei and his brothers kidnapping her from her husband. Yesugei was almost certainly poisoned by his Tartar enemies, though exact details are sketchy.

With his father gone, the tribe chose a new khan and abandoned Hoelun and seven children, down to Temulun, a baby girl. I have not included a half brother, Belgutei, in this story, as he did not play a major part and there were too many similar names already. In the same way, I have changed names where I felt the original was too long or too complex. "Eeluk" is far simpler than "Tarkhutai-kiriltukh." Mongolian is not an easy language to pronounce, though it is worth mentioning that they have no "k" sound, so that "Khan" would be said as "Haan." Kublai Khan, the grandson of Genghis, would have been pronounced as "Hoop-lie Haan." It is true that "Genghis" is perhaps better rendered as "Chinggis," but "Genghis" is how I learned it first and the one that resonates for me.

Hoelun and her children were not expected to survive and it is a testament to that extraordinary woman that the first winter did not kill her children. We do not know exactly how they survived starvation and temperature plunging as low as −20°, but the death of Bekter shows how close to the ragged edge they were during that period. That said, my guide in Mongolia slept in his deel in very low temperatures, so that his hair had frozen to the ground on waking. They are a hardy people and, to this day, practice the three sports of wrestling, archery, and horse-riding to the exclusion of everything else.

Temujin killed Bekter much as I have described it, though it was Khasar, not Kachiun, who fired the second shot. After Bekter stole food, both boys ambushed him with bows. To understand this act, I think it must first be necessary to see your family starve. Mongolia is an unforgiving land. The boy Temujin was never cruel, and there is no record of him ever taking pleasure from the destruction of his enemies. He was capable, however, of utter ruthlessness.

When the tribe sent men back to see what had become of the family they had abandoned, they met fierce resistance and arrow fire from the brothers. After a chase, Temujin hid from them deep in a thicket for nine days without food before starvation eventually forced him out. He was captured, but escaped and hid in a river. The bank of blue ice I described is not in *The Secret History,* though I saw such a thing on my travels in Mongolia. I changed the name of Sorkhansira to Basan for the man who saw him in the water and did not give him away. It was Sorkhansira who hid Temujin in his own ger. When the search failed, Sorkhansira gave him a licorice-colored mare with a white mouth, food, milk, and a bow with two arrows before sending him back to his family.

Temujin's wife, Borte, was stolen by the Merkit tribe rather than the Tartars as I have it. He was wounded in the attack. She was missing for some months rather than days. As a result, the paternity of the first son, Jochi, was never absolutely certain, and Temujin never fully accepted the boy. In fact, it was because his second son, Chagatai, refused to accept Jochi as their father's successor that later Genghis named his third son, Ogedai, as heir.

Cannibalism in the sense of eating the heart of an enemy was rare, but not unheard of amongst the tribes of Mongolia. Indeed, the best part of the marmot, the shoulder, was known as "human meat." In this too there is a link to the practices and beliefs of Native American tribes.

Togrul of the Kerait was indeed promised a kingdom in northern China. Though at first he was a mentor to the young raider, he came to fear Temujin's sudden rise to power and failed in an attempt to have him killed, breaking the cardinal rule of the tribes that a khan must be successful. Togrul was forced into banishment and killed by the Naimans, apparently before they recognized him.

To be betrayed by those he trusted seems to have ignited a spark of vengeance in Temujin, a desire for power that never left him. His childhood experiences created the man he would become, who would not bend or allow fear or weakness in any form. He cared nothing for possessions or wealth, only that his enemies fall.

The Mongolian double-curved bow is as I have described it, with a draw strength greater than the English longbow that was so successful two centuries later against armor. The key to its strength is the laminate form, with layers of boiled horn and sinew to augment the wood. The layer of horn is on the inner face, as horn resists compression. The layer of sinew is on the outer face, as it resists expansion. These layers, as thick as a finger, add power to the weapon, until heaving back on it is the equivalent of lifting two men into the air by two fingers—*at full gallop*. The arrows are made of birch.

Archery is what won Genghis his empire—that and incredible maneuverability. His riders moved far faster than modern armored columns and could live off a mixture of blood and mare's milk for long periods, needing no supply lines.

Each warrior would carry two bows, with thirty to sixty arrows in two quivers, a sword if they had one, a hatchet, and an iron file for sharpening arrowheads—attached to the quiver. As well as weapons, they carried a horsehair lasso, a rope, an awl for punching holes in leather, needle and thread, an iron cooking pot, two leather bottles for water and ten pounds of hard milk curd (to eat at the rate of a half pound per day). Each ten-man unit had a ger on a remount, so was completely self-sufficient. If they had dried mutton, they would make it edible by tenderizing it under the wooden saddle for days on end. It is significant that the word in Mongolian for "poor" is formed from the verb meaning "to go on foot," or "to walk."

One story I did not use is that his mother, Hoelun, showed her boys how an arrow could be snapped, but a bundle of them resisted—the classic metaphor for group strength.

Temujin's alliance with Togrul of the Kerait allowed him to build his followers into a successful raiding group under the protection of a powerful khan. If Temujin had not come to see the Chin as the puppet-masters of his people for a thousand years, he may well have remained a local phenomenon. As it was, however, he had a vision of a nation. The incredible martial skills of the Mongol tribes had always been wasted against each other. From nothing, surrounded by enemies, Temujin rose to unite them all.

What came next would shake the world.

ABOUT THE AUTHOR

CONN IGGULDEN is the acclaimed author of four previous Emperor novels: *Emperor: The Gates of Rome; Emperor: The Death of Kings; Emperor: The Field of Swords;* and *Emperor: The Gods of War.* He lives with his wife and three children in Hertfordshire, England.

The thrilling adventure
continues with

GENGHIS
LORDS OF THE BOW

Conn Iggulden

Read on for an exciting excerpt
from the next book in the Genghis saga
coming from Delacorte Press
in April 2008.

Co-Author of The #1 New York Times Bestseller
THE DANGEROUS BOOK FOR BOYS
CONN IGGULDEN
Genghis Khan
GENGHIS
LORDS OF THE BOW

Genghis: Lords of the Bow

On sale April 2008

THE KHAN OF THE NAIMANS WAS OLD. He shivered in the wind as it blew over the hill. Far below, the army he had gathered made its stand against the man who called himself Genghis. More than a dozen tribes stood with the Naimans in the foothills as the enemy struck in waves. The khan could hear yelling and screams on the clear mountain air, but he was almost blind and could not see the battle.

"Tell me what is happening," he murmured again to his shaman.

Kokchu had yet to see his thirtieth year, and his eyes were sharp, though shadows of regret played over them. "The Jajirat have laid down their bows and swords, my lord. They have lost their courage, as you said they might."

"They give him too much honor with their fear," the khan said, drawing his *deel* close around his scrawny frame. "Tell me of my own Naimans: do they still fight?"

Kokchu did not respond for a long time as he watched the roiling mass of men and horses below. Genghis had caught them all by surprise, appearing out of the grasslands at dawn when the best scouts said he was still hundreds of miles away. They had struck the Naiman alliance with all the ferocity of men used to victory, but there had been a chance to break their charge. Kokchu silently cursed the Jajirat tribe, who had brought so many men from the mountains that he had thought they might even win against their enemies. For a little time, their alliance had been a grand thing, impossible even a few years before. It had lasted as long as the first charge, and then fear had shattered it and the Jajirat had stepped aside.

As Kokchu watched he swore under his breath, seeing how some of the men his khan had welcomed even fought against their brothers. They had the mind of a pack of dogs, turning with the wind as it blew strongest.

"They fight yet, my lord," he said at last. "They have stood against the charge and their arrows sting the men of Genghis, hurting them."

The khan of the Naimans brought his bony hands together, the knuckles white. "That is good, Kokchu, but I should go back down to them, to give them heart."

The shaman turned a feverish gaze on the man he had served all his adult life. "You will die if you do, my lord. I have seen it. Your bondsmen will hold this hill against even the souls of the dead." He hid his shame. The khan had trusted his counsel, but when Kokchu watched the first Naiman lines crumple, he had seen his own death coming on the singing shafts. All he had wanted then was to get away.

The khan sighed. "You have served me well, Kokchu. I have been grateful. Now tell me again what you see."

Kokchu took a quick, sharp breath before replying.

"The brothers of Genghis have joined the battle now.

One of them has led a charge into the flanks of our warriors. It is cutting deeply into their ranks." He paused, biting his lip. Like a buzzing fly, an arrow darted up toward them, and he watched it sink to its feathers in the ground just a few feet below where they crouched.

"We must move higher, my lord," he said, rising to his feet without looking away from the seething mass of killing far below.

The old khan rose with him, aided by two warriors. They were cold-faced as they witnessed the destruction of their friends and brothers, but they turned up the hill at Kokchu's gesture, helping the old man to climb.

"Have we struck back, Kokchu?" he asked, his voice quavering. Kokchu turned and winced at what he saw. Arrows hung in the air below, seeming to move with oily slowness. The Naiman force had been split in two by the charge. The armor Genghis had copied from the Chin was better than the boiled leather the Naimans used. Each man wore hundreds of finger-width lengths of iron sewn onto thick canvas over a silk tunic. Even then, it could not stop a solid hit, though the silk often trapped the arrowhead. Kokchu saw the warriors of Genghis weather the storm of shafts. The horse-tail standard of the Merkit tribe was trampled underfoot, and they too threw down their weapons to kneel, chests heaving. Only the Oirat and Naimans fought on, raging, knowing they could not hold for long. The great alliance had come together to resist a single enemy, and with its end went all hope of freedom. Kokchu frowned to himself, considering his future.

"The men fight with pride, my lord. They will not run from these, not while you are watching." He saw a hundred warriors of Genghis had reached the foot of the hill and were staring balefully up at the lines of bondsmen. The wind was cruelly cold at such a height, and Kokchu felt despair and anger. He had come too far to fail on a dry hill with the cold sun on his face. All the secrets he had won from his father, surpassed even, would be wasted in a blow from a sword, or an arrow to end his life. For a moment, he hated the old khan who had tried to resist the new force on the plains. He had failed and that made him a fool, no matter how strong he had once seemed. In silence Kokchu cursed the bad luck that still stalked him.

The khan of the Naimans was panting as they climbed, and he waved a weary hand at the men who held his arms.

"I must rest here," he said, shaking his head.

"My lord, they are too close," Kokchu replied. The bondsmen ignored the shaman, easing their khan down to where he could sit on a ledge of grass.

"Then we have lost?" the khan said. "How else could the dogs of Genghis have reached this hill, if not over Naiman dead?"

Kokchu did not meet the eyes of the bondsmen. They knew the truth as well as he, but no one wanted to say the words and break the last hope of an old man. Below, the ground was marked in curves and strokes of dead men, like a bloody script on the grass. The Oirat had fought bravely and well, but they too had broken at the last. The army of Genghis moved fluidly, taking advantage of every weakness in the lines. Kokchu could see groups of tens and hundreds race across the battlefield, their officers communicating with bewildering speed. Only the great courage of the Naiman warriors remained to hold back the storm, and it would not be enough. Kokchu knew a moment's hope when the warriors retook the foot of the hill, but it was a small number of exhausted men and they were swept away in the next great charge against them.

"Your bondsmen still stand ready to die for you, my lord," Kokchu murmured. It was all he could say. The rest of the army that had stood so bright and strong the night before lay shattered. He could hear the cries of dying men.

The khan nodded, closing his eyes.

"I thought we might win this day," he said, his voice little more than a whisper. "If it is over, tell my sons to lay down their swords. I will not have them die for nothing."

The khan's sons had been killed as the army of Genghis roared over them. The two bondsmen stared at Kokchu as they heard the order, their grief and anger hidden from view. The older man drew his sword and checked the edge, the veins in his face and neck showing clearly, like delicate threads under the skin.

"I will take word to your sons, lord, if you will let me go."

The khan raised his head.

"Tell them to live, Murakh, that they might see where this Genghis takes us all."

There were tears in Murakh's eyes and he wiped them away angrily as he faced the other bondsman, ignoring Kokchu as if he were not there.

"Protect the khan, my son," he said softly. The younger man bowed his head and Murakh placed a hand on his shoulder, leaning forward to touch foreheads for a moment. Without a glance at the shaman who had brought them to the hill, Murakh strode down the slope.

The khan sighed, his mind full of clouds. "Tell them to let the conqueror through," he whispered. Kokchu watched as a bead of sweat hung on his nose and quivered there. "Perhaps he will be merciful with my sons once he has killed me."

Far below, Kokchu saw the bondsman Murakh reach

the last knot of defenders. They stood taller in his presence; exhausted, broken men who nonetheless raised their heads and tried not to show they had been afraid. Kokchu heard them calling farewell to one another as they walked with a light step toward the enemy.

At the foot of the hill, Kokchu saw Genghis himself come through the mass of warriors, his armor marbled in blood. Kokchu felt the man's gaze pass over him. He shivered and touched the hilt of his knife. Would Genghis spare a shaman who had drawn it across his own khan's throat? The old man sat with his head bowed, his neck painfully thin. Perhaps such a murder would win Kokchu's life for him, and at that moment, he was desperately afraid of death.

Genghis stared up without moving for a long time, and Kokchu let his hand fall. He did not know this cold warrior who came from nowhere with the dawn sun. Kokchu sat at the side of his khan and watched the last of the Naimans go down to die. He chanted an old protective charm his father had taught him, to turn enemies to his side. It seemed to ease the tension in the old khan to hear the tumbling words.

Murakh had been first warrior to the Naimans and had not fought that day. With an ululating yell, he tore into the lines of Genghis's men without a thought for his defense. The last of the Naimans shouted in his wake, their weariness vanishing. Their arrows sent the men of Genghis spinning, though they rose quickly and snapped the shafts, showing their teeth as they came on. As Murakh killed the first who stood against him, a dozen more pressed him on all sides, making his ribs run red with their blows.

Kokchu continued the chant, his eyes widening as Genghis blew a horn and his men pulled back from the panting Naiman survivors.

Murakh still lived, standing dazed. Kokchu could see Genghis call to him, but he could not hear the words. Murakh shook his head and spat blood on the ground as he raised his sword once more. There were only a few Naimans who still stood, and they were all wounded, their blood running down their legs. They raised their blades, staggering as they did so.

"You have fought well," Genghis shouted. "Surrender to me and I will welcome you at my fires. I will give you honor."

Murakh grinned at him through red teeth. "I spit on Wolf honor," he said.

Genghis sat very still on his pony before finally shrugging and dropping his arm once more. The line surged forward and Murakh and the others were engulfed in the press of stamping, stabbing men.

High on the hill, Kokchu rose to his feet, his chant dying in his throat as Genghis dismounted and began to climb. The battle was over. The dead lay in their hundreds, but thousands more had surrendered. Kokchu did not care what happened to them.

"He is coming," Kokchu said softly, peering down the hill. His stomach cramped and the muscles in his legs shuddered like a horse beset with flies. The man who had brought the tribes of the plains under his banners was walking purposefully upwards, his face without expression.

Kokchu could see his armor was battered and more than a few of its metal scales hung by threads. The fight had been hard, but Genghis climbed with his mouth shut, as if the exertion was nothing to him.

"Have my sons survived?" the khan whispered, breaking his stillness. He reached out and took hold of the sleeve of Kokchu's deel.

"They have not," Kokchu said with a sudden surge of bitterness. The hand fell away and the old man slumped. As Kokchu watched, the milky eyes came up once more and there was strength in the way he held himself.

"Then let this Genghis come," the khan said. "What does he matter to me now?"

Kokchu did not respond, unable to tear his gaze from the warrior who climbed the hill. The wind was cold on his neck and he knew he was feeling it more sweetly than ever before. He had seen men faced with death; he had given it to them with the darkest rites, sending their souls spinning away. He saw his own death coming in the steady tread of that man, and for a moment he almost broke and ran. It was not courage that held him there. He was a man of words and spells, more feared amongst the Naimans than his father had ever been. To run was to die, with the certainty of winter coming. He heard the whisper as Murakh's son drew his sword, but took no comfort from it. There was something awe inspiring about the steady gait of the destroyer. Armies had not stopped him. The old khan lifted his head to watch him come, sensing the approach in the same way his sightless eyes could still seek out the sun.

Genghis paused as he reached the three men, gazing at them. He was tall and his skin shone with oil and health. His eyes were wolf-yellow and Kokchu saw no mercy in them. As Kokchu stood frozen, Genghis drew a sword still marked with drying blood. Murakh's son took a pace forward to stand between the two khans. Genghis looked at him with a spark of irritation, and the young man tensed.

"Get down the hill, boy, if you want to live," Genghis said. "I have seen enough of my people die today."

The young warrior shook his head without a word, and Genghis sighed. With a sharp blow, he knocked the sword aside and swept his other hand across, plunging a dagger into the young man's throat. As the life went out of Murakh's son, he fell onto Genghis with open arms. Genghis gave a grunt as he caught the weight and heaved him away. Kokchu watched the body tumble limply down the slope.

Calmly, Genghis wiped his knife and replaced it in a sheath at his waist, his weariness suddenly evident.

"I would have honored the Naimans, if you had joined me," he said.

The old khan stared up at him, his eyes empty. "You have heard my answer," he replied, his voice strong. "Now send me to my sons."

Genghis nodded. His sword came down with apparent slowness. It swept the khan's head from his shoulders and sent it tumbling down the hill. The body hardly jerked at the tug of the blade and only leaned slightly to one side. Kokchu could hear the blood rolling on the rocks as every one of his senses screamed to live. He paled as Genghis turned to him and he spoke in a desperate torrent of words.

"You may not shed the blood of a shaman, lord. You may not. I am a man of power, one who understands power. Strike me and you will find my skin is iron. Instead, let me serve you. Let me proclaim your victory."

"How well did you serve the khan of the Naimans to have brought him here to die?" Genghis replied.

"Did I not bring him far from the battle? I saw you coming in my dreams, lord. I prepared the way for you as best I could. Are you not the future of the tribes? My voice is the voice of the spirits. I stand in water, while you stand on earth and sky. Let me serve you."

Genghis hesitated, his sword perfectly still. The man he faced wore a dark brown deel over a grubby tunic and leggings. It was decorated with patterns of stitching, swirls of purple worn almost black with grease and dirt. The boots Kokchu wore were bound in rope, the sort a man might wear if the last owner had no more use for them.

Yet there was something in the way the eyes burned in the dark face. Genghis remembered how Eeluk of the Wolves had killed his father's shaman. Perhaps Eeluk's fate had been sealed on that bloody day so many years before. Kokchu watched him, waiting for the stroke that would end his life.

"I do not need another storyteller," Genghis said. "I have three men already who claim to speak for the spirits."

Kokchu saw the curiosity in the man's gaze and he did not hesitate. "They are children, lord. Let me show you," he said. Without waiting for a reply, he reached inside his deel and removed a slender length of steel bound clumsily into a hilt of horn. He sensed Genghis raise his sword and Kokchu held up his free palm to stay the blow, closing his eyes.

With a wrenching effort of will, the shaman shut out the wind on his skin and the cold fear that ate at his belly. He murmured the words his father had beaten into him and felt the calm of a trance come sharper and faster than even he had expected. The spirits were with him, their caress slowing his heart. In an instant, he was somewhere else and watching.

Genghis opened his eyes wide as Kokchu touched the dagger to his own forearm, the slim blade entering the flesh. The shaman showed no sign of pain as the metal slid through him, and Genghis watched, fascinated, as the tip raised the skin on the other side. The metal showed black as it poked through, and Kokchu blinked slowly, almost lazily, as he pulled it out.

He watched the eyes of the young khan as the knife came free. They were fastened on the wound. Kokchu took a deep breath, feeling the trance deepen until a great coldness was in every limb.

"Is there blood, lord?" he whispered, knowing the answer.

Genghis frowned. He did not sheathe his sword, but stepped forward and ran a rough thumb over the oval wound in Kokchu's arm.

"None. It is a useful skill," he admitted grudgingly. "Can it be taught?"

Kokchu smiled, no longer afraid. "The spirits will not come to those they have not chosen, lord."

Genghis nodded, stepping away. Even in the cold wind, the shaman stank like an old goat and he did not know what to make of the strange wound that did not bleed.

With a grunt, he ran his fingers along his blade and sheathed it.

"I will give you a year of life, shaman. It is enough time to prove your worth."

Kokchu fell to his knees, pressing his face into the ground. "You are the great khan, as I have foretold," he said, tears staining the dust on his cheeks. He felt the coldness of whispering spirits leave him then. He shrugged his sleeve forward to hide the growing spot of blood.

"I am," Genghis replied. He looked down the hill at the army waiting for him to return. "The world will hear my name." When he spoke again, it was so quiet that Kokchu had to strain to hear him.

"This is not a time of death, shaman. We are one people and there will be no more battles between us. I will summon us all. Cities will fall to us, new lands will be ours to ride. Women will weep and I will be pleased to hear it."

He looked down at the prostrate shaman, frowning.

"You will live, shaman. I have said it. Get off your knees and walk down with me."

At the foot of the hill, Genghis nodded to his brothers Kachiun and Khasar. Each of them had grown in authority in the years since they had begun the gathering of tribes, but they were still young and Kachiun smiled as his brother walked amongst them.

"Who is this?" Khasar asked, staring at Kokchu in his ragged deel.

"The shaman of the Naimans," Genghis replied.

Another man guided his pony close and dismounted, his eyes fastened on Kokchu. Arslan had once been sword-smith to the Naiman tribe, and Kokchu recognized him as he approached. The man was a murderer, he remembered, forced into banishment. It was no surprise to find such as he amongst Genghis's trusted officers.

"I remember you," Arslan said. "Has your father died, then?"

"Years ago, oath-breaker," Kokchu replied, nettled by the tone. For the first time, he realized he had lost the authority he had won so painfully with the Naimans. There were few men in that tribe who would have looked on him without lowering their eyes, for fear that they would be accused of disloyalty and face his knives and fire. Kokchu met the gaze of the Naiman traitor without flinching. They would come to know him.

Genghis watched the tension between the two men with something like amusement.

"Do not give offense, shaman. Not to the first warrior to come to my banners. There are no Naimans any longer, nor ties to tribe. I have claimed them all."

"I have seen it in the visions," Kokchu replied immediately. "You have been blessed by the spirits."

Genghis's face grew tight at the words. "It has been a rough blessing. The army you see around you has been won by strength and skill. If the souls of our fathers were aiding us, they were too subtle for me to see them."

Kokchu blinked. The khan of the Naimans had been credulous and easy to lead. He realized this new man was not as open to his influence. Still, the air was sweet in his lungs. He lived and he had not expected even that an hour before.

Genghis turned to his brothers, dismissing Kokchu from his thoughts.

"Have the new men give their oath to me this evening, as the sun sets," he said to Khasar. "Spread them amongst the others so that they begin to feel part of us, rather than beaten enemies. Do it carefully. I cannot be watching for knives at my back."

Khasar dipped his head before turning away and striding through the warriors to where the defeated tribes still knelt.

Kokchu saw a smile of affection pass between Genghis and his younger brother Kachiun. The two men were friends and Kokchu was beginning to learn everything he could. Even the smallest detail would be useful in the years to come.

"We have broken the alliance, Kachiun. Did I not say we would?" Genghis said, clapping him on the back. "Your armored horses came in at the perfect time."

"As you taught me," Kachiun replied, easy with the praise.

"With the new men, this is an army to ride the plains," Genghis said, smiling. "It is time to set the path, at last." He thought for a moment.

"Send out riders in every direction, Kachiun. I want the land scoured of every wanderer family and small tribe. Tell them to come to the black mountain next spring, near the Onon River. It is a flat plain that will hold all the thousands of our people. We will gather there, ready to ride."

"What message shall they take?" Kachiun asked.

"Tell them to come to me," he said softly. "Tell them Genghis calls them to a gathering. There is no one to stand against us now. They can follow me or they can spend their last days waiting for my warriors on the horizon. Tell them that." He looked around him with satisfaction. In seven years, he had gathered more than ten thousand men. With the survivors of the defeated allied tribes, he had almost twice that number. There was no one left on the plains who could challenge his leadership. He looked away from the sun to the east, imagining the bloated, wealthy cities of the Chin.

"They have kept us apart for a thousand generations, Kachiun. They have ridden us until we were nothing more than savage dogs. That is the past. I have brought us together and they will be trembling. I'll give them cause."